KERRY WILKINSON

CROSSING
THE LINE

D0111447

PAN BOOKS

First published 2014 by Pan Books
an imprint of Pan Macmillan, a division of Macmillan Publishers Limited
Pan Macmillan, 20 New Wharf Road, London N1 9RR
Basingstoke and Oxford
Associated companies throughout the world
www.panmacmillan.com

ISBN 978-1-4472-4787-6

1 3 5 7 9 8 6 4 2

A CIP catalogue record for this book is available from the British Library.

Typeset by Ellipsis Digital Limited, Glasgow
Printed and bound by CPI Group (UK) Ltd, Croydon, CR0 4YY

Visit **www.panmacmillan.com** to read more about all our books
and to buy them. You will also find features, author interviews and
news of any author events, and you can sign up for e-newsletters
so that you're always first to hear about our new releases.

CROSSING THE LINE

Kerry Wilkinson's debut, *Locked In*, the first title in the detective Jessica Daniel series, was written as a challenge to himself and went on to become a UK Number One Kindle bestseller within three months of release.

Since then, his Jessica Daniel series has sold over three-quarters of a million copies and he became the first formerly self-published British author to have an ebook Number One and reach the top 20 of the UK paperback chart.

Crossing the Line is the eighth title in the Jessica Daniel series.

Kerry is an occasional sports journalist and can frequently be spotted cycling the hills of Lancashire while trying not to be knocked off. Please drive safely around him. He was born in Somerset but now lives in Lancashire.

For more information about Kerry and his books visit:

www.kerrywilkinson.com or
www.panmacmillan.com

Twitter: twitter.com/kerrywk

Facebook: www.facebook.com/JessicaDanielBooks

Or you can email Kerry at kerrywilkinson@live.com

By Kerry Wilkinson

The Jessica Daniel series

LOCKED IN

VIGILANTE

THE WOMAN IN BLACK

THINK OF THE CHILDREN

PLAYING WITH FIRE

THICKER THAN WATER

BEHIND CLOSED DOORS

CROSSING THE LINE

The Andrew Hunter series

SOMETHING WICKED

The Silver Blackthorn Trilogy

RECKONING

CROSSING THE LINE

The sights juddered slightly before centring on the politician's chest as he straightened his tie. In a line of people messing around with their expensive clothes, smoothing down patches of disobedient hair, and generally trying to make it look as if they weren't cold, his choice of bright pink neckwear blazed brighter than anything.

It also made him an easier target to hit.

As he moved across the makeshift stage, one hand in the air acknowledging the smattering of applause, the sights followed him, the thin black lines and red circle keeping him in their centre as he pulled an obviously fake smile and nodded towards his crowd. Another hand shot through his hair: a sort of vaguely blond quiff but without the grease or height. It definitely involved a lot of back-combing though.

Another nod and a smile. 'Thank you, thank you.'

Meanwhile, the red circle of the sights shifted a few millimetres until directly over his forehead.

Jessica Daniel stifled a yawn. 'You know, you really could just pop the guy's head right off from here.'

Esther Warren had one hand pressed to her ear, the other covering her eyes from the chilled spring sun raging over the top of the bus station, casting an icy glow across Manchester's Piccadilly Gardens. She brushed away a non-existent crease from her suit and tightened her ponytail. 'Yeah, the blood spatter might even improve his suit. Light grey and bright pink? Anyway, it's a bit hard to blow anyone's head off if all you're holding is a pair of binoculars.'

Jessica put them down and squinted instead from where they were standing on the steps towards where the Home Secretary was beginning his speech. 'It's always the little things with you, isn't it?'

Esther snorted. 'I'm an inspector, temporarily in charge of policing special events for the whole of Greater Manchester. I'd hopefully notice a bloody great rifle if it was in front of me.'

'I thought you said you were deputy?'

'I said I was "technically" deputy. The chief's off on the sick and nobody else fancies it.'

Jessica tried the binoculars again, running along the line of gormless-looking men in suits on the stage standing around with their hands behind their backs, smiling on cue as the Home Secretary banged on about something to do with the community. 'I suppose it's a step up from kidnap squad.'

Esther sighed. 'That's how the bastards sold it to me – it's more like a step sideways off a cliff into a giant pile of shite at the bottom.'

'What counts as a special event? Are you managing a riot squad if the cathedral's jumble sale gets out of hand, or is there some fete I've not heard about?'

Esther failed to stifle a laugh. 'I'm glad my fledgling career is so hilarious to you. I'll have you know we're supervising a scout group tonight in case the ging-gang-goolies get out of hand and then we're keeping an eye on the market this weekend.'

'Really?'

'Of course not really. It's mainly football but there's also some outdoor concerts coming up. We only got the call three days ago that the Home Secretary wanted to do something in the centre.'

'Why's he up here?'

'Who knows? This Westminster lot reckon anywhere north of Watford is like a ghetto. They come up here thinking it's a day in the trenches to show they're one of us. As soon as the cameras disappear, it's a first-class train back to London and a cheeky midnight handjob on Clapham Common.'

Jessica took her phone out of her pocket and started fiddling with the screen. 'You paint quite the picture.'

'Aren't you supposed to be helping?'

'I *am* helping, I was just checking work emails – plus I'm here supporting you.'

'Not just skiving off from Longsight then?'

Jessica looked up and re-pocketed the phone in her suit trousers. 'You asked me to come, here I am.'

Esther checked her watch. 'I asked you to bring the gang actually. It's all about numbers to this lot. The Prime Minister gets three dozen officers, two personal handlers, guns on the roofs, a partridge in a pear tree and his PA carries the lube. The Chancellor only gets half that, so the Home Sec's pissed off that he gets even less again. Suddenly his people are on to my people, the chief constable's involved and then the diktat comes down that we need a "presence".'

'I'm sorry it's just me then. We've got some guy in the cells for hiring out his sister to someone he owed drugs money, an off-licence was held up in Eccles last night, then there's an entire family in after a domestic led to one of their houses being burned down. The fumes have apparently caused mass amnesia when it comes to answering questions.'

'How'd you get out of dealing with all that?'

Jessica pretended to polish her nails. 'Delegation.'

'Aye, I heard about the promotion. It's been—' Before she could finish the sentence, Esther turned half-around, pressing her finger to her ear. If Jessica hadn't known she was talking into a radio mic, it would have seemed like she was having an argument with herself, her free hand flapping around animatedly: 'Well, why didn't someone fill it up with petrol then?' Pause, scowly face. 'I don't know; we're only the sodding police – perhaps we'll manage with a herd of camels next time?' Pause, more frowning. 'What? No, camels. You know, big, slow things that live in the desert?' Pause, shake of the head, eyebrows raised in disbelief. 'What? No, I don't need you to get me— Look, just forget it, fill the bloody car up with petrol and get your arse over here pronto.' She shook her head, sighing, and turned back to Jessica. 'I'm surrounded by morons!'

'Whatever vehicle you're talking about is definitely a petrol, isn't it?'

'Oh for God's sake.' Esther turned her back again, restarting her conversation with whoever was on the other end, telling them to make sure it didn't need diesel.

Jessica focused back on the stage across the concrete plaza. The Home Secretary was banging his fist on a lectern, facing slightly off-centre towards a bank of cameras. She pulled her jacket tighter around herself as the sun continued to lose its battle with the cold. She didn't realise Esther was back by her side until the other woman spoke. 'Either his top button is too tight or his head is too big for the rest of his body. He's like a human bobble head.'

'What's he even announcing? Free Kalashnikovs for eight-year-olds?'

'Something like that. They come up here, cameras in tow, a mini army carrying their bags and think it's the Nuremburg rally. By the time you add up the PRs, journalists, hangers-on, TV types clinging onto their skinny lattes for dear life and all us lot, we outnumber the crowd anyway. It's supposed to be a nice day – who wants to listen to this guy?'

'Who are the other lot standing at the front of the stage in suits?'

'Local councillors, party organisers, activists – basically anyone who fancies getting their face on telly. I think Sky News are broadcasting live.'

Jessica looked from one side of the plaza to the other. Behind the Home Secretary, there was an expanse of grass, recently trimmed and neatly framed for the cameras – enough to make anyone who might happen to catch a snippet on the news think that Manchester was a green paradise, instead of a pissed-upon traffic-jammed nightmare. In front of him, the rest of the area was paved, a busy tram station on one side, hotels, restaurants and stores on the other. Shoppers hurried past, glancing briefly towards the man in a suit before deciding they'd somehow find a way to continue their lives without stopping to listen. Just for good measure, the workmen refitting the giant clothes shop behind them started with the pneumatic drill to add a background din of chuntering concrete to the mix.

'They always show them to the decent bits,' Jessica complained, continuing to scan the area. 'Nice bit of grass, some sun. If it was down to me, we'd wheel 'em out to a burned-out bingo hall in Eccles in the pissing rain. That'd give 'em a wake-up call.'

Esther didn't reply and when Jessica turned around, she was a few metres away, finger in ear, having a conversation that sounded like it was about who they should call to get petrol drained from a diesel engine.

As the Home Secretary said something about either empowerment or impairment, one of the shoppers hurried across the back of the hundred-strong crowd and then stopped to chat to one of the uniformed police officers.

'I'll bet he's either asking what's going on, or he's trying to find out where he can get a dozen eggs,' Esther said, rejoining Jessica.

'Everything all right?'

'Don't ask. Your lot can't be this bad, can they?'

'We got called out to some disturbance at a bowling alley last week. Someone reported a bloke waving a knife around and we sent a team in through the fire exit, not knowing it opened onto the alley itself. Three uniforms went through just as little Jonny-it's-my-twelfth-birthday lobs a ball down. He ends up wiping out the lot of them and then some other kid thinks it's planned entertainment for the party and throws another. Before our boys know it everyone's having a go. They ended up needing the parents to protect them from the kids. One bloke lost his front teeth.'

'Ha! You did well to keep that out of the papers.'

'I think someone threatened to nick the lot of them for assault with a deadly bowling ball or something.'

'What happened to the guy with the knife?'

'There wasn't one – it was one of the chefs that someone had seen walking into the kitchen. You'd have thought the oversized hat and white overalls might've given it away. I was on a day off so I can't be blamed for any of it. I was just responsible for the giant bag of Skittles that was left on night shift's desk.'

Esther laughed as the man chatting to the police officer on the plaza gave a cheery wave, picked up his supermarket carrier bags, and continued walking away from the stage.

Finger pressed to her ear again, Esther breathed a sigh of relief. 'The minister's car is on its way, so he's nearly done. We're one short for the escort to the train station but I doubt he'll notice.'

'Which station?'

'Piccadilly.'

Jessica pointed to the road adjoining the plaza directly in front of her in between a coffee shop and a bank. 'What, the Piccadilly Station that's five minutes' walk that way?'

'Don't ask. The PM had an escort, so he wants an escort. If we get away without the sirens going, it'll be a miracle.'

Esther picked up the binoculars and did another sweep of the area. 'Let's hear it then.'

'What?'

'Your old DI went on gardening leave, didn't he, and never came back?'

'Jason?'

'Reynolds, or something. Was it true he leaked that story about the teacher and the student?'

'More or less.'

'Good man. Wish I'd had the balls to leak a few things over the years. And you got his job?'

Jessica tugged at the sleeve of her jacket, feeling uncomfortable. 'Something like that . . .'

Esther's description of events wasn't that far away from the truth – but Jessica's promotion had only happened after a period away from the job which she didn't particularly want to talk about. She'd been trying to move on and the new job was at least helping, partially because of the amount of paperwork she had to either fill in or sign off.

A large group of student-types – jeans below their arses, expensive trainers, smiling – walked out from Oldham Street and started to cross the area from one side, just as a tram pulled into the station on the other and a horde of commuters emerged.

'You do realise this is the worst perimeter I've ever seen for an event?' Jessica said.

'The minister didn't want it closed off because he wanted the public to be able to "get involved". I think "accessible" must be some buzzword at the moment because his advisor mentioned it a dozen times.'

'So he wanted us to have a "presence" but he also wanted to be in public, with everyone able to "get involved"?'

'I think he wanted his arse wiping too but he's got all those blokes on stage lining up to do that. This is the best I could manage.'

There were seven uniformed officers standing at the back of the crowd and another two on the stage. Off to the side, a dozen more were fighting to get a clear view through the shoppers.

'Chilly, innit?' Jessica said, changing the subject.

'They reckon it's going to get even cooler next week. Some grinning weatherman was saying last night it was the coldest start to a May on record.'

'Knobhead.'

'Quite. It's like they relish giving bad news. Imagine sending one of them round on a death knock – they'd take party balloons.'

Jessica pointed towards one of the students with hair gelled into thick spikes jutting off in various directions. 'Look at that guy – he's got shorts and a T-shirt on. It's just above freezing.'

'We should nick him just for the hair.'

As the two groups met in the middle of the plaza, it almost doubled the crowd in front of the politician. Perhaps buoyed by the increase in audience, the man in the pink tie leant into the lectern, angling towards the camera, and said something that he at least looked like he believed, punctuating each word with a pump of his fist. It got a limp round of applause, which was more than it deserved.

Esther was on the radio again, louder this time. 'Well

tell him to pull his finger out – and if he doesn't, tell him I'll rip it off and shove it sideways up his—' Another angry flap of her free arm. 'No, I don't need you to write it down, just tell him.'

As Jessica was beginning to wonder if the pins and needles in her leg meant it was colder than she'd thought, she realised it was actually her phone buzzing in her pocket. She plucked it out and tried to read the text message before tutting and hunting around in her jacket.

'What's up?'

'Bloody glasses. I'm always losing them.'

'I've never seen you wearing glasses.'

'I only need them for reading close up. Plus I look like an idiot in them.'

'Weren't you on your phone a minute ago?'

'That was just arsing around to look busy. Do it around the station, tut a lot as if you've got stuff on and no one bothers you half the time.' Jessica finally found her glasses in her top pocket and put them on, only to delete the message instantly. 'Some spam saying they'll get me compensation for an accident.' She re-pocketed everything. 'Go on, you can say it.'

'What?'

'I know you want to.'

'Fine, you do look a bit . . . *weird* . . . with them on.'

'Thanks.'

'Not in a bad way, just . . . all right, I'll stop digging. Anyway, we're keeping an eye on that Heaton ParkFest shambles at the end of the month. I could probably sort you a ticket or two if you fancied it?'

'Don't even get me started. I've already got tickets – not my choice.'

'Ha! I was just being nice, I didn't think it'd be your thing.'

'If I wanted to spend a freezing afternoon swaying gently in a field, I'd—'

Jessica's sentence was cut short as a woman's scream rippled across the plaza, followed by another and another until it sounded like the entire crowd was braying at the top of their voices. Jessica set off at full pelt but Esther was already barrelling ahead, bellowing into her radio mic for details. The cold air filled Jessica's lungs in seconds and by the time she was close enough to have an idea of what had happened she could barely breathe. People were running in all directions, the thin line of uniformed officers struggling to maintain anything approaching a perimeter, let alone keep control.

As Jessica put her hands on her hips and tried to catch her breath, sirens blared in the distance, drowning out a man's hysterical cries: 'He's down, call an ambulance'.

2

DCI Jack Cole sat in the sparsely filled temporary incident room on the first floor of Longsight Police Station, looking at Jessica and the four unfortunate PCs who had been walking through reception when Jessica had grabbed them to make the event look busy. The actual incident room in the basement had been closed the previous week for renovations, with no one seemingly thinking CID might need somewhere to work in the meantime. As an alternative, some of the far smaller, damp-riddled storerooms had been cleared out upstairs. The fact there was no adequate heating system in rooms usually filled with boxes didn't appear to be a priority for anyone, meaning coats and gloves were a necessity.

The chief inspector seemed to be losing hair by the day, sporting a receding hairline that could have been parted by Moses. The worry lines across his forehead were now permanent features, although if Jessica had had to tell a superintendent about the bowling-ball incident, then she might have them too.

Cole stared at Jessica as the PCs shuffled nervously, probably wondering why they were there. 'So to sum up, I've been in meetings since first thing this morning,' he said. 'The Home Secretary's back in London on the warpath, telling all and sundry that there weren't enough officers on duty and that he'll be pushing for a full investigation.'

Jessica was feeling defensive. 'I wasn't even officially there! I was doing Esther a favour and it wasn't her fault either – he said he wanted to be accessible, how were we meant to know some loon would turn up with a bottle full of acid?'

'Aylesbury's gone bananas – it's been on the news channels non-stop all day.'

'I'm surprised the super found time to get himself off the golf course. It's not as if it was raining.'

Cole silenced Jessica with a 'you're-an-inspector-now' look, something she had seen a few times recently. No wonder he was losing his hair.

'Where is everyone?' Cole asked.

'Half of them are still out cleaning up from the weekend, the rest are on it. We're a DS down too . . .'

Jessica had constantly been onto the DCI about the fact she hadn't yet been replaced, meaning that, although she had technically been promoted, she was now doing an entirely new workload as well as much of what she had handled before. 'Budgetary constraints' and 'I'm aware' were his favourite responses. Cole ignored her, nodding towards the empty whiteboard.

'Someone keeps nicking the pens or there'd be stuff on there,' Jessica explained. 'If you don't nail it down around here, some bugger walks off with it. Someone should get the police in.'

Cole wasn't amused.

'All right, fine,' she added. 'Councillor Luke Callaghan

was hit in the face with some sort of acid thrown from something we're not sure about yet. We're going to have to wait for the results but the paramedics reckon it was nitric. It's not the type of thing you can buy over the counter, so we're trying to get a list of suppliers and potential buyers. Izzy says there are loads – plus some of the businesses who store it have thousands of staff on their books. It was only a small quantity, so we're looking at all sorts of places, mainly labs. Don't expect anything any time soon – we're getting nailed on overtime, so the late boys might have to help out.'

One of the PCs had found a marker and written the victim's name on the board. In Jessica's mind, this made him prime suspect for the spate of pen thefts.

'Who's Luke Callaghan?' Cole asked.

'He's a councillor for the Old Moat ward – got in at the last election with a narrow majority. Thirty-five, married, runs some sort of technology company.'

PC Pen-Thief wrote 'Old Maid ward', 'techno comp' and 'nitro acid' on the whiteboard in appalling handwriting.

'How is he?'

'He's still in surgery. The acid hit him in the face but we've not heard anything else. The media haven't got his name yet but it's not for the want of trying. We caught some master-of-disguise journalist trying to sneak into the ward wearing a white coat. He'd managed to wander through reception, past hospital security and was outside the door getting out his camera phone when one of our boys nabbed him.'

'Who does he work for?'

'No idea – he'd probably sold his mother to get the coat, you know what journalists are like. Either way, his phone was accidentally trodden on by one of the officers as he was being escorted out. We've been trying to get hold of Callaghan's wife but with no luck. There's no answer at the family home and we don't know where she works.'

Cole turned to the board, new worry lines joining the old ones as he scowled at the spelling. 'I'm judging by the focus on the victim that there's no news on who actually threw the acid?'

Jessica had long been worried by how transparent she apparently was to Cole. They had been working together for far too long. 'We've got half-a-dozen people going through every CCTV camera in the area.' She pulled a folded-up printout from her pocket and handed it to PC Pen-Thief, who attached it to the board with a magnet. 'We've got our guy getting off the tram, mingling through a group of students and then joining the back of the crowd who were listening to the Home Secretary. As you can see, he kept his hood up.'

Jessica realised the 'as you can see' was an exaggeration given how poor the photograph was. Cole turned to look at the photo, tilting his head to the side and creating another worry line.

'That's a snap taken from the camera on the tram station,' Jessica said. 'We've been trying to get one from the actual tram but some little shite had covered it with duct tape and no one apparently noticed. We've got a couple of shots from the back but I doubt we have too many people who can ID him from that. If they can, I've got a stack of

CCTV hoody shots they can have a go at first. The only other ones we have are from the side but it's nothing useable – the media will have a field day if we stick any of them out.'

PC Pen-Thief wrote 'hoddy' on the board.

'Witnesses?' Cole asked.

'Our hoody gradually made his way to the front of the crowd. It wasn't tightly packed so he didn't have any problems. Most of the people there scarpered as soon as the screaming began, so we're trying to identify them too and we've got the usual appeals out for help with our inquiries, blah, blah, blah. The only ones who didn't make a break for it, predictably, were the ones who didn't see anything.'

Cole dragged a chair towards the board, screeching it along the hard floor like a nail down a blackboard. 'Do we at least know where he or she escaped to?'

Jessica pointed towards the printout on the board. 'We're assuming "he" – roughly five foot nine or ten – and it looks like he might have a hint of a beard on that picture. It could just be the dodgy camera though.'

The word 'Man' appeared on the board, spelled correctly but in such dreadful handwriting that it looked more like 'Nom'.

'We've got him heading along Oldham Street and then disappearing into the Northern Quarter alleys. We're trying to get the CCTV enhanced but it's the same old story. After that, there's nothing. We're checking number plates just in case he had a car waiting but there's nothing so far and I wouldn't expect anything anyway – he knew where he was going. He could easily have changed his clothes and gone back to the centre. We're checking the alleys in case any clothing has been abandoned but I've just got a load of people complaining about hunting through rubbish. Dispatch told me one of our lot found a pile of used condoms under a flower pot. Knowing the area, it could've been some sort of modern art thing but then it could just be a bunch of daisy-chaining teenagers. Either way, they're pissed off.'

'Is there actually any good news?' Cole asked.

'I wouldn't call it that. We've been talking to the news channels to see if they captured our hoody on camera without making it too obvious that we've got nothing ourselves. We've given them the old "maintaining relations" line and slipped in that we could get a warrant – but if they had any footage of the guy, they'd be running it themselves. There's nothing so far and we're not expecting anything.'

Jessica saw the little colour that was left in Cole's face drain away as he rubbed the skin above his left eye until it began to flake. She guessed he was picturing the conversation he was going to have with the superintendent: no suspect, hardly any camera footage, no witnesses, one councillor in hospital – all in a daytime attack in the city centre as the Home Secretary watched on.

It wasn't one of Greater Manchester Police's finer moments.

'What exactly are the news channels saying?'

Jessica peered over his shoulder towards the board, deliberately avoiding eye contact. 'The usual – some ex-Met police guy was on, saying that security should have been tighter and that he didn't believe something like that would happen in Westminster.'

'They really think we're all monkeys up here, don't they?'

'Well we do get paid peanuts . . .'

Another hint of a worry line creased onto Cole's forehead, a tram map of interconnecting concerns. Definitely not the time for jokes.

Jessica continued quickly before he could reply. 'They're speculating it was a failed attack on the Home Secretary but we've got nothing to confirm that. In fact, the few vague witness statements we do have say our hoody didn't go anywhere near the stage. Callaghan was standing in the front row with a few other councillors and the attacker dashed across the front of them before disappearing across the plaza.'

'So was Callaghan the target?'

'Perhaps. He was on the Internet last night publicising the appearance, so if someone did have it in for him, they'd know where he'd be.'

The door at the back of the room banged open as a slightly dishevelled-looking PC stumbled through, arms wrapped around himself, hair limp and flat. 'It's bloody freezing out there,' he said through chattering teeth. When he realised he wasn't talking to a sympathetic audience, he pulled out a cardboard folder from inside his jacket. 'I've been told to bring a few things up for you, Ma'am—'

'It's just Jess.'

No matter how high she was promoted, Jessica didn't think she could ever get used to being called anything other than her name. At a push, she could live with 'Inspector' and would even settle for 'the gobby one' if it meant not being called 'Ma'am' or 'Guv'. Anything official made her feel even older than she was.

'Right, er, *Jess* . . . we've managed to get a shot of the hoody from one of the hotel cameras facing the plaza. It was taken as he was crossing from the tram.'

Jessica reached out to take the folder. 'Have you got a face?'

'Not exactly.'

He wasn't wrong. If she squinted, Jessica could just about make out the shape of the hooded figure's head. The face was partly in shadow but even the lighter bits were a speckled blur. 'What am I looking at? This is worse than what we've already got.'

'Look at his hand.' Because of the fuzziness, Jessica couldn't say for certain that it was definitely a hand but whatever it was had hold of a white blob. 'Our guys say it's probably some sort of flask, or possibly a coloured glass beaker.'

'Are you sure it's not a coffee cup?' Jessica asked, looking up.

The PC checked a Post-it note he was carrying. 'Er, I don't think so. Wouldn't the acid have gone through that?'

'No idea but if it was someone carrying around some skinny latte thing, then we could have brought in any of those TV people hanging around.'

'Right . . .'

Definitely not the time for jokes.

'Anything else?'

19

The PC checked a second Post-it note and began to read. 'The team searching the Northern Quarter alleys said to tell you that . . . oh . . . this is more a stream of abuse than an actual message. Fat Pat's on the desk today – I'm not sure why he kept this.'

Jessica snatched it away, read it quickly and then screwed it into a ball, before launching it at – and missing – the bin. 'Sodding thing.'

'There's one more. Apparently Luke Callaghan's wife called 999 last night to say he was trying to attack her.'

3

Jessica edged around a rusting skip filled with scrap metal and hopped over a patch of mud onto a crumbling path. Landing unsteadily, she narrowly avoided falling over what looked like some sort of ancient boiler, made sure no one had been watching, and headed for the front door. The crimson paint and cracked glass of the opening led into a concrete hallway that gave off the unmistakeable smell of eau de piss.

Considering her husband was a councillor and ran his own business, the area of Hulme in which Debbie Callaghan lived was quite the comedown.

Jessica went up the steps, being careful not to touch anything, as she made her way to the third floor. The wall in front was decorated with the spray-painted slogan 'fuk da policje' – which was either part-English, part-gibberish, part-Polish, or someone local went to the same school as PC Pen-Thief. The other option was that it was a post-modern comment on the integration of Eastern Europeans into British society – but given the swastika drawn above, Jessica doubted it.

A middle-aged woman with greying brown hair pulled back into a ponytail invited Jessica into the poky phone box masquerading as a flat and apologised for the mess. She was wearing an unflattering jumper and a pair of jeans that were too long and hanging over her socks. As she entered the living room-cum-kitchen-cum-bedroom, Jessica had to admit that, compared to the outside, the flat's interior wasn't too bad. Bright prints took the edge off the flaking grey walls and Debbie's cushions, throws and ornaments at least made the place look hospitable. As for the mess, if she thought this was untidy, Jessica thought Debbie should come to her house.

Debbie invited Jessica to sit on the blanket-covered sofa as she fussed around the room, moving her ornaments, wiping away specks of dust and moving onto the next. 'Sorry about this, I've not been in long and it's . . . well, it's a complete dump around here. Your people last night said someone would be round.'

With nothing in their official records, Jessica had used the details given to the 999 operator the previous evening to find the address.

'This isn't quite about your reasons for calling 999 last night,' Jessica replied, before explaining that Debbie's husband had been attacked that morning. If she knew anything about it, the woman had a good poker face, even if she didn't seem too concerned.

Debbie continued to move around the room, glancing over her shoulder towards Jessica as she replied. 'I suppose I'm not listed as Luke's next-of-kin any longer. It's not a surprise no one called. I moved out around three months ago but we've not had much of a relationship for years.'

'What happened last night?'

'I told them I didn't want to make a statement.'

'It didn't sound like that when you called 999 – you said your husband was attacking you.'

Debbie paused by a small heater and crouched, using a cloth to wipe between the grooves. She didn't look up. 'I made a mistake. It doesn't matter now, does it?'

'When you phoned, the operator heard a male voice shouting abuse in the background.'

'It was someone down the hallway – you can see what it's like around here.'

'You do realise that wasting police time is an offence and that you could be jailed for making a hoax call?'

Debbie sighed, sitting on the floor and turning around to face Jessica. 'Fine, he was here – but I still don't want to make a statement.'

'Perhaps we can just have a brew then?'

Debbie didn't reply, so Jessica stood and crossed to the kitchen area, filling the kettle and clicking it on before starting to hunt through the cupboards.

'Tea bags are under the sink with the sugar, mugs are next to the cooker, milk's in the fridge. Mine's a Julie.'

'A what?'

'A Julie – as in Andrews. A white nun: milk, no sugar. Sorry, my dad was in the navy.' Jessica leant against the cooker and waited for Debbie to meet her gaze. 'It was a last resort to call you,' Debbie said. 'Luke's been round here every few days since we split up. At first he was begging me to go back to him but when I kept saying I didn't want to, he'd turn up drunk and shouting. Yesterday was the worst.'

'Why did you leave him?'

Debbie picked herself up off the floor and moved to the

sofa. 'We've been married since we were seventeen. When I left, I'd just turned thirty-five and it took me most of those years to realise that it's not normal to be in a relationship where the other person wants to know where you are all the time.'

The kettle started to steam and Jessica filled the two mugs before crossing to the sofa and sitting next to the woman, offering her the drink.

Debbie took a sip before continuing. 'After we left college, I gradually lost all of my friends because he didn't like it if I went out by myself. He'd stay up and then want to know exactly where I'd been and who I'd spoken to. Then he'd keep going on about men that were out, wanting to know if I'd talked to anyone or if they'd tried to chat me up. If I said I'd only been with my mates, then he'd go on about how I must have something to hide but if I said someone tried to buy me a drink, or held a door open for me, he'd hit the roof. He'd accuse me of wanting to sleep with them. Eventually, I stopped going out.'

'How old were you?'

'Twenty-three? Twenty-four? It was the same everywhere. If I went to the supermarket, he'd want to know if I'd been served by a man or a woman. When I got home from work, he'd want to know what I'd done all day. I worked in an office and Luke was obsessed with my boss because he was a bloke. He kept saying I wanted to sleep with him to get a promotion. Eventually I ended up quitting. As my career fell apart, his took off with his business and then the politics thing.'

Jessica couldn't stop herself. 'He sounds like a right charmer.'

Debbie had another sip of her tea. 'Quite. When he got elected, he liked having me there just for the image of having an adoring wife behind him. But then he'd have meetings and other business, so I'd be alone at the house a lot. Have you been there?'

'Not yet.'

'We've got this beautiful place out Withington. We bought it when Luke's business started to do well. Because I was at home all the time, I had nothing to do except tidy the place up. By the end, I was staying with him more because I couldn't face leaving the house.'

'What made you change your mind?'

Debbie finished her tea and put the mug on the floor. As she leant back, she rolled her sleeve up, waiting for Jessica to digest the criss-crossing red scars on her bicep.

'Did you—?'

'I didn't tell anyone, least of all your lot. He came home drunk one night. There'd been a problem with the washing machine and an engineer had been round. He wanted to know what he looked like and how old he was, then if I'd made him tea. I said that the guy just came, fixed it, and left but Luke wasn't having it. He pinned me up against the wall, screaming in my face, calling me a bitch and a slag. He said he'd slash my throat in my sleep and bury my body where no one would find it.'

'Why didn't you tell us? We have people—'

Debbie's demeanour changed instantly, shuffling away from Jessica and standing quickly, knocking over the empty mug with her foot. 'You must think I'm stupid. Luke might have had his problems but I'd rather trust him than your lot.'

'Mrs Calla—'

Debbie cut her off, shouting: 'No, you listen. I told you I didn't want to make a statement and I don't. If you've just come here to tell me about what happened to Luke then you've done that, so you can leave.'

Jessica didn't stand, rolling up the sleeves of her jacket and blouse until the thick red marks around her own wrists were visible. She sat with her palms facing up, feeling Debbie's eyes on them, before pulling the material back down. 'It's not what you think,' she said.

Debbie picked up the mug and sat back on the sofa, wrapping her fingers through the handle and closing her eyes. 'Sorry . . .'

'You don't have to apologise.'

Debbie shook her head, remaining silent for a few moments, gaze fixed on Jessica before she started to speak slowly. 'I said my dad was in the navy but that was when I was a kid – he died in prison when I was a teenager. He was no angel but he always said one of you lot fitted him up for some post-office job. Said he wasn't even in the city at the time. I don't know the truth – but he was my dad, y'know? And he hated you lot.'

'I'm not sure what you want me to say.'

Debbie tugged at her jumper, shrugging. 'Two days later when Luke was out, I packed up my stuff and came here. I saw an advert in the paper and phoned the landlord. I don't know how he found out where I was but Luke came knocking a few days after, crying, saying he was sorry and that he missed me. Then he was back a day later, asking if I'd return. Two days later and he was angry again, going on about how I was going to ruin his career because politicians needed to be married. Then he was laughing and saying that I was in this shithole and that he'd make sure I didn't get a penny of his money. I didn't even want anything.'

'What happened last night?'

'He was drunk, shouting worse than ever, saying that I was a whore and all the usual stuff. He said no one would want me because I'm too old. Then he pulled out a knife – which is when I called you.'

'What did he do?'

'Not much. When I told him I was talking to the police, he said that I'd keep and then he scarpered.'

'And you've not seen him since?'

'No.'

'I've got to ask you this—'

'I was at an AA meeting this morning. I used to drink a lot around the house – there wasn't much else to do – but when I moved out, I decided I was going to get myself clean. I can give you the name of the guy who runs it. He'll vouch for me.'

Debbie crossed to the kitchen, hunting through her handbag. Jessica knew the alibi would check out but there was still a possibility that if the woman was desperate for revenge she could have hired someone else to attack Luke for her.

Debbie passed Jessica a scrap of paper with the name

'Shane Donovan' and a phone number on, adding: 'You can't think I'm involved. I'm just a normal person. I've hardly got any friends and the ones I do know work in bakeries, hospitals. I go out for coffee once or twice a week with the woman who lives next door and we moan about the people downstairs. She lost her dad recently, so it's been hard for her.'

'Do you know anyone who might have it in for Luke?'

'You name it. He wasn't exactly popular with the main rival candidate when he got elected. The guy Luke beat had been in the same seat for twenty-odd years but these leaflets went out to a bunch of houses in the area, saying he was a paedo. Luke denied all knowledge and the election board said it wasn't provable. I don't know for sure and Luke never said anything about them but it wouldn't surprise me – it's the kind of thing he'd do. He ended up winning by a couple of hundred votes. Then there's Michael, of course.'

'Who's that?'

'Michael Cowell. We all knew each other at college. He and Luke used to be business partners but it all fell apart. I don't know the ins and outs but Luke used to rage about him all the time up until a year or so back.'

'Do you have any details?'

'Nothing that would have been recent – plus I left almost everything at the house. I only took what I could carry when I moved out.' She indicated around the room. 'Most of this stuff comes from charity shops.'

Jessica turned down a second cup of tea and checked a few more things, before leaving Debbie her card. She told her which hospital Luke had been taken to but wasn't entirely surprised by the reply: 'At least I'll be able to sleep tonight without worrying about him coming round here with a knife.'

At that, Jessica was gone; past the swastika, down the pissy stairs and back across the obstacle course of a garden to her car.

'Bloody . . . bastard . . . bloody . . . thing. Can you hear me?'

Detective Constable Izzy Diamond's reply echoed clearly through the speakers in Jessica's car. 'I can hear a lot of swearing, so if that's you, then yes.'

'It's this Bluetooth thing, I never know if it's working. It used to be quite the skill to hold a phone between your ear and shoulder, steer with one hand, change gear with the other, overtake a string of cars and talk someone through an interview all at the same time. Then they went and banned it and now we're at the mercy of technology. Philistines.'

'I think there's a few officers around here still suffering from post-traumatic stress after being in a car with you, so perhaps they were onto something?'

Smart-arse.

Jessica waited behind a row of parked cars as a dustbin lorry sat in the middle of the road leading off Debbie's estate. The early morning sun had given way to the usual grey skies and a biting wind and the bin men – or hygiene technicians as they were probably known nowadays – were draped in an array of hats, gloves and scarves, their breaths spiralling into the air. They pulled a succession of wheelie bins into the road, blocking both directions of traffic, as Jessica checked the car's clock, knowing it was going to be one of those days.

'I didn't quite catch that,' Jessica said. 'The line is all crackly. Anyway, I've got some names for you.'

'From the wife?'

'Yes, she's Debbie Callaghan; married Luke not long after leaving school. He sounds like quite the shite. She says he used to beat her, mental abuse, made her stay indoors, probably cheated at Cluedo too. A right nasty bastard.'

'Do you believe her?'

Jessica leant on her horn as the bin men stood having a chat in the middle of the road. 'Probably – she's got the marks, plus there was a lot of detail she would have had to make up on the spot. She's got an alibi for this morning too – she was at an AA meeting run by some Shane Donovan bloke. I've given him a call and will go have a word.'

Jessica heard the sound of a keyboard rattling. 'So you reckon Luke might have been the target?' Izzy asked.

'Maybe. She had quite a story.'

'So could she be involved, with an accomplice?'

'I doubt it but check her out anyway.' Jessica also asked Izzy to find some details on Michael Cowell, the candidate Luke beat in the election, and Debbie's next-door neighbour. If in doubt, cover your own arse. 'How's the CCTV hunt going?' she added.

'How do you think? We've got a marginally better

image from a camera just off the square but it's still a fuzzy grey mess. The tech guys are going to see what they can do but we'll probably end up with a slightly less fuzzy mess. Witnesses are a waste of time – and they're the ones we can find.'

'The Guv?'

'He's not left his office. One of the girls said she heard shouting and that when she walked past it looked like he was untying his shoelaces.'

'I hope she bloody stopped him – we've got enough paperwork.' Jessica continued to speak as she undid her seatbelt and leant across the passenger's side to see what was going on with the unmoving dustbin lorry. It was apparently nothing, while there was now a string of traffic behind her. 'The poor guy's had a shite year since his missus left him. Every time we have a conversation, it's about what an arse the super's being – or how much of the budget he has to cut. Who'd be a chief inspector, eh?'

'At least he's not cleaning used johnnies out of plant pots.'

'You heard about that?'

'There's a whole search team gunning for you.'

'That's what they're getting paid for.'

'Anything else?'

'See what you can dig up about Debbie Callaghan's father – he apparently died in prison twenty years ago. Got put away for holding up a post office. It's probably nothing but you never know. Give it to Dave.'

'He's on holiday, remember?'

Another long beep of the horn. 'Still? How long's he

been gone? If he's off for any longer, it counts as emigrating, doesn't it?'

'He only left four days ago.'

'I thought it'd been quiet. Right, I've got a group of dustmen to kill—'

'There's one other thing. We're still checking but there was a post on some anarchist web forum congratulating them for the success of the attack.'

'That's all we need. Isn't there enough porn on the Internet to keep this lot occupied? What do the tech guys reckon – is it legit?'

'Not sure, it could be a hoax or someone getting the wrong end of the stick. It relates to a group called Anarky.'

'Spelled with a K-Y?'

'Exactly, do you know them?'

'I know a man who does. Well, either that or a certain pen-thieving PC has been answering the phones again.'

4

Jessica walked carefully through the tight streets of the Northern Quarter, just in case any of the search team were still out and wanting revenge. Stray carrier bags fluttered between the grimy buildings as the arctic breeze was joined by a thin film of mist, just to make the day even better. One lone police van was parked on the main through road but, aside from that, the back alleys were a mix of the usual shoppers who'd got lost and locals using the area as a shortcut and potential toilet.

With its live music, pubs, cafes and independent shops – not to mention the 'characters' often found roaming the alleys along the backs of the main streets – the Northern Quarter provided its own unique form of entertainment.

After one full circuit through the zigzagging maze of streets, Jessica had barely seen anyone, let alone the man she was looking for. It also looked like the search team had done quite the clean-up considering the general lack of rubbish and half-eaten abandoned takeaways that would usually be on the streets.

Jessica returned to her car wondering what to do next when she figured there was no harm in trying the obvious. She headed towards a nearby pub and the adjacent white plastic door with the shabbily scrawled '43' that was written on in permanent marker. The door buzzer was hanging on by a thin wire but Jessica pushed it anyway, feeling the vibration in her finger as a low angry rumble echoed from inside. She waited for a few seconds and had already stepped away, ready to head back to the station, when she heard a chain unclinking as the door opened inwards.

It took Jessica a few moments to realise that the person in the doorway was who she was after. 'Toxic' Tony Farnsworth was an alcoholic drug user who, despite having this flat, often lived on the streets. He had a long string of convictions, generally for low-level thefts, and had once been banned from every licensed premises in the city centre. Then he'd had shaggy unkempt hair, a track of razor nicks across his cheeks where he'd tried to shave and a thin nothingness of a frame from years of living on little but booze and the contents of a syringe. The man in front of her had almost the same features but everything was tidier. His hair was short and flat, his cheeks fuller and covered with a thin layer of stubble. Instead of the enormous coat he used to wear, Tony was in skinny jeans and a tight-fitting long-sleeved sweater. Although he was still lean, his chest and arms were larger and he no longer looked like a government warning poster for anorexia.

'Tony?'

His eyes widened. 'Do I know you?'

Jessica pulled out her ID card. 'We've met before – quite a few times.'

Tony squinted at her card and withdrew into the entrance of his flat, hugging his arms around himself. 'I don't exactly remember that much about the past few years. Daniel . . . Daniel . . .' He rolled the name around his tongue a few times. 'Did you once arrest me in an off-licence?'

'Twice. One time you'd tried to steal some brandy from the top shelf, slipped and knocked yourself out on the ice-cream freezer; another time, the shopkeeper hit the panic alarm and left you alone in the shop. You'd panicked and—'

'Pissed myself . . . I remember. You were blonder then, bit younger. Told me to stop fucking my life up or I'd end up dead or in prison.'

'Sounds about right.'

'You bought me breakfast another time too.' Tony rubbed the back of his head nervously, making the hair stick up. 'I've not done anything wrong. I know you lot used to be around all the time 'cos I'd been out nicking but I'm clean now.'

'That's not why I'm here.'

At first Tony seemed confused but then his eyes widened. 'Oh, it's not me ma, is it?'

'It's to do with Anarky.'

'Oh . . . you better come in.'

Tony led Jessica up a flight of stairs into a flat that was bigger than Debbie's but much emptier. Aside from a tiny portable television, a sofa and flat-packed ready-to-fall-apart coffee table, the living room was bare.

Tony headed straight for the doorway at the back of the room. 'Fancy a tea? That's what you lot drink, ain't it?' Indeed it was – Jessica was drowning in the bloody stuff. A police officer's opium. Tony continued without waiting for an answer, his voice echoing through the open door. 'I've got ginseng, Earl Grey, Lung Ching, Bancha, mixed berry, Koslanda, Assam, Darjeeling, Covent Garden and a bit of Oolong somewhere. Any one in particular?'

He'd replaced one addiction with another. Jessica didn't know which was worse; she might even prefer the hard drugs. 'Whatever you're having.'

Jessica would usually have had a poke around but there was nothing to poke at, so she sat on the sofa instead. A few minutes later, Tony returned with two dainty china teacups on a tray with a matching teapot.

'I went for the Bancha,' he said, putting the tray on the table and sitting on the floor. 'Best leave it for a bit to let the leaves do their thing.'

Junkie.

'So, Anarky . . .'

Tony glanced away towards the corner of the room. 'I've not been on any of their marches for ages. I left all that behind.'

'But you used to be a part of everything they did. You were on our watch list – probably still are – because every time there was a protest march through the city, there you were.'

As he reached towards the teapot, Tony's hand was shaking. He plucked off the lid, took out the strainer, and dunked in a spoon, swirling the liquid around manically. 'I was different then. Those guys used to meet in the pub, so I'd see 'em there. I was so pissed half the time, I didn't even know what they were on about. I thought they were on a pub crawl.'

'Come on, Tony . . .'

He filled both cups with a steaming green liquid that smelled vaguely of tree bark and offered Jessica one, the saucer rattling in his hand as he passed it over. 'Okay, it wasn't quite like that but I still didn't really know them. They'd go on about how big government was run by rich men and that we were all puppets. They bought me a few drinks, so I tagged along.'

'What about the other marches?'

Tony sat back on the floor, sipping his tea, his eyes on Jessica's feet. 'I don't remember everything but it was always a day out – a bit of excitement. I remember this pink one where they had biscuits at the end.'

'Pink one?'

'Yeah, a bunch of girls all wearing pink going on about stuff. I remember the colour.'

'I think that was a breast cancer awareness march.'

'Whatever – I'm just saying that I don't remember much. Whenever I saw the groups around, I thought free booze or free biscuits. Then someone would say, "Let's smash something up", and I'd be all "Yeah, let's stick it to the man, man". It was all the booze.'

'I take it you're not talking about the breast cancer march. They don't tend to do much smashing.'

The corners of Tony's lips curled into a smile and Jessica realised he was actually quite good-looking. Now they weren't hazed over by a drug-related fog of confusion, his eyes had a glint, mischievous but not shop-smashing. She couldn't remember but perhaps that's why she'd told him to stop mucking his life up all those years ago, rather than

37

just slapping on the cuffs and chucking him and his pissy pants into a van.

'How much do you know about Anarky?' she asked.

'Not much – there was some Tom bloke, I really don't remember. I know everyone tells you that but I actually *don't* remember and anything I could come up with could potentially be a dream anyway. I'm not entirely sure everything I recall is accurate – well, unless I once sat down for tea with a giant green elephant and we talked about the onset of global capitalism.'

It was Jessica's turn to grin. She picked up the tea and sniffed it, thinking it smelled a bit like her back garden after a solid weekend of rain. She sipped it anyway, surprising herself by not gagging. It wasn't that bad, so she took another drink, thinking about the impending, swirling shit-storm that awaited her back at the station and concluding she was best hiding here for as long as she could.

'How does it feel to be clean?'

Tony's smile became a laugh. 'A bit boring really – I don't know what to do with myself half the time.' He lay back on the carpet, giggling to himself. 'No, it's good, like there was this grey fog which has gone now. Before, I used to look at everything as a means to getting something else to drink, or go up my arms.' He sat up again, eyes back at Jessica's feet, with a sigh. 'You'd see mobile phones in shop windows and think, "that must be worth a few quid, I wonder what I could get for that". You'd hang around cashpoints hoping someone gave you something or dropped a note. One time this woman walked off with her card but left the cash in the slot. There was about a hundred quid, so I took it and pegged it before she noticed. It only hit me a few days later that she was some woman with a kid in a pushchair, run off her feet, knackered, probably taking out her shopping money for the week. I thought about that kid going hungry, p'raps her old man giving her a slap, like, and I'd spent all her money on shite. I couldn't stop thinking about her but then it just made me depressed, so I went and nicked some shoes from this shop on Deansgate. Got twenty quid for them and guess where that went.'

'What were you on?'

Tony shrugged. 'You name it, I probably tried it. I think I was into paint-thinner for a while.'

'Why'd you get clean?'

'Me ma. When I dropped out of uni and ended up doing this, my dad said he didn't want anything to do with me. I think that made it worse 'cos that's when I moved on from the booze. But me ma came to see me one day – she sat where you are now, crying and saying that I was capable of much more. I was buzzing but there was something in her face. She kept saying she'd help. You know they've got a few quid, don't you?'

'I've heard.'

Jessica was aware that his parents owned a string of properties around the country, which Tony stood to inherit. He'd come to the city for university but dropped out during his first year for a reason no one seemed to know and ended up living rough. When his parents reported him missing, it was left to the police to tell them that their son was perfectly fine – he was choosing to live on the street.

Tony nodded: 'She was saying they'd pay for the clinic if I wanted to, p'raps sort me out with a job. I thought I could take the money and spend it on . . . y'know . . . but every time I kept thinking of me ma's face, saying she was disappointed. I mean, she's me ma – what was I supposed to do?'

'So you got help?'

'Yeah, this place out Stockport. Costs a bomb but when I got out, I thought "fair enough". It was sound, not having that fog all the time – being able to go into a shop and not seeing everything as something I could sell on. Honestly, it's the best thing I've done.'

As he continued speaking, Jessica noticed how much of the Manc twang he'd picked up; stretching out the vowels, making the Os sound like Us and pronouncing the letter Y as an E-H.

Tony finished his tea and poured a second cup, including another for Jessica. When he sat again, he tugged up his sleeve. It seemed like a day for that type of thing but his marks were far worse than either hers or Debbie's. Etched along the inside crook of elbow was a train track of scars and scratches, a web of blue, purple, black and pink indelibly a part of him.

'I've got a contact who could look at those for you,' Jessica said. 'They do good work removing things and restoring the skin.'

Tony shook his head. 'I kind of like them – it's a reminder whenever I have my top off, letting me know what I used to be.' He pointed his thumb back over his shoulder. 'Some dude with a gallery out that way wants to take photos of them. Bit weird, like, but I might do it.'

Jessica thought of the flower pot filled with used condoms that they'd found in the back alleys – perhaps it really was an art exhibit. 'What are you going to do now?' she asked.

'Me ma wants me to leave Manchester and go home.'

'Where's that?'

'Just over the border in Yorkshire. Nothing there but p'raps I need a new start? I've been working in this cafe round the corner – cleaning tables, taking orders, that sort of stuff. It feels weird taking people's money and not wanting to go off with it. It's nice – like being a normal person. That's how I got into me tea. Me ma says they'll find me something proper to do.' Tony pulled a battered mobile phone out of his pocket and pressed the screen. 'Look, I've gotta go – I've got a shift at the cafe, it's only a few hours but I've been on a trial period and don't want to be late. I really don't remember anything about Anarky.'

Tony slurped down his tea in one go as Jessica finished the dregs of hers and then helped him carry everything into the kitchen. 'It's good to see you've sorted yourself out. Given the number of man-hours you've cost us over the years, we'll probably throw a going-away party for you if you do go.' Tony took it in the spirit it was meant, laughing and picking up a denim jacket. 'What happened to your old coat?' she added.

'That giant thing with the yellow foam spilling out?'

41

'It was how we identified you on CCTV a few times – like your calling card.'

As he unlatched the door to the flat, Tony pointed towards a cupboard built into the wall. 'In there – I wanted to throw it away with everything else but it's like an old mate.'

He led her down the stairs and out of the front door. 'Do you need a lift?' Jessica asked.

'It's only around the corner. I—' Tony stopped himself, peering across the road where a man in a sharp suit and long expensive-looking overcoat was leaning against a lamppost, staring at the front door. He had a shaven head and was wearing a pair of leather gloves. Jessica saw the man's eyes flicker from Tony to her and then back again. He tapped his wrist as if to indicate a watch and then removed a phone from his pocket and turned his back.

'Who's that?' Jessica asked.

'No one.'

'It looked like he knew you.'

'Never seen him before.'

Before she could reply, Tony began hurrying along the pavement, hands in his pockets, nervously glancing towards the other side of the road where the bald man still had his back turned, phone pressed to his ear. Jessica had no idea who he was but even from a distance, she could smell something distinctive: trouble.

5

Izzy stuck a small pile of Post-it notes on Jessica's computer monitor and stepped backwards, narrowly avoiding tripping over a haphazard stack of cardboard folders and collapsing into a chair. 'Are you ever going to move office?'

Jessica skimmed the top note. 'I don't want to cause all that upheaval for everyone.'

'You mean you don't want to move all your crap?'

Jessica peered over her glasses at the constable, nodding towards the back corner where a grubby pile of cardboard document boxes were stacked. 'That too, Christ knows what's back there.' She paused, before adding: 'You know, you've become a lot more cynical since you let your hair go back to its natural colour. When you were red or purple, you were nice happy-go-lucky Izzy, now you're all "isn't everything shite".'

Izzy started tugging at her hair. 'Perhaps it's just that my level of cynicism is directly related to how long I've worked with you? Either that, or it's since I had Amber.'

'How old is she now?'

'Twenty-five months.'

Jessica counted on her fingers. 'Two then?'

'Pretty much.'

'I've never got that with parents – ask them how old their kid is and it's like: "Ooh, little Billy's thirty-eight months now". You don't get that off adults, do you? Take your first boyfriend home and you tell your dad he's one hundred and seventy-nine months, or whatever.'

Izzy let her strand of hair go. 'Fancy a tea before I talk you through everything?'

'No chance – my body's about forty per cent Earl Grey at the moment. Before I started here, I never drank the stuff, now I can't get through to lunch without ten cups.'

In the other half of the room, a phone started ringing. Izzy started to stretch towards it but Jessica told her to leave it. 'They've not managed to redirect Louise's calls to the sergeant station yet, so everything comes through here.'

'Doesn't that mean we should answer it?'

Jessica took off her glasses and rubbed her eyes. 'How long have you worked here?'

'Three, four years?'

'Lesson number three is never answer a phone unless it's your own. If you can get away with it, don't even answer your own, it's only ever bad news.'

'What's lesson one?'

'I'm always right.'

'Even when you're wrong?'

'Especially when I'm wrong.'

'And lesson two?'

'Always get someone else to make the tea. If it's your turn, make a shit one then nobody asks again. And don't trust the tea machine – whatever they put in there isn't tea, it's more like dishwater.'

Izzy ignored her. 'If all the sergeants have been moved into their own office, what's happening in here?'

Jessica put her feet on the desk at the same time as the phone stopped ringing. 'They're apparently hiring. They need a sergeant to replace me, perhaps another one too, a DI and a constable or two. And if you believe that, you'll believe anything – they'll end up promoting someone, getting somebody in on work experience and that'll be about it.'

'What do you want first – Anarky, Debbie or a surprise?'

'Always the surprise.'

'Okay, it's not much of a surprise though. There's been a pile-up on the M60 out Audenshaw way, some lorry driver in the fog wiped out a Peugeot. The traffic is chaos already because everyone's coming through the city. Half the people we had out doing stuff are stuck in traffic jams – well, either that or they've buggered off home, which I wouldn't blame them for.'

'I thought it was quiet around here. I turned the radio off in the car before they got to the traffic news – somehow they've got hold of Esther's name, poor cow. It's not even her job but the bastards will try to get her sacked. I left her a message but her phone's off. Don't blame her – if it was me, I'd be leaking email after email from the minister bloke saying he wanted to be accessible.'

'Is she the kidnap woman?'

'Used to be. We've stayed in contact on and off since that Lloyd Corless kid went missing. You'd like her.' Jessica picked up a Post-it note and held it in the air. 'Anyway, what about Debbie Callaghan's dad?'

Izzy shuffled through a stack of papers on her lap. 'Ivor Callaghan died in Strangeways almost exactly twenty years ago. He got life after confessing to robbing a post office with a sawn-off shotgun. He got away with fifty grand – money never recovered. String of other minor offences; mainly drink-related. The usual.'

'He confessed?'

'That's what it says.'

'Funny, Debbie reckons he always protested his innocence. Perhaps that's just what he told her? Anyway, what else?'

'I've got you an address for Luke's former business partner, Michael Cowell.'

Jessica picked up the relevant note, relieved that Izzy had written it as it meant it was actually readable. 'I'll take him. I'm going to see the AA guy who's giving Debbie an alibi too. I'm always nervous when someone gets hurt who has a long line of people gunning for them. Too many suspects.'

'I got you some stuff on Debbie but not much. There's nothing formal to say she and Luke have separated; no divorce application, no DV complaints – just that 999 call. Her parents are both dead, no children. They've got a joint bank account but she's got one of her own too. Nothing suspicious has gone in or out – she's got less in hers than I've got in mine.'

'Next-door neighbour?'

'Works as a nurse, nothing special there.'

'Election rival?'

Izzy half-laughed, half-sighed. 'There's a bunch about

him on the Internet – he sodded off to the south of France after the election. It looks like the poor bastard got stitched right up. He'd been on the council for a couple of decades and then all these leaflets went around about him touching kiddies up because he used to work for the scouts. Callaghan was suspected but he denied it, turning things around to say that someone was trying to frame him. I've got someone digging but it doesn't make much sense. If this guy wanted revenge on Callaghan, why would he wait until now when he's off in France? Why would he get someone else to do it in public?'

'The public thing's bugging me too. It sounds like Callaghan's a bit of a shite but why not hit him when he's on the way back from the council after some late-night circle-jerk? Or knock on his door and throw the acid in his face? It's either someone who wants the attention, or a person who doesn't care. Bad news either way.'

'It could still be a botched attack on the Home Secretary.'

'True but we've not had any witnesses say our hoody made any move towards the stage. He might have abandoned his plan when he saw the security but all we can work from is that we've got one guy in surgery and a list of people who have it in for him. What about this Anarky lot?'

Izzy shuffled through her papers and handed over another Post-it note with a web address on. 'It's a private forum where some of our known nutters post their plans. Although it's not public, people can sign up easily, so it's not exactly hidden either. It's mostly harmless – conspiracy theories, planning their meetings, some football stuff. In your email, you've got the exact post. Our geeks are tracing the IP. All it said was, "Nice work at Picc. Get out OK?" Only one reply, which just said "Eh?" and then it got deleted. One of our monitoring lot picked up on it but there's no major chatter, so it could be a hoax or something else entirely.'

'Does the Guv know?'

'He's been talking to your mates at Serious Crime—'

'Pfft.'

'I knew you'd like that but it's their thing because of the gangs. SCD say there's no specific intel that Anarky or any similar groups were planning anything. It might be someone trying to talk the group up, or even a rival trying to smear. They say that even if they get the IP, they'll have to tread carefully because they don't want the forum to be shut down. I'll leave it to you and the Guv but he didn't seem convinced you'd get much backing.'

'All right, great stuff – as ever.'

Izzy stood, ready to leave, but turned as she got to the office door. 'DSI Hambleton's in today, if you didn't know.'

'Niall?'

Izzy giggled. 'Ooooh, *Niall* is it. Very cosy.'

Jessica balled up the messages and threw them towards the bin, missing again. 'What else am I supposed to call him? He's not a superintendent any longer – and he's twice my age.'

'Sugar daddy then. He's nice – and he's got a thing for you. When he spotted me, he specifically asked where you were.'

Jessica untied her hair, flicking it behind her shoulders. 'He's good to talk to – full of stories plus he gives good advice. Perhaps if these miserable bastards stopped gossiping for half an hour they'd get a decent CCTV shot of our hoody.'

Izzy grinned. 'Getting defensive too – very suspicious.'

'All right, sod off. There's fingertip search duties going if you fancy it?'

'Who's going to run all your errands then?'

'Dave – if he ever gets back from holiday.'

Jessica's attempt at not giving the station's gossiping bastards anything to talk about immediately came crashing down when she ran into Niall Hambleton as she was heading through reception. The former DSI had retired almost a decade previously but was working voluntarily for a day or two a month looking into cold cases where they hadn't managed to find the culprit for a certain crime. It fell under the current policy of 'let's see how many people we can get to work for free'. Jessica was sure it wouldn't be long before they had someone doing a CID job for nothing, probably under the guise that as enough people watched police shows on TV it couldn't be that hard.

Izzy was right that Niall had a soft spot for Jessica but what she hadn't said was that it was mutual. There was a little of Jessica's father in Niall – the quick, wicked humour, the fact he didn't seem to miss anything. Jessica knew it was probably the type of thing psychologists had wet dreams about – that her father had died less than a year ago and now an older man wanted to take her under his wing – but she didn't care.

As she was heading out of the front door into the car park, she heard Niall calling her name as he came down the stairs. When she turned, he hugged her, much to the amusement of desk sergeant Fat Pat, who got a middle finger behind Niall's back and a mouthed obscenity. Not that it bothered him as he carried on tucking into the remains of the steak and kidney pie he was hiding under the counter. What a fine example they set to the unsuspecting public. 'Your son's gone missing? Give us a minute because Fat Pat's still chomping on a pie.' Still, he was pretty much the only person in the station who actually knew what everyone else was up to, so staying on his good side was essential. Even if he did eat everything put in front of him.

Niall eventually released Jessica, grinning down at her. Although he was in his late sixties, he had aged well and, if anything, looked younger than DCI Cole. He still had a full head of white hair, with sharp eyes and a trim physique. Aside from the traditional red-and-white striped grandpa jumper, which Jessica assumed was compulsory once you hit a certain age, he could have been twenty years younger and still working. He probably weighed ten stone less than Fat Pat, too.

The older man was beaming, using both his hands to get the words out as if he couldn't contain himself: 'Been quite the day, hasn't it? The attack and everything. These are the days I miss the most, where everyone's running around and the media are going crazy.'

Before Jessica could reply, her phone started to ring. She checked the caller and refused it. 'Sorry, it was my mum. She knows I work . . .'

Niall nodded: 'Aah, but when you get to an age like mine, you can't do much else but wonder what your pride and joys are up to.'

'Yeah, I'm sure it's that. Anyway, I'm on my way out . . .'

'Oh, right, of course. Busy day and all that. I'm working upstairs – just came down to get a tea from the machine.'

That couldn't be a good thing at his age.

'The constables have a kettle squirrelled away – I'm sure someone will make you one.'

'I can't find a pen either. Is there some sort of stationery cupboard?'

Yeah, he's called PC Pen-Thief.

'Check with Fa— Patrick on the desk. He'll sort you out.'

Niall moved his weight from one foot to the other, clearly wanting to ask something. Eventually, as Jessica motioned towards the door, he got to the point. 'I was wondering if you fancied going to the pub at the bottom of the road later? I'm here until six and the roads are blocked. It would be nice to pick your brain.'

Fat Pat coughed but it might have been to disguise a snigger. Either way, this was going to be all around the station within half an hour. Thinking she could probably do with a drink after the afternoon she had planned, Jessica surprised herself: 'All right, I've got a couple of people to visit but then I'm coming back anyway. See you at six.'

51

6

Jessica signed out a pool car and used the sirens to skim through the gridlocked streets towards Ancoats. If anyone asked, someone had tried to attack the Home Secretary and she had witnesses to talk to.

As she walked through the back door of the church hall, Jessica couldn't help remembering the gym from her primary school: a stage at one end, varnished strips of wood running diagonally across the floor, a climbing frame folded onto the wall and a general sense that no one had done the place up in twenty years. The high windows were misted with condensation and it was bloody cold too, even by Manchester's standards.

Shane Donovan was everything Jessica expected from someone who did social work for the council – he looked directly into her eyes, nodded when she spoke, tilted his head slightly to the side to show he was listening and sat with his fingers interlocked on his lap. In fact, he did everything which would usually make Jessica take an instant dislike to someone. She figured she must be getting old if she couldn't bring herself to make rash judgements about a person. He even wore jeans tucked into a pair of Rockports and a plaid shirt over a T-shirt with a bird pattern on it, despite being in his mid-thirties. He looked like a teenager who couldn't quite accept he wasn't eighteen any longer – but he did at least have the boyish grin to match.

He apologised for the length of time that the heating took to turn itself on and offered her his coat, which she didn't take. After that, he explained that he worked on an outreach programme for the council, which involved going into schools to host workshops and provide a little one-on-one counselling. Other days, he would help with rehabilitation programmes. Despite what Debbie had said, it wasn't an official Alcoholics Anonymous setup, instead a session run by the council for people who didn't want the stigma of actually visiting something called AA. He ran two sessions, one in the morning, one in the early evening. He'd returned to the empty hall to set it up for the later session.

From everything he said, it wasn't just the police who were having their budgets crapped on; he explained that he was doing the job of what used to be four individually trained people. Perhaps it was the fact he was still smiling that made Jessica like him. Well, not like – tolerate.

After the explanation, Jessica finally got to the reason she was there. 'Debbie Callaghan's husband was attacked this morning a little after ten. She told us she was here with you and the rest of the group.'

'That's correct.'

'Is there anyone else who can verify that?'

Shane licked his lips, his eyes flickering away from Jessica momentarily. He had shoulder-length, slightly greasy dark blond hair, not entirely unlike hers but a little shorter. 'Anyone that comes here is offered complete discretion. If Debbie admitted she was here then I don't mind confirming that. I'll sign anything you want, or make a formal statement, but I won't pass on the names of any of the other participants who were here – not without a court order. Even then, I'd want to make sure they didn't object. The anonymity we offer is priceless, both to them and me.'

He even had morals. If he liked shopping, some woman somewhere was going to fall head over heels for this guy.

Jessica's reply echoed gently around the empty space, her breath following it. 'I can't promise I won't be back with a warrant at some point but there's no need to come down to the station at the moment. Debbie's not suspected of anything.'

'Was that her husband who's been on the news all day? I knew he was a councillor.'

'Yes.'

'You can't think she'd do that, I know she's had problems but—'

Jessica saw her way in. 'What exactly do you know about her problems?'

Shane began stumbling over his words. 'Well, I wouldn't say I know that much – only that she's here for a reason. I can't tell you what she talks about within these walls. The news has been saying the person was after the Home Secretary anyway.'

'They'd probably report the earth was flat if someone sent them a press release about it. I wouldn't believe everything you hear.'

'It's just I'm interested in the people who come here. It's always nice when someone gets better and beats their demons.'

'What brought you into this?'

Shane was instantly back on message, re-locking his fingers and leaning forwards like a praying mantis with better hair and a shorter neck. 'I got sober twelve years ago – it's a battle every day but being among so many people with the same problems keeps me on my toes.'

Before Jessica could stop him, he was away, giving her a history of everything he had done over the past dozen years. Perhaps he wasn't such a catch after all, well, unless he fell for himself as it was clear that was the person he was most in love with. By the time he got to the end of year six, where he'd gone to Tibet to try to meet the Dalai Lama for spiritual enlightenment, Jessica had to put a stop to it. If she'd let him continue, she'd still be here the following morning hearing about how he knitted Ecuadorian grass into a friendship bracelet for some homeless person he met in the Brazilian favelas while simultaneously teaching the local kids how to do a stepover.

She said her goodbyes, told him she might be back in contact at some point – and that if he really did intend to potentially ignore a court order, then he should probably get a solicitor. Either that or piss off back to Tibet.

In the forty-five minutes Shane had spent giving Jessica his life story, the pool car had managed to ice over. Jessica sat in the driver's seat with the heaters on full blast remembering the old days of her little Fiat that had two settings for the blowers: furnace hot or arctic cold. Half the time it didn't start, the other half the exhaust sounded close to death. Now she was stuck with some new-mobile that had no personality – a car in which everything worked and she didn't open it up in the morning to find a random piece of plastic sitting on the passenger's seat. A car where she turned the key and it actually started without having a think about it. Perhaps because of that, since she returned to work, Jessica had been using the pool cars where she could, enjoying the clunky gearboxes and glove boxes which sprung open for no apparent reason. She could live without the vague whiff of sweat, curry and chips though. It smelled like whoever had signed this one out last had done so to go on a night-crew takeaway run to the local kebab shop. Either that or Fat Pat had borrowed it.

After another blast of the sirens helped her loop back to the other side of the city centre, Jessica parked in a director's named space outside an office building and headed inside.

Michael Cowell was already waiting for her in a side office, squeezed into a brown polyester suit, face like a split coconut, straggly hair sticking out of a disproportionate amount of his face, including his ears.

Especially his ears.

Jessica found it hard to stop herself from staring at the brown wiry tufts fluttering in the air-conditioning. They were hypnotically horrific.

He was sweating, out of breath, and reeked of fags, making quick glances towards the door every few seconds as Jessica introduced herself. 'Are you all right, Mr Cowell?' she asked, not adding: 'Except for the ear hair, of course.'

'When you called, I had to have a word with my boss to

let me off the floor for a few minutes. It's a bit awkward with the police visiting me at work.'

'What do you do?'

'I'm a senior telecommunications happiness enhancer.'

It sounded like a sex toy.

'You do what?'

'I'm a telecommunications happ— I phone people up and sell them stuff.'

'Right, well, I'm sure you appreciate that time is of the essence, which is why I had to visit you here. The alternative was the station.'

'You didn't say on the phone what you wanted to talk to me about.'

'Luke Callaghan.'

Cowell's face darkened, his bushy unibrow deepening in the centre. 'What about him? Whatever he's told you, it's bollocks.'

'What do you think he's told us?'

'I don't know, last time it was some shite about me covering his car in paint. He's a maniac, he—'

'Someone threw nitric acid in his face.'

The unibrow shot back up again. 'Y'what?'

'In Piccadilly this morning – he's been in surgery all day.'

Cowell's features hung in place for a moment before they cracked and he burst out laughing, huge guffaws until he ended up bent over double, coughing in a way that only a smoker could. When he recovered, the grin was carved onto his face. 'That's the best thing I've heard in years – I hope I've got some Champagne in. Actually, fuck that, I'm

all in at Obsessions tonight – I'm going to get utterly bol-
locksed. Come along – everyone's welcome. I'll even invite
this bastard lot along.'

Charmer.

Jessica stopped her eyes from rolling. 'Much as I'd like
to join you at the strip club, I've got other plans. Now
would you like to say what exactly it is you find hilarious
about a local councillor being attacked in public?'

Cowell smoothed the hair away from his face, or about
thirty per cent of it, and then wiped a tear from his eye.
It wasn't one of sorrow. 'All right, all right. Look, I know it
looks bad me laughing and all that while he's in hospital
but you've got to understand that Luke Callaghan is one of
life's C-words. I would say the actual word but, y'know,
you being a lady and that.'

This time Jessica didn't bother to stop her eyes from
rolling. 'Okay, perhaps we should continue this at the
station.'

She stood, reaching into her pockets as if going for the
handcuffs but Cowell was on his feet too, holding both
hands out and bobbing them up and down as if patting a
Great Dane. 'No . . . I mean, all my workmates are out
there and everything. If we could get through things here?'

'If we're going to talk here, you're going to have to actually answer the questions, rather than take the piss.' Jessica
re-took her seat, as did Cowell, who took a literal sigh of
relief, or perhaps the exertion of standing had knackered
him so much that he needed the extra breath. 'Let's start at
the beginning. How do you know Luke?'

'We used to be friends when were at college together

years ago. I hung around with him and his girlfriend, Debs, and a couple of others.' Jessica noted the details to check, asking what happened after that. 'When we were getting close to finishing college, Luke was always going on about starting a business – "I don't want to have a boss", that's what he'd say all the time. He'd go on and on about it. My grandmother had died and left me some money about six months before, so he'd say we could use my money and his brains and make a fortune. I was young and stupid and he was my mate, so in the end I gave in. We set up this company fixing computers.'

'Callaghan Computers, right?'

Cowell shook his head furiously, making his ear hair waggle. 'That's not what it was back then. It was CCC – Callaghan and Cowell Computers.'

'What happened?'

'The bastard stole my money. CCC went bankrupt but somehow all of its assets transferred over into his new company. It was basically the exact same thing we were already doing but with him as the sole director. I got nothing. He had this fancy lawyer to sort all the paperwork and by the time I realised what he'd done, it was all gone.'

'How long ago was that?'

Cowell mumbled under his breath and used his fingers to count. No wonder his mate stole all his money. 'I'm thirty-four now, so that's five, six, seven . . . er, what year is it?' Jessica told him. 'Right, so that's eight, nine – nine years ago.'

'When I first mentioned Luke's name, you thought he'd been on to us about you – why was that?'

Cowell tugged at the collar of his shirt, looking as guilty as anyone ever had. It was a good job she hadn't taken him to the station.

'We, er, had a few, er, run-ins, er, over the, er, years. But he stole my money – I mean the bastard got a quarter of a million out of me, what would people expect me to do? I'm not just going to bend over and take it up the—'

'All right, I get the picture.'

It was an image that was more than enough to put her off any type of tea tonight. If his face was that hairy, she didn't even want to think what the rest of him looked like. He had almost certainly committed a bunch of petty acts of vandalism directed towards his former friend over the years but there was little they could do about those.

'For now,' Jessica continued, 'can we skip the incidents you might or might not have been involved in over the years and bring things a bit more up to date. What are you doing now?'

'Well, I had no money, did I? I had to start again. I got taken on here a few years ago and worked my way up to senior telecommunications happiness enhancer.'

Don't ask, don't ask, don't ask.

'What were you before that?'

'Junior telecommunications happiness enhancer.'

Shouldn't have asked.

'Where were you at ten o'clock this morning?'

Cowell nodded towards the door. 'Out there, on the phones – and don't go thinking I hired someone either, I know what you police types are like, all CSI Manchester and NYPD whatever it is. I've got a shit flat – though not as bad as the last one, shit car, shit job, all because of Luke bloody Callaghan. I only wish I'd been there to see him getting his comeuppance. Check my bank accounts – there's nothing in there, and there'll be even less after tonight.'

Jessica didn't doubt it – he certainly didn't have enough in his account to buy an ear trimmer. Aside from double-checking with his boss he was actually at work that morning, Jessica knew there was little more she could do here.

As she stood to leave, Cowell ensured he had the last word, holding his hands up to indicate his innocence. Given his guilty look from before, she doubted he'd be able to cover anything up now. 'Honestly, love, if I had a bloody clue what nitric acid was, or where to get it, I'd have done it years ago. Like I said – Luke Callaghan: one of life's C-words. Now, if you'll excuse me, I have a trip to a strip club to organise.'

Jessica left the office feeling sorry for the pretty young teenager who didn't yet realise she was going to spend the evening with Michael Cowell's ear hair jammed between her breasts.

7

Outside of the office, the pool car was frozen again, so Jessica sat in the driver's seat with the heaters on full listening to some moron on the radio say that whoever was in charge of policing that morning should be sacked.

Poor Esther.

Jessica tried calling again but her phone was off.

When the windscreen had cleared and Jessica had got the feeling back into her fingers, she returned to Longsight, signed the car back in, told Fat Pat she'd get him a vanilla slice if he stopped gossiping about her, and then headed for the pub.

The evening air was even colder than it had been during the day, with frost glistening on the pavement, despite it still just about being light. Although the longest day of the year was barely a month away, the fixed dark clouds meant it might as well be night time. The unfortunate motorists who hadn't heard about the gridlock had their headlights on, heading into an hour-long traffic jam whichever way they were going.

The closest pub to the station was on Stockport Road, opposite a primary school, presumably because the only way the teachers could get through a day was to nick across at lunchtime. Niall was already in a booth by himself cradling a pint of bitter and nursing the sad sense of someone who didn't have much going on in his life. If he was younger, he would have had his phone out; pretending to be busy, pretending to have friends. Instead, he sat with his head bowed, striped jumper standing out like a decorated Christmas tree in an empty room, inhaling the fumes of his half-finished drink. Jessica slid in opposite him with a glass of wine and dropped two bags of prawn cocktail crisps and a packet of flaming hot Monster Munch on the table between them.

Niall's face lit up like Fat Pat with an iced bun. 'Jess, I'm so glad you came.'

'I even brought tea. You should be grateful – I don't usually share crisps.'

Jessica tore open the first packet of prawn cocktail and split it along the side, splaying it onto the table in front of them and putting three in her mouth.

Niall took a crisp and sniffed it, before biting it in half. 'It's not like the old days. Back then, we'd be in the boozer straight after lunch, getting pissed with the journos and hoping nothing happened. Even if it did, we'd get in the car anyway and head off. I know it sounds alien to you young ones but it worked in its own way. Somewhere like this place would've been drowning in smoke, reeking of booze . . .' The older man tailed off but it was clear he was pining for the past. 'Now, it's the grandkids, of course. They keep me busy since my wife died. You don't have children, do you?'

He realised instantly from Jessica's expression that it was the wrong question. 'Sorry, I didn't mean—'

'It's fine.'

As Niall took another sip of his drink, Jessica launched into the Monster Munch, eating one of those and a crisp at the same time. Sod your celebrity chefs – how many of them could create a flaming hot prawn cocktail corn-and-potato-based snack?

She didn't expand on the children comment, so Niall picked up where he left off. 'Poppy and Zac are my little 'uns – seven and five. My son Brendan usually brings them around with his wife on Sundays and we'll go out for lunch and then do something if it's not raining.'

He didn't have to spell it out but Jessica could see it in his face; aside from the odd times he was at the station, it was the one day a week he got to do something with his life. No wonder he didn't mind working on cold cases for free.

Jessica stretched forwards for a crisp but her sleeve snagged on the table, exposing her wrist and the mishmash of red gouges. She felt Niall's eyes run across them and then he tried to catch her gaze as she picked up another crisp and rolled the material down again, deliberately avoiding looking at him.

'Something you want to talk about?' he whispered.

Suddenly, Jessica knew what it was to be like to be opposite DSI Hambleton in an interview room. She could feel his eyes boring into her and the silence from the other side of the table as the sound of clinking glasses, laughs, burps and faint pop music reverberated around the rest of the pub. He waited for the reply, allowing the suspect to begin sweating and incriminate themselves. It never worked on people familiar with an interview room, of course, although most people couldn't help themselves but fill the gaps in a conversation. Jessica knew the rules; she played the game herself and yet . . .

'They've not healed properly. I keep picking at them.'

'Where did they come from?'

'I was in a stately home for a case, helping out another force. The people there used cable ties on my wrists, then they handcuffed me not long afterwards. It was too tight – like we'd do if we wanted to hurt someone.'

Glasses continued to clink, people were still chatting to each other, laughing, the jukebox flicked onto another tune, but still DSI Hambleton said nothing, knowing there was more. All she had to do was remain silent herself, but . . .

'I had to twist one of my wrists to free myself. I didn't even realise how badly I'd hurt it until everything seized up a few days later. The doctor said I'd done something to the tendons. He said I blocked it out at first because of the shock. It's been healing but . . .'

Pick, pick, pick. That psychologist was having another mucky dream.

Finally, DSI Hambleton became Niall again. 'I saw the newspapers – some cult they were saying – plus people talk around the station, of course. You know what it's like. I didn't realise you were still—'

'I'm not, I'm fine. It was just on the news a lot.' Jessica knew she was sounding too defensive. Keep saying you're okay and eventually you will be.

'They didn't name you, did they?'

'No, it wasn't about me. There was another officer,

Charley, who was featured a lot and came over positively. Well, everywhere except the *Daily Mail* and the *Guardian*, where they called her a "he" – but it's not as if it's hard for a national newspaper to get someone's gender correct, is it? There was talk about her being promoted. Anyway, I'm not the only one who's been in the papers . . .'

Niall smiled slightly, recognising the obvious subject change. This is why Jessica rarely hung around with officers other than Dave and Izzy outside of work.

'Some Ashford bloke called me at home but I told him I didn't want to talk about it – they must have got the information from elsewhere. He must have decent sources because he did a good job actually.'

'He's someone I know – he phoned me and asked for your details but I told him to sod off. Twenty-five years since you put away the Stretford Slasher, though, it's not a surprise the *Herald* was doing something. He told me there might be some sort of documentary in the works.'

Niall seemed hesitant, puffing his chest up and taking a large mouthful of bitter. 'I told them "no" as well. They said it would be too hard to make without my contribution, offered me money. When I still refused, they said they'd make a donation to the victims, trying to guilt me into it. Eventually they went away.'

'It was a massive case though – even I remember it as a kid and I didn't live in Manchester. I think my dad had it on the news when you arrested the guy.'

Niall used his pint to shield his mouth. 'Some things get blown out of proportion.'

His modesty was admirable but Jessica knew how big

the case was and the recent newspaper spread had brought it back to the fore for at least a couple of days. She tried the silence trick but he was happier to say nothing than she had been.

'How many victims was it?' she eventually asked.

'Eight.'

Jessica nodded towards his almost-drained pint. 'Another?' Niall nodded and a few minutes later, Jessica was back juggling a pint of bitter, two more packets of Monster Munch and another glass of wine. It might have been him who invited her out but if Niall was going to give her the retired DSI stare of steel, then she was going to get something out of him too. 'So, eight women . . .'

'It was a long time ago.'

'What rank were you?'

'A DI, like you.' Niall picked up the new glass but didn't drink. 'You're not going to let this go, are you?'

'It's the job to be a bit nosey.'

A flicker of a smile. 'Fair enough. What do you want to know?'

'I suppose the scale of it. We've had big things around here, but in that feature it called the city a ghost town for women after dark, saying that females stopped going out. We've had serial killers, rapists, people targeting women – but never anything like that.'

Niall nodded shortly. 'I was on duty when we were called to the first victim, Stephanie Miller. I can see her now. She'd been out for a few drinks after work and was walking home by herself. He slit her throat, raped her as she was bleeding and dying and then covered her in bleach, before dumping her in a bin in Stretford.'

It sounded so much worse hearing it than reading it. Niall's grandfatherly features now seemed darker, blackened rims around the lines in his face that hadn't been there moments before.

'And there were seven more?'

'Always the same; their skin tinged with that blue from the bleach, a woman out by herself. He didn't mind whether they were older or younger, fat or thin, blonde or brunette, white or Asian. It was just about the women and power.'

'Was it true people stopped going out?'

'Pretty much. They sent officers up from the Met to give us a presence but there were more of us out in the centre than there were normal people. Pubs, cinemas, restaurants – you name it, they were closing because no one was visiting. It felt like the whole city was dying.' He paused for a sip of bitter. 'Sorry, wrong choice of word.'

'What happened?'

'It pushed him out to the edges. The final two victims were found in Altrincham and Bury. That took it out of Manchester and then the politicians started to notice. There was this pub hidden away in the back streets near Ardwick Green that we used to go to but you know what journalists are like – they can smell a boozer from five miles away. As soon as they knew where we were, we had all the nationals in there – and then it went massive. Front page of all the papers, TV news, Prime Minister threatening to send the army in to patrol the streets if need be.'

Jessica puffed out her cheeks and breathed heavily, before opening the next bag of crisps.

'Exactly.' Niall continued. 'I'd been a DI for a couple of years and generally knew what I was doing but this case was too big. The DCI was trying to run things – this big guy called Thorpe – then the super was around plus everyone and anyone. No one knew what they were supposed to be doing because we didn't know who we were reporting to. If a victim had shown up in Liverpool or Birmingham then God only knows the panic it would have caused. You could have had a whole nation of women afraid to go out in the dark.'

'But you got him?'

Niall took a large mouthful, swilling it in his mouth before swallowing and reaching for a crisp. He seemed sheepish, almost embarrassed, not wanting the credit. 'It's never just one person, is it? The media need a name they can build up or knock down. You've seen it today with that inspector—'

'Esther.'

'Yes. Back then, they were after a hero, and it was me.'

'How did you get him?'

'It was the bleach. Now you have the forensics and all the fingertip teams but it wasn't like that. We assumed he'd got a bottle of the stuff from the supermarket, or wherever, and tipped it over the body to wash everything away. It had pretty much been overlooked because everyone just thought the guy was some sicko and we were looking for certain types of profiles. I went looking at local cleaning companies and that's where we found Colin Rawlinson. He was working at this factory where Stretford meets Eccles. I was going from place to place and spotted him one afternoon loading a large bottle of this blue stuff into the back of his car. He'd split with his wife and she'd taken the kid but there were all these women's clothes at his place. Thorpe and I brought him in for questioning and the guy cracked. We found the knife buried in his garden, we had the connection to the bleach and that was that.'

Jessica finished her second glass of wine, letting Niall's story sink in. No wonder he wasn't keen to talk about it; the pressure must have been horrendous.

'The paper said you were promoted afterwards.'

Niall shrugged. 'We both were. I got the DCI's job and he moved up too. I think everyone was so relieved it was over that we could have pushed for whatever we wanted. I didn't even ask for it.'

'What happened to Thorpe?'

'Died a few years ago – heart attack. It comes to us all.'

Jessica's phone began to ring, her mother still trying to get through, but she stopped the call before it rang a second time.

Niall raised his eyebrows, finishing his own drink. 'Mother again?'

'She always calls at the worst times.'

Niall finished the last of the crisps, leaving the table a mass of empty packets, frothy glasses and crumbs. 'I said before, when you get to our age, sometimes your kids are all you've got. Perhaps she has something she needs to tell you?'

'I know why she's calling.'

'Oh . . . well, I suppose I'll unstick my nose from your business.' He grinned, returning to being grandfatherly Niall. 'Would you like a bit of advice?'

'About my mother?'

'About the job.'

'Okay.'

'When you're at the bottom looking up, you always think your bosses are incompetent, that they spend the day sitting around doing nothing, making everyone else do the real work. To a degree, it's true – you do delegate more but the higher you go, the more stick you take. It's one thing to get some abuse from your boss – but what if it's the chief constable? Or the Home Secretary, like today? Or the Prime Minister? All I'm saying is that you're new to this job – you're probably annoyed at all the form-filling and thinking about budgets, then you've got to do the actual job as well. Just trust yourself and know where the lines are. It's not all black and white, there are shades of grey everywhere.'

With that, he was on his feet, both glasses in hand. 'Another?'

8

Jessica caught the bus to work the next morning, getting off two stops early to pick up a vanilla slice and then walking the final half-mile in a temperature even polar bears wouldn't venture out in. It had snowed lightly overnight but it was hard to tell where that began and the frost ended. Jessica's thick winter coat and padded gloves offered little respite as it felt like the wind had grown teeth that gnawed away at everything in its path. Opposite the pub from the previous night, there were schoolchildren hurling snowballs at each other, screaming and giggling. Given the area, it was at least a step up from trying to stab one another.

If he'd been faced with triplets covered in jelly then Fat Pat wouldn't have been happier than he was when Jessica shivered her way into reception and handed over his cake. 'The Guv wants you upstairs,' he said through a mouthful of pastry.

'Is it a Velcro shoe day?'

Pat nodded, cream oozing between his teeth and down his chin. Jessica didn't bother waiting for the actual reply, heading up to the first floor.

Contrary to Pat's warning, Cole was in a marginally better mood than the day before. Jessica would still have taken his shoelaces though. He told her Luke Callaghan was still in hospital with no details about whether he'd keep his sight after the acid attack. The word 'witness' was a loose term when it came to the people they had managed to track down from the plaza, with the fuzzy CCTV image all they were likely to get. The condoms in the flower pot had been the highlight for the search team and they'd dug up nothing suspicious on Luke's wife Debbie, his former business partner Michael, or anyone else. All in all, given the lack of progress on anything, he seemed to have taken it rather well, although that was perhaps because the Home Secretary had stopped bleating overnight, likely down to someone reading his own advisor's emails back to him.

After buttering her up with praise for the work she'd done with Debbie and Michael the previous day, Jessica knew Cole was about to drop her in it.

'I do, er, have a job for you,' he finally said, not looking her in the eye.

'I have a few things this morning; forms and the like.'

It was always unlikely to work and Cole dismissed it with barely a wave. 'I've been speaking to the super this morning and he's been liaising with the SCD . . .'

Cole continued for a few minutes, explaining how important it was and that it could only be trusted to a senior officer who they all had faith in and blah, blah, blah, but the essence was clear. 'Can you visit the leader of Anarky and find out what, if anything, he knows about the attack on Luke Callaghan? Oh, and if you could do that without letting on that the SCD are secretly monitoring him and his group then that would be really helpful. And if you could do it by yourself, it would be even better because we need all the officers we can get, plus we want to do things softly so he doesn't get edgy. Oh, and when you're done with that, if you could get your arse back here because we're all snowed under – literally and figuratively – then that would be great too. Any questions? No? Good.'

Jessica wondered if she should get a pair of Velcro shoes for herself.

Under strict instructions not to blow the Serious Crime Division's monitoring of Thomas McKinney and his Anarky group, Jessica did one of the things she had specifically been instructed not to: she wound him up. As she sat in McKinney's living room, deliberately disobeying strict commands, Jessica already had her reasoning laid out. It was the exact one she'd used when she got sent to the headmaster's office in primary school for punching a boy in the face: he started it. Back then, little seven-year-old Jimmy Francis had pinched her bottom. In this instance, McKinney started it by generally being a cocky so-and-so.

He was in his late thirties, with oiled hair parted down the centre. After inviting her in, he sat in his reclining armchair, feet up, wearing sparkling, chunky gold jewellery, designer jeans, designer T-shirt and designer stubble, ranting about the fact that society was too commercial. He had an orange glow about him that either came from a bottle or a sunbed and a fake-sounding cockney accent.

And he used to be an estate agent.

What was there to like?

Jessica was interviewing McKinney under the pretence that they'd had an anonymous but credible threat made against him and that she had to find out certain details to see what action to take. It was what they called in the trade 'trying it on'.

She was attempting to keep her voice level but there was a natural level of annoyance she couldn't hide. 'So, Mr McKintey,' she said, deliberately getting his name wrong, 'you used to be an estate agent but what do you do now?'

'This is a full-time job, sweetheart, we're looking to go national.'

'Isn't "going national" a bit organised for a group whose overall aim is a society without government or law?'

'It's a means to an end, innit? You only get that end goal if you can get yourself into that position in the first place? Plus, we're in favour of the more up-to-date definition of what you might call "anarchy".'

'Which is?'

'We believe modern governments are in the control of bankers and corporations. That makes the rest of us sheep and democracy a sham. We don't want to do away with all government, we just want to get rid of this setup and abolish capitalism so we can start again.'

Well, there's a long weekend planned, what was he going to do after that?

Jessica pulled a printout from her jacket and began to read. 'Did you believe that when you were given sixty hours community service for dealing speed four years ago? How about when you got a conditional discharge for selling stolen packets of Temazepam? Or the supervision order for dealing mephedrone? Then there's a caution for threatening behaviour?'

'Hey! I thought you were here because I was in danger? What have those got to do with anything?'

'I'm covering all bases, Mr McKinley. Perhaps there could be someone in your past who has it in for you? Drug-dealing friend? A supplier? Punter? Is there anyone you can think of?'

Stony face: 'It's McKinney – and no, I left all of that behind.'

'Okay, what about your organisation? I gather from the Anarky website that you're the founder and chairman but there's also a secretary, a spokesman, a few people you call "officers", there's a bank account . . . could it be that there's any friction there? It sounds like it's a very organised setup but obviously that can create tensions.'

McKinney shuffled awkwardly in the seat, his jewellery clanking together. 'Well, y'know what it's like but it's never a big deal. I can't believe any of the lads would've made any sort of threat. Besides, they're not really the type . . .'

He tailed off before stating the obvious conclusion that if they were going to do something, they wouldn't make a threat, they'd just do it. It was interesting that the group had tensions, though, giving Jessica at least one thing to take back to the SCD.

'What about the money, Mr McKenny?'

'McKinney. What money?'

'On your website, it says there's an annual joining fee, which covers administration costs. That must go some-where.'

'It pays for the website and then I need some left over

to pay for the other organisational things, like renting out places for our meetings. It's all accounted for.'

As far as Jessica could tell, McKinney charged people whatever he wanted in order to pay himself a salary so that they could go on the occasional march to protest against the type of capitalism that allowed him to wear designer clothes. It was no wonder Toxic Tony didn't have a clue what the movement was about.

'Do you think there could be any animosity in relation to that?'

'I don't see why.'

'I'm trying to think of reasons why someone could have it in for you, Mr Mackie, and I found this.' Jessica passed across a printout of an article from the *Manchester Morning Herald*'s website from the previous summer. In it, an Anarky rally in the centre had spiralled out of hand, resulting in half-a-dozen shops being smashed up and looted. McKinney had avoided prosecution as he pointed out he was in a pub a mile away. He was, of course, as were his lieutenants – but he was the one who had whipped up those involved and watched them go.

The man leant forwards in his chair, popping the reclining part back into place. 'It's McKinney.'

Jessica peered down at her notes. 'Sorry, what did I say?'

'Mackie.'

'Apologies Mr, er, McKinney – I'm wondering if you can talk me through what happened last summer.'

He looked at the pages before tossing them back at Jessica. 'I told your lot at the time, I had nothing to do with this. We had a peaceful meeting at a local pub and then a few of the younger members had a bit too much to drink and took things too far.'

'But they were members of your group?'

'Look, if some geezer at your place gets sent down for corruption, that doesn't mean you're involved too, does it? I told you then and I'm telling you now – this was nothing to do with me.'

'But you've been involved in marches in the past that have got out of hand, haven't you?'

'I'm sure you've been involved in policing things where your officers have got out of hand too – a bit of police brutality here and there. It doesn't mean it's your fault, does it?'

'All I'm trying to establish, Mr McKay, is how far these things go. You're not a fan of capitalism but some of your members get the wrong end of the stick and smash up some shops. But what comes next? You're not a fan of democracy, so they attack politicians? You're not a fan of anything organised, so they come after you? How far do you think some of your members might go?'

As subtle as a sledgehammer. Given the media coverage of the attack on Luke Callaghan over the past day, he had to know what she was getting at. His eyes narrowed slightly and she could almost see the cogs whirring. At least she hadn't mentioned the web forum.

For the first time, his accent dropped, no longer cockney, now a gruff Mancunian. 'It's McKinney. Are you fucking stupid?'

Jessica kept her reply level and calm. 'Sorry, I've had a lot on.'

'None of the members would make threats against me – I'm like a god to them.'

Standing, Jessica brushed her papers back into a tidy stack. 'All right, I'll feed that back and we'll be in contact if there's anything else to report. For now, remember to call 999 if you're worried in any way – and I'd keep your doors and windows locked if I were you. Coldest May on record, they're saying. I'll let myself out.'

Wind-up job complete, Jessica called Cole from her car as she headed back to the station. She told him she'd spoken to the Anarky founder and, although he was far from squeaky clean, she didn't think he knew anything about the attack. She also hadn't blown the SCD's cover, so they could pucker up and get her a vanilla slice at the absolute least.

The call was punctuated by the sound of shuffling papers and tapping keys ahead of Cole dropping the real bombshell: Luke Callaghan had lost his sight.

9

The rest of the day was a write-off, with Luke Callaghan's doctors saying he was in shock and unable to speak to anyone. That meant they hammered the same lines as before: Luke's former business partner, his wife, and the person he defeated in the election. Jessica had been angling for a free trip to France to interview the beaten candidate – but he was on holiday in New Zealand with as solid an alibi as anyone could ever have. With all the CCTV checked and eliminated and the witnesses anything but, that left them firmly in the shite. The only comfort was that the national media were more interested in an alleged affair between a footballer and a soap star. If in doubt, you could always rely on a professional sportsman unable to keep it in his pants to get you out of a hole . . . while getting himself into one.

Jessica sat in the restaurant area of Sam's Chop House in Manchester city centre reading through the menu, making a vague attempt at small talk but not fooling either Caroline or Adam, both of whom knew her too well. Caroline was her best friend from school and they had spent almost ten years living together and Adam . . . well, their up-and-down relationship was firmly up and he knew her better than anyone. Annoyingly so.

Adam's sister, Georgia, was determined to enrol Jessica

into some sort of shopping trip, which definitely wasn't going to happen, while her new boyfriend Humphrey thought everything was 'fascinating'. The final person around the table seemed more interested in gazing back through to the bar area, where the life-size bronze statue of L.S. Lowry sat with one elbow on the counter.

Caroline was as dressed up as ever for what was meant to be an 'informal' get-together: tight dress, big shoes, bigger hair, and enormous coat hanging over the back of her chair. 'I just can't get used to them,' she said, staring over her menu at Jessica.

'They're only glasses,' Jessica replied, putting the menu down having decided on the wine, possibly with corned beef hash. Definitely the wine though.

'Yes but *you're* wearing them.'

'Good to see you're observant enough to notice.'

Caroline started tugging on Hugo's arm. He was wearing green cord flares with a matching smoking jacket and a T-shirt which read 'out and proud' – despite the fact he wasn't gay. 'Hugo, hon, what do you think about Jessica's glasses?'

Hugo turned away from the statue to face Jessica, sweeping his long hair away from his face. 'Glasses?'

'She's wearing glasses.'

'Okay . . .'

'It's the first time we've seen her with them.'

His eyes focused in tighter on Jessica. 'I thought you always wore them?'

Jessica shook her head. 'I only got them a couple of months ago.'

'Didn't you used to have that pair with the sticky-up black things?'

'No.'

Hugo leant forwards, squinting. 'Never?'

'Never.'

'Maybe it was another Jessica?'

With that, his attention was back to the statue, Caroline clinging onto his arm, as he took a pack of cards out of his pocket, absent-mindedly shuffling them one-handed.

'Hugo's just got back from Oslo,' Caroline said proudly. 'He's massive there, aren't you, hon?'

The mumble sounded a bit like a 'huh?' but it could have been a 'yes'.

Jessica couldn't quite get her head around their connection. Caroline's recent relationships had been – in her own, admittedly drunken, words – 'a great big bollocking disaster'. She'd planned to move in with someone before finding out he was a serial killer who subsequently went after Jessica, then she'd fallen for someone on the rebound, married him, and then divorced almost as quickly. When the wine got talking and it was just them, it all came out about how she knew she was making a mistake getting married but she wanted someone to be with. At first Jessica had wondered if going out with Hugo was another rebound thing but there was something there . . . even if it was hard to define.

Hugo, for his part, was exactly the same as when Jessica had first met him years before – constantly distracted, odd, strangely dressed, odd, living above a betting shop, odd, a collector of stuffed animals, odd, and a magician. He was also odd. All that had really changed was that he'd gone from being a part-time performer to being a full-time one, appearing on television shows, touring the country and being invited to do things internationally. Some people would be changed by fame; Hugo didn't seem entirely aware that he was recognisable.

As Jessica followed Hugo's gaze towards the statue, two young women were walking through from the toilets towards the bar area. Both were wearing dresses entirely inappropriate for the weather, although Jessica saw Adam's eyes drifting towards them too. 'Mr Wandering Eyes' she called him whenever they were in a car together. His point was that just because they were living together, practically married, technically engaged – although it was complicated – that didn't stop him having the same raging hormones as another male who wasn't in his position. Being the geeky scientist that he was, he even explained the chemical re-action – which seemed a fancy way of excusing himself from ogling other women.

As soon as he spotted that Jessica had noticed where he was looking, Adam turned back to his sister and her boy-friend. Meanwhile, the two women stopped on the spot, heels scraping across the floor as one of them whispered to the other, pointing at Hugo. Caroline didn't remove her hand from Hugo's arm as the two girls click-clacked across the floor, hoiking up their collective cleavages, and asking him for his autograph. If looks could kill, then Caroline would have been off down the station bang to rights but Hugo seemed, as ever, unaware. He signed a pair of nap-kins, drawing a doodle of Lowry for one of the girls, and had his picture taken with each of them – all without moving from his seat. Caroline glowered but she should have probably been more jealous of the Lowry figure. In the war between a bronze statue of a nineteenth-century Mancunian artist and two pairs of bra-related feats of engineering, there was only one winner in Hugo's mind.

When the women had disappeared in fits of giggles back towards the bar, Caroline finally settled again, shaking her head and mouthing the word 'cows' at Jessica.

Everyone around the table was still in their thirties, with the exception of Humphrey, who was in his fifties and struggling to fit into the conversation – although that might have been because of the presence of Georgia's hand on his thigh. Georgia had been trying to get Jessica and Adam to meet her new boyfriend for weeks but Jessica's work, as usual, had interfered with every suggestion. He was dressed smartly, wearing a suit with a waistcoat and an expensive-looking watch which he kept glancing towards. He'd spoiled it slightly by wearing a bright green blazer but no one else had said anything, so Jessica let it go.

'What was Oslo like, Hugo?' Humphrey asked, trying to make conversation.

'Huh?'

'Oslo – what was it like?'

Hugo turned back to the table. 'It's very Norwegian. I only said yes because I wanted to go to the Edvard Munch museum.'

'He painted "The Scream", didn't he?'

Instead of replying, Hugo pulled the face from the

famous painting, with the added bonus of the pack of cards still being in his hand.

'Hugo's off to Germany next week,' Caroline said after an uncomfortable silence. 'He's getting really big in Europe now. It means he's away a lot, though.' Hugo shrugged, his attention now on the menu. 'He's got an agent and a publicist, all sorts of people, haven't you, hon?'

Another shrug.

'I've always wondered what they actually do,' Humphrey said but Hugo didn't seem to know.

The waiter took their orders, with Jessica and Caroline sharing a bottle of wine. Caroline nattered about how well her job was going, peppering everything with how much she missed Hugo when he wasn't around. Jessica ummed and aahed in all the right places but couldn't stop herself from being distracted by Humphrey. The way he checked his watch was like a nervous tic – a flick of his wrist to see the time and then back down again. It happened so quickly that she wondered if anyone else had noticed – perhaps he didn't even know he was doing it. The problem was that because Jessica had seen it once, she couldn't stop seeing it. Every four or five minutes, he would roll his sleeve back, spin his wrist around, glance down and return the sleeve, all within a couple of seconds.

Caroline quickly became distracted by the walking cleavages taking stools at the end of the bar that meant they had a view of Hugo, using their phones to take photographs of him. As Caroline went off to find a waiter, bouncer or contract killer, Adam leant in to whisper into

Jessica's ear. 'Your mum called the house earlier. She said she couldn't get through to you.'

Since moving back into their Swinton house, Adam had let his stubble grow and was now sporting a tidy dark beard. His black hair was shorter than it had been in a while, flopping around his ears.

'What did she want?'

'To talk to you.'

Jessica had a large mouthful of wine, keeping it her mouth so she didn't have to reply. After the death of Jessica's father, her mother had sold their house in Cumbria and moved herself into a community home for retirees just north of the city. Her reason was 'to be closer to you' but Jessica was struggling to get used to it. They'd never had a bad relationship and not fallen out in any way other than a teenage girl battling with her parents, yet Jessica didn't feel the same connection to her mum that she had to her father. She had always been a daddy's girl but when it was just her and her mum alone, there was nothing to talk about, other than the usual 'How's work, how's Adam, how's the house'.

Then there was the other thing.

'What did you talk about?' Jessica asked.

'The house, the weather, you, me. She was telling me about some of the friends she's making. You should visit her.'

More wine.

'I'm too busy at work.'

'She said she's been trying to call.'

'She always phones when I'm busy – either at work, or in meetings, or on overtime. I have things to do.'

Adam lowered his voice even further. 'Is it about—?'

'Of course it bloody is.' Georgia and Humphrey stopped their conversation and turned to her. Realising she had shouted, Jessica lowered her voice to a whisper. 'If she wants someone to visit her, you do it.'

'It's you she wants to see.'

'She only ever wants to go on about the same thing.'

'So tell her to stop.'

Jessica called over a waiter and ordered another bottle of wine. Sod Caroline, she was getting through this by herself. 'I have! At first it was just "Are Adam and you still trying?" but then she started talking about articles she'd read about conceiving and asking if we'd thought about IVF. She never stops.'

Adam smiled in the infuriatingly understanding way he always did, seeing both sides. Sometimes, he was *so* annoying. 'She's had a really bad eighteen months – we all have. She's feeling lonely and living in a place where, to be honest, everyone is winding down their lives. After your dad, she's thinking that she would love to have a grand-child before . . . you know . . . it's only natural. Just tell her the truth – she'll understand.'

Why did he always have to be so rational? Foolish fly-off-the-handle reactions Jessica could understand; calm, measured responses were beyond her and only made her more annoyed.

Jessica was saved by the waiter arriving with their food and Caroline returning in a huff, presumably because she hadn't succeeded in having the other girls chucked out for daring to take photos of her semi-famous boyfriend. Jessica hid herself behind forkfuls of corned beef hash whenever anyone wanted to talk, continuing to observe Humphrey. Aside from the watch thing, there wasn't anything particularly wrong with him; he had grown into his looks in the way some older men did – and she could see the attraction for Georgia, despite the age difference. Georgia hadn't gone as over the top as Caroline in getting dressed up but her bleached hair had been curled into a bob and she was wearing skinny jeans and a tight jumper, showing off a figure that made abundant at least one of the reasons why Humphrey was with her. Despite all of that, there was something about him that made Jessica uneasy. Avoiding eye contact could be seen as shifty but he was the opposite, staring directly at whomever he was speaking to. In many ways, that was even more unnerving.

As Jessica glanced up from her plate, she accidentally caught his gaze, dark brown beads staring into her. Even though he was smiling, she didn't feel it. 'What's it like having my girl living with you?' he asked, squeezing Georgia's arm.

Jessica had mistimed picking up her glass and had no option other than to answer. 'It's nice to have another woman around.'

Sometimes she really was a terrible liar.

Georgia thankfully didn't seem aware of the fact that Jessica preferred having the house to herself on her days off. 'It's only temporary,' Georgia said, flashing a toothy smile for her boyfriend. 'I'm looking at a flat on Monday evening if you want to come?'

Humphrey did the weird thing with his watch before nodding. 'Remind me this weekend and I'll see what I can do.' He turned back to Jessica, waiting for her to finish chewing before adding: 'Do you mind if I ask you a personal question?'

Yes.

Fake smile, feel for Adam's hand under the table, hope he doesn't ask about children, curl your toes so the rest of you doesn't tense, stay calm.

'No, go for it.'

He nodded towards Jessica's hand, which was gripping the fork far too tightly. 'You wear a wedding ring but you're not . . .'

Whew, an easy one.

'We sort of are but we're not,' Adam replied, saving Jessica the job. 'We did the whole ceremony thing but there was a problem with the paperwork. There are pictures and everything but we're not legally married.'

'Any plans to have another go?'

Adam squeezed Jessica's hand under the table but didn't glance sideways at her, didn't offer that stupid knowing grin that couples always saved for each other. Bloody hell, he was good at this. 'We're happy as we are for now.'

Good answer, she should have thought of that, shouldn't she?

Georgia interrupted, pointing towards Adam excitedly. 'What's that thing we're going to?'

'What thing?'

'You know, that park thing. What's it called?'

'I don't know, you're telling me.'

Georgia flapped her hand around in the air, umming. 'You know . . . I know you know.'

'ParkFest?' Caroline said.

'Yes!' Georgia turned to her boyfriend. 'Ads, Jess and me are all off to ParkFest – you should come. One of my mates was going to come up but she can't make it.'

Humphrey didn't seem so sure, checking the diary on his phone, but Georgia wouldn't take no for an answer. 'If you're at work in the morning, I'll give you the ticket – then we can meet there. Go on, you can come, can't you? For meeeeeeeeeeee?'

'I'm sure I can figure something out.'

That got him a kiss on the cheek and another squeeze on the thigh. Humphrey nodded towards Jessica again. 'Sounds like you should be busy at work with everything that's been on the news the past couple of days?'

'What, the footballer shagging around?'

Laughter. Ha, ha, ha, that was good. Be funny, keep joking, then no one asks The Question. Adam squeezes her hand again; only he knows. He sees both faces – this Jessica, the work Jessica, the funny one. Then there's the other Jessica; the broken one who miscarried Marcus. She hates him knowing that the other Jessica exists. That's why she avoids places like this, new people with their questions. Work, work, work and then nobody asks.

Jessica pushed her chair away from the table and excused herself to go to the toilet. Adam pressed his fingers into hers one more time. He knew. The bastard.

10

Lisa Dawes knew she'd made a mistake in giving her kids a treat. It wasn't taking them to tea after school, nor was it missing the five o'clock start time at the cinema, meaning they had to watch the half-five show. It wasn't letting them have an ice cream while they were waiting – it did at least shut them up – but it was definitely allowing them to share that bag of sweets during the film. The crunching, shuffling, fidgeting and double toilet break she could handle; what she was less happy about was the running. They flew out of the cinema, chasing each other and leaping the bollards before nearly knocking an older woman off her feet.

Lisa apologised, helping the woman pick up her shopping, before turning and shouting at the boys to stop running. She hated being one of *those* grown-ups: the ones who bellowed at their kids in public, letting everyone know what bad parents they were. The pair slowed to a fast walk but still stayed ahead of her, desperate to charge on again, despite the shopping centre being full of early evening bargain-hunters. Didn't these people have homes to go to? Somehow, Lisa had to get them to bed when they got home, despite the fact they were flying high on the produce of Mr Cadbury. She really was an awful mother, wasn't she? That's what the custody counter-claim said anyway: Bad

Mother. Still, he had his bimbo and she had the kids, so who was the winner there.

Wishing she still had the reins from when they were small, Lisa allowed her sons to lead her along the top floor of the shopping centre, through the double doors and into the lifts. Except they didn't wait for the bloody lift, did they? As they screamed their way up the stairs, Lisa followed, legs aching, back sore, wanting to go to bed herself. At least she didn't have to go to work tomorrow – a rare weekday off. No boss gawping at her tits, no stupid Nicole banging on about how her kids had just got straight As in their exams. They might have got good marks but they were still spoiled little shits. Sure, *she* might take her lads to the cinema once in a while but they knew the value of money and that their mum couldn't afford to buy them everything they wanted. They understood the difference between want and need. Unlike that bitch Nicole's little shitbags, mooching around the estate in their brand-new trainers, expensive mobile phones they were too young for welded to their pierced ears. Lisa took consolation from the fact they'd have some young girl up the duff soon enough and then what would happen to their straight As? Just because Nicole's husband had some job off drilling oilfields or something and they had a bit of money about them. If he had any sense, he'd be off drilling something else – anything had to be better than looking at Nicole's walnut face.

Lisa emerged onto the correct floor of the multi-storey car park relieved that at least her kids could count. She expected them to be haring across the tarmac, hopefully not into the path of a car. Why wouldn't they slow down? She was tired; it had been a long day.

As she rounded the thick concrete pillar, Lisa's two sons were standing still, staring towards the corner where someone in a dark blue hooded top was standing close to a dirty white van. It took a few moments for her to see what they were looking at but when she did, she gasped, stepping forwards and putting her hands over the boys' eyes.

Next to the van's front wheel, a second man was on the floor. The hooded figure lunged ahead, cracking a bat over the unconscious man's back with a grunt of effort and a deep cough. Lisa couldn't stop herself from squealing, the sound popping out before she knew it was there, echoing around the concrete space like the squeak from a trapped mouse.

When the hooded figure turned to face her, she expected to see a face but there was a white mask with a red letter 'A' painted across the front and a diagonal line through it. She could see the whites of his eyes glaring across the car park, illuminated in the blue haze of the strip lights. The person straightened up to full height – which wasn't much – chest rising and falling quickly as he tried to catch his breath.

'Please don't hurt us,' Lisa said, her voice cracking. She still had her sons' eyes covered, somehow balancing her bags at the same time, but the children were beginning to squirm.

The figure said nothing, glancing slowly in both directions before nodding his head ever so slightly towards her. Somewhere below, a car's wheels screeched around the corner but the person remained calm, wiping the bat on the ground and then walking quickly towards the far end of the car park.

11

Jessica stared up at the enlarged photo of the victim pinned to the incident room's whiteboard and turned back to the assembled officers. 'I think we can safely say someone didn't like this guy.'

A dozen officers were squeezed into the makeshift room, a mix of CID and uniform. As she faced them, Jessica couldn't stop looking at the speckled patch of black and green mould above the door. The incident room in the basement was hardly state-of-the-art but at least there was a heater and she didn't feel at risk of Legionnaires' disease just by showing up to work.

Jessica still had her jacket on, as did almost everyone else. She waited for one of the constables to stop picking his nose, giving him the raised eyebrow treatment, before continuing. 'This is Alan Hume – he's in his fifties, un-married and a self-employed builder who owns a dozen or so houses around Manchester. He was working on a shop refitting yesterday afternoon at the Trafford Centre and, miraculously seeing as he's a builder, he didn't knock off at half two. Some time a little after seven, Lisa Dawes and her two sons were heading back to their car after a trip to the cinema when they saw a man in a dark blue hoody introducing Mr Hume to Mr Sawn-Off Baseball Bat.'

A voice at the back piped up: 'Sawn-off?'

Jessica nodded to Izzy, who pressed a button on the laptop, changing the image on the screen. It was a good thing somebody knew how to set the damned thing up – Jessica had spent a day on a training course and was none the wiser.

'We've not recovered the weapon but the CCTV system around the shopping centre picked this up. As far as we can tell, it's a baseball bat that has had the top third cut off. Our colleagues in North Manchester—'

A low grumbling began at the back – the usual sound-track whenever a division other than their Manchester Metropolitan one was mentioned.

'All right, it's not like we're dealing with the Met or anything.'

Actual boos.

Jessica grinned. 'Anyway, one of the lads up north says it's something that's been breaking out among the gangs – apparently it makes the weapon quicker through the air. In my day it was Rubik's Cubes and Hungry Hungry Hippos, now it's crack cocaine and ten-year-olds getting each other pregnant. Apparently this makes it easier for kids with weaker arms to smack each other over the head, plus they can hide it better in their clothes. There's no specific gang we can tie it to but it's something to bear in mind. Lisa Dawes gave us a description of the attacker but it's not much use, neither is the CCTV.'

Izzy changed the screen to another still from the camera, showing the hooded figure wearing the mask. The A with the diagonal line through it was framed perfectly in the centre.

'This is the logo for Anarchy. You might think that gives us a lead by linking it to various protest groups but unfortunately these things are widely available on the Internet.'

The next slide was of the mask itself, taken from a website.

'The night crew started to put together a list of places where these masks can be bought but stopped when they reached a hundred – and that's just online. We don't have the staff to begin getting together a list of locals who could have bought these so we're going to have to give it to the media and rely on people to call in if they're suspicious of anyone who owns one.'

Izzy clicked through a selection of stills from the shopping centre's CCTV cameras as Jessica talked everyone through them. 'The Bradford Park geeks have been comparing the full-length camera shots of the person who attacked Luke Callaghan to the full-length ones we have here. Ask them some random fact about Doctor Who in the 1970s and they'll give you an answer straight away. Ask them to match two photographs and they give you a bunch of bollocks about a bunch of procedures. Off the record, they say it's almost certainly the same person. On the record, they're too busy watching Star Trek marathons to give us a direct answer any time soon. Anyway, we've got this hooded guy walking into the centre via the ground-level car park entrance, heading up two floors and then waiting for almost an hour and a half. There are no cameras pointing towards where the attack took place. He was likely waiting next to the victim's van but we don't know for sure. Shortly after the attack, we have him walking out the exact way he came in, still wearing the mask, and then he disappears.'

With another nod, Izzy picked up the account. Because they were still a DS short and DCI Cole was busy getting his daily bollocking from the superintendent and other higher-ups, Jessica was leaning on her friend. 'I've been talking to the camera operators around Trafford Park, Eccles and Davyhulme but there are no spots of our guy,' Izzy said. 'We've cross-reffed the ANPR of cars leaving the city centre on the morning of the Callaghan attack to anything leaving the Trafford Centre but it's clear. I've not been able to find out whether the attacker left the area on foot or in a car.'

Jessica finished drinking her second mug of tea of the morning. 'Right, whichever one of you lot makes the best teas can stay here – fight it out among yourselves. I'm milk, no sugar. Iz is milk with one and the Guv has it black. Don't ask me why, I've got it on good authority that nine out of ten serial killers also have their tea black. Anyway, the rest of you: we've nicked some uniforms for a search team to check the bins around—'

'Not the bloody bins again?' Everyone turned to see one of the female constables looking particularly pissed off. Jessica didn't blame her. 'Sorry,' the woman added. 'It's just those bastards downstairs have been calling me Joy Bag Jane ever since I found those johnnies in the flower pot the other day.'

Jessica tried not to laugh but as the rest of the room burst into giggles, she couldn't stop herself. 'Sorry,' she smiled. 'I'm not laughing at you, more with you.'

'It's not funny.'

More giggles. 'No, it's not.' Jessica just about composed herself to get the rest of the sentence out. 'As I was saying, we've got to search the external bins around Trafford Park in case our guy ditched the clothes and the bat on the way out. We've got some uniforms helping, plus DS Cornish—'

More groans. 'DS Grumpy Bitch,' an unidentified voice piped up at the back.

'Christ, what is it with you miserable bastards today? You don't want to sort through other people's rubbish, you don't like finding piles of used condoms. What do you want to do? Look, someone needs to make sure you lot know how to pick through a bin properly and then fill in the forms at the end of it and it's not going to be me, so Louise has been drafted over. Half of you are going over there, so make sure you take a bloody coat – if someone gets frostbite and loses a finger, you can fill in your own health and safety forms.'

Jessica picked up her mug and looked at the dregs in the bottom as if to prove the point that someone had a job to be doing.

'Right, the other half of you are what we call "lucky" – you're here trying to find a connection from Luke Callaghan to Alan Hume. Assuming our hoody friend is the same person, why has he gone after these two? We all know Callaghan's a piece of work, so let's get digging on Hume. He's a builder so he's obviously got a long stream of annoyed customers behind him wondering why he rolls up at ten and sods off at two after having an hour for lunch and drinking cups of tea all morning. There's got to be more to it than that though. Go back and look at Callaghan's wife, the councillor and Michael Cowell too – are they connected to Hume in any way? I want a motive and a link by this afternoon. I also want a packet of chocolate biscuits in here within the hour but whatever you do, don't let Pat catch you bringing them up – he's borderline diabetic as it is.' Jessica paused for breath. 'Right, any questions?'

The only noise was people blowing into their hands as the department collectively tried not to turn into human icicles.

'Right, Louise is on her way up – she'll sort out the lucky ones on bin duty. Iz, you're with me.'

DCI Cole's office was barely warmer than the incident room and he was wearing a hat and scarf when he waved Jessica and Izzy in. 'I've got some good news for you,' he said, wearing a look that didn't have the word 'good' in it. He looked like he hadn't slept in days, dark bags offset against his pale skin.

Jessica wondered why he had his hands under the desk and then it dawned on her: 'Have you got a heater back there?' His eyes shot downwards and then up again, giving her the answer. 'All right, shift up, I'm coming round,' she added.

Without giving him an option Jessica walked around to the other side of the desk and sat on the floor, holding her hands out for the small oil radiator to offer its heavenly glow. Cole shuffled his chair backwards, poking his sock-covered feet out towards the heater, his shoes tucked neatly under the cabinet behind him.

'No wonder you've been holed up in here all week,' Jessica added. 'You've got your own little snug on the go.'

'It was cluttering up the garage – we never used it because it eats too much power but I sneaked it in the other morning.'

'I'm surprised Pat didn't confiscate it for health and safety.'

'Aah, I had a simultaneous steak and kidney pie discovery which may have distracted him.'

It was the first time Jessica could remember Cole smiling properly in weeks and it felt good to see again. If it wasn't for him, she'd probably still be in her house moping. She owed him a lot and yet there was little she could do to help either his personal situation or the professional one.

Jessica waved Izzy around and they sat next to each other on the floor, hidden by the desk, warming their hands. 'Everything I told you about is under way,' she added. 'What's your news?'

'I spoke to Serious Crime today and they're convinced the anarchist mask is a coincidence. They say there's a difference between the *concept* of anarchy and Thomas McKinney's Anarky *group* – but they are looking into the fact that our hoody suspect could have placed that post on the website to incriminate the group and then wore the mask for the same reason. It's out of our hands though. They said to thank you for your work with McKinney.'

'Did they really?'

Cole shuffled uneasily in his chair. 'What do you think? They didn't say a word.'

'Ungrateful sods. Anything else?'

'The super was on the line this morning—'

'I suppose the golf course is closed because of the frost.'

Not even a hint of a smile this time. 'He was pondering if these could be random attacks.'

It was Jessica's turn to squirm. The thought had crossed her mind – she'd even written it on the pad in her office before crossing it out, screwing the paper up and missing the bin. It was their worst fear: a person attacking random targets in public. The biggest reason she was desperate to link one victim to the other was because the prospect of them not being connected meant that anyone could be targeted. If that was to get into the news then there could be real panic.

'It isn't random,' Jessica said, not even convincing herself.

'Let's hope not. Now if you don't mind, I'd quite like my radiator back.'

Jessica sat in her office next to the main radiator wearing her jacket, hat and scarf. Although the central heating was working on the ground level, it was still freezing – the eighth consecutive day temperatures had gone below zero. Instead of snow, the heavens were treating them to a cocktail of freezing rain and sleet. The blue sky from the morning of Luke Callaghan's attack was a distant memory, with spring apparently picking a scrap with winter and getting its arse kicked. The weatherman that morning kept banging on about isobars, a pressure system and the jet stream but he might as well have kept it simple: it's bloody cold and it ain't getting better any time soon.

Jessica stretched the desk phone cord across the room and called Esther, who surprisingly picked up.

'I thought you'd be hung, drawn and quartered by now,' Jessica joked.

Esther sounded tired: 'Just hung out to dry – these arse-holes are desperate for me to stay because if anyone ends up getting sacked for the Piccadilly incident then they can make sure it's me. If I quit before then, one of my bosses will get it in the neck.'

'So you're a human shield?'

'Exactly.'

'If it's any consolation, we're pretty sure the Home Secretary wasn't the target. The blinded guy had a long list of people who had it in for him.'

'I left a message for his chief advisor saying that if he didn't call the attack dogs off, then a certain email with the word "accessible" in capital letters would be winging its way to the newspapers. It went quiet after that. Now I just have to deal with the fact my bosses are willing to stitch me up. Then we're supposed to be policing some concert on the canal next week but it's going to be frozen if this keeps up.'

Jessica said they'd sort out going for a drink some time and then hung up, pleased that her friend wasn't getting sacked. Well, not yet.

She finally wheeled herself away from the radiator, parking herself by her desk and turning her attention to her other job for the day. She began by searching for 'Humphrey Caton' on the Internet. The search engine threw up a host of matches, mainly people in America, but no one who seemed to match Georgia's boyfriend. A couple of years ago, an officer in North Manchester had got himself in trouble for running police checks on his girl-friend, her mum, dad, and everyone she had ever gone out with. Everyone was a lot more careful about logging who they looked for and making sure the reasons for using the system were legitimate. None of that meant there weren't ways of finding things out if an officer wanted to. The records were only ever checked if there was a complaint but Jessica logged the reason as relating to known associates of Anarky and checked for Humphrey's name in the police system, finding no exact matches. There were far more Humphreys than she would have guessed but none with a similar last name. Of the few dozen Catons, there was no one with the alias or middle name 'Humphrey'.

Whoever Georgia's boyfriend was, their system had no record of him existing anywhere. That left Jessica with one major problem – she couldn't tell either Adam or Georgia what she'd found because she'd broken the law to get the information.

Damn.

As she was wondering what she should do, there was a knock at the door and Izzy entered, wearing a pink deer-stalker.

'Where'd you get that?' Jessica asked.

'Boot of my car. I put together a pack of stuff in case the car broke down and I got trapped somewhere overnight. I've never been near it but radiators on the main floor are starting to creak, so I reckon the system's on the blink. The rain was lashing down earlier and now it's frozen – the car park's like an ice rink.'

Jessica thought about asking Izzy to look into Humphrey Caton because she was so good on the system but didn't want to get her in trouble.

'Have you got your glasses?' Izzy asked.

Jessica checked the pockets of her jacket, then the top drawer. 'Sodding things – I had them this morning. Why?'

'Well, the headline's going to be big enough for you to read but I think you're going to be more interested in the rest of the words.'

Izzy pulled a copy of the *Manchester Morning Herald* out from in between two cardboard folders and held it up for Jessica to see. Her eyes might be dodgy but the headline was clear: 'GANG WAR' – alongside a photograph of the second victim, Alan Hume, making a Nazi salute.

12

Jessica snatched the paper from Izzy and squinted, trying to read the top line. 'How did they get this before us?' Izzy waited with her hand out as Jessica returned it sheepishly. 'Sorry, you're going to have to read it to me.'

'Basically it says that last night's victim is a member of a right-wing group. They say the fact he was attacked by someone in an anarchist mask shows that there's a war between the two factions.'

'Who wrote it?'

'It was—'

'Actually, don't bother, I already know. It's always him – Garry bloody Ashford. Right, I'll deal with him later – let's cover our arses first.'

'Already done – there's nothing in Hume's file and he's not on any watch lists. Even the material stuff is clear – his head isn't shaven, no tattoos. For all intents and purposes he's just a builder.'

'Good – can you get that upstairs to the Guv and then brief the press office? I've got a journalist to lynch.'

'Are you going now?'

'Why?'

'Because if you are, I'm going to stay and watch you try to cross the car park.'

*

Jessica could feel her colleagues peering from the windows and made sure she spoiled their fun by heading around the edge of the car park where the ice was thinner. It was still slippery but she reached her car without falling on her arse and then turned and proffered a middle finger to whoever was watching.

The journey across Manchester could have been described as stop-start but there wasn't much starting. The radio said there had been accidents at three separate places on the ring road and that Mancunian Way was closed because of an oil spill. Even by Manchester's standards the traffic was abysmal. As soon as Jessica left the station and turned onto Stockport Road, she was stuck in a long row of red tail lights stretching into the murky grey haze.

After an hour of solid clutch-work that would go un-appreciated by her colleagues who claimed she was a bad driver, Jessica eventually reached Chorlton, hoping the *Herald* receptionist had her facts correct. Garry Ashford lived in one of the new-builds, meaning he must be on a better salary than she would have guessed. The red-brick Lego boxes were lined up in parallel rows at the end of an incomprehensible maze of roads leading onto the estate. It would have been bad enough to negotiate at the best of times but with the climate building up for the arrival of penguins and the roads frozen solid, Jessica skidded her way into three incorrect cul de sacs before eventually finding the correct address.

Garry answered after the first ring of the doorbell, standing in his socks and tracksuit bottoms, wearing a Dangermouse T-shirt. He'd not shaved in a few days, rough stubble peppering his chin and cheeks. 'Oh, it's you,' he said.

'Bloody hell, it's nice to see you too. I come all the way out in the middle of the next ice age just to say hello and have a friendly brew – and that's how you greet me.'

He half-blocked a yawn with his hand. 'It's my week off, Jess.'

'I know, that's why I thought I'd drop around – y'know, like the old days but without the curry and beer. Can I come in then? It's freezing out here.' Garry sighed before stepping to the side and letting her pass. She took off her coat, gloves, hat and scarf, passing them to him, and heading through the closest door which she correctly guessed was the living room. 'Blimey, it's all right in here, isn't it? Who's the DIY fan? It's can't be you – how is Mrs Ashford?'

Jessica made herself comfortable in the recliner, putting her feet up as Garry sat on the sofa, moving a copy of that morning's *Herald* out of his way. 'I know why you're here.'

'What? We're mates, aren't we? What's the world come to when a friend can't drop in on another friend to say hello when he's on a week off?'

'How did you know I was on holiday?'

'Called your office, told them I was working on a TV documentary about the Stretford Slasher and that I wanted you on as a star guest after your feature. I thought they'd give me a bunch of bollocks about data protection but whoever answers your phones caved straight away. She'd have given me your inside leg measurement if I'd asked. Not that I want to know. So, anyway, how is Mrs Ashford? What's her name?'

Garry glanced towards the television where a photograph of him and his girlfriend grinning was proudly displayed. 'It's not *Mrs* Ashford but she's fine – she couldn't get the whole week off work. We're supposed to be going away tomorrow but I can barely get the car off the drive.'

'How's her cataracts? Didn't she have some sort of personality disorder too?'

Garry rolled his eyes. 'Haven't you got any new jokes?'

'The old ones are the best – now aren't you going to brew up? I'm a guest and you're being rude.'

'Fine. How do you have it?'

'White, no sugar – but not too much milk. You should see this new constable we've got, he's all over the bloody place. He gets the shakes whenever he gets a milk bottle in his hand. It's like drinking a tea latte. If it was down to me, we'd sack 'em – if you can't make a half-decent cuppa then you can't be trusted to go hunting for murderers, can you?'

Garry finally cracked, a hint of a smile creeping across his face. 'All right, I'll get your tea – but if you're going to have a poke around in here, can you at least not move anything? Beth knows where everything goes and it's me who'll get it in the neck.'

'Aah, the basis for all solid relationships – complete fear of moving anything in your own house. Fine, I won't move anything, just toss over that paper and I'll have a good look at what's going on.'

Garry smacked Jessica across the head with the paper on his way into the kitchen, knowing what he was going to walk back into but unaware that Jessica had lost her glasses and couldn't read any of the stories.

A few minutes later, the journalist returned from the kitchen, passing Jessica a Muppets mug with Walter on the front. The tea was a perfect caramel colour. 'Do you want to come and work for us?' Jessica asked. 'Minimum wage, four weeks' holiday, no bank holidays, my personal tea-maker.'

'You're all right.'

'Fine – be like that but don't come running to me when they come to their senses and boot you out over made-up stories.'

Another roll of the eyes. 'Here we go . . .'

'What? Don't take it out on me just because you're making up stories for your front page.' Jessica held up the *Herald* to prove her point. Even though she couldn't read it, Izzy had given her enough of a rundown so she could bluff her way through. 'It says here that Alan Hume is a member of some right-wing nutcase group and yet there's nothing in any of our files that says that. I've been onto the Serious Crime Division this morning who monitor gang behaviour and they've never heard of him. Very serious thing, making up stories like that.'

There was a definite smirk on his face as Garry took the paper back. 'It's not made up.'

'Come off it – how would you know something like that when our gang experts don't? Admittedly they can't tie their own shoelaces and half of them aren't potty-trained but they are experts.'

'I'm not telling you how I know, I just know.'

'Where'd you get the picture of him heiling Hitler?'

'Never you mind.'

Jessica took a sip of the tea, which was good. 'Come on, Garry, how long have we known each other? We've got all these mutual friends, you tried it on with me at a wake – I mean how would that go down with Mrs Ashford? She's got over a personality disorder and then she finds out her boyfriend's the type to chat up girls after a funeral.'

Garry's smile became a full-on grin. 'How come when I called you to ask for details of DSI Niall Hambleton, you told me to, and I quote, "sod the sod off" – and yet when you want to know something, it's all smiles and cups of tea?'

He had her there.

'All right, fine. I didn't give you Niall's details because he didn't want them giving out. You found them out anyway but he wouldn't talk to you, would he? I did you a favour. But fair's fair, what do you want?'

'The next time something huge is happening, I want a tip-off so we can get a photographer there. The nationals have been hammering us, the BBC is always sniffing around and we barely get a look in. Not just a "we've found that guy nicking bags of peas from Tesco" tip, I want an actual exclusive.'

'Fine, whatever, just make sure you keep your phone on and I'll see what I can do.'

'Really?'

'I thought you were going to want sexual favours or something – compared to that, sending a text message is a piece of piss. Come on then, how'd you know about Hume?'

'One more thing—'

'I've told you before I'm not touching you there, you'll have to do it yourself.'

Garry grinned. 'I think you're getting worse. Eighteen months ago we could have had a conversation where every response wasn't a punchline at my expense.'

Jessica had more of the tea. 'What do you want?'

'I was wondering what you thought of the Stretford Slasher piece. Did Hambleton read it?'

'Why do you want to know?'

Garry bit on his bottom lip and shrugged slightly. 'I put a lot of work into it. I really wanted to interview him but I suppose I hoped he at least had a look at it.'

'All right but if you ever run into him, don't tell him I told you this.'

'I won't.'

'I mean it – he won't talk to me again if he knows I've spoken to you about it.'

'I won't!'

'This is a direct quote: "He must have decent sources because he did a good job actually".'

'That's what Hambleton said?'

'Well it's not something I'd say, is it? I'd say, "What bollocks has he been making up this time?"'

The smile was now fixed on Garry's face as he leant back onto the sofa. 'That's really nice of him. We'd planned it as this big pullout but when he said he didn't want to speak to us, it became complicated. The old DCI is dead too and they were the main two involved in the investigation.'

'I thought it was a decent piece too – it's just you lot

and your alliteration. I mean, "Stretford Slasher", it must have been a media thing.'

'How'd you mean?'

'Come off it, it's all headlines with you. In the past few years we've had the Tameside Tit-Grabber, the Gorton Groper, the Didsbury Dick-Flasher, the Prestwich Panty-Sniffer and the Fallowfield Flasher – they're just the cases I've worked on.'

Garry laughed. 'I remember that Fallowfield guy, whatever happened to him?'

'We had him in on a line-up but the woman ID'd the wrong guy.'

'She wasn't looking at . . .'

'What? Penises? Of course she wasn't. How old are you? Grow up.'

Garry tried to apologise but Jessica had the giggles, sending a spray of tea across the carpet and Garry scarpering for the kitchen muttering about how Beth was going to notice the stain. Still, it served him right for putting the image in her mind of half-a-dozen naked men lined up having their genitals examined by an already traumatised victim.

After Garry had scrubbed the floor amid a series of tuts, he finally returned to the sofa. 'Right, let's hear it then,' Jessica said.

Garry nodded over the back of her. She turned to look at the wall where there was a row of pig ornaments on top of a bookshelf.

'Are you calling me a pig?'

'No, that's how I know Alan Hume is a right-wing nutball.'

'How?'

'He lives next door. He had a bunch of his racist, idiotic mates around over Christmas. They were all in the back garden listening to punk music, pissed off their heads, chanting "Paki, Paki, Paki – out, out, out". That photo on today's front page is one I took from our bedroom. The stupid bellends were marching around giving Nazi salutes. It's only our house that had a view of it because of the high fences. You think of them with tattoos and skinheads but this lot were all respectable types – suits, smart shoes, posh cars.'

Jessica turned to stare at the wall. 'I didn't even clock his address. We saw that he was single and because he was in hospital, there was no point in coming round.'

'I'm pretty sure he owns another place anyway because he's hardly here. I think he bought this to sell it on.'

'What about the "Gang War" headline?'

'Not mine – I'm on holiday. I have newswire access at home and was checking through things last night when I saw a name that rang a bell. I emailed the copy and picture and they did the rest.'

Jessica finished the last of her tea, swallowing it this time. 'Do you have any photos of the other Nazis from Christmas?'

Garry booted up his laptop and showed her the two-dozen images. It was always going to be a long shot but there was no Luke Callaghan there. He put them on a pen drive, with Jessica saying she'd send them on to the SCD to go into their gang files.

'I do have one other thing for you,' Garry added, handing over the drive.

'If there are naked pictures of you on here I don't want to see them.'

'It's about Hume – you know he's a builder and a land-lord, don't you?'

'We might be incompetent but we're not complete numpties.'

'I've heard rumours a lot of his tenants are unhappy and that his houses are in terrible states. I was thinking about doing an exposé but it's a little too close to home.'

'You're sure?'

'Definitely but I'm not going to put this on a plate for you, you'll have to do the legwork yourself.'

Jessica didn't mind that – she just wondered if they'd been thinking too big.

13

As she sat in unmoving traffic that had somehow become even worse than before, Jessica phoned Cole to give him the information about Alan Hume and then called Izzy to give her the news too.

'What else is going on?' Jessica asked, half-wishing she had a pool car so she could use the sirens and then realising it was probably a bad idea to drive at speed given the conditions.

'Not much,' Izzy replied. 'There hasn't been any web chatter about this attack, so if Anarky or anyone else are responsible then they're keeping it quiet. The DCI says the SCD reckons the first post could've been someone trying to claim credit to make a name for themselves.'

'What about the search team at Trafford?'

'They're stuck out there because the roads are gridlocked. I think they've all gone to the food court.'

'Did they find anything?'

'There was a rotting seagull in one of the bins.'

'Ugh, who found that?'

'Who do you think?'

Jessica thought for a few moments. Her first idea would always have been DC Rowlands but he was sunning himself somewhere and leaving them to do the work. Then it hit her. 'Not Joy Bag Jane?'

'Yep. They were singing "The Birdy Song" at her, apparently.'

'Y'know, the people we work with really are a bunch of bastards. If it's not making up lies about my driving, then it's giving a constable rude nicknames.'

'Firstly, I've been in a car with you and the reputation is deserved. Secondly, you're the one who sent her out on both searches, so don't be surprised if that seagull finds its way into your office. Not that you'd notice given the amount of shite that's in there.'

'Whose side are you on?'

'No one's but I'd sleep with one eye open if I were you because Joy Bag's on the warpath.'

'That's all I need; another constable gunning for me. What else is going on – have we spoken to the SCD about the gang war thing? Garry says it wasn't his headline.'

There was a rustle of papers and the line went quiet for a moment as Jessica heard the faint sound of Izzy shouting at someone. 'Sorry, Pat's going off on one,' she said, returning to the call. 'The canteen's closed today because the cook can't get in.'

'We have a cook? Imagine having that on your CV. I hope no one here gives them a reference, the food's bloody awful.'

Izzy ignored her. 'Serious Crime say there's no evidence and no chatter. The press office is putting out a statement rubbishing the news piece.'

'If I'd known that, I would have hung around at Garry's to wait for his editor to call.'

'Luke Callaghan has spoken to a victim support officer

this morning with one of our lot present. I think it's the best we're going to get, statement-wise.'

'What did he say?'

'Not a lot. We asked if he knew anyone who could have targeted him but there were no names we didn't already know. He kept going on about his wife – plus his old business partner, that Cowell guy. He even mentioned the councillor he defeated but we know he's in New Zealand. We've already eliminated everyone.'

'Anything else?'

'He said something about getting a lawyer and suing us for not protecting him but he's just angry. Whatever he's done in past, he's still lost his eyesight – the guy's entire life has changed. Oh, and you owe me a tenner.'

Jessica finally moved forwards an entire car's length before putting the handbrake on again. It was going to be a long journey back. 'Why?'

'We had a book running on whether you were going to slip over in the car park heading to your car. I put ten quid down that you were going arse over tit but then you crept around the edge. If I'd known you were going to do that, I wouldn't have told you how icy the car park was.'

'You bet against me?'

'Obviously. I don't take cheques though, cash only.'

'Why would I pay you the ten pounds you bet against me?'

'Because I tipped you off! If it wasn't for that I would have had my tenner back, plus the twenty quid from the two-to-one odds. I should really get thirty quid off you but I'll settle for my stake back.'

'Who was running the book?'

'Who do you think? Pat.'

'Bastard – I even gave him a vanilla slice and this is how he repays me. If you'd said something, I could have given you fifty quid to put on, faked falling over and then we could have gone halves.'

Izzy wasn't listening. 'Where are you?'

'Just outside Chorlton – the traffic's not moving but the rain's finally stopped. Some bloke in front has one of those massive exhausts.'

'I've got a list of properties that Hume owns. There are four close to you – if his houses are that bad, you can go and have a chat to some of his tenants. It doesn't sound like you're going anywhere quickly.'

The row of traffic heading towards the centre of the city was unmoving but the line in the opposite direction was at least crawling along.

'Fine, text them to me and I'll see what I can do. Has anyone got a connection between the two victims yet?'

'No, but I'd be more worried about Joy Bag getting vengeance if I were you.'

The first address Jessica checked was a two-bedroom semi-detached house with once-red-brick walls that were stained with black soot as if it had recently been on fire with a tatty flowery curtain hanging across single-glazed windows. It looked like it had been built some time shortly after the Second World War and hadn't been renovated since. To call it a shithole would insult any holes that had been dug in the ground and filled with shit. No one answered the door.

The second place Hume owned was a terrace in the middle of a row that stretched the entire length of a street. Although the roads had been tarmacked, the alleys that ran in between the houses were still made of the same cobbles that had been laid a hundred years previously. The house didn't look as if it had been done up much since then either. Although every other house in the street had new gutters plus a double-glazed door and windows, Hume's property had a metal gutter hanging off its brackets and a flaking wooden door that Jessica felt confident she could put her boot through if she felt like it.

Jessica knocked on the door and heard an instant scrabbling from the inside. She couldn't see anything through the letterbox but when she pressed her face to the living-room window, she spotted a pair of legs hiding behind the sofa.

This time she knocked on the window. 'Hello? I can see you in there.'

The legs twitched but the figure didn't stand. After another few attempts, Jessica gave up – but it didn't bode well if Hume's tenants were hiding when the door went.

After the first two houses, Jessica didn't think it could get any worse but the third place somehow managed to be a step down. This was a flat above a pizza shop that was hard to find even with the address on her phone and the sat nav in her car telling her she was facing the front door. Jessica eventually realised that what she thought was an alleyway for the shop's bins was actually the entrance to a stairwell that led up to a flat. Even holding her breath, Jessica couldn't avoid the smell of rotting food as she edged around a pile of pizza boxes. For the first time since the bad weather had begun, she was grateful for the freezing cold – if it had been a hot day, this area would have been crawling with ants and who knew what else.

At the top of a rickety set of wooden steps, there was a once-green door that was smeared with grease and dirt. In the muck, someone had used a finger to inscribe the somewhat poetic 'fancy a fuk?'

Courtship wasn't what it used to be.

Carly Dennis answered after one knock, cigarette hanging from her mouth, Manchester facelift in full flow, her hair scraped back so tightly that it made the rest of her features bulge like a squeezed frog. She was somewhere in her forties, her best days long behind her, if they'd ever existed. Despite her strong local accent making every sentence sound like she was offering to rip your ears off, she was quite pleasant.

The last thing Jessica expected was to be invited in for a cup of tea. Well, that was until she walked into the living room where there was a life-size poster of Liam Gallagher pinned to the wall. It was from his younger days in Oasis when he still pronounced 'sunshine' as 'sunshiiiiiiiine', long hair hanging across his face, sunglasses shielding his eyes, snarl in full effect. If that wasn't the last thing that anyone would expect, then Jessica didn't know what would be.

'Don't mind Liam,' Carly said, leading Jessica across a bare unvarnished wooden floor into a kitchen covered with patchy, ripped lino and green cupboard doors straight out of the 1970s.

She filled the kettle up, plugged it in and flicked the switch.

Nothing happened.

'Bloody thing,' Carly cursed, jabbing a fork into the socket as Jessica leapt out of the way in surprise. 'Oh don't worry about this; it's about finding the right spot, innit?'

Jessica wasn't sure she wanted to know but after a gentle popping sound, Carly plugged the kettle back in, switched it on, and the red light appeared.

'Is it always like that?' Jessica asked.

'Oh yes, the electric's been buggered ever since I moved in.'

'That's sort of what I was here for – I wanted to ask about your landlord, Alan Hume.'

'That dirty bastard? He doesn't like my Liam.'

Jessica peered back towards the living room where the Oasis lead singer was still pinned to the wall, still snarling. 'What's not to like?'

'Oh, I'm with you, darlin'. Alan wouldn't know a real man if he got hit in the face by one.'

Jessica didn't point out the irony of Alan having been hit repeatedly in the face by someone who might turn out to be a real man. Probably not Liam though.

'I wanted to ask you about the flat you're living in. We've been talking to a few of Alan's tenants.'

''Bout bloody time. Look at this place.'

Carly pointed to the ceiling where a large patch of damp was spreading inexorably towards the light fitting which itself was hanging by two wires. As Jessica looked around the rest of the flat she could see mould and damp in every corner. Carly said that every power point was on the blink; the sofa sagged in the middle, the springs had gone in the mattress, the hot tap in the sink didn't work and she had to leave mouse traps out each night.

Jessica wondered what Liam would think of that. She didn't want to but as she sipped on another perfectly made cup of tea, she had to ask the question. 'If it's so bad, why do you live here?'

The woman tightened the flowery tie in her hair, stretching her skin even tauter. 'Darlin', if you ain't got nuffin, then where else are you meant to stay? Me mam reckons this is an elf 'azard but I ain't got a job, 'av' I? Where else can I go?'

It took Jessica a few moments to realise that Carly meant 'health hazard', rather than the flat being a direct threat to pointy-eared mythical creatures.

'If I were to tell you that Alan Hume was seriously injured last night, what would you say?'

'Good – the dirty bastard prob'ly tried it on with one too many girls.'

'How do you mean?'

'He's a fuckin' perv, innee? When I were struggling wiv me rent, he said I could give him a blowie and we'd call it even. I told the dirty bastard to piss off and borrowed some money off me mam.'

Charming.

Jessica had seen and heard enough. She said goodbye to Carly and Liam and returned to her car, hoping it was still there and hadn't been bricked up. Luckily all the wheels were still present, although the smell of gone-off pizza and rat shite had drifted across the road and, now the rain had stopped, it felt even colder. As she was about to call the station to tell Izzy that an obvious connection between Luke Callaghan and Alan Hume was that they were both shitbags, her phone rang anyway.

'Iz?'

'Are you on your way back?'

'Yes, I've got a sort-of connection from Callaghan to Hume.'

'Good, we've got one too.'

'Really?'

'Guess who one of Hume's former tenants is?'

Jessica didn't have to guess because Michael Cowell's words suddenly flitted into her head: 'I've got a shit flat – though not as bad as the last one'. Luke Callaghan's hairy-eared former business partner used to live in one of Alan Hume's houses.

14

Michael Cowell invited Jessica and Izzy into his living room by eyeing DC Diamond up and down and saying: 'Blimey, why didn't you bring her last time?'

Ever the charmer.

The heating was cranked up in his flat, providing a welcome relief from the howling, frost-ridden gale outside, but any satisfaction was immediately forgotten at the sight of him wearing shorts and a white T-shirt exposing a freakish amount of hair. Jessica had seen wildlife documentaries on primates where the subjects had less fur than Michael Cowell. Thick black hair coated his legs and arms, as well as sticking out from the V in his shirt. When he turned, the T-shirt was so tight and thin, she could see the dark hairs through it.

As soon as Michael led them into the living room, Izzy asked where the toilet was. Jessica didn't blame her – she was close to vomiting too. The worst thing was that none of it distracted from the quite extraordinary ear hair, as if he had crammed a small dark mouse above each lobe. Jessica couldn't stop staring at it.

With Izzy gone, she felt out of her depth, overwhelmed by the sheer amount of hair. It was like making small talk with a gorilla. 'How was the strip club?' she asked, not wanting the answer.

'Amazing. There's this nineteen-year-old Ukrainian, Alanya. I had the night of my life.'

Ugh. Jessica doubted Alanya would be saying the same.

When Izzy returned looking paler than she had been before she left, they sat down. 'I do have some more news for you, Mr Cowell,' Jessica said.

'Call me Mike. Or Mikey. That's what Alanya called me.'

Double ugh. 'It's about someone else you know. Alan Hume was attacked last night. He's in intensive care.'

'As in the builder Alan Hume?'

'Your former landlord.'

Jessica didn't think he would collapse to his knees and confess, nor did she think he would be upset. She definitely didn't expect the reaction that came. Cowell leapt up from his armchair, blubbery stomach releasing itself from the bottom of his T-shirt, exposing the hairiest belly-button Jessica thought she would ever see. He punched the air. 'You little beauty. I've definitely got some champers around here.' Before either Jessica or Izzy could say something, he had scuttled across to the open-plan kitchen and opened the fridge.

'Mr Cowell, you do realise we are looking for suspects for both attacks and you're the only person we can find who links the pair?'

He stuck his head out from the fridge. 'When was he attacked?'

'Last night at around seven o'clock.'

'I was still at work – we'd been out to the strip club and me and Alanya, well, it was a late one. I was delayed getting to work yesterday, so had to stay late. Check with my boss, check the call records, whatever.' He plonked a bottle on the counter top. 'Now, do you want some Blanc de Noirs, or don't you?'

'I was hoping you could tell us a bit more information about your relationship with Alan Hume. We could visit the station.'

There was a loud popping sound as the cork hammered into the ceiling. 'Aww, bollocks, we can't do that now, can we? I've opened the bottle.'

'Perhaps if you answer the questions in a calmer manner, we can do this here.'

'Aye, good thinking. Do you want a glass?'

And so the conversation continued. Cowell could barely contain his excitement, telling a similar story to Carly's about the state of the flat in which he'd lived, albeit without Hume's invitation to give him a 'blowie' instead of rent money. He did say that Hume had kept his deposit and an extra month's rent for no reason and refused to answer his phone calls. Three-quarters of a Champagne bottle down and he wasn't flagging, talking about 'getting the lads round' for a 'big night'.

He might have been glad to hear of the attacks on Callaghan and Hume – and certainly had a motive – but with his alibis, they had no reason to arrest him. Jessica thought he was relatively harmless anyway, unless you were a nineteen-year-old Ukrainian, in which case he was likely your worst nightmare.

On their journey back to the station, it was already beginning to get dark. Gentle flurries of snow were fluttering to the ground with the radio weatherman predicting a cold night – as if it wasn't something they could figure out for themselves. Izzy called in for an update but no one had uncovered anything else on Michael Cowell. Everything he had told them about his history checked out and his alibis were sound. They had looked at his bank accounts but there were no suspicious deposits, transfers or withdrawals. He was as clean as could be. Not literally of course, not with that hair.

There were updates from the hospital, though: Hume had been moved from critical to stable, although he wouldn't be giving a statement any time soon. Callaghan wasn't coping with his blindness too well and was demanding to be allowed home.

Izzy hung up as Jessica pulled into the stream of traffic heading towards Longsight. 'Are you off this weekend?' Jessica asked.

'Yes, Mal and me are doing nothing for two days: telly, takeaways and beer. Well, that and looking after Amber. I'm turning my phone off, so don't even bother.'

'Good for you. Me and Adam are going to IKEA.'

Izzy laughed. 'What have you done to deserve that?'

'I think it's all the swearing and this is payback. We need a few new cabinets for the spare room.'

'I hope you've put aside seven or eight hours – once you get in that place, there's no getting out. It's a giant flat-packed hall of doom.'

'I've never been. Adam got talked into it by his sister – he thinks it's going to be a quick in-out, then back to the house with the furniture. I'm not putting any of it together so he'd better know what he's doing.'

'How are things between you?'

'When we're actually together, it's like we're an old married couple. Having Georgia at the house is awkward but she's looking for her own place.'

'What about . . . ?'

'No.'

Jessica pulled onto Stockport Road for the final part of the journey. Traffic had started to clear but the red lights still stretched far ahead, eating into the grey of the early evening as the snow eased off, replaced by a light drizzle.

Izzy remained quiet for a few moments, before adding: 'If you want to talk, we can.'

Jessica didn't reply. The low rumble of the engine rippled around the vehicle alongside the gentle scrape of the windscreen wipers flip-flopping across the glass. 'We've not done . . . *that* . . . in a couple of months,' Jessica croaked. 'It's not him. After they said I couldn't get pregnant, it's all the tests and the inspections and the talk about it. It feels so mechanical – everything's talked through with the doctor to make sure you're doing it at the right time and you just end up going over it all so much that it's like changing a tyre or . . . putting together a flat-pack cupboard.'

'Have you ever done either of those?'

Jessica forced a laugh. She hated talking about these things to anyone, least of all with a doctor she didn't know. Izzy was seemingly good at everything – if you wanted a job doing, give it to Iz. Parenting tips? She was a natural. And the fact the constable had made her laugh about this proved it was something else she was good at.

'Of course I've never done either of those. I just mean that it's not about being together, or having fun, it's just another chore. I've not felt right since I got back to work. Adam's really good about it – infuriatingly good – he's so bloody nice about everything and everyone that it drives me mad.'

'What are you going to do?'

'You end up wondering if it's worth it? When I was pregnant before, I was used to the idea of leaving this behind and going to do something else.'

'You wouldn't have come back?'

'I'm not like you – you can multi-task, you're naturally good at everything—'

'I'm really not.'

'It seems like it. My point is that I just want to be good at one thing. If I'm going to be a mother, then I'll have to make sure I'm brilliant but I don't think I could do that and this, not now, not after the promotion.'

'So why did you accept becoming a DI?'

Jessica sucked in the warm air spewing from the vehicle's heater. In front, the traffic surged forwards a dozen car lengths before stuttering to a halt again. Jessica wrenched the handbrake into place and rested her head on the driver's side window. 'Because it was there. It's a justification of everything from the past few years, isn't it? Having a stun gun used on me, the injection, the fire, the shotgun – even the house. There are other things that you don't want to hear. You go into these places hoping to come out the other side and when you do, and they offer you a reward for it, you feel like you should take it.'

'Perhaps you should think about what makes you happy. Is it the job or is it the idea of being a mother? Could it be both? Or something else entirely?'

'It's not this sodding weather, that's for sure. It's nearly summer – I'm off to that ParkFest thing soon but everyone's going to be wearing coats, scarves and hats at this rate.'

Izzy wasn't fooled by the attempted change of subject. 'What about Adam?'

Jessica allowed someone to pull out from a side street and edge in front of her.

'Bloody hell, you really aren't yourself, are you?' Izzy said, reaching over and putting her hand across Jessica's forehead.

'You're hilarious.'

'What about Adam?'

Jessica knew she had started the conversation and now her friend wasn't going to let her finish it without answering the question. 'Can I tell you something I've never told anyone?'

'Of course.'

'And you'll keep it to yourself?'

'Promise.'

'Have you ever totally loved and utterly hated the same person all at the same time?'

Izzy didn't reply instantly and Jessica felt like it made the admission all the worse. It had been on her mind for such a long time but now she'd said it, it was somehow real.

'No I haven't.'

Jessica laughed hollowly. 'Just me then. It's hard to explain. He was at an overnight thing for the university a couple of weeks ago and I couldn't sleep. It's the first night we've spent apart since I got back from the house. I was rolling over, reaching for him, not to do anything, just to have him there. I felt empty, like there was a part of me missing. Then, when he was back, he was lovely. I'd been at work and when I got home he'd been shopping and cooked us tea. He said he'd missed me and talked me through his day but I couldn't help but think that he knew me too well. He knew I would've had a long day and couldn't be bothered to get any food in – and that I'd have got a takeaway or not bothered eating. He did everything I needed and it comes so naturally to him. Then I find myself wondering if that's what I want, which makes me guilty because I wonder that if it isn't, then what *do* I want? Sometimes, I wish he'd get annoyed. Like that day – if he'd got home after being away and wondered why I hadn't bothered to do any of those things instead of doing it himself.'

'And that makes you hate him? It's a strong word.'

Jessica sighed. 'I know . . . but I shouldn't feel like that, should I? I shouldn't resent him for being nice and trying to see both sides of an argument. I know I shouldn't – but the fact I do has me hating the way it makes me feel. Because of that, I suppose . . . I end up hating him too.'

She accelerated through a set of lights into traffic that was actually moving, albeit slowly.

'No one has the answer to this except you. Every time

I've seen you with Adam, you seem happy. He's a really good guy. You're great at work too, although it's hard to tell whether you enjoy it because you're in the thick of everything all the time. Perhaps you shouldn't be so hard on yourself – you've had a tough time, you do a stressful job. Not everything has to be a laugh a minute; sometimes things don't work out, so you get up and go again. Remember when Mal first wanted kids and I didn't? I never thought I would but then, when I was pregnant, it felt right. Sometimes, I wonder if you treat everything that happens away from the station as if it's still a case.'

Jessica didn't reply straight away, taking a breath and thinking over Izzy's words. 'How do you mean?'

'At work, everything needs a motive and a method, doesn't it? You watch the police things on TV or you read a book and you'd think the world was full of nutters who do things for no reason – but it isn't like that. There's always a reason why people kill or hurt others – even if it's just that they like it. So when you go home and Adam's done something for you, you're wondering why, or what you've done to deserve it. Or you feel guilty that you haven't done anything to make it up to him. It doesn't have to be like that though – sometimes you can let it go and accept that he doesn't have a motive, other than the fact that he's a nice person.'

The psychologist would be reaching for the tissues again.

Jessica didn't reply but as the clock ticked over to six o'clock, the time their shifts were due to finish, she turned the radio up as the news came on, wondering what they'd have to say about the gang war story from earlier. The top story was the traffic chaos, which linked into the apocalyptic weather report. Overnight snow was the start and it went downhill from there.

The newsreader had a hint of a local accent but had obviously been on some sort of elocution course because she was doing her best to hide it. She sure knew how to drop a bombshell, however: ' . . . Also in the news: Colin Rawlinson, the infamous Stretford Slasher who terrorised the streets of Manchester a quarter of a century ago, has been found dead in his cell . . .'

The weekend's news was full of end-of-a-monster-type stories, following on from the Stretford Slasher anniversary articles. Niall Hambleton was apparently unwilling to contribute, meaning Garry Ashford was somehow the next best thing. Over the course of the Saturday, Jessica heard him on local and national radio, plus he showed up on the evening news – and that was just where she spotted him. She never would have told him to his face but he was a natural, speaking clearly and concisely about a subject on which he had clearly done a lot of work.

On Sunday, Jessica and Adam went through the ritual perhaps more sacred than wedding vows: a weekend trip to IKEA. The Warrington store was heaving with similarly depressed-looking couples mooching up and down the endless one-way aisles, dwarfed by towering piles of furniture and boxes.

'What type of cabinet is it you want?' Jessica asked, already bored.

Adam was squinting into the distance, hands in his pockets. 'I don't know, I didn't realise this place was so big. I thought we'd turn up, pick up something we liked and drive home. We've already been here for an hour and I'm not sure we've found the right aisle yet.'

'You should've brought Georgia. She reckoned her flat down south was full of this stuff.'

'She's out with Humphrey, it was a last-minute thing.'

'What do you think about him?'

Adam paused before answering, as ever a step ahead, knowing that she'd asked because she was unsure. 'He seems all right – they met on the Internet, so they spent some time getting to know each other before meeting in person. You don't have any brothers or sisters and for all these years, I didn't know I did either. I reckon older sisters should know best about these things. You?'

'I've only met him once.'

Adam laughed. 'Once is enough with you.'

'I'm not sure about him. Perhaps it's the age thing? I'm sure he's fine.'

She couldn't say that she'd checked him out and found no record of him.

Adam stopped, staring up towards the enormous ceiling where signs hung saying where everything was. 'Haven't we been down here?'

'I have no idea, they all look the same.'

'Shall we ask someone?'

'That'd be admitting defeat – do you think Churchill would ask someone and give up, or do you think he'd keep going?'

'*Churchill?*'

'I couldn't think of anyone else. Anyway, the point is that he wouldn't give up.'

'I think he probably had more on his mind than navigating Swedish furniture stores.'

They tried the next aisle across, even though it was one they had definitely been down. 'Do you remember when we were younger?' Jessica said. 'You'd spend all your time talking about booze, fags or going out. Wondering who was shagging who, all that stuff. Now, it's dressers and sideboards and whether the bedding matches the carpet. It's bloody depressing.'

'Perhaps we should get matching dressing tables to make us a proper couple?'

'Do I look like I'm in my sixties?'

Adam put an arm around her. 'Only first thing in the morning.'

Jessica elbowed him in the ribs but her mind was whirring, trying to remember what Shane Donovan had been wearing when she'd visited him in the church hall. If it was what she thought, then Adam had just given her an idea.

15

Jessica sat on a low wooden bench watching a group of children stand in a circle flapping their respective corners of a parachute up and down. The church hall was a lot warmer compared to the last time she had visited, with the gust of air whipping around the space like an enclosed tropical storm. Shane Donovan was off to the side, arms folded, a huge smile on his face. He called out a name and one of the kids dropped their corner and dashed under the parachute, emerging moments later, out of breath, clutching a handful of silver and gold pieces of paper. He dropped his takings into a bucket and then retook his place around the parachute before Shane called out another name.

As well as the whistle of the warm air, the main thing Jessica could hear was laughing. After their run under the parachute, each child would emerge beaming as the others chanted, sang and cheered.

When the time was up, the children separated out into teams according to the colours of their shirts and counted up the number of papers they had collected. Each team whispered their result to Shane and he stood in the middle of the room as they stomped on the floor, creating a thunderous drumroll. When he announced the winners, the whole team erupted into more cheers before Shane made sure the teams shook hands with each other.

The children's parents had gathered at the back of the hall and almost every one of them thanked Shane personally before heading back out into the maelstrom, their happy and exhausted kids in tow.

'I don't suppose you want to help me clear up, do you?' Shane asked Jessica when it was the two of them remaining. 'There's usually more than just me but Sarah's snowed in. Some of these kids only get out once a week, so I didn't want to cancel.'

Jessica sat on the wooden floor next to him and started to pile the silver pieces into one pile, the gold in another. 'What is this?'

'Every Sunday, I run an activity evening for children who've become known to the council or social services for whatever reason. Some of them come from extreme poverty, others have had a parent die, some have been excluded from school. There's no hard and fast rule and we don't turn people away, even if it's local kids knocking at the door wanting to join in. As long as they respect each other, I don't mind.'

'I would have thought it'd all be screams and carnage but it was quite well organised.'

Shane shrugged, dumping a pile of golds onto Jessica's. 'You'd be surprised what it's like when you treat them with respect. Some of them have had the worst possible upbringings. I know it's not an excuse when they continue to get into trouble, but sometimes they just need someone to give them a chance. In schools today, it's all about being non-competitive but that misses the point. There's nothing wrong with them playing games against each other, as long as they respect their team-mates and the opposition. We always make them draw teams at random for the games to split up any potential cliques and then everyone shakes hands. It's little things.'

'What do you do if any of them play up?'

Shane picked up Jessica's pile of silvers and placed them into a box. 'They self-police. If they all wanted this group to be a place where they come to act up, shout, swear, bully or whatever else, there's not much I could do to stop it. They outnumber me and that's not what *they* want. If someone's acting up, I encourage them to deal with it – and they do. A couple of months ago we had a session where we didn't play any games. Everyone sat down and it was like an intervention – one of the kids had been messing around, doing all those things I just said, and the others decided it wasn't on. They said he could either stop doing it, or go home.'

'What did he do?'

'Everyone's under fourteen here but some of them are still headstrong. They've had to grow up quickly and think they know everything. He stormed away, telling them to fuck off. Two weeks later, I got here to open up and he was sat by the side door. He asked if he could come back and I said it wasn't up to me. Inside, all the kids agreed that the lad he'd been bullying should have the final say.'

'So he sent him packing?'

Shane grinned. 'They shook hands and that was that. No one said another word. The first kid, the angry one, was here because his grandfather had been touching him up until he was eight when we got him away. The other one's mother was killed in a car crash and he's been brought up by his dad who couldn't care less about him. What they end up realising is that even when they don't have anything else, they've still got each other – so why piss it away with all the stupid squabbling.'

Shane finished packing the papers away and carried the case across to a store cupboard, Jessica just behind him. The hall was empty and the squeakiness of the floor made their movements echo eerily. 'Now, I'm sure you didn't come here for a chat about my kids, so how can I help you?' he added.

'When I was here the other day, you weren't entirely honest with me . . .'

'About Debbie? She was here. I'm not giving you any names of others present if that's what you think.' His voice was steady but there was a hint of anger.

'I know she was – we had two other members of your group come forward to confirm that both of you were here at the time that Luke Callaghan was having acid thrown in his face.'

'You checked up on me too?'

'We've had a full look into every aspect of your life.'

'Why?'

'Because Debbie Callaghan had as good a motive as anyone to go after her husband, so if you were giving her an alibi then we needed to make sure you were the person you claimed.'

'Well . . . I suppose . . .' Shane stumbled over his words before concluding: 'I don't have anything to hide.'

'Sure?'

'You can't make me admit to something I haven't done, I know my rights and—'

Jessica held a hand up to stop him mid-flow. 'Everyone knows their sodding rights nowadays, except they actually don't. You have far fewer rights than you might think. Anyway, do you know what I thought when we first met? "Some woman somewhere is going to fall head over heels for this guy".'

Shane stared at Jessica, unsure what to say.

'Oh don't worry, I'm not flirting with you – you'd drive me nuts. What I didn't realise is that I'd already met her. Why didn't you tell me you were seeing Debbie Callaghan?'

His mouth continued to hang open but Jessica was happy to wait for the reply. When it eventually came, it only confirmed what she already knew. 'How did you know?'

'I was out with my fiancé earlier and he was joking about getting matching dressers. My brain works slowly but it gets there in the end. I remembered your T-shirt with a bird pattern. Debbie had these little puffin ornaments everywhere. After a quick check with the RSPB, I found out you were both members. Contrary to popular opinion, two plus two doesn't always make four in this job – but it does here, doesn't it?'

Shane leant back against the storeroom door, his head sinking onto his chest. 'After one of the sessions here, we got talking. I've always been into birds and found out that she was interested too. Her husband never let her out but she'd paint them and collect the ornaments. I said she should join. A group of us go walking on Saturday and Sunday mornings. I suppose one thing led to another. I didn't take advantage – I told her we shouldn't at first – it was all her. It's very recent.'

Jessica shook her head. 'What you do is your own business – but one of you should have told me. We're investigating a major incident and she has a motive. The fact you withheld information is serious – if we'd found out another way, or at a later date, we could have had you both in – fingerprints, lawyers, interview rooms, some idiot leaking your names to the media, all that.'

Shane gulped. 'Does that mean you're not going to do that now?'

'I called the DCI earlier and he agrees with me. You told me the other day that you were in a relationship and I forgot to write it down. Silly me. It's in the documents now.'

'So nothing's going to happen?'

'Not unless you've got something else on your conscience.'

Shane started tapping his chest, coughing. 'Thank God, I'm so sorry . . . I was going to tell you but I thought it would get her in trouble because it'd look like she left him for me and then you'd arrest us both. She was on the phone crying the other night, thinking you'd find out.'

'One of you should have said.'

'I know and I'm grateful – but why would you change the statement for us?'

Jessica shrugged. 'I don't know – perhaps I'm going soft. Maybe it's just because I know Debbie has been through a lot.'

'She really has. He was a shit to her.'

'That doesn't mean he deserved to have acid thrown in his eyes.'

'I'm not saying it was. I—'

'All right, don't dig yourself a deeper hole. You can answer something for me though.'

'What?'

Jessica turned to face the room. 'The children. You say they're "your kids" and I sort of get why – but what's it like looking after ones that aren't yours?'

Shane bit his bottom lip, thinking. 'Out of everything, I think it's the most rewarding thing I do. There are always those kids who slip through the net, who you want to help but they don't want it. Finding that one who goes the other way and turns their life around is enough. If you had your own kids, you'd expect them to listen and learn. With other people's, so many are broken and you end up helping to put them back together again. You watch them becoming an adult.'

'What's it like when you see them leave each week?'

Shane began walking towards the main door, slowing so Jessica kept pace. 'Good and bad. Hopefully they learn things here which you want them to take away and act upon. They can't do that if they're supervised every minute of the day. When they come back the next week and you can see the slow changes, you know it's actually them and not just something happening because you're with them all the time. There are always kids you have soft spots for – that you worry about because you know they're going home to an environment that's not safe, or they're back on the streets with older kids who'll push them to do things they shouldn't. That's the other side because you'd love to be able to make sure they stay safe but you can't.' He paused as he reached the door, an icy chill creeping through the opening. 'Do you have children?'

'No, I was just wondering.'

Shane thanked her twice more before locking up and saying goodbye.

Because of the abundance of parked cars around Ancoats, Jessica had left her vehicle at the back of the Northern Quarter. It was only a five-minute walk but the wind was whistling between the tight buildings, biting viciously through her coat. The dusting of snow from before had been trampled into the pavements and started to refreeze, so Jessica walked in the road. The yellow-white street lights cast a spooky erratic glow around the surroundings, long shadows stretching into the night. Jessica could feel the cold air tickling the top of her lungs as she rounded the final bend onto the street where her car was parked. She sighed as she saw the rear window had already frosted over, hoping the de-icer on the back seat hadn't run out.

As she was contemplating calling Adam, Jessica heard a low groaning from the cobbled alley running off the main street. The breeze flitted along the passage, carrying the noise a second time and sending a sodden carrier bag spiralling past her into the side window of her car with a splat. Jessica patted her pocket instinctively, even though she knew her pepper spray wasn't there.

Armed with only a mobile phone and her own stupidity, Jessica edged into the shadows of the alley. The moan was there again. It definitely sounded like a person, probably a man, someone in pain.

'Hello?'

As soon as the word left Jessica's mouth, it was gobbled up by the wind and gone again. The narrow trail of light made barely an imprint on the gloom but Jessica could see a small patch of yellow almost glowing a short distance in front of her. She took another step ahead, crouching but leaning back on her heels, ready to spring away if needed.

'Hello?'

The figure rolled onto its back; definitely human, definitely a man. As her eyes adjusted, Jessica could see the thick padding of the once-shiny jacket. Along a slit in the side, yellow foam was spilling out.

'Shite.'

Jessica knelt, the freezing cobbles rubbing on her knees through her jeans. She rolled the figure back onto his side, brushing the hair away from his face, and used the light from her phone to illuminate his face. Toxic Tony's eyelids twitched, before a deep gurgle erupted from his stomach, closely followed by its contents all over her lap.

16

'Eeew. Tony, you dirty bast—' The smell hit the back of Jessica's throat, making her gag. 'God's sake, it's everywhere.'

Tony's lids flickered open but his eyes flopped lazily to one side. Vomit clung to his chin, dripping onto the ground. The stinking, chunky liquid was already soaking through Jessica's trousers and she could feel it on her freezing thighs.

She patted his cheek gently, getting more of the mush on her fingers. 'Come on, Tony, wake up for me.' He slumped onto her lap, mashing the bile into his hair and deeper into the denim of her jeans.

'Muuh.'

Jessica turned her head to the side, taking a gasp of cleanish air, stifling the swearing. 'Tony, what happened? I only saw you a few days ago and you were fine.'

She helped him sit against the wall, manoeuvring him away from the puddle of sick that was already beginning to crystallise between the cobbles. He giggled to himself as Jessica shone her phone into his eyes, trying to get them to focus. The pupils were pinpricks, staring past her into the distance.

'Tony, I'm going to take you to the hospital, all right?'

He began struggling but his frail arms were so weak that she could barely feel them flapping against her. 'No.'

More vomit dribbled down his chin, his lips hanging limply. 'Have you got a key for your flat anywhere?' she asked. He motioned towards the pocket of his coat but it was hanging open, filled with lumpy stomach stew.

'There's no way I'm reaching in there, buddy.'

His eyes drooped closed again. 'Muuh.'

'Hospital?'

'No!'

Jessica supported his head, peering along the alley towards the street, where the carrier bag was still stuck to the side of her car. 'Bollocks. Adam's going to kill me.'

'Can you still smell it?' Jessica could tell from the slight curl to Adam's top lip that he could. 'Shite, I'm going to have to burn everything I was wearing.'

Adam held a blanket out towards her. 'You'll have to burn that too. Who is he?'

Jessica wrapped the cover around herself and sat at the kitchen table being careful not to touch anything unnecessarily. 'Half an hour I spent in the shower too – someone's going to have to clean up in there.' Adam raised his eyebrows knowingly. 'All right,' she added, 'I'm asking if you'll clean up in there. I don't think I can take any more. The car reeks of it too. I might petrol bomb the bloody thing and claim the insurance.'

Adam sat waiting for a reply, sipping a cup of tea.

'Tony Farnsworth,' Jessica said, drinking from her own cup and pulling the blanket tighter, covering her bare shoulders. She was wearing clean underwear and yet the vomit smell was still there. 'I've known him on and off for a while. He's one of those people you see around; junkies, alkies, often in trouble.'

'Why have you brought him here?'

Jessica shook her head, sighing. 'I don't know. I saw him the other day and he was fine. He said he was thinking about moving out of the area and that he'd turned his life around.'

'He didn't look fine when you dumped him in the bath with his clothes on, covered in his own sick.'

Jessica wrapped her fingers around the mug, letting the warmth flow into her hand. 'Is that your qualified medical opinion? "He didn't look fine".'

'Call me Doctor Compton.'

'Anyway, you're right – he's not fine. I hosed him down with the shower and got rid of his clothes—'

Adam was grinning, mock-outraged. 'You undressed another man?'

'We had a nice romantic moment in the bathroom; lights, candles, soft music, puke-covered clothes – the works. Anyway, he wasn't really with it. He has track scars on his arm but there was bruising too.'

'So he's been using again?'

Jessica nodded. 'Don't worry, I used gloves. It looks like the skin had been growing back because the mark in his vein is wider than it should be, like he had to go hunting for it.'

'Is he still up?'

'No, it must've worn off a while back – there was

alcohol in his stomach too. I would've taken him to hospital but every time I mentioned it, he started panicking. I couldn't leave him on the street, he would have frozen to death.'

'Did he say anything?'

'He kept muttering "sorry" in the car but most of it was gibberish. He's sleeping it off in the box room. I managed to wash the worst of it out of his hair and threw a couple of duvets over him. I borrowed one of your tatty old jumpers and a pair of jeans I never liked and left them in there too.'

'*Borrowed?*'

'If you want them back, I could probably arrange it.'

'You're all right.'

Jessica finished off her tea, pulling the blanket tighter again. 'Thanks.'

'For what?'

'Not throwing a wobbly. I'd guess that if most women brought home a drunken, high-as-a-kite bloke covered in sick, their fiancés would probably have a word or two to say about it.'

Adam shrugged. 'I trust you. I'd rather it didn't become a regular thing, though. Wednesday night: pizza. Friday night: curry. Sunday night: spew-covered stranger.'

Jessica grinned narrowly. How could she not be in love with him when he could say things like that and make her giggle when she felt so awful?

'Will you tell Georgia?' she asked.

'I'll wake her now and let her know we've got a mate staying overnight.'

'And will you—?'

'Yes, I'll clean it. Go to bed and I'll see you tomorrow. I'm not firebombing the car for you though.'

Jessica flitted in and out of sleep, the Callaghans, Shane's kids, Izzy, Adam and Tony peppering her dreams. For once, it had been nice to think that someone had turned their life around. When she'd seen Tony the other day, she wanted him to get away from Manchester – not because it would have any effect on her workload but because it was comforting to think that he'd come out the other side. She remembered Shane's words: 'Finding that one who goes the other way and turns their life around is enough.' He'd been talking about his children but it was true of Tony as well. She'd been thinking it was nice someone she knew had done the same. In a way, it made what they did worthwhile – all the petty arrests, the drugs, the drink, the abuse – and yet Tony had got himself clean while he was still young enough to start a new life. Now, he was just another junkie.

Bollocks.

As her alarm clock flipped over to read 05.05, she heard the bump from the room at the far end of the hallway. She'd been waiting for it since she first started trying to sleep. She slipped on her dressing gown and padded barefoot to the box room, knocking gently and heading inside. Tony was laid on his back, trying to put Adam's jeans on the wrong way around.

'Where's the fly?' he croaked, the words sticking in his throat.

'Do you know where you are, Tony?'

He kicked the trousers off, sitting on the bed in a pair of boxer shorts, his pale, thin frame almost see-through in the overhead light. His words slurred into one another but were clear enough. 'You told me you were taking me to your house and that if I threw up again, you'd chop my bollocks off.'

'That sounds like me. I didn't realise you were awake. What happened?

Tony put the trousers on the correct way and pulled the jumper over his head. His face was white, his pupils still small.

'Where's my coat?'

'By the front door. I've washed it but it stinks. Your key's in the pocket where you left it.'

Tony stood abruptly, heading past Jessica through the door onto the landing. He looked both ways, disorientated and then stumbled towards the stairs.

'Tony—'

Jessica hurried to catch him but he had half-walked, half-fallen down the stairs into their hallway. She snagged him as he reached the front door, taking his still-damp coat off the radiator.

'What happened? When I saw you last week, you were talking about being clean, having a job and going home.'

Tony heaved the enormous jacket around himself. His hair was still damp from where she had washed him and hung across his face. 'It's all messed up.'

'I can get you help – you don't have to leave the house. Let's have something to eat and then I'll make a call, yes?'

Tony paused, one hand on the front door, the faint smell of vomit still clinging to him – or perhaps it was her. He took a deep breath and Jessica thought he was going to answer but instead he burst into tears. She reached out to touch him but he pulled away, stumbling backwards and clattering into the still flat-packed IKEA boxes. She tried to stop him but Tony yanked the door open and fell through it, slipping on the icy welcome mat before righting himself. As he disappeared into the early morning in a cloud of freezing breath, Jessica could hear his sobs echoing behind him. 'It wasn't me.'

17

The first person Jessica saw at the station was Niall. He was pacing through reception, distracted and pale as he headed towards the canteen. She caught him as he was passing her office.

'Bit early for you, isn't it?' Jessica said, tapping him on the shoulder.

The former DSI spun around. 'Oh, Jess . . . sorry. I'm not due in today but it's been a long weekend and they said we could come in whenever we wanted as long as we signed in and out. I think it's a health and safety thing.'

'I didn't mean it like that. You didn't look like yourself.'

He was wearing the same sweater as when she'd last seen him and his black suit trousers were creased, almost as if he'd worn them to bed. It was as if he had aged a decade over a handful of days. He glimpsed down at himself, sighing. 'I've not slept a lot this weekend. All the news people have been onto me since Rawlinson's death, wanting a comment. I unplugged the phone, so they started knocking on the door. I snuck out this morning, figuring I was safer here. There are so many files in storage, there's always something to be getting on with.'

'It's no wonder they're interested in you – it's the closing of a chapter.'

Niall shook his head, turning back towards the canteen.

'The chapter closed for me when I retired. I only came back to keep myself out of the garden.'

Jessica was already thinking of an excuse for why she couldn't have breakfast with him but Niall didn't ask, mumbling something about the weather and then hurrying into the canteen, apparently keen on giving himself stomach cramps as quickly as possible.

Given the way she had folded under his imposing stare in the pub last week, the journalists must have been relentless to rattle him so badly.

Jessica headed into her office, closing the door too quickly and sending stacks of papers scuttling across the room. On her desk, someone had left a pile of flavoured condoms, thankfully still in their wrappers. Probably Joy Bag Jane's idea of a joke – at least it wasn't the dead seagull. Wincing at the idea of a bubblegum-flavoured one, Jessica swept them into her top drawer.

She fumbled for her glasses, finding them in a coat pocket, and logged onto the system as she flicked through her pile of messages. The top Post-it note read: 'Call SDC', which presumably meant 'SCD' – Serious Crime Division. She screwed it up and aimed for the bin, missing by a whisker. Almost three points. Sod that – they could call her. Underneath was one which read: 'Ester called', followed by a number. That ball at least hit the rim of the bin before bouncing away. PC Pen-Thief must have been answering the phones today, either that or Fat Pat had overdosed on sugar and forgotten how to spell. She'd already spoken to Esther that morning anyway. Some people wrote anything down.

Jessica used the Internet to search for all the cafes within a half-mile radius of Tony's flat and then began phoning around, asking if they employed him. Her fifth call was answered by a woman who sounded like she was halfway through having a conversation with someone else. '. . . Fried, poached or boiled? Hello.'

'Er, hello?'

The line was muffled for a moment but the woman's words were still clear as she shouted: 'That's a full English with fried. No mushrooms.' Quieter: 'That's four-eighty, love.' Then Jessica could hear clearly again. 'How can I help?'

'I was wondering if you employed someone called Tony Farnsworth?'

'Have you got the exact money, love?'

'Sorry?'

'Not you.'

Jessica waited as what should have been a simple question took five minutes to get an answer, with the woman holding anything up to four conversations at the same time. Eventually the phone went dead before a man's voice came on, asking who he was speaking to. After introducing herself again, Jessica finally got the answer. 'Tony? Yes, he's been working here. I'm paying the National Insurance if that's what yer on about. I'm a bit late with the papers, that's all. I've got a business to run.'

When he finally accepted that Jessica wasn't from the tax office and wasn't trying to catch him out, she eventually got to the point. 'When was the last time you saw him?'

The man huffed loudly. 'Last bloody Tuesday – you give a guy a chance and this is how he repays you. Didn't bother calling in and didn't turn up on Wednesday and then missed another on Saturday.'

It was Wednesday when Jessica had seen Tony outside his flat and he said he was going to work. If he hadn't turned up, then where had he gone?

'Have you heard anything from him?'

'Like buggery, have I. I'm gonna have to get a new ad in now, ain't I? Probably have to settle for some Pole who don't know how to speak English.' Jessica didn't get a chance to point out that he wasn't exactly identifying himself as a defender of the Queen's English either before he finished with a flourish. '. . . And if you see him, you can tell him from me he's fired. F-O-R-E-D. Fired!'

Jessica thought if she did run into Tony again, it would probably be the least of his concerns.

Jessica hurried across the frozen supermarket car park and opened the passenger door of the almost-new Vauxhall.

'Are you Josh?' she asked, offering her hand for the man in the driver's seat to shake.

'If I wasn't then you'd be feeling pretty stupid right about now, wouldn't you?'

Jessica paused half in the car. 'Does that mean you are or you aren't?'

The man reached forwards and took her hand. 'Hi, I'm Josh.'

Josh was around her age, with a muscular chest and strong, thick fingers, although he didn't squeeze tightly. He was wearing glasses but there was steel behind them, dark, determined eyes that met hers as they shook.

'Sorry about the clandestine meeting place and everything,' she said. 'This isn't exactly for work purposes.'

Josh continued to eye her. 'Esther called this morning and asked if I'd do her a favour by doing you a favour. She said your exact request was: "Can you get me someone from the drugs squad who isn't a total tosspot?"'

Jessica squirmed. 'I may have said something like that – but at least it means she doesn't think you're a, erm, tosspot.'

'That's nice to know considering we went out for a year. Anyway, how can I help you?'

'I'm worried about someone I know. I'm pretty sure he's got himself into something stupid and wanted to ask about the supply situation into the city.'

Josh's eyes narrowed on Jessica before he gave a shallow nod. 'Unofficial, yeah?'

'For me too.'

'Fine. The supply in and out is as under control as it's been in years. It's not like we're going to stop it any time soon but we roughly know what's coming in and where it's coming from.'

'Is that the press office bullshit or what's actually going on?'

'Ha! Esther said you were one to watch.'

'Did she?'

Josh laughed again. 'She reckoned you were like her, only gobbier.'

Jessica's neck was hurting from turning to the side so

she shuffled around to face the front. 'That also sounds like me.'

'That's the real story. It could be a lot better but it has been far worse. Coke's at a relative low because the boys out at Liverpool have got tighter on the container ships coming in.'

'I'm more interested in the harder stuff.'

'How hard?'

'The stuff that makes your pupils shrink.'

Josh grinned. 'A bit of the old horse?'

Jessica shrugged. 'If you say so.'

His face was serious again. 'Heroin is the one drug where use went up in the city last year. It's still low compared to the recreational stuff but we've barely made a dent on the supply chain. We don't have the numbers plus we have to prioritise something – and it's not this.'

'Do you know any of the people involved— oh for f—. Sorry about this.' Jessica slipped her phone out of her pocket and pressed answer. 'Mum, I'm at work, I'm really busy. Can this wait?' She mouthed a sorry to Josh, whose sideways smirk was quickly becoming a grin. 'What? Of course I'm eating properly.'

Shite, shite, shite, shouldn't have answered.

'Mum, I'm working. I'm fine, honestly. So's Adam.'

More mouthed apologies as Josh tried not to laugh.

'Well, why didn't you ask him then? Look, I really have to go – I'm in the middle of something.'

Jessica hung up before her mum could reply. 'I'm really sorry about that. She always calls at the worst times. She sees some health scare thing on the news and then wants to make sure I'm all right.'

Josh was still smiling. 'At least yours calls – mine sodded off when I was a kid.'

'I was wondering if . . . ?'

Josh reached into the back seat and grabbed a cardboard folder, opening the top flap. 'I'm way ahead of you. I'm only doing this as a favour to Esther, okay?'

Jessica checked her front jacket pockets, then her trouser ones, before finding her glasses in the jacket's internal pocket. 'Bloody things. That's fine.'

Josh slipped a glossy photograph out of the folder and handed it across. 'There was a bit of a scramble when Nicholas Long died and his son ended up in prison. They weren't even big-time players but their clubs were an outlet for this type of thing. Then there was that whole episode with Harry Irwell. Their deaths have left a bit of a hole in the scene but with these powerful crime guys, if you cut off a head, two more grow back.'

He showed Jessica pictures of a handful of people they believed were at the top of the drug chain, explaining that much of their information could never be presented in court.

'These guys themselves are more or less untouchable – but it's like a Christmas tree, with these at the top and all sorts of interesting characters lower down. These next ones are the lieutenants. They do a lot of the dirtiest work but still have that level of protection below them if we come calling. They're loyal and it's not usually about money, more the power. These are the ones we *really* want because they know the detail of what's going on below them with the street dealers – as well as above them with the bosses and the importing. Every now and then we'll get enough on one of them to take them down – but then it's trying to get them to turn, which almost never happens.'

Josh handed the first picture to Jessica, talking her through the list of things the man was suspected of doing. It was the usual rundown for an average scumbag: trafficking, pimping, violence, drug-dealing, money-laundering, eating the last Rolo; that sort of thing.

When he passed her the third photo, Jessica froze, finger pressed to the image, taking in the man's bald head and sharp suit. It was the person she had seen standing across the road from Tony's flat.

18

'Who's that?' Jessica asked.

Josh paused, peering from the photo to Jessica and back again. 'Do you know him?'

'Not personally.'

'Lucky you. That's Scott Dewhurst – a real piece of work. His dad died a couple of years back but drug-dealing has always been in the family.'

'What else is he into?'

Josh began to reply but stopped himself, seeming more hesitant. 'Why do you want to know?'

'My friend.'

Josh sighed, biting on his lip, sucking his teeth. He straightened his shirt and took the photo back. 'If your friend has anything to do with Scott Dewhurst then he's either involved in something serious that he shouldn't be – or he's managed to stumble his way into a situation he almost certainly won't get out of. Either way, he might as well be dead. Is he someone I should be interested in?'

'No.'

'You sure?'

Jessica remembered how pathetic Tony had been the previous evening; the way she had stripped and washed him, then put him to bed. She'd known him on and off for years – a pest but nothing more. When she'd spoken to him in his flat she saw in his eyes that he wanted to be free of his past – but she'd also seen how scared he had been, hurrying down the street when he noticed Scott opposite the flat. There was something there.

What had he got himself into?

'I'm not sure,' Jessica said.

Scott packed the photographs back into the folder, shaking his head. 'You know we can't go through this. I'm here as a favour to Esther – but I can't give you details if I don't know why you need them.'

'I'm not dirty.'

Scott shrugged, tossing the folder onto the back seat. 'It's not like you'd say anything different whether you were or you weren't.'

'But Esther—'

'Look, Esther's great – we went out and I'd trust her if *she* was asking but *she* isn't. I don't know you and if our roles were reversed, I doubt you'd say anything different.'

Jessica knew he was right – but so was she. 'All right, come with me.' Josh moved reluctantly at first but she led him across the car park steadily, opening up the passenger side of her car and holding the door open. 'Go on then, get in.' As soon as he was inside, Jessica slammed the door and pressed the button on her keyfob to lock the vehicle. At first Josh stared at her, confused, but then she saw his nose twitch. Within a second, he was hammering on the window and scrabbling on the door itself to find the lock, not knowing it could only be unlocked from the driver's side.

Jessica let him stew for thirty more seconds, his face turning greyer until he eventually clamped a hand over his mouth and nose. When she eventually unlocked the door, Josh fell out of the side, landing on all fours on the frozen tarmac of the car park, gasping for breath.

After a long stream of expletives, he finally managed to get a sentence out. 'What's that smell?'

Jessica had her hands on her hips. 'Last night I found my friend in an alleyway on his way down. His pupils were tiny dots and he was sick everywhere. EV-ERY-WHERE. Mainly on me. If you really think I'm dirty, then fine. Fuck you. But if you think I welcome puke-covered junkies into my car for a laugh, then you're very, very wrong.'

Josh clambered to his feet, still gasping for air. 'You could have just bloody told me.'

'Yeah and you could've not been a knobhead. Now are you going to tell me about Scott Dewhurst or do I have to go hunting myself?'

Josh began walking back to his car rubbing at his face, trying to remove an invisible spot. His voice was croaky. 'Esther said you were sound – she didn't say you were mental.'

'It's my middle name, now get a move on – you bloody stink.' Back in Josh's car he took the photo out again, clicking his tongue against the top of his mouth, trying to get rid of the taste. 'It's not that bad, stop being a baby,' she added.

'I can still smell it. How did you drive here in that?'

'I had the window open and a massive coat, now stop whingeing and tell me about Scott's dad.'

'Oliver Dewhurst – he was sent down a decade ago for

various things, mainly involving drugs. He died in prison a couple of years back, no suspicious circumstances.'

Jessica peered at the photograph again. 'What about Scott?'

'We don't know much about his mother but she was never really in the picture. His dad was on Greater Manchester's police radar a long time before either of us were around, building up from thefts to drugs, plus plenty more they never pinned on him. Scott's a little different, mainly keeping himself out of trouble and generally learning from his old man's mistakes.'

'Does he have a record?'

'Not much. He was arrested for a drugs offence four years ago but there was no evidence and the charges were dropped. We had him nailed for a serious GBH a year ago when he attacked someone outside a nightclub. We had witnesses, his blood at the scene – everything except CCTV. Two weeks before the trial, the victim changed his story. He said he'd been the aggressor and attacked Dewhurst and then slipped, smashing his own nose on the floor. Surprise, surprise, our witnesses suddenly had a change of heart too. Obviously Dewhurst got to them but how are you supposed to prove it? If he paid them off, we've not found the money. More likely, he sent someone round with a crowbar. Anyway, Dewhurst's solicitor said that explained why his blood was at the scene and with no witnesses and no compliant victim, the CPS dropped the charges.'

'What a surprise.'

'Exactly. Since then, he's kept himself cleaner than a wet wipe. We've been keeping an eye but he lives in this smallish three-bed house and doesn't spend much money. The only thing he does have that would make you notice him is this flash soft-top sports car and a few suits. No expensive holidays, no credit card bills, no huge parties – nothing to say he has much more money than me or you. And I'll bet his car doesn't smell of sick.'

'How do you know he's still in drugs?'

'Officially, we don't. Unofficially, some of those who just happen to be visiting pubs and clubs at the same time as him are people very much on our radar. You'll never see them together but the messages somehow get across. He's got smart since we nearly nabbed him and he's moving up too. He'll be in the big leagues soon.'

'Can you send me anything else you have? I'll give you a home email address.'

'You know internal will get into your non-work emails if they really want to?'

'So send it from somewhere secure that doesn't have your name attached. It's not like I'll say where I got it from if they ever come asking – which they won't.'

'You know we shouldn't be talking about these things.'

'Who's talking? I've come to the supermarket to use the car wash next door. I didn't meet anyone here other than the valet attendant who will surely remember the girl whose car smells of sick if he's ever asked. Josh who? I don't know a Josh.'

A smile crept across Josh's face. 'Esther said you were sharp.'

'Like a Stanley knife. Now are you going to send me what I need?'

'I'll sort something.'

'Good – then you should take a shower.'

Given the queasy look on the valet's face after he had spent twenty-five minutes cleaning the inside of her car for the princely sum of eight pounds, Jessica was pretty sure he would never forget her. The poor guy looked about sixteen, although she had consoled herself in the knowledge that she had given him a valuable life lesson: everyone starts with a rubbish job. By the time he was forty and running a billion-pound multi-national technology company, he'd be giving after-dinner speeches about this moment. Either way, she told him to keep the change from her ten-pound note and headed back across Manchester, her car smelling ninety per cent less vomity.

As she passed the Printworks entertainment plaza, trying to imagine what Tony had got himself into, Jessica noticed a small huddle of people standing by the traffic lights. Groups of tourists and shoppers weren't unusual but as she waited at the red light, more people spilled out of the glass-fronted Arndale shopping centre, standing on the kerb and talking excitedly among themselves.

Jessica pulled her car onto the wide pavement, leaving her hazard lights flashing and offering a terse 'piss off' to the know-it-all gobshite giving her the evil eye for parking on the path. A quick flash of her ID and he soon went scuttling back to wherever he came from.

As she headed into the Arndale, more and more people

were hurrying out, couples and groups, until it was one large sea of shoppers chattering in a mixture of excitement and confusion. Overhead, the alarm blared into life but Jessica knew this wasn't just a fire. She rounded the corner, passing W.H. Smith, to see a group of security guards at the other end standing in a small circle. One of them was on a walkie-talkie, two others were on their mobile phones. Apart from a handful of shop workers stumbling out of their stores, confused looks on their faces, the place was empty. Her footsteps would have been echoing from the high ceilings but were instantly drowned out by the unending blast of the alarm.

The tallest security guard held his hand up as he saw her approaching, bellowing something impossible to hear over the din. Jessica took out her ID, her walk becoming a run until she was at the far end of the rank close to the toilets.

Jessica shouted into the ear of the security guard who had tried to stop her, asking what was going on. One of the others was still on his walkie-talkie, although Jessica couldn't imagine how he could ever be heard. He pointed towards the toilet and leant in to yell back into Jessica's ear. 'Someone's been stabbed.'

'Dead?' Jessica mouthed.

He shook his head and angled in to shout again. 'Not a knife.'

Jessica dashed forwards, heading into the men's toilet where the smell was only marginally better than in her car an hour ago. Another security guard tried to stop her but Jessica showed him her ID and continued past. Slumped inside a cubicle was a youngish man, somewhere in his mid-twenties, his hair dark and patchy, eyes wide in terror. As Jessica approached, he held up his hands, shouting 'stay back', even though she could only lip-read.

Jessica edged closer but he pointed towards a spot on the floor next to him where a needle lay, the plunger thrust all the way in, droplets of blood clinging to the pointed tip. She didn't have to be a world-class lip-reader to work out the next thing he said: 'H-I-V.'

19

Jessica sat in the makeshift incident room shivering as the pilfered heater failed to make much impact on the wintry temperature. The operation to steal the small convection device from the basement room given over to solicitors had been as ruthless in the planning as anything Jessica had been involved in. A three-man team created the distraction, with a further two-woman party doing the actual thieving. Getting it up the first set of stairs was simple enough but negotiating past Pat on reception had involved a Holland's meat and potato pie, plus a Bakewell tart. Jessica had made sure Cole was otherwise engaged and in less time than it would take for a drug-dealing scroat to get bail, an eight-person team had taken thievery to a new level. Execution: A+. Effectiveness: D. The bloody thing was useless, producing more cold air than hot.

Izzy blew into her hands, wisps of breath spiralling through her fingers into the air. 'For all your military operation to nick this fan, we could've chipped in a fiver each and bought something that actually worked.'

Jessica checked her watch, glancing at the door. 'Where's the fun in that?'

Izzy stretched out her foot, nudging the heater. 'Blowing into my hands creates more hot air than that does.'

'Yeah, but for every minute the solicitors are distracted

by freezing their balls off downstairs, that's one minute they're not trying to get some thieving shite off the hook.'

As Jessica finished complaining, the door clicked open and Detective Constable David Rowlands walked in, hands in pockets, turning from Izzy to Jessica. 'Did you miss me?'

Jessica stood and began slow-clapping. 'Well, well, well, look who it is. The adventurer returns: Marco Polo Rowlands.'

Rowlands sat next to Izzy, blowing into his hands. 'When I flew out yesterday, it was thirty degrees, blue skies, no breeze, beautiful pool. I got back here and it was so foggy we couldn't see the ground, the roads are frozen, there's still snow on my road and it's about minus ten out.'

Izzy reached forwards and rubbed his cheek. 'I thought it was fake tan. You make me sick.'

Dave leant back in his chair, hands behind his head. His skin was bronzed, his hair tall and spiky. Jessica would never tell him but he looked more relaxed than she'd seen him in a long time. He nodded towards her, grinning. 'Your glasses look ridiculous, by the way.'

'At least I can take them off, you're stuck with that face.'

'Blah, blah, blah. Same old jokes.'

'Where did you go again?'

'Majorca.'

'Broadening your horizons then? It's not quite Scott of the Antarctic or Columbus finding America, is it?'

Rowlands dismissed her with a 'pfft' as the doors re-opened and a stream of PCs and DCs entered, with a weary-looking sergeant at the back who had been sent out to round them up. Jessica waited until they'd settled and then Izzy started the projector, flashing up a passport-type image of the man Jessica had seen in the Arndale toilets. He had short dark hair but his hairline was already receding, despite him only being in his twenties. He looked like the bottom of a plimsoll: rubbery grey-brown pock-marked skin, a flat nose and thick lips – one of those faces you'd never tire of punching.

'Three days ago, Victor Todd was attacked in the toilets of the Arndale centre—' Jessica began.

'So he was approached by a man from behind in the toilets and there was a prick involved?' PC Pen-Thief seemed particularly proud of his remark but Jessica didn't flinch, despite the smattering of sniggers around the room.

'I'll make the jokes. Anyway, it's taken us almost this long to piece together everything that happened. At first the Arndale gave us footage from the wrong day, then the bus company got the arse. Despite every bus, train and tram in the city being fitted with CCTV, it seems that any time something happens, they're either broken, not set up correctly or – in this case – they lost the bus.'

Joy Bag's turn to pipe up: 'How do you lose a bus?'

'They hired it out to a tour group who'd gone to Torquay for two days. By the time they figured out it was the bus we were looking for, it was three hundred miles away. In the end, it wasn't worth it anyway.'

Izzy started the footage, which showed Victor getting onto a bus, paying his fare and then sitting at the back. Directly behind him, a figure with his hood up paid and sat in the seat slightly hidden behind the stairs that led to the top deck.

'Todd and his assailant got onto the bus at the stop closest to Todd's house in Moss Side. We're assuming this is the same person responsible for the attacks on Luke Callaghan and Alan Hume because of the clothing, build and the other things you'll see. They rode the bus to the centre where they both got off at the same stop. Our guy in the hood then followed Todd for a few hundred metres into the Arndale.'

The next set of images from the camera within the shopping centre showed Todd entering, walking around a clothing shop as the other figure waited on a bench outside, and then heading into the toilets, closely followed by his attacker. As the person looked directly at a camera, the screen froze on a shot of the mask with the A-shaped anarchy logo on the front.

'At some point between getting off the bus and attacking Todd,' Jessica continued, 'our hoody put this mask on. Usually you might think a figure walking around a city centre wearing such a thing might attract some attention but our guy wasn't the only one.'

The projector changed to show images of five other people sporting similar masks and then finished on a top-down map of the area.

'On the day Victor Todd was attacked, there were four separate stalls between the bus stop and the toilets selling these masks. We've checked with the stall-holders but they don't remember anyone specifically buying one – perhaps not surprising considering it seems to be the hottest new accessory at the moment.'

Flash, flash, flash: two dozen more images flickered across the screen.

'These things are everywhere, selling for a quid each not just in Manchester but across the country. With this story in the news, it's made them more popular. Our hoody might have been concealing his own mask anyway before putting it on but the wider point is that we have no clear image of him. We're assuming a man because of the height. He walks a little awkwardly but that might be because he's slowing himself to keep pace with his target and not stand out. We've spoken to the driver of the bus, plus the passengers we traced, but no one remembers any details – perhaps not surprising for anyone who's been on public transport recently, it's a zoo out there.'

Jessica nodded to Izzy, who took over, standing and reading from a sheet of paper. 'Victor Todd was at a urinal when he felt somebody standing close behind him. He says he felt something puncture his neck and then the person said something like, "Enjoy getting HIV". He says it was a gruff male voice, which backs what we've been assuming for a while. There were no traces of anything alien in Todd's system, other than cannabis – which he denied using at first. Eventually he admitted he'd been smoking some the previous evening but it does seem likely the syringe was either empty, or filled with water or saline. That doesn't mean it wasn't tainted with HIV – but the blood tests aren't back yet.'

A male PC's hand went up. 'Why didn't he fight back if there was nothing in the syringe?'

Izzy continued: 'Probably because he was still weeing at

the time he was attacked. Not having a penis myself, I can't say for sure but I suspect you'd put it away before fighting anyone.'

There were a few more sniggers around the room.

'There are obviously no cameras in the toilets but on the footage, the attacker moves quickly out of the toilets and away from the shopping centre. There was someone locked in a cubicle who heard a commotion but no specific words and then two people who entered in the immediate aftermath. All we have is Todd's statement and it's fair to say he was in shock – and possibly had piss down his leg.'

Izzy sat and Jessica took over again. 'We've spent the last couple of days looking into every aspect of Victor Todd's life. He has no criminal record, not even a speeding ticket. That doesn't mean he's whiter than white. In short, it's not just the Arndale toilets where he's been flapping his naughty bits about.'

The screen flicked back to the initial snapshot of Todd.

'If you can restrain yourselves, ladies, this thin-haired, rubber-faced twenty-four-year-old Casanova is such a catch that he's already got six kids by five different mothers. If his ravishing good looks aren't enough to make you throw those rabbits away then the fact he left school at fifteen and now works in a chicken-processing factory might just tip you over the edge. He is apparently single but with the sheer number of relations he has, it's been a nightmare checking everyone out. We're still getting there, so some of you will be out today talking to the supermodels he's got up the duff over the years. There's clearly some animosity towards him but it's a bit of a step up from shagging around to all of this.'

Jessica waited to see if anyone had anything to add but no hands went up, so she continued. 'Victor Todd's out of hospital and back at his house awaiting his blood test results. Obviously if he *has* been infected with HIV, then it is worryingly serious. We've kept it away from the media so far, giving them the line that there was an assault at the Arndale and leaving it at that. We've been in contact with local clinics to see if they're aware of anyone who might have particular grudges relating to the disease, or who might match the description of our hoody, but we've had nothing solid. For now, that leaves us chasing the same lines.'

Jessica nodded to the sergeant at the back of the room who had been drafted in from East Manchester CID to help out as the DS recruitment process dragged on. He was in his early forties and a bit too normal for Jessica's liking but she had given him the job of trying to connect everything together.

He stood and coughed loudly, clearing his throat and pulling his coat tighter. 'Morning, everyone.' An awkward pause as nobody said anything. They must be bloody wet out east. 'Er, okay . . . right . . . we've cross-reffed everything we've got on the other two victims with our most recent one and there's nothing to connect them. Different ages, different family members, interests, schools attended, everything. At best, we've got that they're all from around Manchester. The previous link we had from Luke Callaghan to Alan Hume was that they had both annoyed Michael Cowell.'

Izzy pressed a button on the laptop to change the screen's image to one of Cowell.

'Cowell was Luke Callaghan's former business partner and Alan Hume's tenant – but he has no connection we can find to our third victim. As well as our failure to link them, they deny knowing each other.'

A hand went up: 'Could this be a copycat?'

The sergeant sat and Jessica took over. 'Perhaps – but our forensics team working on enhancing the video frames are convinced it's the same assailant for all three attacks. They say it's less than a two per cent chance of it being someone else. We've got to assume it's the same guy – but if Cowell is nothing to do with this then we need something, or someone, who connects our three victims. After the "Gang War" fiasco, we've checked Victor Todd's possible connections to extreme groups but he has no links to anything. Having spoken to him myself, I think he's too stupid to understand the difference between right-wing and left-wing if he's not talking about football.'

She paused for breath, wanting to make the point extra clear.

'We need that link between our three victims. The alternative isn't worth thinking about – random attacks in public on total strangers. We've been lucky with the media so far because they're taking our line of one attacker, motives unknown, blah, blah, blah – but if they start reporting these are random attacks, we're going to have a panic.'

She couldn't help but think of how Niall had described the media pressure building up to his capture of the Stretford Slasher. Public attacks, few leads, a police force seemingly inept and a worried community. This wasn't there yet but it could go the same way.

Izzy turned the projector screen off and the team began fidgeting as Jessica handed out the day's roles. As they all headed to the exit, Jessica called back Izzy and Dave, who sat opposite her. When it was just the three of them, she turned to Rowlands: 'Let's hear it then.'

His eyes flicked left and right. 'What?'

'You obviously got some while you were off gallivanting – so who was she?'

His eyebrows curved downwards. 'What?'

'Come on, I can read you like a book – and not a good book. One with pictures and a rambling plot that doesn't go anywhere.' He tried his best to look innocent but Jessica was on a roll. 'Right, was she blonde or brunette?'

Rowlands shook his head. 'Haven't you got work to do?'

'Brunette – your right eye twitched.'

'It did not.'

'There – you raised your hand, a classic sign that you're lying.'

Dave lowered his hand slowly, chewing the inside of his mouth, rattled. 'You're making this up—'

'Right, is she older or younger than you?'

'There is no she!'

'Ooh, older. How much older? Forties? Fifties?' Rowlands' chair rocketed backwards as he stood too quickly. 'She's in her fifties? You're a sly one.'

The constable stared at Jessica, one eye cocked, confused.

Izzy was stunned: 'How did you know all that?'

'Because I know him too well – coming in here all cocky and relaxed because he's shagged a granny.'

'She's not that old.'

Jessica turned back to face him. 'Aha! But she *is* old. Who is she?'

Rowlands didn't know where to turn, even though he couldn't stop the sheepish grin from sliding onto his face. 'All right, sod off, I've got work to do. I'm putting in a workplace bullying complaint.'

'You do that.' Before he could leave, Jessica turned to Izzy. 'Right, I want the name and number for the head of the Majorcan police on my desk within the hour. One way or the other, I'm going to find out the name of the granny that Dave copped off with.'

As they left, Izzy clapped an arm around Dave's shoulders. 'You all right, Romeo?'

He sounded dejected: 'I've only been back for an hour and it's like I never left. How did she know?'

Jessica hid the heater underneath the desk in case anyone came looking for it and then headed along the hallway to DCI Cole's glass-fronted office. He was on the phone but waved her in, jabbing a finger at the chair on the other side of the desk as she couldn't help but hear his half of an irate argument over a direct debit payment. He slammed the phone down with a plastic-sounding clatter. 'British Gas really are useless.'

'So I've heard. We've still got nothing linking our three

victims, by the way. I gave 'em a bit of the old bum-booting but we're flagging.'

'I've been onto Serious Crime but they're convinced the gang link was a red herring.'

'Any chance they're saying that because they don't want us to jeopardise any of their ongoing investigations?'

'No, the assistant chief constable's been onto them too. Stop being so cynical. How is everything?'

'Not too bad. We could do with an extra sergeant but we charged a guy for the Eccles off-licence robbery yesterday and our guy was remanded for the Salford arson attempt. Everything's ticking over except for this.'

Cole twisted his head away but couldn't stop himself from yawning.

'You look tired,' Jessica said.

'The job isn't what it used to be.'

'That's what Niall told me.'

'Aah . . . DSI Hambleton.' Cole took a deep breath, fighting back another yawn. 'He had just been promoted when I moved in here. It was a different time then.' It sounded as if Cole was going to add something before he stopped himself mid-word. 'That's not exactly what I meant. Since the divorce, I think I've been preparing to get out.'

'Sir?'

Cole rubbed the bridge of his nose. 'I know what I look like in the mirror – I'm an old man now and feel like it.'

'You seem fine to me – nothing that a holiday and some good nights' sleep wouldn't solve.'

His smile was narrow, not fooled. 'You used to be a better liar.'

Jessica chuckled. 'I'm just saying you shouldn't make any rash decisions. The only reason I came back was for you.'

'And how are things?'

'Great, except that I keep losing my glasses.' Cole widened his eyes, wanting the proper answer. 'I'm fine, Sir,' she added.

'Would you tell me if you weren't?'

'Probably not.'

Another thin smile, which his eyes didn't match. 'Keep me updated if anything comes in – I've got a conference call with the assistant chief constable and the superintendent later.'

Jessica stood to leave but Cole waved her around his desk, lifting his feet into the air. 'What?' she asked, confused.

'Slip-ons.'

'Sorry?'

'Not Velcro shoes, slip-ons.' Jessica started to apologise but Cole held his hand up with a smile and a wink. 'I have spies all over – there's life in the old dog yet.'

Jessica grinned back, apologised again and then headed for the stairs and her office, wondering who had blabbed.

Halfway down, she ran into Izzy. 'I was looking for you,' the constable said.

'Have you got me a number for the head of the Majorcan police yet?'

Izzy laughed. 'How did you really know all of that about Dave?'

'A PC I know from Northern CID was on holiday out there with his missus too. He saw Dave in some bar copping off with an older woman and sent me a text. I have spies all over . . .'

20

Considering the time of year, darkness had dropped across the city ridiculously early. The work day was over but Rowlands rested his head against the window of Jessica's car as she edged along the roads connecting the Northern Quarter to the rest of Manchester's city centre.

'It smells odd in here,' he protested.

'Stop whingeing.'

'What is it?'

'Probably whatever gel you use, now stop complaining and help.' Jessica slowed the car to a crawl as they reached the opening to the alley where she had found Tony four nights previously. 'See anything?'

'Fog.'

Jessica pulled the car over to the side of the road and parked. 'You're hilarious. I don't know why I bothered asking you for help.'

'Because I'm a big strong man and you need protecting?'

'Keep telling yourself that. The sun must've really gone to your head.'

Jessica got out of the car and rounded it until she was on the pavement. Dave was wearing a coat down to his knees, gloves, a scarf and a thick woollen hat pulled over his ears.

'It's freezing out here.'

Jessica was wearing much the same but her coat was at least practical to run in. 'You're not the first to notice.'

She led him into the alley, looking both ways as she moved slowly. The shadows weren't quite as large as the other night and it was marginally warmer but there was still a faint trace of vomit stuck between the cobbles.

Dave kept on her shoulder. 'What exactly are we doing?'

'I told you – looking for Tony.'

'Why?'

'Because I asked you to do me a favour and you very kindly said yes.'

'Are you being sarcastic?'

'No, I'm being nice, can't you tell the difference?'

Dave used his shoe to nudge a bin bag, revealing nothing underneath. 'I don't think so.'

'Well I do appreciate it – it's dark, it's colder than the polar ice caps and this area is full of weirdos.'

They reached the end of the alley having not seen anyone, so Jessica walked along the road parallel to where she had parked and started along the next cut-through. Rundown buildings covered in grime rose above them, blocking the street lights and leaving them in near-darkness. In the distance, the city hummed with people out for the evening and traffic buzzing towards its destination.

'Let's hear it then,' Jessica said, 'who's your granny?'

'She's not a granny.'

'So who is she?'

'I still don't know how you knew but her name's Lynn. She's in her *early*-fifties but you wouldn't guess it – she's thin, she's—'

'All right, I don't need to hear all that stuff. So was it just a holiday romance?'

Dave's deep breath swirled into the surrounding gloom. 'I don't know, we had a fun time and swapped numbers. We'll see. I'd be happier if everyone at the station wasn't calling me a granny-shagger.'

'Don't blame me.'

'You told them!'

'I did not – I told Pat and he told them. If you'd been planning ahead you could've bribed him with a giant bag of mini Cheddars.'

'He did tell me that old DSI guy's got a crush on you. The phrase "love-sick puppy" was mentioned.'

'Sod off and stop changing the subject. So are you going to see her again?'

'I don't know, I'm leaving it with her. She's not had it easy.'

'How do you mean?'

'She's divorced but her husband used to smack her around. She was on holiday with her mates and I think they were all out looking for a bit of fun. No one expected anything more but we got chatting on my second night there and then we spent the rest of the holiday together.'

'That's really nice.'

'And . . .'

'And what?'

'I thought you were going to add something like: "That's really nice . . . when's she getting her hip replaced?" or "That's really nice . . . when's she having the sex-change operation?"'

'Actually I was going to say, "That's really nice . . . let's hope you don't wake up to find your kidneys on eBay."'

Dave laughed. 'That's actually pretty funny.'

'It won't be when they sell for five hundred quid.'

At the end of another empty alley, Jessica said they should try Tony's flat. He'd been in the last time she was around and although she wasn't expecting him to be there now, it was worth a go. They hurried along the streets hands in pockets, Jessica trying to stop her teeth chattering.

'It's nice to talk like this again,' she said.

'What, for you to take the piss?'

'Essentially – you give as good as you get though. It's just nice after everything that happened with you and your big mouth.'

Dave didn't reply straight away, unsurprising considering he'd told her that he loved her only a couple of years ago and hadn't been in a relationship since. It had taken her enough time to talk to him again. 'Izzy says you and Adam are still trying for kids . . .'

It was Jessica's turn to stay silent. Although she didn't necessarily mind, she didn't know Dave and Izzy spoke about things like that. Izzy couldn't have passed on what Jessica had told her about not being with Adam for months . . . 'We're seeing how it goes. The doctors say it can't happen but they've been wrong about other things in the past.'

They continued heading through the streets, falling into silence as they reached Tony's flat. Despite ringing the bell attached to the front door, knocking loudly, and throwing tiny stones to bounce off his window, no one answered.

'Pub?' Dave asked, nodding towards the building next door.

'You buying?'

'I've only got euros. Not had time to change them back yet.'

'Okay, no worries.'

Jessica headed for the door but Dave caught her arm. 'What are you grinning about?'

'Nothing. Just a cosy drink with a mate.'

'So you're going to go in there, buy a drink for the pair of us and that's why you're grinning?'

Jessica pointed to a scrawled note pinned to the window: EURO'S ACCEPTED. 'They might not know how to use an apostrophe – but at least they'll take your money.'

Inside and the barkeeper did take Dave's leftover euros, much to his annoyance. The floors were sticky, the lighting dim and orange and the clientele a mixture of people they spent their time trying to lock up and student-types slumming around with multi-coloured hair and T-shirts sporting slogans.

They found a booth near the window next to a radiator underneath a sign that read THURSDAY NIGHT IS PARTAY NIGHT. It was also apparently karaoke night. As Dave told her about the rest of his holiday, the students and pissed-up locals took it in turns to sing out-of-tune Britpop songs to a largely uninterested crowd.

Jessica eventually crossed the booth to sit next to the

constable so they could hear each other over the sound of a Goth girl murdering a Verve song.

'Why Tony?' Dave asked.

Jessica left Scott Dewhurst out of it but told him how she'd seen Tony clean, sober and ready for a new life one day, and then drunk and high a few days later.

'That's just him, isn't it?' Dave said. 'We've all picked him up over the years.'

Jessica shrugged. 'Don't you ever want to believe that we make a difference?'

'We do – when we get people away from their abusive families, or someone gets sent down.'

'It's all small stuff though. Drunken idiots, wannabe gangsters. I don't mean that, I suppose . . .' Jessica took a deep breath, trying to block out the crime being committed by the Goth with the microphone. '. . . I suppose there's not that much difference between Tony and me.'

'What do you mean? You an inspector – he's a junkie.'

Jessica shook her head. 'You're missing it. He's a little younger than me but we share a lot. Neither of us comes from around here but we both came to the city to see if it could give us something better. Something happened when he was at university which made him turn to the drugs and the drink. It could happen to anyone if they didn't have the support around them. I lived with Caroline and became a PC but if I'd had someone who'd wanted to take advantage of me, maybe I'd have gone for it too.'

'I can't imagine anyone taking advantage of you.'

Jessica didn't reply because he didn't understand the point and didn't know her then. It was easy to think of her as the person she was now but she'd hardened through all her years as an officer at various levels. As an impression-able twenty-something, perhaps she'd have made bad choices too?

She looked around the room and could see it here as well: weathered, long-in-the-tooth locals trying it on with a group of female students at the bar. Some of them would play the game, get a few free drinks and then go home. More power to them. Others would be less experienced at dealing with older people and feel under pressure, even though all they'd done was accept a drink.

The Goth girl thankfully finished singing but that wasn't the end of the torture. Up stepped her boyfriend, face like a drawer full of paperclips, who launched into a Metallica track.

Jessica downed the rest of her wine in one. 'Sod this, let's see if we can find anyone else on the street – someone must know where Tony is.'

Back outside, it felt even colder after the time they had spent next to the radiator. Jessica headed into the nearest alleyway, Dave close behind. It didn't take them long to find three bearded men huddled under a couple of sleeping bags next to a pair of large wheelie bins, passing a bottle of cider between them. As she and Dave approached, their mutterings went silent as they withdrew under the covers.

Jessica stood in front of them, framed by the street light. She took a twenty-pound note out of her pocket and stretched it out between her hands so they had a clear view.

'If any of you know where Tony is, this is yours.'

The three heads shot out of the bag at once, like a triple-headed tortoise looking for food. She could see their beady eyes registering what was in her hand, remembering how Tony described it – they weren't seeing the banknote, they were seeing a means to an end: booze, fags, drugs.

'Tony,' she repeated.

The one in the centre half-mumbled, half-coughed a reply. 'Norff.'

'North what?'

He took his hand out from under the cover, stretching it towards her. 'Norff.'

'You're not getting the money until you say where he is. "North" doesn't count.'

'Great Norff. Trains.'

Jessica dropped the note on his lap and turned to walk away, listening to the scurrying behind her as the homeless men scrambled for it.

'I take it you know where he's on about?' Dave asked.

'Out the back of the cinema down by Deansgate station there are a few cobbled alleys. Some of the homeless community beg around there because it's close to the bars on the locks and you get all the drunks going home that way towards the taxis. There used to be a pickpocketing problem when I was in uniform.'

Jessica took the car, driving the short distance across the city and parking outside the station. She led Dave along Great Bridgewater Street, asking him to wait as she moved into one of the cobbled ginnels engulfed by the long, freezing shadows. Mist clung to the top of the overhanging buildings, bathing the cobbles in a hazy orange burn from the dim street lights. Jessica could feel the glacial air filling her lungs as she approached a small group of people-shaped silhouettes slumped against a wall smudged with filth. The person on the far end scuttled away as soon as he saw her and although she didn't recognise one of the remaining shapes, Tony's coat was unmistakeable. She sat next to him on the ground, feeling the harsh frost eating through her clothes. Again.

'Tony.'

He gurgled something incomprehensible and Jessica edged away, flashing back to the last time he had done that in an alley. This time he spoke almost clearly. 'It's so cold.'

'Why don't you let me take you home, Tony? I've got the car. I could take you there, or to my house if you like. I could even take you back to your parents' if you really want?'

'No.'

'You can't stay out here all the time. I can get you help.'

The man sitting next to Tony picked up a bottle of strong-smelling alcohol and drank deeply but didn't seem to be aware of the conversation going on around him.

'Tony?'

The sound of footsteps made Jessica glance up, peering towards the opposite end of the alley from where she'd entered. Each step was heavy, echoing loudly around the tight walls. The closer he came, the larger he seemed until the outline morphed into the tightly cut suit, slim-fitting woollen jacket and bald head that made Scott Dewhurst so recognisable.

21

Scott stood still for a few moments, breath disappearing into the atmosphere, eyes scanning across Jessica, Tony and the other homeless man.

'Scarper,' he said sternly.

The man she didn't know slid across the cobbles and then dashed past Scott into the night. Jessica didn't move. From where he was, Scott couldn't have known she was female; her heavy coat shielded her slender figure and her long hair was bundled up inside her hat.

'You fuckin' deaf?'

Jessica slumped to the side, head resting on Tony's shoulder. He tried to shake her off but she clung on.

'Fuck's sake.'

Scott stepped towards her but Jessica spoke softly, making it clear she was female. 'Who is it, Tony?'

The bald man quickly backed away from them. 'Christ, you didn't say you had a fuckin' tart on the go. Get her out of the way – I'll be back soon and you better be around.'

Tony mumbled something but Scott had turned and was striding back to the end of the alley where Jessica could see the outline of a sports car. She tried to hold him down but Tony was on his feet, groaning something she couldn't make out. He tried to run after Scott but tripped, falling into the wall with a smack.

Jessica scrambled across the floor until she was by his side. Tony's coat had taken the brunt of the blow but she could smell the booze as he turned to face her.

At the end of the alley, the car roared away in a choked cough of diesel. 'Who was that?' Jessica asked, helping Tony to straighten up.

'No one.'

'Tony—'

She tried to make sure that his face wasn't bleeding but Tony pulled away, stumbling to his feet. Jessica tried to go with him but he was surprisingly nimble, shaking her off and breaking into a run. As she reached out, Jessica could only hang onto his pocket, pulling the material and feeling a solid thump as something fell out, hitting the floor. Tony spun, but Jessica got to it first, grabbing the brown package from the ground and holding it up into the light. The paper of the folded envelope had frayed but the top was open and the contents clear: money.

Lots of it.

Jessica ran her finger across the notes, a mixture of tens and twenties – thousands of pounds. She didn't have a chance to count anything before Tony snatched the bundle back, pushing her in the chest with his forearm. He might have done it by accident but Jessica stumbled backwards, more in surprise than from the force, feeling the cold damp of the frosty cobbles through her trousers again. By the time she had picked herself up, Tony had turned on his heels and dashed at full speed into the night.

*

At the station the next day, Jessica was struggling with a sore arse and elbow from the fall. She'd told Dave that she hadn't seen Tony, not wanting to mention Scott and the information she wasn't supposed to have. Josh had forwarded her the files but they only expanded on what he had already told her. Scott Dewhurst was quite the piece of work and Jessica wasn't sure she wanted to know the reason why Tony had a bundle of money apparently meant for him.

That didn't mean she wouldn't keep digging.

In the morning meeting, Izzy told them that Victor Todd's blood test had come back negative for HIV, hepatitis A and B, plus anything else that he could have been infected with. He did, however, have herpes, which wasn't a surprise given his apparent promiscuity. Izzy had spoken to him and he was shaken up but generally okay. He'd probably have another child to celebrate if he could find someone who wasn't too bothered about the whole genital warts thing.

Everything else was going nowhere: they still didn't have a link from Luke to Alan to Victor; Michael Cowell was a dead end; all five of the women who had given birth to Victor's children had been interviewed and eliminated; and there was little else to go on. All they had found out was that Victor's chicken factory wages unsurprisingly didn't stretch too far in terms of child maintenance. What a credit to society he was.

Jessica had ranted about how every scroat and his mother had a camera phone nowadays and yet none of them had bothered to use it when someone was being attacked in broad daylight. The moan hadn't even made her feel better. Niggling at the back of her mind was Niall's warning about a public panic and things getting out of hand. Another attack and it would get to the point where they couldn't keep things under wraps and away from the media any longer.

The only link Jessica could see between the three victims was that, in their own way, they were all total shits: a thief and a wife-abuser; someone who tried to extort sexual favours and who made his tenants live in squalor; and a person who could make good use of the condoms which kept being left on Jessica's desk.

When she thought of it like that, it all seemed so low-level. Jessica had dealt with a vigilante in the past – someone who went after murderers and drug-dealers. This felt entirely different, less dangerous in one way but more vicious in another because it was so public. She wondered if that was the key – was this meant to be a shaming for their apparent sins and, if so, who connected them?

No one, least of all her, had a clue.

Jessica sat in DCI Cole's office talking him through the non-progress. He nodded wearily, as ever, and then stopped mid-sentence when his desk phone rang. His eyes flickered towards her, saying silently that something had happened. When he hung up, his message was short but it at least gave her something to do: Anarky's founder, Thomas McKinney, had been attacked with a crowbar.

22

Jessica sat next to Thomas McKinney's hospital bed eating from a plastic tub filled with grapes. 'Want one?' she asked, offering them towards him.

The reply was gruff and coarse. 'I hate fruit.'

'Really? I got seedless just for you.'

'Sod off.'

'Well that's gratitude, isn't it, Thomas? I go out of my way, nip to Tesco, pick up a few clubcard points, get you some grapes and that's all you can say to me.'

'Thomas now, is it? I thought it was McKenny, Mackie and McKay.'

'I figured we were on first-name terms now we've met more than once.'

The Anarky founder wasn't even attempting to hide his local accent any longer. His hair that had been neatly parted when she first met him was now almost entirely buried under a bandage, with a few damp and floppy dark strands sticking out. His jewellery had been removed and his designer clothes replaced by the latest range in hospital gowns, complete with a tie-at-the-back opening and straight, unflattering lines. With his over-the-top tan, he looked like a squished pumpkin crammed into a torn napkin.

Jessica peered more closely at his bandage. 'Either that's

part of the latest spring collection, or you've not had a good morning.'

'Piss off. I'm not pressing charges.'

'What an odd thing to say. I've seen the CCTV and it's pretty brutal – you're walking along the pavement around the corner from your house having a cheeky smoke. Then along comes some guy on a moped, mounts the kerb, out comes a crowbar and down you go. If it had been a few centimetres lower and caught you at the top of the spine, you could be paralysed. A tiny bit either way and it would have missed the harder part of your skull and you'd be dead. Surely you want the person responsible charged?'

'No comment.'

Jessica bit into a grape, chewing it slowly. 'Not even an "ouch"? It must be hurting? Still, I suppose they've got you hopped up on all sorts on painkillers.'

'No comment.'

'You really don't have to say that to everything, I wasn't even asking for a comment. Anyway, my point is that there have been a few public attacks recently – you might have read about them. When I first heard you'd been smashed in the back of the head with a crowbar, I thought it was another but it's not that at all, is it?'

'No—'

'Yeah, yeah, I know, "no comment". The fact is, it doesn't matter what you want to do because we've got the camera footage and we've got a number plate from the moped. Your attacker was clever enough to cover the plate on the roads close to your house but as we followed him on the street cameras, he stopped to remove the bag and then merrily carried on through the streets. He's what we call in the trade "a moron".'

Silence.

Jessica offered the tub of grapes again and this time Thomas took a small handful.

'I thought you didn't eat fruit?'

'Changed my mind.'

'So are you going to say something, or do you want me to keep telling you what you already know?'

'I guess I sound like a bit of a tit now, don't I?' Jessica didn't mean to laugh but it was the resigned way he said it with a mouthful of grape that set her off. Even Thomas joined in with a knowing smile. 'You got him, then? He never was the sharpest match in the box.'

'I think you mean knife in the drawer but, yes, we got him. He left the moped in a lock-up garage where we didn't have a camera but then walked onto the street where we did. We matched his face to the one on your own website: George O'Reilly, moped-riding, crowbar-wielding, Anarky Secretary. By the time he got off his bus, we already had someone waiting outside his house.'

'Wanker.'

'Not quite a god to them after all, then?'

Thomas sighed. 'It was that bloody newspaper headline. "Gang War?" What gang war? That idiot took it as a call to arms.'

'So when you disagreed, he decided to take things into his own hands by attacking you and blaming one of your rival groups. Don't worry, we've already got an email he sent about it, plus his mobile records, the crowbar, the bike, the CCTV. I wouldn't be here otherwise.'

'Why *are* you here?'

Jessica offered him the grapes again. 'Probably my world-famous bedside manner. Well, that and to tell you that we're not going to let anything like this go any further. If you clowns want to batter the shite out of each other in private, then knock yourselves out. Literally. Your protests, your marches, your meetings – they're all things we can manage but this crosses a line.'

'It wasn't—'

Jessica didn't miss a beat. 'I'm talking, you listen. I don't care if it's him attacking you, you attacking him, one group on your group, yours on them, or if you all give each other one giant reach-around – keep it off the streets. You might be fine but your idiot mate's going to be up for GBH or attempted murder and all he's done is bring attention to your petty little battles. You might bang on about being anarchists but it's still us who cleans up the mess when you get in over your heads.'

Thomas didn't reply, chewing another grape.

'Got it?' Jessica added.

'Whatever.'

'Good. In the meantime you can help me with something else.'

He laughed again, humourlessly, peering over the top of Jessica towards the wall. 'As if. Why do you think I'm going to help you?'

Jessica held up the tub. 'Free grapes.'

'You're the maddest copper I've ever met.'

'Flattery will get you everywhere. Anyway, I've got two words for you: Scott Dewhurst.'

23

'Who?'

It wasn't exactly the reply Jessica expected, considering what she'd read in the Dewhurst file Josh had sent her. Not that she could tell him that.

'C'mon, Thomas, let's not be shy. Big bald guy, smart suits, looks a bit like an egg. Perhaps you know him as "Scotty" or "Dewey"? Something unimaginative with the letter Y on the end.'

Thomas shuffled into a sitting position on the bed. 'I don't know what you're trying to stitch me up for but it ain't gonna work. I don't know no Scott Dewhurst.'

'Sure?'

'Listen, sweetheart, I've never heard of anyone called Scott and even if I had, why would I tell you?'

'Remember the community service you did four years ago after you were done for dealing speed? Sixty hours picking up litter, cleaning kerbs, cottaging in the parks, that sort of stuff. I've seen your record and guess who you were arrested with?'

'I don't know what you're on about.'

Jessica took an envelope out of her bag and slipped out a mugshot of Scott Dewhurst. She held it up, watching the recognition on Thomas' face.

'How do you know him?' she asked.

He shook his head, reaching for a grape. 'What's in it for me?'

Jessica put the photo back in her bag and took a grape herself, squashing it between her teeth as she stood and moved to the bottom of the bed, resting on the bedframe.

'What do you want? If it's a helicopter to Switzerland and three million in used notes then I don't think our budget will cover it.'

'I want it out of the papers. He only battered me this morning, so you can keep it quiet.'

'How do you think we're going to manage that when your secretary mate goes to court?'

'It'll only be a remand jobbie and no one will go unless you flag it up. You could easily keep it quiet and by the time it gets to court properly in a few months – *if* it does – I'll have had a chance to talk to my guys.'

Jessica got it perfectly. George O'Reilly had made his move but it was unlikely he'd done it by himself. Thomas wanted to get back into the arms of his members and head off the prospect of an internal war before it actually happened. If he was still in hospital and the media got hold of it, then it could already be too late.

She said nothing, clucking the back of her mouth as he watched her.

Thomas cracked first. 'Well?'

'Well what? I've got a bit of grape stuck between my teeth.'

'Are you going to sort it?'

Jessica stepped closer so he could see her better, making

sure he was looking into her eyes. 'Of course I'm not. I don't owe you anything and I definitely don't do deals.'

Thomas held her gaze for a few moments, wondering if there was anything else. When it was clear there wasn't, he rolled over and shouted for a nurse, adding: 'Fuck you then. I want you out of here.'

Jessica picked up her bag and headed for the door. 'Fine, I've got a busy afternoon anyway. First I've got to get to the magistrates' court, wake some of them up and get a warrant for your house. We've heard some rumours that the reason your secretary attacked you was over unpaid drug debts. Vicious things, rumours, aren't they? Anyway, I'm sure you won't mind us taking your hard drives, digging up your floorboards, checking in your attic, going through your fridge and eating all the cheese. A fine upstanding citizen like yourself obviously has nothing to hide.'

Jessica had one hand on the door when it swung inwards. A nurse entered but stopped on the spot, sensing the atmosphere and glancing between the two of them. 'Everything all right?'

'Fine,' Jessica replied. 'I was just leaving.'

Thomas shouted so loudly that he took both women by surprise: 'No—'

The nurse looked at Jessica accusingly. 'I told you that you could only talk to him for a short while.'

Jessica shrugged, pulling the door open further. 'I'm finished.'

Thomas had one leg out of the bed, sending the nurse scurrying across to tuck him in again. 'I've still got information for you,' he said.

The nurse peered between them again, looking at the clock on the wall. 'You've got five more minutes and that's it – the doctor won't be happy about this.'

When it was just them, Jessica retook her seat, tidying her bag. 'You must really have something you want to keep hidden. What is it, a collection of Cliff Richard vinyls?'

'You're so fucking clever, aren't you?'

'Hopefully, now get on with it: Scott Dewhurst.'

Thomas shook his head, swallowing and turning away. His eyebrow was twitching with anger, features lined with deep wrinkles; his pumpkin face now looked as if it had been left out for a week after Halloween. She could see the person behind the fake tan and large jewellery. This was the Thomas his group members got to see as he wound them up and set them loose to smash up a city centre.

When he spoke it was almost too quickly for her to pick up properly. 'I was at a house party four years ago, this right dive out in Salford – music, booze, drugs, girls, the usual. Your mate was there, built like a tank. I didn't say a word to him all night, didn't even know him. We were just there. For whatever reason, your lot raided: bells, whistles, guns, "everyone on the ground", the full works. They let all the girls go and arrested all of the men. I got my sixty hours, some of the others got off. I suppose they had better lawyers but I've never seen your bloke before or since. Happy now?'

Jessica munched on another grape, nodding towards the clock. 'That nurse reckons you've got four more minutes, so you better start giving me the real version before I get my warrant.'

'That's the truth!'

'Bollocks is it. I went to parties four years ago and there would have been people there I never spoke to but I wouldn't remember them now. If someone shoved a photo of them under my nose, I wouldn't hold my breath for a couple of seconds as my pupils dilate in recognition. Three and a half minutes, now get on with it.'

Thomas glanced towards the clock, licking his lips. She could see his foot bobbing under the covers, as he pondered what to do. When he spoke, his tone was softer, more distant and he was a different person again – calmer and sadder: 'Chris Carmichael.'

'Who's that?'

'My best friend growing up – we used to play football, go into town, try to pick up girls. You know what it's like when you have a best mate. When we were out and about, we got into a couple of things. Believe it or not, I've never done drugs – not once. Not coke, speed, dope, blow, whatever you want to call it. Not my thing. But we'd get our hands on some and sell it on. Easy money, except that Chris couldn't leave it at that.'

'He got a taste for the merchandise?'

Thomas tutted in annoyance at being interrupted. 'Right. That night, he'd taken me to the party to meet this guy he knew who he reckoned was going to make us rich. It really was a shithole, a total dive – but there were girls everywhere and no one seemed to care. Some of them were high as kites, others were snorting stuff off the floor. I'd only gone for Chris and he'd nicked off to talk to your man. The girls didn't have much on but the lads wore jeans, T-shirts, nothing special – except for him. Shiny shoes, expensive suit, big watch, head like a fucking egg. Anyway, he wasn't happy about something Chris said but before anything happened, your Rambo lot stormed in, shouting and telling everyone to get down. Like I said, out went the girls and we all got carted off to the station. I never saw 'em again.'

'Scott?'

Thomas shook his head. 'Neither of 'em.'

Jessica felt the atmosphere change as she was drawn into the story, not wanting the pay-off but knowing she had to hear it. 'What happened?'

Thomas' voice cracked. 'No idea what happened to your mate but Chris . . . it says on his death certificate that he choked on his own vomit while in police custody.'

Shite.

Jessica could remember the name now he'd put it in context. Four years ago she had been a DS. One of their sister teams from Greater Manchester had handled that raid but it was on a busy Friday night and those arrested had ended up in cells in the north of the city. The investigation had cleared anyone of any wrongdoing – but it still stank. People arrested shouldn't die in custody and when they did, the entire city, fuelled by the media, became anxious about what was really going on behind closed doors. Their bosses got nervous and everyone had been sent on a three-hour refresher course for prisoner care. Some dickwit had come up from the Met, peering over his glasses, talking down to them as if they were untrained baboons while he was from the cultured south. She'd spent the entire session doodling and trying to make a rubber band ball. It seemed so silly now – someone had died, not just a nameless face but Thomas McKinney's best friend.

Now it made sense. Thomas used to be an estate agent and wasn't a stupid person. He spoke clearly and eloquently. Anarky wasn't just about the money he could get out of people, it was his way of taking his anger out on society, on them. Wind people up and let them loose. Light that flame and let it burn. He liked his material possessions too much to be a real anarchist but that didn't mean he couldn't play people who were.

Thomas' voice was low and determined. 'How did it happen?'

'What?'

'Chris.'

'I don't know – it wasn't me and I wasn't there.'

'Did you throw him down the stairs to get some sort of confession? That's how it works, isn't it? One of your hardmen handcuffs his hands behind his back and then beats him to death? Dress it up as a nice little choke to death, rather than murder by cop?'

'He would have had a post mortem, no one could cover up something like that.'

'Bullshit, you're all in it together – and I'll tell you one other thing. I don't know why you're interested in your Scott guy, whether bald guys are your thing, but he ain't scared of you boys in blue. When your guys came in, guns in the air giving it the big I am, we all hit the floor scared shitless but your mate, he was standing there in the middle of the room, arms out wide, laughing his cock off. If they didn't have the guns, he'd have taken the lot of them on and walked out of there without a scratch on him. I've never seen anything like it.'

He burst out laughing, swearing under his breath at the memory. Before he could add anything else, the nurse walked back in, fresh pillow in hand, pointing at the clock.

Double shite.

24

Jessica sat in the station's canteen opposite Rowlands, playing Russian roulette by sipping a tea from the machine. It tasted like week-old puréed sprouts with the consistency of soggy toilet roll. Dave was tucking into a meal that was twenty per cent fish, twenty per cent chips, ten per cent baked beans and fifty per cent ketchup.

As she swallowed her tea, Jessica winced – a worthy punishment for four days of inaction. There had been no other linked attacks and their clean-up jobs on the CCTV images of the hoody with the anarchy mask had come to nothing. Luke Callaghan had said nothing since being released from hospital and with the Home Secretary now silent, there was little pressure to solve things. Alan Hume and Victor Todd were all but forgotten, except for having their names on a whiteboard among a lot of misspelled words.

Thomas McKinney was out of hospital and had been correct that no journalists had bothered to visit his secretary's committal at court. The police press office hadn't sent out the details, not because Jessica had stepped in but because they didn't want the possibility of this assault being linked to the other random attacks. Either that or incompetence.

Lucky Thomas.

The only reason she wasn't under greater pressure was because everything else was going surprisingly well. Someone passing dodgy money around pubs in the centre: solved. Cashpoint smashed open next to the arena: man in custody. Series of knife muggings around the university: got him. Jessica's team were consistently getting results – it was only on her main case that they couldn't get a break-through.

'What's up with him?' Rowlands was chewing on a chip with his mouth open, nodding towards Niall. The former DSI was standing at the counter with a tray, leaning for-wards to look at the menu board.

'No idea – he was in almost every day last week, barely saying a word to anyone.'

'Is it something to do with his Slasher guy dying?'

Jessica took her glasses off and rubbed her eyes. She couldn't get used to using them for close-up things and taking them off for anything in the distance. Her eyes hurt, which at least gave her an easy excuse for why she couldn't sleep. 'I suppose so but he doesn't want to talk about it. He's either in that room upstairs reading through files, or shambling around the corridors down here.'

'It must be tough when your career is defined by that one catch.'

Another sip of tea. Yuk.

'He's not interested in any of that. When they were after interviews for the twenty-five-year anniversary, he didn't want to be a part of it.'

Dave shrugged. 'I don't know the guy but every time you hear anything about him, it's always that he's the one who caught the Stretford Slasher. I don't reckon it matters whether you want to remember it, or if you want to do interviews – if that's how everyone thinks of you then your legacy is already set. Once the Slasher died, there was always going to be a part of his life that was over too. We all know what it's like when there are big things going on – you're in the middle of it and can't think of anything else. Day after day you're hunting down those leads, talking to people and then you get home and watch it on the news. The next day you wake up, listen to it on the radio, and do it all again. You hate it but you love it. When it's over and you've got the guy, you wake up in the morning and have that thought, "Oh shite, it's finished". You hate yourself because the bad guy's off the street and you shouldn't be sad about it but you are.'

He paused to have a swig from his drink. 'You wonder what you're going to do. Some thugs getting pissed and having a fight on a Friday night isn't quite the same. We get that buzz – and we never caught anyone like he did when he had the whole country watching him. Now imagine you wake up some day and not only is it over – but that guy you've been tied to for a quarter of a century has died. It's no wonder he doesn't know what to do with himself.'

Jessica let Rowlands' words sink in. He was spot-on about those feelings and probably right about Niall. It was just a shame that one of the most profound statements he'd ever made had come at a time when there was ketchup smeared across his chin.

Dave nodded beyond her again to where the former

superintendent was walking towards them, tray in hand, face blank. Jessica stood. 'Niall?'

He almost dropped the tray in surprise at someone speaking to him. 'Jessica, I, er . . .'

'Are you all right?'

His eyes darted both ways, wanting out of the conversation. He tried to laugh it off but his other features betrayed him. 'Yes, just a busy morning – so many things to work through up there.' He stepped past her, heading for a single table.

'If you need me, you know where my office is.'

Niall nodded, muttering, 'Of course', but she knew he had no intention of visiting her.

When Jessica sat down, the sauce had disappeared from Rowlands' chin. 'He really has got it bad, hasn't he?' Dave said.

'He's probably just lonely – his wife died, now this. Slowly, it's happening to everyone who has been a part of his life.'

Before she could stop herself, Jessica was yawning. When her eyes had finished watering, Dave was staring at her. 'Sodding hell, that was like being hit by a cyclone. You've not been out looking for Tony since that night we were out, have you?'

He picked up a piece of fish, meaning he wasn't looking straight at her as Jessica lied by telling him she'd not even thought of Tony since the night they'd gone out together.

She'd spent each evening trawling the back streets of Manchester city centre trying to find Tony or any possible reason why he was connected to Scott Dewhurst. She'd been propositioned by drunken weekend revellers, ended up with frozen bits she didn't know she had, and hardly slept. Meanwhile, Thomas' warning kept drifting around her head.

He ain't scared of you boys in blue.

There was nothing new in that. When she had worked in uniform, Jessica had arrested drunken women fighting each other who wouldn't have stopped scratching, biting and kicking until they'd killed the other person. They were so much worse than the men and, when restrained, they'd thrash around, try to headbutt the arresting officer, spitting and saying they were going to kill everyone and anyone.

The drink made them fearless.

Then there were the groups of youngsters who'd roam the streets, throwing stones at cars and giving anyone who tried to stop them a mouthful of abuse. They knew swear words Jessica had never come across when she was their age, jeering that they were below the age of criminal responsibility and couldn't be touched.

Their age, upbringing and sense of invulnerability made them fearless.

With Scott, she'd seen it herself because it was a part of him. The way he'd stood across the road from Tony's flat with a sense that what he wanted would inevitably happen. Then in the alley, she'd seen his cocky swagger. It wasn't something brought about by money, it was the absolute knowledge that he was untouchable. Jessica had even seen it through Josh's reaction when she had been in his car going through the photographs. He'd faltered, wanting to make sure she was talking about the right person.

Scott Dewhurst wasn't fearless because of booze or naivety, it was because he didn't have that emotion. He didn't care about the police and would have no concerns about her. Not only that but people were naturally scared of him.

Perhaps she was?

She'd looked up everything she could find on Scott. His record was so sparse that they had next to nothing on him in their system and Internet searches had thrown up little more. All she really had was the confidential SCD files Josh had emailed her. She had read and re-read the notes until she could practically recite them word for word. Josh had told her that Scott wasn't top of the tree in Manchester's criminal underworld, so she had even started investigating the person to whom he answered.

Christian Fraser ran an empire of low-level clubs and pubs around the city that were almost certainly a front for dealing drugs and laundering money. He was the one the SCD *really* wanted, with Scott someone they thought could potentially turn. The pair's combined criminal records were almost nothing – two smart guys building a fortune on the backs of the easily manipulated. What could either of them possibly want with Tony?

For Jessica, things had already gone too far. Dave had done enough for her in the past and how could she ask Izzy to help when she was a mother? She was supposed to be an inspector now and yet she'd done the same stupid thing she always did – got involved. This time it was worse because she'd allowed Tony to get to her. Stupid, alcoholic, tea-loving junkie Toxic Tony Farnsworth was in her head and she couldn't get him out.

What on earth had he got himself into?

'Jess—'

Rowlands' voice brought her back into the room. 'Wuh . . . what?' she replied.

'You're worried about him, aren't you?'

'Who?'

'Tony.'

'Don't be wet.'

Jessica hid behind her plastic teacup but Dave wasn't fooled. 'Have you ever looked into his background?'

'What, the sleeping rough?'

'His parents.'

'I know they own some houses and that they've got a few quid.'

Dave shook his head, stuffing the final three chips into his mouth in one go. 'Mmmf, pfft, mmph.'

'Attractive.'

He swallowed. 'Come with me.'

Jessica threw the remains of her tea into the bin thinking she wouldn't be surprised to find out days later it had melded with Dave's leftover baked beans to create some sort of toxic superbug. Rowlands led her through the corridors towards the main floor where the constables worked. It was one of the warmest areas of the building, largely because they were packed in so tightly. There was a clatter of keyboards, slam of phones and general undercurrent of swearing. At the back was a large whiteboard listing everyone's outstanding cases – or at least it should have done.

'Hasn't anyone updated that?' Jessica asked, nodding towards the board.

'No one knows where the pens are – they keep going missing.'

'You're detectives – do some detecting and bloody find them. Either that or get creative and nick them from somewhere else.'

'Is that official GMP policy?'

'Unofficially, yes. Now what have you got?'

Rowlands' desk was a clutter of folders, paperwork and magazines. He leafed through the top one which had a half-naked girl on the front.

'If it's some gran-bang porn mag starring your girlfriend then I'm not interested.'

Dave wasn't listening, picking up the stacks of work papers and putting them down again, checking under his keyboard, and then starting to go through the drawers. Rubber bands, biros, a can of Fosters, paperclips, a laser pen, coins, a packet of matches, buttons . . .

'Wow, you've got more crap in your desk than I've got in mine.'

Dave held out a small carved wooden frog. 'Want that?'

'Why would I?'

'No idea – I think it was in here when I moved in . . . Aha!' From the bottom drawer, Dave pulled out a glossy, slightly ripped magazine covered with tea-mug rings. On the front was a photo of a scantily clad female with her arms and legs fully outstretched in a way that couldn't be comfortable.

'I thought I said no granny porn?'

Dave began flicking through the pages. 'It's from a Sunday newspaper a year or so ago. The picture on the front's from some photographer's profile. They like to pretend they're all arty, instead of just taking porno pics. Not that there's anything wrong with that.'

'Why'd you keep it?'

Rowlands thrust the magazine into her hand, pointing at an entry at the bottom of a page. 'They do a rich list every year. I'm not really fussed but I got reading for some reason and look who popped up.'

Number 397
Anthony and Sylvia Farnsworth, property, £188.5m

Anthony Richard Farnsworth's father was a miner, his mother a baker and housewife. He grew up in Bradford, West Yorkshire. By the age of nineteen, he had married his grammar school sweetheart, Sylvia, and founded Farnsworth Properties. Initially, he renovated run-down houses bought at auction but quickly developed a reputation for the speed at which he could work. What could have been a risky investment in buying a large plot of land outside Halifax turned into a windfall when the council commissioned him to spearhead their social housing push. The custom-built estate was completed ahead of schedule and he received additional praise for the high-quality builds. Farnsworth's hands-on, personable approach has garnered him a solid reputation throughout the industry, leading to a succession of housing contracts from local councils. He currently lives close to Huddersfield in West Yorkshire with his wife, Sylvia. This year they will celebrate their golden wedding anniversary. They have one son, Anthony Junior.

Jessica had spent so much time looking into Scott that she'd not bothered to do her research properly on Tony. She knew his parents were rich – but this was on a different level. Suddenly she had a little over one-hundred-and-eighty-eight-million reasons why a person like Scott Dewhurst would be interested in Toxic Tony.

25

Jessica stared at the heavy red lights of the lorry in front beaming through her car's windscreen like two giant Catherine wheels. She pulled the handbrake up for the umpteenth time and turned to the man in the passenger seat. 'Has there ever been a bigger crime inflicted on the British public than the M62? The bloody thing's always chocker – usually some jackknifed lorry. If they wanted to keep Lancastrians and Yorkshiremen apart, they could have just built a wall instead of a hundred-mile-long traffic jam.'

Niall glanced up from his newspaper. 'I was warned not to go in a car with you.'

'Who by?'

'What's the name of your desk sergeant? The portly fellow.'

'Pat?'

'He said – and this is a direct quote: "I hope you've made a will".'

'Bastard.'

'There were a few others too.'

'It's a myth!'

'Your friend with the spiky hair—'

'Dave?'

'He had some article from the *Herald* about how the number of cyclists on Manchester's roads had fallen by fifteen per cent in the past four months. He pointed out that the number coincided almost exactly with the length of time since you returned to work.'

Jessica started to speak but it wasn't coherent phrases that were coming out, more a long stream of previously unrelated swear words that had now been linked together to form entirely new descriptions of her colleagues. 'I'm not that bad,' she eventually managed.

Niall peered around the lorry at the blue sign on the side of the road. 'I have to say that in the fifty minutes it's taken us to move fewer than ten miles, you've been perfectly fine.'

'Thank you.'

'There was that incident on the roundabout but—'

Jessica's eyes flashed sideways and the former DSI stopped mid-sentence. How was she supposed to know the other driver was going the entire way around the round-about and not getting off at the junction? That's what indicators were for.

'I've had to take a holiday day for this too,' Jessica grumbled.

Niall folded his paper away as the traffic picked up again. Jessica eased into the outer lane to overtake, only to see the lorry zoom away from her as the cars in front crawled. Finally the other vehicles started to move and Jessica managed to get the car into fifth gear for the first time in a while. She could feel Niall watching her.

'I've been meaning to ask why you invited me,' he said.

'You've seemed a bit bored around the station over the past week or so and I thought you'd be able to give me a hand.'

'But this isn't official business?'

'No.'

'Are you going to tell me?'

'We're visiting the parents of someone I know. He's got himself into trouble and I'm wondering if they might be able to help.'

Niall didn't reply instantly but must have sensed there was a lot more to it than that. Sometimes when you did this job, you learned not to ask.

Wherever Anthony and Sylvia Farnsworth lived, it was remote. When they finally got off the motorway at the Huddersfield junction, Jessica's sat nav seemed intent on taking her along narrow winding roads that seemingly went nowhere. The wintry weather had taken more of a hold on the wrong side of the Lancashire–Yorkshire border, snow clinging to the tops of the bushes, frost lining the edge of the roads, but the sun was at least out. The bright blue sky felt like a stranger, with the fields steaming as the temperature gradually crept above freezing. Compared to the endless cloud that had been hanging over Manchester, this was practically the Caribbean.

Jessica's car hopped over a humpback bridge and she rounded a corner that narrowed into a single-track road. Three more miles and one terrified cyclist later and Jessica pulled up next to a thick stone pillar and pressed the buzzer. The heavy metal gates swung inwards and she accelerated along the wide, long, straight driveway. With the frosty white-green expanses of lawn on either side and the trees in the distance, Jessica couldn't help but be reminded of the other big house she had spent time in.

Niall noticed it too. 'Everything all right?'

'Yes.'

'You're shaking.'

Jessica glanced away from the driveway to see the whites of her knuckles as they clung onto the steering wheel. He was right: her wrist was trembling. She felt something on her arm and jumped with surprise, accidentally pulling the car to the left before righting herself with a gasp.

Niall had placed a comforting hand on her arm but removed it sharply. 'Sorry.'

'It's fine.'

Jessica pressed the brake, slowing the car as she parked next to an almost-new Bentley. The house in front was enormous – three storeys high, each a dozen windows across with a tall, thick wooden front door with white marble-looking steps leading up to it and impressively carved pillars. Jessica had never visited Washington DC but it looked like a sandstone-coloured version of every picture she'd seen of the White House.

Large houses only ever made her think of one place. Her heart was thumping and she didn't have to look into the mirror to know her face was flushed.

'It's a different house, Jessica.'

Niall spoke calmly, facing the front. Good – she didn't want anyone staring at her, not when she felt like this.

'I know.'

'I'm here. It's all right.'

Jessica breathed in through her nose, thinking of that fictional bloody psychologist again. He didn't even have the decency to exist anywhere other than in her head. Bastard,

bastard, bastard. Not now – it's only a house. Bricks, cement, wood. Pull yourself together.

Slowly, she breathed out through her mouth and opened the car door. Her legs were unsteady and she held onto the roof as she closed the door with a pitiful slam.

Only a house – and it didn't even look like *that* one.

Before she could properly get a grip, she heard a woman's voice and turned to see someone she assumed was Sylvia Farnsworth standing between the two pillars at the front. 'Hello? Are you Jessica?'

One step at a time, hand outstretched, smile. It's not bloody hard, is it?

'Hi, I'm Jessica Daniel and this is my colleague Niall Hambleton.'

Sylvia gripped her hand, with a smile like it was painted on, make-up immaculate, smart, expensive clothes. She hadn't noticed, had she?

Jessica let Niall go ahead of her as they entered the house. She was expecting a huge hallway and a giant painting but it was nothing like that. No wood panelling, no thick rugs. Definitely not the same house. Instead the interior was like her place but bigger – carpeted, a small side table for keys and mail, a cupboard where coats went. The ceiling was higher and the room larger but Jessica instantly knew the people she was dealing with – Anthony Farnsworth Senior was the son of a miner and came from Bradford. She knew the area, knew the people. It wasn't the type of place where you'd be allowed to get above yourself. He'd made a fortune from good-quality social housing, not ripping people off.

Sylvia led them through a hallway into a dining room laid out like an old Victorian tea room. There were four round tables with green baize covers and varnished wood around the edge. The chairs, curtains and carpet all matched. 'I'll fetch Anthony,' she said, pronouncing the H in her husband's name.

Jessica and Niall sat opposite each other, taking in the room, chandelier and all.

She was beginning to think she'd misjudged the couple when Sylvia re-entered with Anthony at her side. In contrast to his son, Anthony was a brute of a man: tree-trunk thighs, saucepan hands, a neck as thick as his waist. Six and a bit feet of pure Yorkshireman but somehow he didn't feel intimidating. He reached in to shake her hand, his brown eyes staring into hers. His grip wasn't overly strong but the moment he let her go, his attention turned to Niall, the same fixed stare.

As they sat, he failed to mask his discomfort, glancing around the room unhappily. Jessica didn't need to ask to know what the problem was. They had been childhood sweethearts but Sylvia was prim and proper. This was her room, perhaps something she'd dreamed of having since she was young. Anthony was old-fashioned, a product of the mining family in which he'd grown up, gruff with an accent as thick now as it had likely ever been. Opposites really did attract.

'I was hoping to ask you about your son,' Jessica said, looking between the pair.

'I bloody told you!' Anthony practically broke the back of the chair as he spun to face his wife. It wasn't through aggression, more that the setup was far too dainty for him.

Jessica expected Sylvia to shrink away but despite her size, she wagged a finger in her husband's face. 'Don't you take that tone with me.'

Anthony cowered under her gaze, turning back to Jessica. 'What's he done now?'

Jessica felt bad for lying but didn't know if there was any great benefit – at least for now – in telling them their son was back doing drugs again. 'He's not done anything. I was wondering if either of you have had any contact with him in the past few weeks or so?'

Sylvia replied. 'I've been up to see him a handful of times. He's been sorting himself out.' She emphasised the final few words, clearly for her husband's benefit.

'Tony's been helping us with a couple of things – nothing for you to worry about – but I've not seen him in around a week. I'm sure he's fine but he told me he was thinking about getting out of Manchester and perhaps returning home. I wondered if you'd heard anything?'

Jessica could have asked on the phone but sometimes it was better to see people's faces. All she could see in theirs was concern – from his mother especially. His father had an 'I-told-you-so' look of annoyance on his face but the eyes gave his disappointment away.

'I could try calling him?'

Sylvia left the room, returning moments later with a mobile phone, muttering that he might answer if he saw it was her. She tried three times back to back before giving up, putting the phone on the table in front of her.

'I really thought he'd turned himself around,' Sylvia said, eyes fixed on the phone, willing it to ring.

'No one's saying he hasn't—'

Anthony's snort of derision interrupted her. 'You do know the types of thing he was into?'

'Tony's been in and out of my life a lot over the years.'

'Then you should know what he could have had. I've worked my whole life for this – back-breaking stuff, early mornings, late nights.' He stretched out a hand towards his wife. 'Sylv couldn't have children after him. She dedicated her life to that boy and this is how he repays her. We told him we'd support whatever he wanted – if he wanted a job, or if he had some idea that he thought he could make a go of, then we would have invested. But oh no, he had do things his own way in that God-forsaken hellhole. Look at him now – a stupid, thick junkie.'

Before Jessica could reply, Anthony was on his feet, sending the chair spiralling to the ground behind him. He was at the door in three strides and away down the corridor, the heavy echo of his footsteps booming behind him. Niall must've clicked that this was what Jessica had feared because he was quickly on his feet too, saying he'd be back and heading out of the room after the other man.

Sylvia stood and picked up the fallen chair. 'Sorry about that.'

'No need . . .'

'He's always been like this – he wants people to think he doesn't care so he gets angry and stomps away. The truth is, he's hurting as much as I am. He always wanted a son.'

'He's right about one thing.'

'What?'

'Manchester: it really is a God-forsaken hellhole sometimes. I've not seen blue sky in weeks.'

Sylvia smiled wearily. 'I thought it was different this time.'

'When I saw him a couple of weeks ago, I thought that too. He was into his tea and talking about coming back here.'

'What happened?'

'Who says anything did?'

'Why else would you be here?'

Jessica didn't have an answer but still didn't want to tell Sylvia about the state in which she'd found her son. 'All I can say is that we've not seen him in a few days – that's the truth.'

Sylvia peered back towards her silent phone again. 'I can't help but feel that so much of this is down to us. I know it sounds stupid but I suppose we were the ultimate in pushy parents. We didn't spoil him, that's not our way, but we kept on and on at him about what he was going to do for his future. He was never going to work for his father, we both knew that, so we offered to give him some money to set up a business if he could find something investable. Anthony asked for a proper business plan, costings, the lot. He was only eighteen. We were trying to be hard on him but probably pushed it too far. We thought we were giving him an opportunity not many eighteen-year-olds got but that was the point, wasn't it? He didn't want that, at least not then, he wanted to go out with his mates, meet girls, get into trouble.'

'I'm sure you did what you thought was best.'

Sylvia shrugged, which didn't seem quite right given her otherwise straight-laced appearance. 'When he said he was going to university, we weren't exactly unhappy but we were surprised. I suppose it was because neither of us went and we assumed. He had great grades at school and we had the money. We would have paid for him to study abroad, or if he'd wanted to go to one of the big universities, it wouldn't be a problem. But then he said he was going to Manchester and we didn't know what to think. I know you'll think I sound like a snob but it wasn't like that. It felt like we were offering him the world – giving him everything we never had – and then he turned around to say he'd rather live down the road.'

Jessica had often felt that herself, especially when she had been younger. It sounded ridiculous considering the hell some children went through but sometimes, a person's upbringing was almost too good. It wasn't about being spoiled, but things were put on a plate, not giving an individual the chance to go out and find out what the real world was like. Making mistakes was as important a part of life as getting things right.

Perhaps this was why Tony was in her head – Jessica had seen it in him and now she knew it was true. He'd gone to the city for the same reason she had: to get away from home. Here he would have had a huge bedroom, support, money, opportunity; but they were their own prisons too. Perhaps sleeping rough or in a poky flat offered him the freedom that this didn't. He had certainly made his own mistakes.

Jessica asked a few more questions, finding out that Sylvia had visited Manchester half-a-dozen times in the past six months, seeing an improvement in her son on each occasion. Jessica asked if Tony had ever been with anyone but his mother insisted he was always by himself. She'd not heard of anyone named Scott.

When Niall returned, letting Jessica know with the merest nod of his head that he wasn't going to get anything else, she started to say her goodbyes, giving Sylvia her card and telling her to call if she heard anything.

'Will you phone me too?' Tony's mother asked.

'If we find him, I'll get him to call you himself.'

Sylvia nodded but the gulp exposed her real fear. 'That's *if* you find him.'

Jessica negotiated the tight turns away from the property a lot better than she'd managed when she was coming in the opposite direction. Niall didn't speak until they were back on the main A road leading to the motorway.

'I had an interesting conversation with Anthony. It sounds like his son is quite the character.'

'That's one way of putting it.'

'What's going on with the pair of you?'

'I'd rather not say.'

'But you're not here on official business, so it's something personal . . .'

Jessica didn't reply, remaining silent until they were back on the motorway, where the traffic was thankfully moving.

'Did you visit your mum yet?' Niall's question came so out of the blue that Jessica answered without thinking.

'Not yet. I've been busy.'

'You really should.'

If anyone else had told her that, they would've been impolitely informed to mind their own business. With Niall, she let it go, replying with a simple: 'I will.'

He was about to say something else when his phone started ringing. Niall hunted through his pockets until he found it. She thought whoever was calling was going to ring off but he eventually pressed the right button to answer. She only heard one half of the conversation but the increasing agitation in his voice put her on edge too, the mention of his grandchildren's names sending a shiver rocking through her: 'Right . . . Are you sure? . . . Poppy and Zac? . . . Both of them? . . . Where was Rebecca? . . . They've got to be somewhere . . . I'm on the motorway, I'll be there as soon as I can.'

Warm air was spewing from the car vents but the atmosphere still felt icy. 'Where do you need me to take you?' Jessica asked.

'My son's house.'

'Brendan?'

'Yes.'

'What's happened?'

'Zac and Poppy are missing.'

Jessica put her foot down, blazing around a BMW into the outside lane and barrelling past a caravan, wishing she had a siren. There was nothing she could say but Niall's final word left her dumbstruck anyway. It was barely a whisper, almost lost in the sound from the heater, but it was there nonetheless: 'Slasher.'

26

Rebecca Hambleton sat at the kitchen table in her house, still shaking. A support officer was at her side, trusty cups of tea at the ready. Even with all of their training, there was still little that ranked above being able to make a good cuppa. Rebecca's long dark hair was covered with a small bandage courtesy of the paramedics but Jessica could still see strands stuck together. Despite the head wound, she had refused to leave the house and go to hospital, even though the paramedics said she was concussed. DCI Cole was with Niall in the living room, talking to his son, Brendan.

Jessica tried to take things slowly with Niall's daughter-in-law, aware of her injuries, but it was Rebecca who kept pushing things, wanting them to take her seriously and 'get out there and look for them'. Jessica tried to explain that the best thing Rebecca could do was tell them as calmly as possible what had happened.

'I need you to go back to the start of the day,' Jessica said. 'What time did you get up?'

'How's that going to get my kids back?'

'Please can you trust me? The more information you can give us, the better it will be. Sometimes the things you think might be innocuous end up being important.'

Rebecca breathed noisily through her nose and then replied: 'The alarm went off at five to seven, the same as always.'

'What then?'

'Brendan went to have a shower and get ready for work. He does it every day.'

Jessica already knew that Niall's son worked in a bank in Manchester city centre. Rebecca was a housewife and they shared a large-ish semi-detached in a nice area of the city. They clearly weren't struggling financially but there was little extravagance. Brendan was a mid-level manager but had no access to money outside of the branch. If you were kidnapping children because you wanted a ransom, there would have been so many more viable targets.

Niall hadn't mentioned it again but Jessica couldn't help remembering the way he'd said it in the car: *'Slasher'.*

'What's the rest of your morning routine?' she asked.

'We eat breakfast together at around half past seven and then Brendan goes to work. I take the kids to school at around ten past eight. They usually watch a bit of television.'

'Do they go to the same school?'

'Yes. Poppy's seven and Zac's five – they're at the same primary.'

They already had the details – a cosy little building attached to a church hall a couple of miles away. Solid results, a respected headteacher, nothing unusual. Officers had gone to talk to the teachers who hadn't already gone home for the day.

'Was there anything unusual about your journey?'

Rebecca shook her head. The tears and shattered expression weren't enough to hide how pretty she was. 'There are those roadworks over by the roundabout but they've been there for weeks. You get stuck in the traffic lights but I started leaving a couple of minutes earlier.'

'What about when you get to the school? Do you hang around for a chat with the other mums? Come straight home?'

'Zac and Poppy usually go off to run around with their friends in the playground if it's dry but it's been so cold. Today they went straight into the school. I was talking to one of my friends close to the gates, another mum, but it was freezing. We might have gone for a coffee on another day but I had a class today.'

She nodded towards the corner where there was a gym bag propped up against the wall, a yoga mat rolled up behind it. A calendar was stuck to the fridge by a magnet, exercise class times written on for Monday to Friday. If it had been in front of Jessica, she wouldn't have been able to read it without her glasses; across the room it was clear. Rebecca obviously looked after herself.

'What class was it?'

'Rumba. I did that and then half an hour on the bike, before driving home.'

'What time did you get back?'

'Quarter past eleven? I'm not really sure. I left the gym at eleven.'

'What did you do then?'

'Just things around the house: cleaning up, washing

clothes, watched a bit of television, paid a few bills online. Normal things.'

'But you didn't leave the house?'

'No.'

'Did anyone visit?'

'No . . . Oh, I suppose the postman. There was a bill or two – they're still on the side.'

'He didn't knock though?'

'No.' The support officer handed Rebecca a tissue as she began to sob quietly again. 'Can you please just get out there and look for them?'

'We do have officers doing their best. We've almost finished here. Everything you've said has been really helpful.'

'But I've not said anything.'

'You have – we know what times the house was empty. We know you stuck to a routine – if anyone had been watching you over a period of time, they might have noted that. It's all important, which is why we need to know these things. What time did you go to pick your children up?'

Now she understood, Rebecca stopped hesitating and ploughed on. 'Three fifteen. They finish at half past and I was there a couple of minutes before. I had a quick chat to a couple of the other mums again but it was cold, so as soon as the kids came out, we set off.'

'Do you remember anyone suspicious there? Anything unusual?'

'Nothing, I wasn't really paying attention.'

'What about the journey home?'

'Same as usual, perhaps a bit less traffic.'

'What happened when you got home?'

'I parked on the drive – then I came in here. The kids had gone to put their things away upstairs in their bedrooms and then they were watching TV in the living room.'

'What were you doing in here?'

'Making their tea. On Wednesdays, I always let them choose what they want as long as they can agree. It was Brendan's idea – teaching them young that if they can negotiate with each other and come to an agreement, then they can get what they want. They usually squabble a little bit but I was doing them sausage, beans and chips. Not exactly gourmet, I know . . .'

'It was one of my favourites when I was a kid.'

'I'd barely even started. I'd got the beans open and then the doorbell went. Sometimes you get parcels late in the afternoon around here, so I thought it was either that or one of those charity collector types. I should have put the chain on, or looked through the fisheye, but you don't even think, do you? It's second nature – the doorbell rings, so you open it.'

Rebecca stopped herself, crossing to the sink and running the water into a glass, sipping it at first and then taking a large gulp. She looked a little better afterwards, her eyes slightly more focused. She leant on the sink, peering across to Jessica. 'Anyway, when I opened the door I wasn't really looking because Zac had cried out from the other room. I had one hand on the door handle and was facing away as I opened it. There was this sort of grunt and I turned back to see this shape there – a man, something dark, I'm not sure. I just remember something coming towards me, like a bat or a paddle, something flat. It was only a fraction of a second and then—'

'You called us at exactly eighteen minutes past four. Do you remember what time the doorbell went?'

'No, I wasn't paying attention.'

'But a little under a fifteen-minute journey from the school to here, so you would have been in by quarter to four, ten to at the latest. The kids had put their things down and you'd sorted out what they wanted for tea, so what time do you think you might have started thinking about cooking? Four o'clock? Five past?

'It was definitely after four. Five past at the latest.'

'So you were likely unconscious for around ten minutes – fifteen at the absolute most. That gives us a window where whoever attacked you escaped. Do you see why that's helpful?'

'Yes.'

'Okay, so tell me what happened when you woke up.'

'I remember feeling cold. My hands were chilly and something was tickling my nose. I thought I was dreaming for a few seconds and then I realised I was lying in the hallway and the door was open. It was just the breeze that was making me cold. I had a headache from where I'd been hit. I was running through the house calling for Zac and Poppy, panicking, crying. As soon as I knew they were gone, I called you – then I called Brendan. I think Brendan called his dad and then there were police everywhere . . .'

'I know this is going to sound like an obvious question

but can you think of anyone who could possibly be involved? Someone you might have fallen out with . . . ?'

Rebecca's voice cracked completely, tears running down her face onto the floor. 'I've been trying to think but we're not like that. We say hello to the neighbours, I've got the gym, Brendan goes circuit training at the rugby club, then we visit Brendan's dad once a week or so. Other than that, we keep ourselves to ourselves.'

The story was terrifying because it was so simple. It was the type of thing they would say was every parent's worst nightmare but it went beyond that because there was no sophistication. If someone could come to your house and walk away with your kids in broad daylight then what couldn't they do?

'What about the message?' Jessica asked, half-turning towards the front of the house.

Rebecca shrugged. 'I have no idea what it means.'

Jessica thanked Rebecca for her time and left her with the support officer, before heading into the hallway. There was a patch of blood dried into the light brown carpet but no other signs of a struggle. Whoever attacked her had stolen her car but the single spray-painted word on the wall was altogether more worrying.

Jessica popped her head around the door into the living room and gave Cole the nod to say she was ready. He joined her outside on the front step. It was staying lighter this evening but only because the cloud was so high, making it significantly colder than it had been during the day.

'What was she like?' Cole asked.

'More or less as you'd expect, slightly calmer. Everything she told me is the same as from the emergency call plus the first quick statement. What about Brendan?'

'He's all over the place – got home from work to find his kids gone, wife covered in blood with the paramedics and police here.'

'Niall?'

'Not said a word – he just sat and listened. He's taking it badly.'

'Did Brendan have any potential suspects?'

'No, he said they don't have a large field of friends.'

'Exactly like her. She didn't have a description of the attacker either. What about the message in the hallway?'

'Brendan says he doesn't know anything.'

'Rebecca says the same. Have you told them the rest?'

'Not yet, I had to nip out to take the call. ANPR picked up their car but we lost it heading away from the city. We sent patrol cars out that way and they found it dumped in a field on fire.'

'I suppose we at least know this was planned – someone would have had a separate car there waiting. She says she kept to a similar routine most days, so it's either someone who knows her or someone who's been watching. Izzy texted me from the station to say that she found their full address in under a minute on the Internet – they're on the electoral roll and in the phone book. Uniform say one of the neighbours across the road saw the front door open but thought it was just the kids playing. No one seemed to notice the car pulling away, let alone see who was driving. Do we have any shots of the driver on camera?'

'Not that we've had verified but we might. I'm waiting on the call.'

'I'm going back to the station if you don't mind – Izzy's staying late, so we can plough through things before the morning.'

Cole nodded. 'I'm going to remain here for a while. We'll talk later.'

Jessica turned to head to her car but Cole called her back. His voice was even lower this time. 'I had the thought coming over and I can't be the only one. The Slasher died just under two weeks ago. Brendan and Rebecca share Niall's last name – anyone could have found that out . . .'

Jessica wondered if she should tell him about Niall's single hushed word in the car but figured he didn't need to know, at least not yet. At some point, she needed to talk to the former DSI himself. Before she left, Jessica glanced back through the open door of the house. The single word had been sprayed in green capital letters on the hallway wall, clear and simple against the light purple wallpaper.

'CONFESS'.

Back at the station and Izzy wasn't the only one still hanging around. At least a quarter of the day shift were overlapping with the evening crew, frantically doing everything they could to find out what had happened to Poppy and Zac Hambleton. It would have been busy anyway but Jessica couldn't help but think some of the attention was due to the fact that Niall was one of them.

Izzy and DS Cornish had already compiled an incredible amount of information in the almost three hours since the children had gone missing. Brendan was never really under suspicion but his alibi had been cleared with people at the bank and they had his car on camera making the rapid journey home. Reports from the neighbours had been compiled, although aside from the homeowner who lived opposite, they didn't have anything. Two of the fellow parents from the school had been spoken to, confirming the time that Rebecca left.

The other concern was that it could have something to do with their three other random attacks but it didn't feel right – they were public, targeting people who had a crypt full of skeletons in their cupboards. This was more private and almost certainly a targeted act, especially given the spray-painted message.

Jessica pulled Izzy to one side as the bedlam continued around them, leading her into the corridor. 'How's it been working with Louise?'

Izzy's hair was greasy but her eyes attentive. She was in her element when she had a dozen things to do at the same time. 'Fine, I don't know why everyone has such a problem with her.'

'Did you manage to get the other stuff for me?'

'Half of it. You must've called as soon as you got to the house because it had all kicked off here and I had a hundred things to do.' She passed Jessica a small pile of Post-it notes. 'The Stretford Slasher – Colin Rawlinson – had a son, Jake. He would have only been nine or ten when his dad was jailed. He had been living with his mother but ended up being taken into care until he was sixteen.'

'Any up-to-date details?'

'Not on a Jake Rawlinson but I did some digging. There's a "Jake Forester" who lives not far from here. He's claiming jobseeker's allowance under that Forester name – but his national insurance number matches the one given to Rawlinson.'

Jessica flicked through the notes until she got his address. 'Is Dave still here?'

'Louise has been hammering him to get stuff done – I've never seen him work so hard.'

'All right, I'll go and rescue him.'

Jessica started to walk back towards the main area but Izzy stopped her. 'Jess . . .'

'Yep.'

Izzy sounded reluctant to ask, half-facing away. 'It can't be Jake, can it? The Slasher's son taking the grandchildren from the officer who arrested his dad? It seems too . . . I don't know, clean – obvious.'

'I'm only checking all the scenarios. I'm sure it's nothing but it can't do any harm to go and say hello. Are you going to go home any time soon?'

Izzy shook her head. 'I could ask you the same thing.'

'Touché. If you are going to stay around, can you check the prison thing for me?'

'I've already put the request in. Someone's doing me a favour.'

Jessica thanked her again, called Adam to apologise for working late – again, promising she'd make it up to him even if he'd have to put it on her 'tab', and then she went to save Dave from having to do some real work for DS Cornish.

They were only halfway to Jake's house when Jessica received the text message from Izzy. Dave read it for her, but she had already expected the outcome. The Stretford Slasher had had a single visitor in prison the month before he died: J. Forester.

27

Jessica had seen many things around the estates of Manchester. When she had been in uniform, she'd once been called to Trafford to reports of a robbery at a toy shop. They'd arrived with the full lights and sirens treatment, sending the robbers scarpering. As the police spread out, Jessica had arrested someone making their escape on a liberated Space-Hopper with a blow-up Spider-Man under their arm. Another time, she'd been on a drugs raid at a house in Eccles, where the owners kept a pet pig that was given the freedom to roam wherever it wanted, including the bedrooms. Straw lined the hallway and the stench had seeped into every part of the house to the extent that the bricks themselves reeked of pig shit. Out in Levenshulme, someone had tried to build a do-it-yourself extension on their house – but instead of removing the tree that sat next to it, they had built around it, making it part of an extended living room.

Even with those memories, the area in which Jake Forester lived just outside Longsight was extraordinary. At the edge of a green in the middle of a U-shaped block of flats, a collection of traffic control items had been re-arranged into a sculpture of a couple having sex. The 'woman' was made from scaffolding, plastic barrier boards and a beer-garden umbrella, all topped off with traffic-cone breasts. Her male friend had a bin for legs, a wooden-board chest, a rounded bush for a head and a three-foot night-owl bollard sticking out of this groin. In its own way, it was one of the most incredible pieces of community art Jessica had ever seen, especially given the delicate lighting from the overhanging street lamp. If she had been a member of the public, she would have had her picture taken in front of it. Unfortunately, she knew there would be unsignalled roadworks somewhere nearby with someone waiting to fall into it. Jessica called it in – and then she and Rowlands took each other's photographs in front of it.

The rest of the estate didn't share the same creativity: long terraced flats spread across two floors, dirty once-red bricks, missing roof tiles, grimy doorsteps, barking dogs, screaming babies – and satellite dishes jammed onto every stationary surface. Somewhere on the far side, dance music thumped out of one of the flats, echoing across the green. Even though there should be at least another hour of day-light at this time of year, darkened clouds were massing, the hazy glow of lights from inside the flats pooling into the centre of the clearing.

Jake lived in a top-floor flat facing the square. The route to his front door took them up a concrete stairwell that smelled of any number of bodily fluids and along a pas-sageway lined with front doors on one side but open to the elements on the other. Up close, everything looked even dirtier than it did from a distance. A trail of oil led along the stairs to an engine that had been left opposite some-one's front door, blocking half the path. A few doors down, there was an upturned bicycle missing its wheels. Along from that was a mound of rubbish bags, its corners torn open by rats, the contents spilling onto the ground.

The force's health and safety department could have spent a week here and not cleared the place into somewhere they'd be allowed to work safely.

It was the type of housing block even Jehovah's Witnesses would look at and think, 'Sod that'. In their suits, Jessica and Rowlands stood out like pensioners in a nightclub. Not wanting to attract any attention they didn't need, Jessica knocked quietly on Jake's front door. The window was covered in a thin layer of grime, with tatty crimson curtains obscuring all but a sliver in the centre. Rowlands leant in close to the glass, trying to peer inside.

'See anything?' Jessica whispered.

'There's too much glare.'

'So push yourself against the glass then.'

'It's filthy.'

'Stop moaning.'

Rowlands leant closer, pressing onto the window. 'Eew, I think this is shit.'

'Who'd smear shit on a window?'

'I don't know, who'd leave half an engine outside their front door?'

'Perhaps you're right – if you want to stop someone peering through your window, there can't be many better ways to do it than by covering it in shite.'

'It's in my hair . . .'

'Stop whingeing and tell me what you see.'

Jessica heard a slight squeak as Rowlands' hands slid

around the glass. 'There's a light on at the back. Telly's off, couple of chairs – it looks empty.'

Jessica crouched and quietly opened the letterbox, pushing the bristles to one side and staring into an empty hallway. She eased the flap back into place and sorted through the Post-it notes in her pocket. When she'd found the right one, Jessica dialled Jake's phone number. Inside a shrill pop song began.

'Something's flashing,' Dave said.

'It's his phone, you dimwit. Is he moving towards it?'

'No, it's on the arm of the chair.'

The phone stopped ringing.

'I think we can safely say that he's not in and has probably forgotten his phone. There's no way he could have resisted going for it otherwise.'

Dave extracted himself from the window, using his fingers to rub away the dark smear from his cheek. 'Are we going to get a team down here?'

'Everyone's off searching and we're only here on a hunch. Hang on.'

Jessica took her phone out and called Izzy, who answered while halfway through shouting at someone else. Jessica waited until she got the 'hello'.

'Gone home yet?'

'What do you think?'

'When you were looking into Jake's national insurance number, did you notice what day he signs on?'

'Where am I supposed to find that out?'

'I don't know, where do you ever come up with stuff?'

Jessica could hear the general bustle of the station in

the background and somebody shouting a request that sounded anatomically impossible. Izzy sounded distracted: 'I know someone who knows someone but the office will be shut. Give me ten minutes and I'll see what I can do.'

Eight minutes later, back in the relative warmth of the car with Rowlands scrubbing at his skin with a tissue, Izzy text-messaged Jessica a one-word answer: 'Monday'.

'What time do you knock off?' Jessica asked.

Rowlands looked at his watch. 'Forty-five minutes ago.'

'What are you doing tonight?'

'Not much.'

'There's a dingy little all-night cafe around the corner. How do you fancy going home, having a shower, and then meeting me back here for a late-night dodgy fry-up at eleven o'clock?'

'Who's buying?'

'As an extra-special treat, I'll pay up to the value of five pounds.'

'Wow, last of the big spenders. Want to tell me why?'

'No – if I'm wrong then we're just out for a late tea, if I'm right then I end up looking like the genius that I am.'

To call the cafe a greasy spoon was underplaying it. A greasy, grimy, oily, lardy, scuzzy spoon was a far more accurate way of describing the all-night breakfast place where Jessica sat opposite Dave eating a black pudding and fried egg sandwich. Aside from the Rottweiler-faced owner scuttling between the kitchen and the counter, muttering under his breath, banging saucepans around, the place was empty. The brown plastic table and matching chairs were bolted to the floor, giving the place the feel of a post-riot prison canteen. Jessica and Dave were sitting in the window, dressed down in jeans and warm tops as the outside frosty air crept through the thin glass.

Dave held a cup of tea in one hand, using a piece of toast in the other to mop up the remains of a fried egg. 'If this was a date – which it obviously isn't – it would comfortably be the worst one I've ever been on.'

'What's not to like?' Jessica replied. 'Fried food, relative peace and quiet. If you were someone else, this would be straight into my top five.'

She polished off the final bite of her sandwich and then stole a piece of Dave's toast to start mopping up the remaining egg on her plate.

'Oi!' Rowlands protested.

'I paid for it.'

'The first meal you've ever bought me and you're eating it yourself anyway.'

'How's your granny?'

'She's—'

'Yeah, yeah, not a granny. How's your age-challenged girlfriend?'

'We're meeting up this weekend – well, hopefully, if this all blows over.'

'No sign of the kids yet but the night crew are working their balls off as we speak. Izzy said they've got a partial shot on a traffic cam of our kidnapper – but only from the nose down. He had his sun blind down and we haven't got a full face. Definitely a bloke though – well, either that or a very hairy woman. No idea what the "confess" message means. Stop changing the subject. Where does she live again?'

'I've never told you.'

'Maybe I'll just do my mind-reading trick then. North or south?' Jessica leant in, narrowing her eyes to stare at him.

Rowlands waved his hands in front of his face. 'Sod off. All right, she's from the north-east. She's coming down here.'

'Are you going to dazzle her with the best of Manchester? Trafford Centre, canal boat, curry mile, quick feel in the bushes and then home?'

Dave checked his watch. 'Something like that. Why are we here?'

Jessica let the change of subject go, peering at the clock on the wall above Dave's head. 'What time have you got?'

'Eleven fifty-one.'

Jessica nodded across the road towards a bank of shops that had their metal shutters clamped to the ground. The only thing exposed was a cashpoint sticking through a gap in the metal and a beer company's neon logo burning out from a sign high on the wall above a minimart. 'The clock above your head's five minutes fast, so let's say eleven fifty-six on your watch and see what happens.'

Jessica knew she was going to look like an idiot if she was wrong but three and a half minutes later a woman with pyjamas and slippers sticking out of a long overcoat began hovering on the pavement next to the shutters. A minute later and there was a second woman there with a pram.

Dave finished his tea and blew into his hands. 'What's she doing out this late with a kid? It's freezing.'

'Just wait.'

Over the course of the next five minutes, seven more people turned up, half of them in pyjamas and slippers, the others wrapped up in hats, scarves and coats.

Jessica took a folded-up piece of paper out of her pocket and held it up for Dave to see. 'This is our guy. We've got two possibles over the road, both with their hats down. Don't let him run.'

'Why are they there?'

'You get it most days of the week around here. Everyone gets their benefits paid into their account three days after they sign on. If you go in on Monday, you get paid at midnight on the Thursday. They all come to the cashpoint to get their money out as soon as it drops. Why do you think places like this stay open? There's an offy round the corner too that's open until one in the morning.'

Jessica waited for the women to draw out their cash from the machine before heading across the road. She deliberately walked along the line, glancing at the faces, before joining at the back.

'Two in front,' she whispered to Dave.

The line was as orderly as any queue Jessica had been in, everyone shivering in silence as the freezing atmosphere sent their breaths drifting into the air. The cash machine clicked and chuntered its way through each of the requests. Each time, the recipient flicked through the notes, stuffed them in their pockets, and headed back in the direction of the flats.

By the time the man in the hat got to the front of the line, there was only one other person waiting between them. The machine spat the money out and, as he turned to walk away, the street light shone down on the unmistakeable ratlike face of Jake Forester. His nose twitched, as if scenting trouble, but Jessica was already on him, clamping one arm through his as Rowlands took the other.

'Bit late to be on the streets with all that cash, isn't it?' Jessica said breezily. 'I thought you might need a police escort back to your flat.'

Jessica wasn't tall but she had at least four inches on Jake and, along with Rowlands, they were practically dragging him along.

His voice was high and weaselly, his breath reeking of booze, though he didn't bother to question their identities. 'I ain't done nuffin'.'

'All right, calm down. We only want a quick word.'

The two officers escorted him back to his flat as he tried to free himself. He wasn't violent, simply so small that his limbs and stride pattern made him difficult to keep hold of. The fact that he didn't question why they were there was enough to tell Jessica that it wasn't exactly uncommon on this estate. As he unlocked his front door, Dave and Jessica stayed close behind, pushing their way in after him to avoid being shut out.

Inside and Jake hurried through to the living room, Jessica in close pursuit. He snatched his phone from the arm of the chair. 'Always losing the bloody thing.'

'Do you know why we're here, Jake?'

Jake flopped in his armchair and began playing with his

phone. His rough red skin burned from the alcohol, making him look at least fifteen years older than the thirty-four that he was. Jessica didn't know where he got the money from considering he was on benefits but she could probably guess.

'What is it this time?' Jake said, not looking up. 'Nicked TVs? I ain't seen 'em. Something kicked off outside? I've been down the boozer. I don't know nuffin' 'bout those dodgy tenners been going round either. It's always summit with you lot. Don't you know what time it is?'

'Perhaps if you took your phone with you, we'd have been able to get hold of you earlier.'

'Bah! Ain't you got a home to go to?'

'I wanted to talk to you about your dad.'

Jake's demeanour changed in an instant, his phone dropping into his lap, head spinning around. 'I don't have a dad.'

'I could talk you through the birds and the bees to point out how that's impossible – but it's late and you've got Channel Five for that. Let's just say we know about the whole name-change, being taken into care thing.'

'Oh.'

'Oh indeed. When was the last time you saw your father?'

Jake's eyes darted both ways. 'Er . . .'

'Surely you remember?'

'Yeah, yeah . . . it was a few years ago. I visited him in prison.'

'How many years?'

'Three? Four?'

'Which prison?'

'Strangeways.'

'And you're one hundred per cent sure that's where he was a few years back?'

'Er . . . my memory's sometimes a bit hazy, like.'

'Right – but you definitely haven't seen him at any time since?'

He looked her dead in the eye, putting on his most honest face, which was about as genuine as a used car salesman selling you the front of one car and back of another. 'Definitely.'

Jessica glanced up at Dave, letting him know he was up and then turned back to the flat's owner. 'I'm going to let you into a secret here, Jake. I've been drinking tea all evening. I also had a black pudding and fried egg sandwich which was probably a mistake at this time of night. I'm going to find your toilet and then I'm going to return and ask you the same question I just have. I'd like you to have a really good think about the answer.'

Closing the door behind her, Jessica headed into the hallway for an impromptu poke-around. In the kitchen, a green plastic toaster was on the counter surrounded by crumbs, with a matching microwave sporting a murky brown film across the front. The bin was packed with plastic tubs and cardboard sleeves from microwave meals – an uncomfortable reminder of her old flat. Aside from that, the lack of use made it surprisingly clean. No notes on the fridge, no interesting letters in the bin – or at least none near the top, there was no way Jessica was going delving.

The bathroom could have fitted into a similar space to the ones found on planes. There was a shower, a toilet and a sink all crammed almost impossibly into a cupboard in which it was barely possible to turn around.

The bedroom wasn't that much larger; a computer desk was wodged into the space at the end of a double bed and there were tall built-in wardrobes on the walls. Everything was so tight that there was no room to walk around without climbing onto the bed. Jessica checked through the wardrobes and under the computer desk before finding something vaguely interesting.

She walked back into the living room clutching a handful of items, placing them on the table in front of the television. Jake protested the entire way through, telling Jessica he knew his rights and that she couldn't go through his things without a warrant.

Jessica looked to Dave. 'The strange thing is, I distinctly remember being invited in, DC Rowlands, don't you?'

'Aye, very accommodating, our friend Jake. Walked us over from the cashpoint, invited us in, offered us tea and biscuits.'

Jessica focused on Jake again. 'That's your problem – when you invited us in, it isn't my fault if I was looking for the toilet and accidentally walked through the wrong door into your bedroom and stumbled across all this stuff.'

'I didn't invite you in!'

'That's not how I remember it. Anyway, we need some explanations here.' She used the tips of her thumb and forefinger to hold up a crumpled porn mag. '"OLD AND BOLD",' she read, handing the offending article to Rowlands. 'Here's one for you. Check there's no animal stuff in there.' She looked back to Jake, pointing to the stack of magazines she'd taken. 'Nothing illegal in here, is there?'

Jake crossed his legs uncomfortably, his pointed rodent face twitching again. 'No.'

Jessica took the next one from the pile, pulling a face. '"GLAMMED-UP GRANS". Christ's sake. Where do you even get this stuff?' She handed it to Rowlands again, who had the other magazine open lengthways, looking slightly queasy.

After flicking through the rest of the stack, Jessica conceded everything Jake had was probably legal, if a little 'specialist'.

Jessica pointed towards a stack of DVDs in individual plastic wallets. Each of them had a title written on in black marker pen. 'Right, what's this lot?'

'Just a few movies.'

'What type of movies?' Jessica nodded towards the magazines. 'Not more porn? I don't know how you've not gone blind from that lot.'

'All sorts.'

Jessica flicked through the top few and held one up for Rowlands to look at.

'Ooh, I've been meaning to see that,' the constable said.

'Me too – it's still in cinemas. What does this look like to you, DC Rowlands?'

'It looks like that DVD might have been pirated.'

Jessica peered back at Jake. 'And not just one copied DVD – there are hundreds here. Do you know what that says to me? Piracy ring. We're going to have to get the big boys in and rip this place apart. There could be disc-burners hidden anywhere, thousands of copied discs being distributed to the entire estate. There's no tax being paid and all sorts of copyright infringements going on.'

Jake shrunk back into his seat. 'It's only a few films. You can buy 'em down the pub – three for a tenner.'

Jessica shook her head. 'That's not what this looks like to me; this looks like a major international attempt to defraud the film industry.'

Jake's reply was more like a squeak. 'It's only a few discs.'

'Who sold 'em to you?'

More panic on Jake's face. 'I can't remember 'is name, like . . .'

'What did he look like?'

'It was . . . er . . . dark.'

'Definitely a he though, good. White, black, Asian?'

'Er . . . It's only a few discs.'

'I'll give you a bit of advice here, Jake. You're best off admitting it. If you beat up some old dear, you'll get a slap on the wrist, your name in the paper and a bit of community service. We know some right nasty bastards in the police – but I've never met anyone quite as evil as those copyright Nazis. Copy a DVD and they'll chop your cock off, feed it to you with a side salad of bollocks and sling you in a cell for forty years. If you think the things you've heard about Guantanamo Bay are bad, wait until this lot get hold of you.'

'I haven't done anything!'

'Right, and I might be able to help you out. If you can

tell me the last time you saw your dad without treating me like I'm stupid, I'll see what I can do.'

'I don't know what you're talking about – I've not seen him in years.'

Jessica rolled her eyes. Jake wasn't convincing himself, let alone her. He was making the mistake of too much eye contact, which was infinitely worse than not looking at somebody at all. His eyebrows were twitching, Adam's apple bobbing.

'Last chance – when was the last time you saw your father? Think *really* carefully before lying to me again.'

'I'm not lying.'

Jessica dropped the discs back on the table and turned to Dave. 'All right, nick him.'

28

DCI Cole didn't exactly approve of Jessica arresting Jake but he hadn't shut her down either. She wanted to talk to the man about the kidnap but had no reason to bring him in if it wasn't for the copied discs. Cole's initial words were, 'Not again', followed by, 'I hope you know what you're doing', and then, 'Whatever you do, don't hand him over to those copyright Nazis'.

Cole had taken charge of the search for the missing Hambleton children, with Jessica sitting in on the briefing. Using a combination of different angles from the traffic cameras, they had around two-thirds of the kidnapper's face. He was definitely male, with grey-black stubble on his chin, a thin face and plain dark clothing. It wasn't much to go on – but it was something. They'd traced the vehicles going onto the estate in the build-up to the kidnapping but couldn't find anything they could pin onto someone specifically. After abandoning the stolen car in the field and setting it on fire, they had no idea what had happened to the children. No footprints, no easy-to-find forensic details in the burned-out vehicle, no cameras anywhere near it and, crucially, no witnesses. If the kidnapper knew what he was doing, Zac and Poppy would be hidden some- where either soundproofed or remote enough that no one would hear them. For the police, the window to catch him in the act had already gone, now it was about getting their pictures everywhere and hoping for the best.

Jessica assumed Niall was still with his son and daughter-in-law because he was nowhere to be seen. He'd been in the force long enough to know they were now relying either on luck or the kidnapper's stupidity. She still hadn't told Cole the single word – 'Slasher' – he'd said in the car. There was no reason not to tell him but she felt there was something she needed to find out for herself first.

By the time Jessica had Jake brought up from the cells, he was looking more like a rodent than ever. His eyes were red and bleary, his crimson skin blotched and covered with a thin layer of stubble. As he was led into the interview room, his eyes darted around, nose twitching as it had the previous evening. For some inexplicable reason, he had refused to even speak to the duty solicitor, let alone bring him to the interview room. Some people were like that – no matter how many times they were told it was free, they trusted people in suits less than they trusted those in a uniform. To be fair, Jessica had come across more shifty bastards in suits than she had in uniform over the years.

Jake slumped in his seat, scratching at the back of his hand. His forehead was sweating, even though it wasn't hot. Jessica had seen enough alcoholics over the years to know he was struggling. 'You've ruined my life,' he said, not looking up.

'Are you ready to tell the truth about visiting the prison yet?' Jessica asked.

Jake slid further down the chair, until his back was

almost parallel to the ground. 'You don't know what it's like having a dad like that. If people find out . . . all the victims' families, they might come for me.'

He sounded so pitiful that Jessica was beginning to feel sorry for him. After a night in the cells and a few hours off the booze, he was reacting in the way most people would if they'd been arrested. 'Jake, we've got two kids missing and I'm hoping you might be able to help us find them. As I tried to tell you, we might be able to put these copied discs to one side if you can help us.'

'What missing kids?'

'Poppy and Zac Hambleton—'

'*Hambleton?*' Jessica saw the recognition in Jake's eyes straight away. 'As in Inspector Hambleton?'

'Have you seen the articles about your father over the past few weeks?'

'I, er . . .'

'It doesn't matter if you have – the important thing is that you know that surname, don't you?'

'I don't know nuffin' 'bout no kids. There was something on the pub TV, like, but I wasn't really watching.'

'I want you to tell me exactly what you spoke about with your father the last time you visited the prison.'

'I've not seen him, I—'

'If you're not going to tell me, I want to know exactly what you were doing yesterday. We're looking into motives for the kidnapping of two children and you're one of the only people with a reason.'

'What motive, I—'

'Police officer puts your dad away, then twenty-five

years later, a couple of weeks after he dies, you take revenge. He stole your childhood, how about you steal theirs? What did you do, follow their mother around for a few weeks, find out her routine, then strike?'

'No, I—'

'Then you're going to have to get talking. Where were you yesterday between three and four?'

Jake squirmed in his seat, the scratching becoming worse until flakes of skin were peeling from the top of his hand. 'In the pub, there were people there.'

'You know we'll check. Are you absolutely sure they'll know you? What if they're not certain? What if you were in a back booth somewhere and no one remembers? What if they're off sick today and we can't get hold of them?'

'I was there!'

'You were also at the prison a few weeks ago, weren't you?'

'No, I've not been there in years.'

Jessica took a deep breath, trying to stay on top of her frustration. 'Okay, fine, when you saw him three or four years ago, what did you talk about?'

Scratch, scratch, scratch. Jessica couldn't let this go on for too much longer. She often felt more nervous when there was no solicitor present. You could push things further, make it appear as if you knew more than you did, but there was always a danger you'd get caught up and forget where the line was. There was still a tape, still a video camera recording, still accountability.

'He'd been trying to get in contact since I turned eighteen. I ignored him for years but somehow he always managed to know where I was. I'd get a letter asking if he could have my phone number, wanting me to visit. Sometimes it'd come to wherever I was living but I used to work in this factory and I got one there.'

It was as coherent a sentence as he'd uttered.

'What did you do?'

'Eventually, I thought I'd go just to say I wasn't interested.'

'What did he say?'

Jake stopped scratching the back of his hand and began rubbing his eyes with his thumbs. 'Can you get a drink around here?'

'I can do you tea, coffee or water – possibly some fizzy Vimto, depending on what's in the constables' fridge, but I can't promise anything.'

Jake was sucking on his teeth. 'Nuffin' else?'

'Not the type of thing you're after.'

'Shite.'

Jessica got up anyway and opened the interview-room door, grabbing the first person to walk past and asking him to bring water. When he returned, Jake drank down three cups back to back and looked a lot better for it, his eyes having a focus to them that they didn't before.

Jessica sat opposite him, waiting, using the silence.

'Dad wasn't what I thought,' Jake said quietly. 'When he was sent to prison, I was only eight or nine and had been living with my mum. I wasn't really aware of everything but there were photographers in our garden. I remember her taking me to school and there were people everywhere, pushing and trying to take our pictures. She sat me down and said that my dad had done a bad thing but I didn't really understand. After that, there were kids at school saying my dad was a murderer and wanting to start fights. They ended up teaching me by myself. I only really remember it as a dream, like I was watching somebody else. One day my mum walked me into a police station and told the man she couldn't cope with looking after me any longer. She said goodbye and I never saw her again.'

He was still sweating but sounded like a different person, pronouncing the words more clearly, looking her in the eye, telling the truth.

'You said your dad wasn't what you thought . . .'

'When I was a bit older, I read about what he'd done, then you always get the anniversary things – ten years since the Slasher, fifteen years, it never ends. I changed my name because everyone knew and I couldn't escape it. I'd been ignoring him and then I was twenty-two, twenty-three, and thought I'd get it over with. I had this vision of some big killer who'd murdered all those people, made my mum leave and ruined my life. He wasn't like that at all, though. He was some little guy; no muscles, only a bit taller than me.'

'What did you talk about?'

'Back then? Nothing really – he wanted to know how I was doing: if I had a job, girlfriend. I had to make things up so I didn't sound so . . .'

He didn't have to finish the sentence.

Jessica left the silence for a moment, then said: 'Didn't you talk about him at all?'

'Not then . . .'

'How often did you visit?'

'Two or three times a year. I was never doing much so didn't have anything to say and he was inside, obviously. We'd talk about TV programmes – or whatever was in the news. He'd want to talk about books but they're not my thing.'

Jessica reached into a cardboard wallet on the table and took out a sheet of paper, then slid it across towards Jake. It was a photocopy of the visiting book from the prison, with the date from a few weeks before, Jake's name and signature. 'We've got the digital record too,' Jessica added. 'We could probably go back and get the CCTV from the prison with a bit of time.'

Jake glanced at the sheet, resigned. He sighed: 'Dad was dying – there's this hospital area where prisoners go for things like that. He could have applied for compassionate leave, or whatever they call it, but didn't think it'd be safe on the outside.'

'What did you talk about?'

Jake shook his head. 'I can't say.'

'Was it about the Hambleton kids?'

Jake shook his head rapidly from side to side but didn't answer. He was scratching the back of his hand again, skin flaking like a dried-out Danish.

'Tell me what he said, Jake.'

'It's private.'

'Did he tell you about any sympathetic friends or cell-mates?'

'No.'

'So what did he say?'

Jake stared down at the table, shaking and picking at the loose skin on his hand. 'Nothing.'

'Stop lying to me.'

'I'm not.'

'You lied when you told me you hadn't visited and you're lying now. What did he say?'

'I don't know anything.'

Jessica stood, her chair squeaking across the hard floor with an ear-piercing screech. Jake was sweating more than before, head in his hands, the backs of both his hands red and raw. He was lying and didn't seem too bothered that she knew.

She kept her voice as calm as she could. 'Jake, we arrested you for suspicion of copyright offences. In the interview you've admitted to lying to us about an unrelated matter regarding the last time you saw your father. Two children are missing, both of whom can be linked back to your dad. You were one of the last people to speak to him, so can you see how that's going to look if you keep refusing to say what you spoke about?'

'He didn't say anything.'

'You're going to be put in front of a court for conspiracy. Your name will be in the paper, everyone will know who your father was. They're going to start looking at who you were working with when those kids were taken. Even if you get off, think how that's going to look.'

'I haven't done anything.'

'By refusing to tell me what you talked about, that's enough. Withholding information, lying to the police, it doesn't look good, does it?'

Jake looked up from the table, tears in his eyes. 'You're going to do it again, aren't you?'

'Do what?'

Jake sniffed violently, eyes rolling into his head. Still the tears came. 'All the times I visited him, we never talked about the Slasher. I didn't ask and he never spoke about it.'

The atmosphere in the room suddenly felt heavy, harder to breathe. 'It was different when he was on his death bed though, wasn't it?'

Jake nodded slowly. 'He said he had to tell me what happened while he still had the chance. He talked about Inspector Hambleton.'

'Did he mention the children?'

A shake of the head.

'What did he say?'

'He told me what happened back then.'

'With the women?'

A nod. Jessica wasn't sure she wanted to hear the rest. Niall's description of the Slasher killings had been enough: the bleach, the rapes as they were bleeding to death, dumping the bodies in a bin as if they were worth nothing. She breathed in through her nose, trying not to show she was nervous. Jake noticed, peering up to stare at her through tear-stained eyes. For the first time, she felt grateful for her glasses. A shield from the rest of the room.

'He told me to be careful with everything and never trust the police. He was right, wasn't he?'

'Right about what?'

'He knew you'd try something – because of what you did to him.'

Jessica was confused, thinking she was going to get a rundown of the Slasher's crimes, or information about the missing children. 'I don't know what you mean.'

Jake stared up towards the camera in the top corner of the room, taking a breath and speaking clearly. When the reply came, it felt like someone had opened a freezer in the room, bitter air searing through Jessica's clothes. 'He told me how your inspector fitted him up.'

29

Jessica listened to everything Jake had to say but it felt like he was interrogating her and she barely had a reply. In the corridor, she asked the uniformed officer to wait outside the interview room, assuring Jake she'd be with him soon but that she had someone to talk to first.

The station was buzzing with activity, full of officers in on their days off to help with the search. Footsteps, voices, phones ringing, noise, noise, noise. Tired eyes, loose ties, unwashed hair. Jessica had spent many years working in and around this place in various roles: she'd seen people come and go, enjoyed wonderful highs and the worst of lows. Through all of that, the station had felt like a second home, sometimes a first home. Now, it felt different: darker, harsher. Perhaps it had always been like this, she simply hadn't seen it. A detective who couldn't see what was under her nose.

Jessica went into reception where Pat was hanging up the phone. 'Bloody thing's not stopped ringing all day. How are we supposed to get any work done when the—'

'There are two kids missing. What do you think's going to happen?'

Pat reeled backwards, the blubber in his face wobbling. 'I'm just saying—'

'Do you know where Niall is?'

'Aye, he came in about half-hour ago – went straight upstairs.'

'Thanks.'

He began moaning about being overworked and under-appreciated but Jessica ignored him, heading up the stairs. There was a hum from the temporary incident room at the far end of the corridor but Jessica didn't get that far. Sitting by himself in DCI Cole's office was Niall, wearing a thick woollen granddad jumper, looking every inch the gentle retiree.

Jessica opened the door to Cole's office and slipped inside, closing it behind her with a quiet click. Niall glanced up, eyes sullen, skin grey. 'How are things going?' he asked.

'Not good.'

He obviously assumed Jessica was talking about the search because his head sunk onto his chest. When he spoke, there was no authority to his voice. 'Those kids are all I've bloody got. Brendan's such a good lad and he struck gold with Rebecca.'

'Do you have any idea what might have happened?'

Niall ran a hand through his hair and looked up again. 'I was with them all through last night – hardly any of us slept. It's all they kept talking about: was there someone they'd fallen out with, something in their past? We went over and over. I was half-expecting a ransom demand but nothing came. Too much time has passed now . . .'

'I asked if *you* knew what happened.'

'Me?'

'Do you remember when we went to the pub? We were

talking about my promotion and you told me to trust myself but know where the lines are. I was wondering if you knew.'

Niall shook his head slowly but his expression was hard to read. 'When we were in the car and you found out the children were missing, you said the word: "Slasher".'

'Did I? I don't remember . . .'

'Everything moved really quickly yesterday but it stuck in my mind – not even that you'd said it but the way you said it. Like you knew something.'

'Rawlinson's dead.'

'I know, I've been speaking to his son. He visited his father in prison a couple of weeks before his death and has a very distressing story to tell. It almost ties in with the message painted on your son's wall . . .'

Jessica wanted one thing to happen – for Niall to look her in the eye and say he didn't know what she was talking about. All it would take was a slight shift in his vision and she'd trust herself to know that he was telling the truth. One second passed. Then another. And another. Niall's gaze didn't move from the floor.

She watched his chest rise and fall: a man ageing in front of her. His reply was more a breath than a statement. 'It was a different time . . .'

Oh, fuck.

He breathed in deeply, finding his voice. 'Is this why they've been taken?'

'I don't know.'

Jessica didn't have a better reply and suddenly Hambleton wouldn't stop. 'You don't know what it was like; there was so much pressure – it was everywhere you looked. You'd come to the station and you'd see it in everyone's face. At the supermarket, filling up the car with petrol, the workers, the members of the public, you'd see how frightened they were, people not wanting to look each other in the eye. It was in every paper, on every news broadcast, day after day after day.'

Jessica had wanted the truth but now, more than anything, she wanted him to stop. Now she was back to asking questions she didn't want to know the answers to.

'What happened?'

'Do you know who's got Zac and Poppy?'

'No – but it's like anything else; the more background we have, the more we have to look into.'

Niall sighed loudly, defeated. He must have known something like this could happen. 'It was like I told you; I'd followed Rawlinson from the cleaning company to his house with the big drum of that blue cleaning fluid in his car. It was a complete fluke that I saw him but I did a bit of digging and he fitted the profile perfectly. He was a divorced male, right age, knowledge of the area – he was what we were looking for. Then we got a warrant for the house and it was all there too. We found women's clothes that weren't his ex-wife's, stacks of pornography – really hardcore stuff, violent movies – and the bleach too. He said the women's clothes were his wife's, then changed his story to say he'd stolen them from washing lines over successive years. He reckoned he'd taken the cleaning solution by mistake, then said he was actually stealing it to sell to a rival company. Every time you'd catch him on something, he'd change his story to something slightly different.'

'What did you do?'

'It wasn't just me!'

And with that, any degree of sympathy Jessica had for former Detective Superintendent Niall Hambleton evaporated. There were plenty of things she'd done that she wasn't proud of but she'd always take responsibility for them if and when the time came.

'Who?' she whispered.

'Thorpe. He was convinced – we all wanted it over with. We *really* thought it was him.'

Jessica had forgotten that both Hambleton and the then DCI Thorpe got promotions following the arrest. 'What did you do?'

'He had no alibi because he lived alone but everything else was circumstantial. He'd lied so often but it was only about little things – stealing, perving.'

'You knew it wouldn't be enough.'

Niall put his hands on his knees, pressing back into the seat and closing his eyes. 'He kept saying over and over it wasn't him. We thought he was goading us because we couldn't find the knife. We had the reports of the type of weapon used, so knew what we were looking for. One day Thorpe turned up with exactly what we were after. It was like a butcher's knife but made from a single piece of stainless steel. I thought it was *the* weapon but he said he'd found it at a hardware store in the city. I didn't understand at first but we both knew Rawlinson was guilty and he said it was the icing on the cake to make sure he didn't get off.'

He opened his eyes, searching for Jessica's, pleading, wanting her to understand, but she couldn't bring herself to look at him.

'We went out to the house and buried it in the garden. Later, the full excavation was ordered and it was found. There were no fingerprints though, so it was still touch and go. Thorpe said we needed a confession . . .'

Niall's Adam's apple began to bob but he just about held himself together. Jessica didn't want to hear the details and he didn't offer anything.

When he spoke again, his voice was a whisper. 'What about the kids?'

Jessica ignored him. 'What happened to the actual Slasher?'

Another sigh. 'There were no more killings and I suppose I convinced myself over the years that it was him after all. There was always the circumstantial stuff and I assumed he was just a tough bastard who wouldn't give it up. Rawlinson denied it throughout the trial but that's what they do, isn't it? Afterwards, Thorpe never mentioned it again.'

'Didn't it occur to you that there were no more murders because you'd given the guy a free pass? He either went to ground, or learned from his mistakes and became smarter. Perhaps the profile was correct and after breaking up with his wife, they got back together? Or he found someone else? Maybe he's been killing women quietly for years but thought of a better way to get rid of the bodies?'

Niall shrugged sullenly. It was so dismissive that Jessica had to ball her fists, digging her nails into her palms to try to control her anger. She knew what she had to do next and being angry couldn't be a part of it.

She kept her tone calm: 'In the pub, you told me things aren't all black and white and that there are shades of grey – but there are no shades in this. You planted evidence and beat a confession out of someone just because you were under pressure. I'm going to fetch DCI Cole, we're going to get the super on the phone – and you can tell them exactly what you've told me. Then we're going to investigate everyone who's got a grudge against you. Once that's done, we're going to find your grandkids. Whoever has them left you a message to confess – and whatever happens to them is on your head.'

30

DCI Cole leant back into his office chair, rubbing the bridge of his nose. Jessica didn't know how he would take things but he'd been like the officer she used to know. No snap judgements, no emotions – he simply acted. Niall had repeated everything he'd told her and more.

So much detail.

It was no wonder Colin Rawlinson had confessed – it was either that or leave the cells in a bag. Throughout, Niall insisted that he hadn't done anything else wrong in his career. It was a one-off, a lack of judgement while under pressure from a senior officer. If the abduction of his grandchildren was related then it could only be something to do with Rawlinson wanting revenge from beyond the grave.

Cole had the superintendent and chief constable on conference call and they'd done all they could. A team of sergeants and constables had been put together to find out everything possible on Rawlinson. Were there any other family members? Sympathetic cellmates? They'd not been given the reason but they would know soon enough.

While that was going on, the most senior members of Greater Manchester Police were in crisis mode. Thankfully it went far above either Jessica or Cole but she could guess what would be happening – either another conference call or tea and biscuits at headquarters. Point one on the agenda: how fucked are we? Point two: how can we make sure none of the blame comes back to us?

Cole looked across his desk to Jessica. After hours of recriminations, it was down to just them. 'Are you okay?' he asked.

Usually, it was the question Jessica hated the most. It was such a woolly nothingness – an endless roundabout of meaningless words that people constantly asked each other. You've just lost a leg in a horrific accident and people want to know if you're all right. Your whole family's gone in a house fire, are you okay? On and on.

This time, she was grateful, even if she didn't have a proper answer. 'It's been a long morning.'

A knowing smile. 'How was Jake?'

'All right, actually. It was no wonder he didn't want to speak about visiting his dad in prison. He was already wary of us and then I brought him in on some spurious movie-copying shite and reinforced everything his dad had told him.'

'You weren't to know.'

It was little consolation.

'I told him about Niall and the missing kids. He really doesn't know anything about the kidnap. He wanted to know about having his dad's name cleared and I said there was likely to be some sort of investigation—'

'More like a full-on inquiry. Front-page headlines, top of the news, bells, whistles. Things are going to change.'

'Quite. Either way, I gave him a lift home and let him have all my phone numbers. He seemed satisfied enough for now. If it was me, I don't think I'd have been as calm as he was. He was still asking if we were going to push charges for the copied discs. I told him we'd let it slide but even that felt wrong – we've got more pirated discs floating around here than he had.'

Cole offered a slight shrug. 'If you'd not got him in here, he'd have never told you about DSI Hambleton. If it leads to the exoneration of an innocent man, charges against a corrupt officer and we find those kids, then you'll have done all right. Better than all right.'

Jessica looked him in the eyes. 'Do you think that's what Niall thought? Does the end justify the means?'

'You can't compare what he did to you bringing Jake in. There are shades of grey in everything.'

There it was again – the same thing Niall had said. The problem was knowing where that line had to be drawn. Jessica wondered if she knew.

'What's going to happen to Niall?'

'He's gone back to the son's house for now while everyone decides what to do with him. You wonder what Brendan's going to think when he finds out the reason his kids are missing is probably down to his dad. Niall's going to lose everything and then he's probably going to go to prison. We need to find the kids first.'

It was still less of a punishment than Colin Rawlinson had been given.

'Louise, Izzy and Dave are all on it but did you think . . .'

'. . . that the Slasher is still on the loose all these years later? We can't run a full reinvestigation of that as well. It'll come.'

'What if whoever was the Slasher took the children?'

'If that's true then we'll have to find it out through our regular investigation into getting the kids back. We have no reason to think that might be the case and no resources to go through all of the old Slasher information. Plus, why would they?'

A knock on the glass behind her saved Jessica from admitting she didn't know. Izzy was waved into the office but Jessica was already on her feet, reading the constable's face. They had a lead on Hambleton's grandchildren.

31

The trip up the M61 to Westhoughton had been the usual mix of blinking red brake lights, frozen verges and fellow motorists panicking when they saw the flashing blue lights in their wing mirrors. And people said Jessica was a bad driver.

Local police had already visited William Overton's house and confirmed there were no signs of life. Jessica was in the back of the pool car with a uniformed PC, another PC was driving and Cole was in the passenger seat. Jessica read through everything they had on Overton. Now in his late sixties, he'd spent large parts of the last thirty-five years in prisons around the country for all manner of offences ranging from defrauding pensioners to battering someone with an axe handle in a pub car park.

He was someone for whom the law was clearly an inconvenience – but what really interested them was the six years he'd spent as Colin Rawlinson's cellmate after being caught trying to drive through the Queensway Tunnel on Merseyside with two kilos of cocaine in his boot.

He'd been released three months earlier on licence but had missed an appointment with probation the previous day and wasn't answering his phone. In the only recent photo they had of him, he was sporting the same grey-black stubble as the kidnapper. It was hardly conclusive but, sometimes, two plus two equalled four. Actually, it always equalled four.

Daylight was just about clinging on as they arrived in a street flanked by long red-bricked terraces. Parked cars were on both sides of the road, funnelling all through traffic into a single line down the centre. Local police had sealed off both ends, with curious residents watching from their doors as officers massed around Overton's end-of-terrace house.

Jessica could feel the pressure from the small army of camera-phone-carrying residents across the road. A handful of officers were trying to make everyone move along, assuring them the half-dozen police cars, collection of suited CID officers and almost two dozen uniformed officers gathering at the end of a usually quiet residential street was 'nothing to see'.

One of the local PCs approached Cole and Jessica, telling them he'd spoken to Overton's next-door neighbour and the residents across the road. All of them had the same story: they'd not seen him in days. He then introduced them to a worried-looking middle-aged man brandishing a large set of keys. Overton's landlord apparently owned around a third of the street and had turned up when he'd heard about the commotion on local radio. 'You don't have to smash the door in,' he insisted as three officers with a battering ram and large boots returned to their van looking disappointed.

There was nothing quite like the sound of boot through door on a fresh-feeling evening to set the pulse racing.

Warrant in place, keys in hand, camera phones filming, honestly there's nothing to see here: 'Go, go, go'.

The uniformed officers went in first, clumping around and making as much noise as possible. 'Clear', 'clear', 'clear'. Time for the boring bit.

The inside of Overton's house was as unimpressive as the outside: the vague smell of damp with matching black splotches above the door, a broken light bulb in the hallway, peeling brown wallpaper and the general sense that nothing had changed in twenty years. If they'd smashed through the door, it might have done the land-lord a favour seeing as they'd have had to replace it and a bit of creativity on his part could have led to a claim for a new carpet as well.

In the kitchen, there was a sinkful of browned coffee cups and an open box of breakfast cereal on the counter. So far, so slovenly.

The living room presumably was already furnished because the rank brown sofas came complete with cigarette burns in the arm and a table decorated with coffee-cup rings that made it look like an out of control Olympics logo. In the corner, a scrunched-up newspaper was sticking out of a mesh bin. Without taking it out, Jessica could already see part of the headline: 'DEATH OF A MONSTER'. It was what had been on the front page of the *Herald* on the day Colin Rawlinson died. The photo of the Stretford Slasher from his arrest a quarter of a century ago stared out at Jessica from the paper; eyes blank. Before, they'd been the eyes of a multiple killer, now they were the gaze of a man spending his life in prison for something he didn't do.

Jessica pointed out the paper to one of the officers to be taken for evidence, before turning her attention to the rest of the room. Not that there was much to see. Two overflowing ashtrays and a small stack of bills were the highlights. From the red-topped notices, it didn't look as if Overton had paid for anything since moving in.

Upstairs and it was a similar story of mould, damp and a vague smell of cigarettes. The first bedroom was empty of anything except a single bed and bare floorboards. The room next to it had more items crammed in than the rest of the house put together. An unmade bed was pushed against the far wall with an empty soft wardrobe at the far end. There was a bedside cabinet next to that and a large computer desk wedged underneath a windowsill. Jessica sat on the bed and opened the cabinet's top drawer with her gloved hand. Inside were piles of letters and receipts which she emptied onto the bed.

Some were on browning, crusty paper with faded dark handwriting. From the dates at the top, he must have received them when he'd been inside. The top one appeared to be from a pen pal and included a host of banal details, followed by some sloppily written, if graphically creative, erotic ideas.

Jessica flicked through the stack, thinking she'd leave it to someone else to check properly before she noticed what the receipts were for. She turned to Cole. 'When you read Overton's file, do you remember if he had kids?'

Cole had his back to her, hunting through the drawer under the bed. 'I don't think so.'

'I don't remember reading about children either. So why

do you think he has receipts for kids' clothing? Two coats, two jumpers – bought a week ago.'

Cole took them from her and skimmed the contents. The items had been paid for in cash. Opposite her, one of the PCs took a laptop out of the drawer underneath the computer table. He looked up to Cole, asking what to do with it.

'Bag it,' came the reply.

'What else is in there?' Jessica asked. The officer held up a handful of discs and a small black plastic square. 'Is that a memory card?'

'Yes.'

Jessica turned to Cole. 'Think the lab will mind if we have a look before them?'

'Probably.'

Back downstairs, Cole climbed into the patrol car's driver's seat, Jessica in the passenger's. Each force vehicle had a built-in spot for a laptop between the front seats, which had received particular attention a few years ago when someone at the *Herald* put in a Freedom of Information Act request to reveal that Greater Manchester Police had had over twenty stolen from their own vehicles in one year. 'Nicked-Book' was their rather weak pun on 'Netbook' but the ensuing three days of coverage had made everyone look more incompetent than usual.

Cole booted the machine, as officers continued to remove items from the house and put them in the back of a van. After logging in, Cole had used up all of his computer expertise and turned to Jessica. Using the USB adaptor borrowed from Overton's computer desk, Jessica inserted the memory card, clicked into the DCIM directory, and began going through the images one at a time. The first dozen appeared to be tests – uninspiring photos of the street they were on and of the empty back yard. There were a couple of others from a local park of someone walking a dog and then the one that made Cole sit up so quickly that his head cracked into the roof of the car.

They had been at Brendan and Rebecca Hambleton's house only twenty-four hours ago and its tidy front was unmistakeable. Each click showed another photo: more of the property itself and then of school railings and a playground. Everything was there: Rebecca's car, Rebecca herself, Brendan, Zac, Poppy – photo after photo each with a neat date and time digitally stamped into the corner.

The simple message was spelled out pixel by pixel: William Overton had been stalking the Hambletons for the entire week leading up to the children's disappearance.

32

Two days later and the missing Hambleton children felt like a solved case that hadn't been solved. William Overton had withdrawn £250 from cashpoints on four successive days leading up to the kidnap. Now they knew who they were looking for, they'd traced CCTV of him close to the school two days before the children were taken – and two of Brendan and Rebecca's neighbours now remembered seeing him hanging around suspiciously. So far, so good – except that they couldn't find him.

Over three decades of being in and out of prison meant there were hundreds of potential associates to check out, plus two dozen places he'd lived on the outside – and they were just the ones they'd found. In their patched history of his life, there were long periods in which they had no idea where he'd lived and who his friends were. His photo had been all over the media but the decision had been made – for now – not to release Niall Hambleton's admissions. The official reason was that the inevitable media storm would detract attention from the missing children; the unofficial one was that everyone who knew was bricking it over what might happen. Because of that, the news broadcasts had been full of 'nasty man kidnaps grandkids of officer who arrested former cellmate' stories. They weren't wrong but when the truth came out, Jessica didn't want to be standing anywhere near the proverbial fan.

Jessica stood in line outside Heaton Park wearing wellington boots, thick socks, jeans and a heavy coat over a jumper – traditional get-up for a British music festival. With only a couple more days left in May, the weather had taken a marginal turn for the better; frosty mornings and freezing afternoons replaced by the relentless grey wash of cloud that defined the city. The one-day ParkFest music event had been billed as a 'party in the park' by the local council but 'cower from the elements in the park' would have been a more accurate slogan. Although it had remained dry all morning, it felt like rain was in the air – although that too could be a motto for the city. Jessica could practically picture it now on the signs leading into the centre:

WELCOME TO THE CITY OF MANCHESTER

Twinned with Los Angeles, Faisalabad, Wuhan, Cordoba, St Petersburg, Rehovot, Kanpur, Chemnitz.

There's rain in the air

Cole had ordered her to take the Saturday off, which meant Jessica had no excuse to wriggle out of having to go. Humphrey – who was inexplicably wearing a bright pink blazer – had made it after all, with Georgia clinging onto his arm as if it was an extension of her own. Considering they'd only seen each other for a few snatched hours during the week, Jessica was finding it relaxing to be around Adam again, even if her mind kept wandering back to Niall, the missing Hambleton children and Tony – of whom she'd seen nothing since he escaped from her down the alley. Sylvia Farnsworth had called Jessica the previous evening to ask if there were any updates on her son and Jessica had to tell her the truth, that she'd been sidetracked. The slow pause followed by a clearly disappointed, 'Oh, okay, I understand', only made her feel worse.

Heaton Park was one of the biggest public parks in Europe and the process of cordoning off the entire area west of the boating lake looked as if it had taken some time. Large metal barriers stretched around the entrance closest to the tram station, with queues of people in long parallel lines winding along Bury Old Road. The gates were supposed to have opened ten minutes ago but the usual levels of organisation were in place with ripples of 'why are we waiting' sounding along the line. Figures weaved in and out of the line offering to buy and sell tickets, seemingly oblivious to the fact that the only reason anyone would stand in lines like this was if they already had a ticket.

'Humphrey!'

Georgia's boyfriend jumped as a man's voice shouted from somewhere behind them.

'Someone you know?' Georgia was tugging on Humphrey's arm as he pushed himself up on tiptoes to peer over the top of the crowd.

'I don't know, I can't see anyone.'

Jessica tried to look too but she was too short to see over people.

'Humphrey!'

The man's voice sounded closer this time but still no

one approached and Georgia's boyfriend insisted he couldn't see anyone he knew.

'Two Humphreys in the same queue,' Adam said, which was a statement that could surely only be true in Britain.

Finally a cheer went up from near the front and the line began to move. Shuffle, shuffle, shuffle.

As they finally reached the entrance and had their tickets scanned with a barcode reader, Jessica saw a familiar face. Esther was wearing a headset, watching the queue of people closely until she spotted her friend. As she waved Jessica over, a grin spread across her face. 'Hello, stranger.'

'Haven't you been sacked yet?'

Esther winked. 'Cheeky bitch – you're the one who hasn't found the attacker yet.'

Jessica gave Adam a peck on the cheek, pointing towards a Ferris wheel at the far end of a row of stalls, and saying she'd meet him, Georgia and Humphrey there in fifteen minutes. He gave her the same raised-eyebrow knowing look he always did when she ditched him for work before heading off into the crowd.

'Who's that guy?' Esther asked, nodding towards the retreating trio.

'Adam? He's my boyfriend-fiancé-husband, depending on who we're talking to.'

'Not him, the human flamingo.'

Jessica laughed. 'Adam's sister's boyfriend. Christ knows where he thought he was going in that thing. He was wearing a bright green one the last time I saw him but no one else said anything, so I thought it was just me who found it odd.' Jessica tugged on the blue waterproof jacket

Esther was wearing. 'Nice anorak, by the way. Have you got the matching thermos and train-spotting binoculars?'

Esther started to reply but her hand shot to her ear. 'No, of course they can't bring it in.' Pause. 'Why? Because it's a giant blow-up giraffe.' Frown. 'I don't care if the sign fails to say "No inflatable safari animals", they're still not bringing it in. Let the air out and leave it at the security hut. They can get it on the way out.' Sigh. 'No, of course I'm not going to look after the bloody thing.'

Out of the corner of her eye, Jessica could see a plastic yellow giraffe's head bobbing along over the top of the fence. Esther was shaking her head. 'I hate this job. I gave them my notice last week. Every time I'm out doing something, it's like I'm babysitting the work experience kids.'

'What are you going to do next?'

'I'm not sure, I've put in for a couple of things. I'd rather do nothing than do this.'

Through the main gate a man walked in carrying an inflatable giraffe that must have been twelve feet tall. He glanced both ways and then strolled past a security guard as if they weren't there.

'Oh for f—'

'I'll go if you want,' Jessica said.

'Forget it, let him keep the bloody thing. At first my bosses were saying they wanted everyone to pass through a metal detector on their way in and to have their bags checked. When I pointed out the length of time it would take to do that for twenty thousand people, they said we'd just do random searches on the way in. After last time, I keep all the emails. No one can make a decision and if anyone's going to get it in the neck, it's not going to be me.'

'Rule number one: cover your own arse.'

'Exactly – anyway, I've been hearing rumours . . .'

'What rumours?'

'Hambleton.'

Jessica puffed out a sigh. 'The GMP's got more leaks in it than the *Titanic*. How we've kept it out of the press, I'll never know. What have you heard?'

'DSI Hambleton fitted up Rawlinson as the Slasher and now Rawlinson's old cellmate has kidnapped his grandkids.'

'We are so totally, unbelievably screwed. When the media find out the reason Overton went after the children, everything's going to kick off like you've never seen before.'

'Any leads?'

'All sorts of sightings but you know what it's like when you get someone's picture on the news – for every thousand phone calls, you're lucky if you get one with anything useful. For everyone's sake I hope they're still alive. I'd rather be working but the DCI's banned me from the building on my day off and we had tickets for this. I've barely seen Adam all week.'

'You look tired.'

'Don't you start.'

Esther nodded over Jessica's shoulder towards the giraffe disappearing into the distance. 'Is the Slasher case going to be reopened?'

'Only after we get the kids back.'

'What if—?'

'Don't even think it. You can't just make two children disappear. Overton will be hiding out somewhere and will pop up at some point. His face is everywhere – someone's got to spot him.'

'What about the person who threw acid at Luke Callaghan?'

'Are you listing everything we've not solved?'

Esther laughed. 'I'm looking for work – if I can get you sacked, that leaves a place open.'

'It's gone ridiculously quiet. We've all been distracted by the kids and so have the media. Perhaps if we leave it long enough, it'll go away. It's just so odd – three unconnected shites. The dodgy councillor's blind, the shifty landlord's recovering after a beating and our resident Lothario's hopefully keeping it in his pants.'

Esther was keeping a watchful eye on the gates as someone entered carrying an inflated giant banana. There was probably some sort of Internet competition over who could get the most ridiculous item into the arena. 'This is what bothered me at the time. If the attacker wanted to hurt Callaghan, they could've done anything in those few seconds – stuck a knife in his guts, sidled up behind and slit his throat, stabbed him in the kidneys. It's not as if it would have been the first time. If anything, slotting in behind someone in a crowd, doing that, then running, would get you less attention and you'd be away quicker. The acid attack was surely harder to pull off – definitely more reckless.'

'We've gone through it all, especially because of the

choice of victims. It's always felt like our hoody was trying to humiliate rather than murder. Usually, attacks would escalate in their seriousness but this went the other way – he started by blinding someone and ended by injecting a guy with something harmless and giving him a scare. It doesn't fit any pattern of anything we've ever had.'

Esther glanced back to the gates, perhaps regretting that there wasn't a metal detector after all. Jessica watched as a complete mix of people continued to enter. There were middle-aged couples holding hands, often completely unprepared for the mounds of mud they were walking into, as well as the ones who were clearly looking to rekindle the festivals from their youth with brand-new wellies and light, floaty hippy clothing. If the weather turned, it'd be like someone spilling water over a watercolour, with pastel shades running everywhere. There were teenagers attending their first festival, skipping happily into the arena alongside Goth kids acting like they weren't interested, even though they'd gone to the expense and effort of getting tickets. Perhaps the strangest group was the twenty- and thirty-something couples with prams. Jessica saw a mother shoving her wheeled monstrosity over a muddy hump and then stopping to berate one of the security guards, presumably for not making a sodden public park friendly enough for pushchairs. That was one end of the age scale but then there were handfuls of older people too, some with the stereotypical array of heavy clothing and blankets but others walking with a spring in their step and wry grins, as if they'd gatecrashed some-where they weren't entirely convinced they should be.

Blacks, Asians and whites mixed, laughed, danced and sang their way into the arena. If nothing else, ParkFest had brought the community together in a way few gatherings in British cities could.

Even if it was just so they could complain about the weather.

Esther and Jessica continued to watch the crowds mill past. So many faces, but neither of the pair Jessica was looking for. Tony had disappeared off into the Manchester night and she hadn't seen him since; William Overton could be anywhere.

Jessica checked the time on her phone. 'I should get going.'

Esther's hand was to her ear again and she half-turned around. 'Well, what do you think you should do with it? We're hardly going to roll it up and smoke it between us, are we? Nick him.' She turned to Jessica. 'Sorry.'

Jessica gave her a cheery wave and headed off into the crowds. The atmosphere felt like a party; weeks of frozen ground and unseasonal snow flurries replaced by a return to normality. It was probably a bit much to expect the sun to come out for the occasion but it was still an improvement. The smell of various festival foods drifted on the air, mixing to create a heady if slightly toxic blend of popcorn, candy floss, beef burgers, chips and beer.

The ground was already becoming squishy from the sheer weight of people. Off to the side, a teenage girl was abandoning an ill-chosen pair of canvas trainers into the hedge and beginning to slop bare-footed through the thicker parts of mud towards her cheering friends.

Oh to be young and stupid again – or at least be able to blame stupid decisions on the naivety of being young.

When Jessica snapped out of her envious haze, she turned to head towards the Ferris wheel, bumping into something solid. She started to apologise before stumbling backwards in surprise. Staring directly at her was someone in a dark blue hoody and white mask with a red letter A for anarchy etched onto the front.

33

Jessica was so surprised that she took another step backwards, tripping over her foot and landing with a splat in the mud. The person in the hoody reached up and pulled the mask down, exposing the face of a sheepish teenager, even younger than the bare-footed girl. He could only have been fifteen at the most, thin-faced, wide-eyed. 'Sorry, er, lady,' he said, offering his hand to help her up.

Jessica's eyes were drawn to a stall between the popcorn stand and a place selling gourmet boar burgers. Across the front were rows of hats and masks – including a large pile of the anarchy ones. As Jessica felt the sodden and sodding mud seeping through her clothes, she tried to think if there was something she could arrest him for.

Assaulting a police officer? No, he hadn't touched her and it would be quite harsh.

Disrespecting his elders? Definitely a possibility, if only it was a criminal offence.

Being a bit too young? Probably should be an offence, especially as she was rapidly getting older. Kids these days.

Wearing a stupid mask? Bollocks, that wasn't an offence either.

Jessica took his hand and allowed him to help her up, making sure her filthy hands got as much of the mud as possible on his sleeve.

In fairness, not that Jessica was feeling particularly charitable, he did seem genuinely apologetic. 'Sorry, I didn't mean to scare you.'

'It's fine.'

Jessica marched past him towards the hat and mask stall. The seller was wearing a soft jester-style hat, with alternating fluorescent colours and bells hanging from the pointed parts. 'What can I do for you, love?' he asked, full local twang in evidence.

Jessica pointed to the stack of anarchy masks. 'Why are you selling these?'

His grin slipped slightly. 'What's it to you?'

'You do realise these are associated with someone who's been carrying out very serious public attacks?'

The seller picked up one of the masks, holding it in front of his face. 'Just a bit of fun, innit? You from the council or summit?'

'Police.'

'There ain't nuffin' wrong with sellin' a few masks, is there? I've got all the receipts, paid all the tax. What is it with you lot pickin' on the honest man, eh? Got three points for doing thirty-five in a thirty the other week. Why don't you catch some real crooks?'

Jessica tried to think of something either witty or withering to fire back but she had nothing. He wasn't doing anything wrong – living in a free country allowed people to sell whatever shite they wanted, no matter how tacky and distasteful. She glanced up at the sign above the stall and made some vague threat about checking his paperwork when she got back to the station. She had no intention of doing so but his incredulous jibe that he had 'nuffin' to hide, darlin',' didn't improve her mood.

It wasn't a long walk to the Ferris wheel but Jessica could now see masks and hoods everywhere. The entire place was a nightmare from a security and policing point of view.

Adam was chatting to his sister, a large smile on his face which morphed into confusion when he saw Jessica. 'What happened to you?'

Jessica spun to show him. 'Slipped in the mud.'

'Your whole backside is covered in it.'

'Thanks – I hadn't noticed the fact my clothes are stuck to me, nor the people pointing and laughing.'

Adam wasn't pointing but he was clearly trying to stop himself from joining those who found it hilarious. Georgia was still clinging onto Humphrey, her bright hair covered by a blue bonnet that matched her wellies. Humphrey was doing the odd thing with his watch again – eyes flicking down to it, then back up in a flash as if it hadn't happened. Georgia said they were going for a wander and set off into the crowds, Humphrey's pink blazer making him look like a giant stick of candy floss.

'What does he look like?' Jessica said to Adam as they watched them go.

'At least he's not covered in mud.'

Jessica scraped some mud from the back of her jeans and then wiped it on Adam's nose as he leant in to give her a peck. 'That'll teach you for laughing.'

They spent the rest of the afternoon exploring the different corners of the field. Teenagers sprinted past at various points determined to get to the front, while families had reserved their part of England by arranging blankets on the ground far away from the main stage and then scowled at anyone who walked a little too close. Jessica wasn't too fussed about any of the bands but followed Adam wherever he wanted to go. They rode the Ferris wheel, ate a crocodile burger – which tasted suspiciously like chicken, walked, chatted and laughed. As they sat on the stools underneath an area roped off for food stalls, they watched strangers from afar, making up stories about the types of wild secret lives they were leading. As the afternoon went on, their made-up biographies got more and more outlandish until Jessica's ribs were hurting from laughter. It was like the old days of when they first got together.

Adam worked at the university, mainly doing scientific research but also with limited teaching. As they strolled towards the main stage, he was spotted by one of his former students, a lad with skinny jeans and too much chest hair who clearly fancied himself. He told Adam he'd got himself a job with a lab somewhere around Lytham and then asked Jessica if she had any other 'fit mates who fancied science geeks'. She sent him packing by saying that if he knew any fit science geeks then he should get in contact and she'd see what she could do. He gave her a wink anyway before scurrying back to his friends. Adam laughed it off and for the first time in a long while, they felt like a proper couple again. They were actually out – together – not stuck at work, not sharing a house with Georgia, not struggling to deal with the death and trauma which had defined their lives over the past couple of years.

As it became late afternoon, the grey swirling clouds began to lift, revealing hints of blue that gradually took control of the rest of the sky. A cheer went up from the crowd as gentle hints of sunlight crept over the tops of the trees, offering natural warmth the city hadn't enjoyed since their week of summer the previous year. Jessica took off her jacket, putting it on the ground not far from the Ferris wheel so they could rest their tired legs. Adam put an arm around her and she rested her head on his shoulder. Jessica tried to remember the feelings from the restaurant, the hate that went hand in hand with the love, but it wasn't there. Everything going on at work would still be there tomorrow but for now, for today, this was the happiest she'd been in a long time.

Modern music was still shite though. This was the city of the Stone Roses, Oasis, the Chemical Brothers, the Smiths, New Order, the Charlatans. Now, the best they could come up with was some fresh-faced tit straight from Saturday-night singing competitions.

On the other side of Adam, Georgia was standing with Humphrey, eating ice cream from a tub. Her hat had gone into her bag, as had her jacket, and her bare fake-tanned shoulders looked a golden brown in the sun. Humphrey was still persisting with his pink blazer, which looked marginally less stupid with the sun out.

'Had a good day?' Georgia asked.

'Better than I thought,' Jessica replied with a weary grin. It was nice not to spend a day sat in a car or behind a desk.

'We've been in the folk tent most of the afternoon. It's the only music Humphrey knows.' Georgia dug him in the ribs with her elbow and they both grinned, like a long-married couple. 'Do you want to meet back at the house, or are we leaving together?'

Adam shrugged Jessica off his shoulder so they could see each other. Jessica said she didn't mind, so they arranged to make their own way home. With twenty thousand people pouring onto trams and buses, it was probably easier anyway.

Humphrey peered down at Jessica and Adam, a knowing half-grin on his face. 'You look good together.'

It might have come from a man who looked like an oversized marshmallow but it felt nice nonetheless. It was the type of thing people used to say. 'Thanks,' Jessica said. 'You should have seen the state of him when we first met – like a reject from a failed rock band. All long hair, black T-shirts and tight trousers.'

'What's changed?' Georgia asked.

'His hair's a bit shorter and his trousers aren't as tight.' Jessica squeezed Adam's upper arm. 'He's finally putting a bit of weight on too. I reckon he's around eight per cent less runtish.'

Adam's fingers slipped underneath Jessica's top and began tickling a little above her waist, making her shriek so loudly that a couple walking nearby spun around, probably wondering if someone was being attacked.

Georgia had finished her ice cream and retaken Humphrey's arm with a grin. 'It's nice to see you both happy.'

They said their goodbyes and, as they walked away slowly arm-in-arm, Jessica wondered if she had misjudged Humphrey. She was naturally suspicious of pretty much everyone but although he had his quirks, he didn't seem like a bad person. Georgia was happy with him too, which was surely the important thing. Her life had changed dramatically since she and Adam had found each other. They'd gone from being only children to having someone else who understood the other's upbringing. Georgia had moved from the other end of the country, starting a new job, making new friends.

Jessica leant her head back on Adam's shoulder, listening to the music drifting across the field. The crowd in front of the main stage had their hands and inflatables in the air, singing along to the choruses. She twisted so she could see Georgia and Humphrey walking towards the food area. The crowds had thinned where they were at the back, with everyone massing towards the front now it was nearly time for the headliners. The mix of the lack of sleep, being on her feet all day, food, and human contact left Jessica with a wonderful feeling of tiredness. She wrapped her arm around Adam's waist and snuggled onto his shoulder. He responded, pulling her tighter as she closed her eyes and let her mind wander. It wasn't Toxic Tony, egg-headed Scott Dewhurst, their unknown hoody or any of his victims that she thought of. It wasn't even Niall Hambleton, the Stretford Slasher, his son, or the kidnapper, William Overton. For once, she let her mind drift, thinking only of herself and Adam. She really did love him, didn't she? This proved it. On the days when she got time away from work, where she didn't have to stay late or start early, where she wasn't drowning in paperwork or sitting in traffic jams, this was what it felt like to be normal.

At first she thought the scream was something in her subconscious battling to get out; a leftover demon from everything she had seen and heard over the past few years. Then Adam's shoulder jolted upwards and there was a second scream.

Jessica's eyes opened into a flash of colour. The bright pink figure of Humphrey was on his back, legs flailing in the mud fifty or sixty metres away. Georgia's vivid blue bag was on its side on the ground, contents spilling out, her flash of blonde hair practically glowing in the sunlight. She was screaming but unmoving as a figure in a dark hoody and anarchy mask leant over Humphrey, spraying something into his face.

34

Jessica tried to leap to her feet but the ground was wet and skiddy and she only succeeded in collapsing sideways onto Adam, her elbow landing in a rather sensitive area. As he gulped in pain, Jessica finally managed to get a footing. Ahead, a few people stood confused as the hooded figure dashed towards the main stage. Humphrey was rolling on the ground, hands clawing at his eyes as Georgia continued to scream. Jessica had little time to choose, so headed after the hoody, slipping and slaloming her way around people swaying in time to the music.

The crowd was thickening the deeper Jessica got into the park and the figure disappeared through a slim gap between two people still wearing coats. They turned in surprise but he was already past them, thinner than Jessica remembered from the photographs they had of the daylight attacker. He wasn't particularly quick, but was more than nimble enough to slide through gaps she would never have got through without wiping out bystanders. As she almost barrelled into a small child clutching a hotdog, Jessica stopped, peering towards the space where she'd seen the man enter the tighter mass of people. Jessica edged closer, trying to get a better view, but most of the revellers were wearing dark clothes. Almost everyone seemed to have their arms in the air and it was like the inflatables were breeding: dolphins, mallets, more bananas – even that bloody giraffe was being waved in the air by someone in the middle.

Jessica pushed herself into the same gap the hoody had gone through, getting an 'oi' for her efforts. She tried to peer over the heads but everyone was packed so tightly, she could barely move, let alone see over the hands.

She backed out, treading on someone's toe and getting a swearier rebuke this time, and then began pacing along the back of the crowd. A handful of individuals were breaking away, heading towards the rear of the field where it was less compacted. The hoody had gone straight for the crowd, not for the gates. Whoever it was had thought it through – if he'd tried to exit, the security staff would have been ready, but by hiding in plain sight, he'd already disappeared. If he ditched or hid the mask, he'd blend in with no problems. There was no way the police or security would be able to stop everyone wearing dark clothing on their way out of the arena. With the headline act next on, the main crowd was at the biggest it had been all day. All he had to do was bide his time and then leave when everyone else did.

Jessica made one more attempt to stand on tiptoes and peer towards the area in which the hoody had gone but even from the one spot, there were at least a dozen people with dark hoods up. Their one might have even put his down, or ditched the outfit entirely.

As she made her way back to Humphrey, Jessica could see a small crowd had gathered around him – almost everyone on their phones. Jessica was less worried about shoving people aside this time, telling them she was police and that if they didn't put their phones away then she'd confiscate them for evidence purposes. Faced with that prospect, people began drifting away.

Humphrey was sitting up, Georgia on her knees behind him supporting his back. He was still rubbing his eyes but they were already red and puffy. Adam was looking a little queasy from having been elbowed but he was standing behind Georgia, trying to calm her down. Jessica threw him her mobile phone, telling him to call Esther. She took a bottle of water that had rolled out of Georgia's bag and crouched in front of them.

'Humphrey, this is Jessica, can you hear me all right?'

He mumbled a yes.

'You've got to stop rubbing your eyes, okay? I'm pretty sure it's some sort of pepper spray and the more you touch them, the worse it's going to get.'

His reply was more of a grunt than anything else. 'It's burning.'

'It's going to burn worse if you keep rubbing. You've got to put your hands down.'

Slowly he did what he was told but the damage was already done. Police guidelines said they were supposed to be at least a metre away from anyone they used the spray on but the hooded figure had sprayed it into Humphrey's eyes from only a few centimetres away. The entire top half of his face had swelled and turned a mix of red and purple, making him look like a misshapen beetroot.

Jessica put on her best bad-news voice. 'Okay, Humphrey, listen to me. Water is not going to do your eyes any good.

I'm going to use a very small amount to try to clear the area at the top of your cheeks and around your eyebrows. After that, all you can do is give it time to clear. When you blink, your eyes will produce tears and that will help somewhat but there's no instant cure for what's happened.'

Taking a tissue from Georgia's bag, Jessica gently dabbed it around the areas she'd mentioned and then took her phone from Adam. Before using it, she turned to Georgia. 'Don't let him touch his face. Sit on his hands if you have to.'

Jessica could see two security guards in their black uniforms making their way across the field – it had only taken them five minutes to realise something had happened – but Jessica told Esther exactly where they were, gave her a description of the attacker, and told her to send one of the standby ambulances across.

With that done, Jessica shooed a few more phone-wielders away before turning back to Georgia. 'What happened?'

Adam's sister was in shock, stumbling over her reply. 'I'm not sure, he came out of nowhere.'

'Did you get a look at anything other than the mask?'

'No.'

'What did he do?'

'Someone tapped Humphrey on the shoulder. He's been getting attention all day because of the jacket and I assumed it was someone saying hello or whatever. It all happened in an instant – Humphrey turned and then the guy just sprayed this stuff in his face.'

There were a few red blotches on Georgia's neck from

where the spray had narrowly – and luckily – missed her face. The biggest problem with pepper spray was that it went everywhere. Officers only used it as a last resort because they were as likely to have it bounce back into their own faces as they were to hit the target. Ask a paramedic how many police officers' eyes they had cleaned out and it would almost certainly outnumber the amount of criminals'. The anarchy mask was not only something to hide behind, it stopped the assailant from harming himself.

'It was definitely a guy?'

Georgia bit her bottom lip, thinking. 'I suppose.'

'How do you know?'

'He spoke.'

'What did he say?'

'It didn't make any sense.'

'Perhaps not to you but it could do to us.'

Georgia was shaking, both hands grasping onto Humphrey's wrist as he tried to reach for his face. The two security guards were now standing over them, listening to the conversation and being no use at all.

'Georgia.'

'Huh?'

'One of you has to tell me what he said before he ran off. It could be important.'

Humphrey was groaning and still battling to touch his face. Adam had taken hold of one arm, with Georgia clasping the other. Her gaze was blank, so Jessica reached out and twisted the woman's face gently until they were staring at each other.

'Georgia.'

'What?'

'What did he say?'

'He said, "Be nice to your wife", and then he started spraying. I don't really remember anything after that.'

'Did he have a local accent?'

'I'm not sure.'

'What about the voice – was it deep? High-pitched?'

'I don't know – it was just normal.'

Jessica glanced up to see the flashing blue lights of the ambulance. Even though its siren wasn't blaring, it was attracting attention and she could sense the crowd building behind her again.

'Right, and when he said, "Be nice to your wife", did he look at you?'

'How do you mean?'

Jessica squatted slightly so she was at the same height as Georgia. 'Did he look at you, point at you or in any way indicate that it was you he was talking about?'

'I . . . I don't know.'

'You've been around the field all day today. Was there a time where you were playing around and it could have looked like you were fighting? Like Adam and I do some-times if I give him a shove or he nudges me – something like that?'

'No.'

'Have you argued at all today?'

Georgia shook her head. 'No, it's been really nice up until now.'

The ambulance had come to a halt next to them, attracting even more of a crowd.

Jessica had time for one more question. 'Is there anything else about his voice you'd remember?'

Humphrey replied this time. 'He sounded croaky, like he had a cold or something.'

With that, Jessica got back to her feet, allowing the paramedics to take over. Esther had got out of the back of the ambulance and Jessica waved her to the side.

'How is he?' Esther asked.

'He'll be fine – it was pepper spray but from very close range. Same guy as before, I think – hoody, anarchy mask, similar build.'

Esther nodded to where someone else was walking by in one of the masks. 'They're everywhere. There's no way we'll be able to stop everyone leaving. Some of the ones with younger children are already going home. He could easily ditch the clothes too. We've got cameras covering the gates, so might be able to check everyone in and out at a later date – but it'll probably give you a few hundred possible suspects.'

Jessica paused to watch the paramedics help Humphrey into the back of the ambulance along with Georgia. Behind them a huge cheer went up as the band on the main stage started a new song. Adam was waiting nearby, hunched over slightly.

Esther nodded in his direction. 'What's wrong with him?'

'I accidentally elbowed him in the balls.'

'"Accidentally"?'

'I wasn't aiming.' Jessica was about to explain when her phone began vibrating in her pocket. She expected it to be someone at the station who had heard what had happened but when she hung up, she could do nothing but stare blankly at Esther.

'What?'

'William Overton just walked into the BBC building in Salford, saying he'd give us the location of Zac and Poppy Hambleton if they interview him on the news.'

35

Jessica watched the news on television that evening, not that she could escape it. The BBC had shared their William Overton interview among the other news organisations and it was running on a loop on television and radio.

Cole had already filled Jessica in on the details before she'd got home. As soon as Overton had identified himself in the reception area of the BBC, a have-a-go-hero security guard had leapt into action, vaulting the desk, eyes lighting up at the prospect of the citizen's arrest to end them all. Unfortunately for him, Overton had far more idea what he was doing and pulled a tyre iron out of his pocket, slapping the man across the temple. As the guard lay in a pool of his own blood, Overton had calmly told the second person on reception to open the main door and take him to the news floor.

Being a Saturday, anyone who was anybody naturally had the day off so protocol went out of the window. Sitting with the tyre iron in his lap, Overton had done a piece to camera explaining why he'd kidnapped the children. He gave chapter and verse on Niall Hambleton and the way he'd fixed Colin Rawlinson up as the Stretford Slasher. One of the production crew had called 999 while that was going on.

The interview hadn't been broadcast live but Overton

refused to answer any questions in custody until he'd seen the footage appear on television. Stuck between the devil and the Mariana Trench, the chief constable had caved, telling the BBC to run it.

An hour later and the children were safe, Overton was chatting merrily away in an interview room, Niall Hambleton was under arrest and everyone even remotely associated with Greater Manchester Police was utterly screwed.

Georgia had called from the hospital to say that she was planning on staying with Humphrey overnight, leaving Jessica curled up next to Adam on the sofa under a blanket wearing only her underwear. Adam had an arm draped around her, sleeping off the effects of an elbow in the balls. Jessica flicked between the news stations watching the interview repeated over and over.

Overton explained how he'd become best friends with Colin Rawlinson in prison. 'Everyone thinks he's a monster but he's a normal guy.' Overton held out his hands, showing off the tattered remains of his own appearance. He looked every inch of his sixty-eight years, although his experience clearly made up for a lack of physical strength given the ruthless way he had dealt with the security guard and the level of planning he'd used to snatch the two children.

For anyone watching at home, he was an old man, wearing ripped tracksuit bottoms and an old Manchester United football shirt, unshaven with that pepper-coloured stubble and short grey-white hair. He sounded perfectly sincere when he spoke and even Jessica thought he was probably telling the truth.

'Look at me, I've wasted my life – I know I'll die in prison but I've had my time anyway. This isn't about me. This is about a guy who had his life snatched away from him.'

He'd obviously planned what to say because he was so calm that even as a list of his crimes skimmed along the bottom of the screen, any right-thinking person would have been left with the opinion that he couldn't be that bad, even with the tyre iron on his lap.

'Colin told me all about Hambleton and Thorpe. They threw him down the stairs, smashed his knuckles with a hammer, gouged him in the eyes – saying that if he didn't confess to being the Slasher then they'd make sure he never left the cells. What would you do?'

The camera switched back to the surprised presenter who hadn't expected the question. He was young, wearing a suit a size too big for him, hair hastily gelled, out of his depth without an autocue to read. 'Well, I suppose—'

It was exactly the hesitation that Overton needed. 'Exactly – so he confessed and said he did it. They'd planted a knife in his garden and because of his job with the cleaning company and the fact he lived alone, he looked guilty. Any jury would have sent him down, no one can blame them for that. Colin didn't – he knew how guilty he looked, it's why he never appealed. He'd been fixed up good and proper.'

The presenter finally took a degree of control. 'Mr Overton, you've bullied your way into our studios and made some very serious allegations and yet you're the one with the weapon – you've even admitted to kidnapping two children.'

Overton bowed his head in a piece of perfect theatre. He'd picked up all sorts of tricks while inside. Some people got by through size and intimidation, others through being smart and learning. There was no doubt of the type of prisoner Overton was.

'All I can do is apologise. As soon as this footage is shown on TV, I'll happily tell anyone where those little wee kids are. This was never about them – it's about justice for a friend.' He reached forwards, passing the tyre iron to the presenter, who clasped it between his thumb and forefinger as if he'd found a flower pot full of used condoms. 'This isn't about harming anyone, it's about getting Colin's story out there.'

The presenter handed the iron to someone off-camera and winced. 'Even with that, there are some who will say that as soon as Colin Rawlinson was arrested, the Slasher killings stopped. Have you considered that he pulled the wool over your eyes too?'

Overton ran a hand over the top of his head, smiling sadly. 'Of course it did. When you spend six years sharing a cell with someone, you get to know everything about them. I knew he was telling the truth – and that's before the real Slasher got brought in.'

Even the presenter gasped at the moment that screwed everybody. Overton named the person he claimed was the actual Slasher. Years after the Slasher killings, the man had been convicted of murdering a divorcee after meeting her on the Internet. While in prison, he had openly admitted to being the Slasher, even laughing in Colin's face that the wrong man had gone down for it. He had died almost two years previously of lung cancer, so there was no way to prove or dispute it, but Overton reckoned there would be at least half-a-dozen other surviving prisoners who had heard the details.

It sounded plausible, not only giving Niall his comeuppance but making the later investigating team who arrested the *actual* Slasher seem incompetent for not pinning any other crimes on him.

As Overton finished, the presenter turned to the camera, announcing that the police were there. The cameras continued to roll as Overton lay on the floor putting his hands behind his back. With the police knowing they were being filmed, it was the gentlest arrest Jessica had ever seen. Overton had planned it to such perfection, knowing that if he'd waited to be found and a firearms squad had become involved, all it would have taken was someone particularly trigger-happy and it would have all been over.

The recorded interview cut back to the studio where the live newsreader could barely contain her excitement, telling viewers that in the past five minutes it had been confirmed that the children were safe and unharmed. Apparently, Overton had kept them in an abandoned flat in which he had lived twenty years ago. Already an official inquiry had been launched, with some bloke seconded from the Met to investigate what had happened in GMP twenty-five years ago. Having some London numpty mooching around asking questions was only going to put everyone's backs up even further.

And to think, a few hours ago, Jessica had been huddled under Adam's arm thinking it was the best time she'd had in as long as she could remember. Now she was lying in an almost identical position on their sofa with another victim of their hoody attacker in hospital, no suspect, and the shit-storm to end them all brewing at her workplace.

Jessica was jolted awake by Georgia letting herself into the house at twenty past two in the morning. She was still curled up with Adam on the sofa but the twist of key in lock got them both moving. Georgia's eyes were red from where she'd been crying but apart from saying that Humphrey was being kept in overnight and that he seemed to be fine, she didn't want to talk about much else. Adam went up the stairs with her, making sure she was all right, as Jessica checked the news once more, wondering if anyone had resigned yet. The only update was a text message from DCI Cole:

'If you're not on the rota, DON'T come in tomorrow. That's an ORDER.'

Jessica wasn't scheduled to be in and if ever she was going to obey an instruction, this was it.

Upstairs and Adam was waiting for her in bed, his bare thin chest as inviting a pillow as any. 'How's Georgia?' Jessica asked.

'She won't talk about it. Perhaps you were right about Humphrey after all?'

Jessica closed her eyes without replying. Sometimes it was nice to be wrong.

*

Jessica hated hospitals. They made her think of fires, dead constables and misfiring shotguns. So many lines on the floor, signs that sent you in circles and that endless smell of cleanliness. She weaved her way through the corridors following a nurse who was asking about what everyone had seen on the news last night and in the morning. 'Is it true the Slasher wasn't the actual Slasher? . . . Awful, isn't it, if some guy spent all that time in prison? . . . What do you reckon's going to happen now? . . . Did you see the picture of that cop who fixed him up in the papers this morning? He looks just like my granddad. . . . Good job those kiddies are back, isn't it?'

A succession of ums, ers, and 'I'm not sure's was the best Jessica could offer but even on a Sunday people were only talking about one thing. They walked up two flights of stairs and kept going until they were at the back of the hospital. Jessica didn't ask but assumed Humphrey must have medical insurance considering he had a small private room to himself. The nurse left them alone and Jessica took a seat next to Humphrey, who was propped up in bed listening to someone with a cheesy voice play love songs on Radio Two.

As if he hadn't been through enough.

His face was almost unrecognisable, the skin on his cheeks and forehead red and scrubbed raw. It was true what she'd told him that water would only make it worse but a constant stream of cleansing solution was one of the few things that would eventually help to clean it away. His nose had bulged to three times its regular size and the skin of his hands was peppered by so many red blobs that it looked like an extreme form of eczema. His eyes were covered by two thin circles of cotton wool.

'Humphrey, it's Jessica. How are you feeling?'

'I told Georgia that I didn't want to see anyone.'

'So she said but someone from the police has to interview you, so we thought it'd be best if it was someone you knew.'

That wasn't true at all – Jessica had simply called the station and said she was already at the hospital with her sister-in-law so she'd do it. Considering the satellite vans parked outside the station's gates broadcasting live, she doubted anyone would notice.

'I don't have anything to say.'

Jessica gently took his hand, careful not to touch the sore areas. 'Who are you married to?'

'What?'

'Let's not go around in circles – you can either tell me or I'll go away and find out anyway. One way takes longer and pisses me off. It's not been the best half-day or so and I'd really like – for once – to do things the easy way.'

Humphrey sighed. 'Are you going to tell Georgia?'

'We're speaking as investigating officer and victim of an attack, so no, I'm not going to tell her anything. That doesn't mean that you shouldn't.'

It was strange talking to someone whose eyes she couldn't look into but when Humphrey replied, he told the truth anyway. 'She's called Beverley.'

'And what's your real last name? I'm assuming Caton is the one you told Georgia and not the actual one.'

'It's Marsh.'

'I'm going to need your address and details and am going to have to speak to her.'

'Why?'

'Because you've been attacked and we need to talk to anyone who might have information.'

'You don't think she'd got anything to do with this?'

'I don't think anything. All I'm saying is that there will be people we need to speak to – starting with your wife.'

Another sigh, which might have been because of Jessica's request, but also coincided with another dedication being made on the radio: 'This is going out to Claudia in Bromsgrove, whose husband Graham says that he loves her very much . . .' Blah, blah, blah. Graham was definitely having an affair. Probably Claudia too, not that Jessica blamed her – if someone had phoned up to dedicate a Barry Manilow song to her, she'd be having second thoughts too.

Humphrey gave Jessica a name and address, asking if she'd tell Beverley for him that he was fine and would be home later. Jessica said she would, not asking the obvious question about why she hadn't been notified already. Sometimes you didn't want to get involved in more personal business than you had to.

'What about Georgia?' Jessica asked.

'I'll tell her this afternoon.' Not a complete coward then, only a partial one. He must have sensed Jessica's disapproval, because he followed it up with: 'It's not what you think.'

'What do I think?'

'We've been going through the motions in the marriage

for a long time. We've been married for over thirty years. At first we stayed together for the kids, then it became more about the house and maintaining a quality of life. If you split up, you end up having to divide everything and neither of us wants that.'

'Does your wife know you're having an affair?'

'Not exactly . . .'

'So, "no", then?'

'She doesn't say anything when I spend nights away from home – it's why she won't be worried today. I've always thought she probably just assumes.'

The bedrock of any relationship: an assumption that your partner is having an affair.

'Your attacker escaped through the crowds. We've got lots of footage of people entering and exiting the festival which we'll get through as and when we can but, for now, we don't have any actual suspects. The obvious question is if you know anyone who might have a grudge against you . . . with the obvious exception of your wife.'

'Who says she has a grudge?'

'That's what I'm going to find out. Is there anyone else? Have you had previous extra-marital relationships, for instance – perhaps with other married people where there might be an angry husband?'

Humphrey reached up and removed the cotton wool from his eyes. He blinked rapidly, reaching for a small bottle of solution that was on the table next to the bed and squirting some drops into his eyes. It was clearly a method to get out of answering the question but Jessica waited anyway. His eyes were bloodshot and unfocused.

Eventually he took a mouthful of water and replied. 'There have been a few but everything ended on solid terms. Usually I would break up with them and we'd move on. If any of them had husbands then I didn't know anything about it.'

'I'm still going to need the names.'

'They're on my email at work. I signed up for this dating site – that's where I met Georgia. At first it would just be a quiet drink or a meal to see if we got on. Every now and then it would turn into more. Georgia said she was moving to the area and wanted to get to know a few people. We hit it off straight away. I'll be able to get you the names of the other women – but not until tomorrow when my office opens again.'

'I also need to know who you told that you were going to the festival yesterday.'

'No one – only you, Georgia and Adam knew.'

'That can't be true.'

'Why?'

'Because if this was a targeted attack – which we have to assume it is given what the attacker said to you – then how else would they have known where you were?'

36

Humphrey continued to insist that no one else knew he was going to the festival, making the point that, although he assumed his wife knew about his affairs, he wasn't going to go out of his way to make sure she or anyone else knew for sure. It was a speck of truth in an ocean of dishonesty.

Jessica contacted DS Cornish at the station, asking if she could begin looking into linking Humphrey to Luke Callaghan, Alan Hume and Victor Todd. If she could do that without letting DCI Cole know Jessica had asked, that would be even better.

When she saw the house that belonged to Humphrey and Beverley Marsh, Jessica could at least understand why he said he was concerned about having to split the property if they divorced. It was a beautiful detached home at the back of a modern estate, complete with its own stables and four-berth garage. From the size, it must have had at least six bedrooms and who knew what else. Having to sell it and then move into two separate smaller houses would have been a comedown.

Beverley was more or less what Jessica expected: late-fifties, her looks gone and she knew it. Some women made the best of what they had; some didn't care and had no reason to. Others had once been pretty and couldn't cope with the fact they weren't any longer, caking on the make-up and bathing in perfume in an effort to maintain what they'd once had. Beverley fell firmly into the final category – dressed as if she was set for a posh night out, rather than a day around the house.

When Jessica introduced herself, Beverley seemed ready for the worst – with a husband who stopped out so regularly, she'd probably been waiting for bad news for years. Jessica told her that Humphrey had been attacked with pepper spray from very close range but that he should be released in the late afternoon or early evening. His wife didn't exactly seem disappointed but there was no pleasure there either – she simply wasn't bothered. Some partners would have been in their cars and roaring their way to hospital but Beverley nodded an acceptance, inviting Jessica in and offering her a cup of tea.

They sat on either side of a breakfast bar in an immaculate bright white kitchen sipping their drinks as if neither of them had a care in the world, with a small yappy dog snapping around Jessica's feet.

'Don't mind Terrance,' Beverley said.

Jessica scowled down at the ball of hair and then back up at Beverley. 'You weren't down as his next of kin.'

The woman shrugged. 'I'm not that surprised – we're not really in each other's lives other than sharing a roof. We've got separate bedrooms, bathrooms, cars. I'll still cook every now and then but that's it.'

'The person who attacked your husband gave him a message just before he sprayed the liquid. He said: "Be nice to your wife".'

Beverley put her mug down so quickly that tea lapped over the top onto the counter. '*Really?*'

'Really. Which leaves me with an obvious question—'

'I wasn't even around – I was at work.'

Yap, yap, yap went Terrance in agreement.

'I'll take the details to verify that but you're getting ahead of me. What I was going to ask was if there's anyone you know who might want to stand up for you – friends, family, that sort of thing.'

Beverley picked up a dishcloth and started mopping away the tea as Terrance did his best to help by running in and out of her legs. 'Did Humphrey tell you about his "indiscretions"?'

'He told me a few things.'

'He's had other women on the go for years. I suppose it's partly my fault for knowing but not saying anything. Have you been asking any of his other women?'

'We'll get to that but the attacker very specifically said, "Be nice to your wife", which is why I'm here first.'

Beverley dropped the cloth into the sink and returned to her mug, eyes fixed on the counter. 'I don't really talk to people about things like this. Who can you tell that you know your husband's having affairs? I don't even mind that much – I just wish he'd talked to me about it, plus he's never as clever with it all as he thinks. Whenever he's wearing new clothes, I know it's because he's off out to meet one of his women.'

'Isn't there anyone you talk to about things?'

'Only Paula and a couple of the girls at work – we both complain about our husbands; the usual stuff.'

As Terrance continued to add his opinion with a series of high-pitched barks, Jessica took the details of Beverley's workplace. It was already Sunday afternoon and she was going to struggle to get much sense out of anyone at this time of day. The chances of getting any officers to help would be zero too – especially as she was supposed to be taking a day off. Jessica pocketed the slip of paper, thinking she'd deal with it on Monday.

Beverley let Jessica out, saying she'd be around for the rest of the day if there were any other questions. Her parting words were perhaps the most biting: 'I know this might all seem strange to a young person like yourself but it comes to us all in the end.'

On that happy piece of advice, Jessica decided she'd finally make the visit she'd been putting off for weeks. Her mother's retirement home was just outside Heywood, halfway between Bury and Rochdale, north of Manchester city centre. It was barely ten miles from her house and compared to the ninety-mile journey she used to take to her parents' place in Cumbria, Jessica really didn't have much of an excuse for not going. Her family had no historical connection to the area and she suspected her mother had chosen the place because she liked the name of the home as opposed to any other reason.

Meadowside Retirement Home gave the impression that it was on the edge of sprawling fields stretching far into the distance with patches of pretty summer flowers constantly in bloom. The truth was that it was probably once quite impressive. The first time Jessica had seen it, she'd been glad Adam was with her because the outside made it look like another large stately home. He'd gripped her hand and told her it was fine and then she'd been all right as soon as she'd gone inside. The smell was difficult to describe; definitely cleaning products but also a large dose of *old*. Jessica couldn't think of a better way to put it. It was probably a mix of the faded flowery carpets and dusty chandeliers. What was good to see was the interaction between the staff and residents. After years of horrendous undercover stories on the news with workers in places like this taking advantage of the elderly patients, here you could sense the friendly atmosphere as soon as you entered.

As Jessica walked into Meadowside, two of the older gentlemen appeared to be racing from one end of the entranceway to the other in wheelchairs, egged on by a twenty-something worker in a white smock and three other residents sitting in armchairs waving their walking sticks in the air. Jessica stood watching as one of the men crossed a line at the far end, where one carpet met another, and raised his arm in victory. The other one instantly accused him of making a false start and they went back and forth, bickering with enormous smiles on their faces as if they were schoolchildren again. When Jessica thought of retirement homes, this wasn't exactly what she pictured.

A woman wearing the same white smock as the younger man sidled up to Jessica and introduced herself as the duty manager. 'Can I help you?'

'I'm here to visit my mother.' Jessica started to give details and then stopped herself, nodding towards the men. 'Were they racing?'

The woman smiled. 'That's Walter and Brian – they're always trying to outdo each other at something, so it wouldn't surprise me. It doesn't matter what we have on – bowls on the lawn, tiddlywinks in the canteen, bingo or quiz night – it always comes down to those two trying to beat each other.'

Jessica watched as the man in the smock got in between the two arguing men, getting poked in the thigh for his troubles as they continued arguing over who was the rightful winner. After taking her mother's name, the duty manager led Jessica up a staircase and along a brightly lit hallway to the room. She knocked, got the 'come in' and then left Jessica to it.

Lydia Daniel kept her room as immaculate as she used to keep the family home. The bed was tidily made with perfect corners, her cosmetics were arranged in straight lines beside the basin and there was a neat pile of clothes on the dresser. She was sitting in a rocking chair by a curved window that looked out over the front of the house, watching television. As Jessica entered, her mum began to stand but Jessica quickly moved across the room to stop her, kneeling and giving her mother a hug before sitting on the floor under the window.

'You'll hurt your back sitting on the floor,' Jessica's mother scolded.

'I've been sitting on floors since I was a kid and I'm fine.'

'Then why did you wince when you sat?'

She had her there. Always one step ahead, even now. Perhaps that was why Jessica's back hurt a lot.

'Fine.'

Jessica climbed up and carried a wooden chair across from next to the dresser and sat by her mum. On the television was a quiz show where the contestants were getting incredibly excited every time they got a question correct. Her mum's eyes flickered towards her and then back to the screen. Although there was still a spark there, physically she was a shadow of the person Jessica remembered when growing up. Then, she'd walked everywhere and carried huge bags of mail at their post office. She refused to let her husband do anything for her that she could do herself and in many ways was the strong woman that Jessica had herself hoped to be. Now, little brown blotches ran the entire length of her arms, which were like sticks. Her eyes had shrunk because of the sagginess of her skin and her hair was so thin and spindly that it was like the wire wool that sat under the sink unused in Jessica's house. The past eighteen months had hit Jessica hard but it'd had an effect on her mother too.

Jessica fixed her eyes on the screen; it was one of the other reasons she hated visiting – it was so hard to see the person who had brought her up in a state like this. She knew that made her a horrible person but it didn't mean she could push back those feelings.

Her mum nodded towards the television. 'Reykjavik.'

On the screen, the man answered 'Helsinki' as his final answer.

'It's Reykjavik, you idiot.'

The presenter informed the disappointed contestant

that the capital of Iceland was indeed Reykjavik, not Helsinki, and that he'd just lost sixteen thousand pounds.

'Buffoon,' Jessica's mother said.

'How are you, Mum?'

Lydia's eyes didn't leave the screen. 'Oh, now you want to visit me, do you? I've been trying to call you for weeks.'

'I've been busy. It's been on the news all the time – first the guy in the mask attacking people, then the missing kids. I've hardly stopped.'

Her mum wasn't buying it. 'So you never get a day off? I'm only up the road. Adam finds time to call me and say hello.'

Of course he bloody does.

'Okay, Mum, can we agree that I'm a bad daughter and have a conversation about how we're both doing before it's time for me to go again?'

'Brian Jones.'

'Sorry?'

Jessica's mother nodded at the screen. 'Founding member of the Rolling Stones. This idiot thinks it's Bill Wyman.'

'I thought Bill Wyman founded the Rolling Stones.'

Lydia peered at her daughter with a didn't-I-teach-you-anything? look. Sure enough, the answer was Brian Jones.

'Can I turn the telly off, Mum? I can't stay all evening and we're never going to have time to talk about anything.'

'I like having it on.'

'Can I at least turn the sound off?'

'Fine.' Jessica stood to pick up the remote control,

leaning across to the windowsill. When she sat, her mother was watching her disapprovingly again. 'What?'

'You're getting very thin. Are you eating properly?'

'I'm eating fine, Mum. I'm just busy.'

'All right, no need to snap.'

Jessica took a breath. She *wasn't* snapping but she bloody well would be if this carried on for much longer. Every time they had a conversation where Adam wasn't present, this is what it ended up like. Adam was the calmest of all influences. Quite how he'd been so awkward around girls when she'd first met him, Jessica had no idea, considering how he always seemingly knew the right thing to say.

'How have you been?' Jessica asked, calmly.

'Not too bad – I've taken up cross-stitching.' Her mum pointed towards a canvas on the bed with a partially completed fabric house. Jessica crossed the room and picked it up, unsurprised by how perfect and neat it was. 'I was watching a documentary the other week.'

Oh God, not this again.

'It was about women who couldn't have babies – some new treatment thing they've been working on.'

Please stop.

'They had this woman on whose doctor said she couldn't have a baby. There was this operation and then she was on these tablets and it happened within a month. They kept saying it was a miracle.'

Jessica continued staring at the cross-stitch frame. This was precisely why she didn't come.

'They say it's going to be available for wider testing this year. I wrote down the name of it.'

'I saw that too,' Jessica lied. 'I called our doctor the day afterwards but he says we've got different conditions, so it would never work on me.'

She might be a terrible liar sometimes, but she was terrific at others.

Her mother had been trying to get out of the rocking chair again but pushed herself back, disappointed. Jessica had no doubt this was why she'd spent the last fortnight trying to get in contact.

'Have you and Adam still been . . .'

Jessica cringed, thinking her mother was actually going to say the word but she thankfully stopped herself.

'Everything's fine, Mum. We're relaxed about things. The doctor says there's no chance of me getting pregnant but if it ever happens, then it happens. I promise, if there's ever any change, I'll call you first.'

'All right, no need to snap, I was only trying to help.'

Grr.

Jessica sat on the bed, listening to her mum give her the lowdown on everyone who lived around the home. There seemed to be two classes of people – the 'idiots', of which Walter and Brian were full members, and those her mum called 'lovely'. With no apparent middle ground, Jessica's mother's mind was made up about everyone.

A few tactical 'uh-huh's were enough to make it seem as if Jessica was listening, when really she had completed a couple of stitches on her mother's house which didn't look *too* dissimilar to the others. She was half-watching the muted television thinking that if the object of the show was to know absolutely nothing, then this contestant was going to win a fortune.

'What do you think of that?'

Jessica jolted back into the room. 'Yeah, really interesting.'

'That's what I thought. I mean Irene's always going on about what a saint her son is but the grandchild could be anyone's. What does that tell you?'

Jessica was halfway through a non-committal 'I know', before she stopped herself. 'Sorry, what did you say?'

'I was saying that you hear all sorts around here. Irene walks around like butter wouldn't melt but then Joyce told me all about her son's little secret. I mean, you've got to think of the kids in all this, haven't you? If he knows his wife's been going around doing all sorts, then you've got to be a brave type to raise someone else's child.'

'I . . . yeah.'

Jessica reached into her pocket and took out the piece of paper with Beverley Marsh's name and workplace on it, reading the words over and over until she'd convinced herself. She spent ten minutes saying goodbye as her mum piled on the guilt about finally coming over and then not staying for very long. Jessica eventually got out of the front door and called Izzy, asking the constable if she fancied meeting her at the station for a bit of Sunday-night digging.

37

Three minutes past two in the ridiculously early hours of Monday morning and they had it. There was no shame in missing the link from Luke Callaghan to Alan Hume to Victor Todd to Humphrey Marsh. All shits, all cheaters, all with one thing in common: they were normal. In the end, it had taken Jessica's gossiping mother to make her see it.

'You hear all sorts around here.'

Unsurprisingly, Izzy knew the theory. Stanley Milgram was a New York scientist famous for his electrocution experiment in which test subjects were instructed to give shocks to other people who answered questions incorrectly. The shocks got increasingly harsher until they were effectively killing the person on the other side of the machine. It was a test that apparently showed the perils of obedience – something of which Jessica could never be accused.

Jessica had heard of that test but what she'd never known was that he was also responsible for the theory of six degrees of separation – the idea that any one person could be linked to anyone else on the planet within six steps. He'd called it the small-world phenomenon.

And that was the biggest problem they'd had in trying to connect the four victims: anyone could be connected to anyone else if they looked hard enough – but how deep can you go? The only reason they had any idea who might be responsible for the attacks was that their hoody had finally gone for someone connected *too* closely.

Humphrey Marsh was married to Beverley Marsh, who worked at the St Trinity Hospice in Swinton. It was barely a mile from Jessica's house.

Victor Todd had a child with someone whose grandmother worked at the same hospice.

The mother of one of Alan Hume's current tenants was a patient at St Trinity Hospice.

Luke Callaghan was married to Debbie Callaghan, whose next-door neighbour's late father had lived at the hospice. Debbie had even told Jessica that her friend had recently lost her father.

All four were tenuous connections but Beverley had told Jessica the only people she spoke to were her friend Paula and a couple of the others from work. Whoever their attacker was had to be someone connected – a male who worked there, someone's husband, a caretaker, cleaner . . . someone who wanted to humiliate those who had been causing misery for other people connected to the hospice. It even explained the reduction in violence; the goal was never to kill anyone but the attack on Luke had gone too far with his blinding.

They knew roughly the type of male they were looking for, including the height and build. Although they had the 'where', the best way they could get the 'who' was to visit the hospice in clothes that didn't make them look too obviously like police officers and have a poke around. They'd have to inform the manager but nobody else, or else risk alerting the person they were looking for.

As the members of the night crew looked on, confused, Jessica and Izzy exchanged mutual yawns and quick hugs, and then away they went – home to get some sleep.

Barely six hours later and Jessica was out of bed, yawning for England. She called Cole to let him know she was close to closing a case but that she needed Izzy. He probably suspected that she simply wanted to be away from the station when the news cameras returned for another day of round-the-clock broadcasting. He wasn't wrong – but he didn't object.

Jessica met Izzy at the bus stop outside the hospice a little before nine in the morning, both dressed down in jeans and jumpers. Add a waterproof coat and that was the unofficial uniform of the north. With the minimal amount of detective work – waiting to see who parked in the manager's space – Jessica and Izzy showed their identification and explained that they needed access to the staff records. The manager was a tall, suited man with too-shiny shoes and an officious manner who blathered on about the data protection act. Jessica pointed out that a lot of the people here were very poorly and the last thing they needed was a full-on search team with a warrant, heavy boots and loud, shouty voices. Put like that, the manager decided she was right and let them into his office, logging them onto the computer and showing them which filing cabinet had the hard copies in.

'Can I ask what exactly it is you're investigating?' he asked nervously, slightly loosening his tie.

Jessica shook her head. 'We can't divulge that but it would be really useful to have a tour of your premises.'

She left Izzy hunting through the computer records as the manager led her into the main area of the hospice. It was a strange mix of the residential home where her mother lived and a hospital. Some of the rooms were almost like her mother's bedroom – televisions, dressing tables, homely rugs, wardrobes – others were whitewashed, equipped with drips and breathing equipment.

Jessica didn't know what to make of it. Everywhere she went there were people who looked as ill as anyone she'd ever seen. Working in uniform, you became used to meeting people who couldn't look after themselves – you became used to that degree of sickness, but what was around her almost needed a new word. The greyness in people's skin, the struggle some were having to lift their arms, let alone do anything else. If she hadn't visited, she would have assumed somewhere like this would be full of older people but it wasn't like that at all. She found herself looking into the faces of people her age – younger – wondering what was wrong with them. It felt wrong to be here, imposing upon their final few months, weeks and days under a false pretence.

'It's hard, isn't it?' the manager said as he and Jessica took a seat in the dining room.

'I didn't think it would be like this.'

'Now do you mind if I ask why you're here?'

A few tables away, one of the nurses was feeding porridge to a patient with a spoon, like a mother with a child. Jessica felt awful for bullying him into letting them into the private records. The thought of ever bringing a search team here – warrant, heavy boots, shouty voices – now appalled her. Why couldn't she keep her mouth shut sometimes?

'We've linked a few crimes to people who might have connections here. I really can't tell you too much more than that. Hopefully my colleague is ruling out as many people as possible.'

'Is it someone who works here? Everyone is fully CRB-checked and there are rigorous interviews. I'm always thorough before I hire anyone.'

'We're really not sure.'

'Is there anything I can help you with?'

Jessica had to make a judgement: the manager would have as much knowledge as anyone about the people who worked here. He was too tall to be their hoody but that didn't mean he hadn't spoken to someone about the issues around the workplace who had then talked to someone else. That was their entire problem in the first place: too many degrees of separation.

'How much do you know about Beverley Marsh?'

The manager's face darkened. 'Beverley? What can she be involved with? She's one of our longest-serving staff members.'

'I'm not saying she's involved in anything. I can't give you details – but anyone I mention could be a victim, remember. All I'm asking is what you know about her. You shouldn't read anything else into it.'

He nodded, apparently understanding. 'She's been here

longer than me. She has a terrific bedside manner, very popular with the patients and other staff members.'

'Has she ever been in any sort of trouble?'

'Not at all. As far as I know she's happily married – no problems away from here and certainly no issues with her work. I think they inherited some money – she certainly doesn't come to work for the pay.'

If the manager thought she was living in wedded bliss, then that ruled him out of being connected to the crimes.

Jessica ran through the names of the people they had linked to the other three victims – two patients and another worker – but the manager shook his head to all of them. She also asked about Beverley's friend, Paula, who worked there but he didn't have a bad word to say about any of them.

The manager led her back to the office, assuring her he'd wait outside but adding he was uncomfortable about them being there for too much longer. Jessica was too – it felt like they were invading the privacy of people when they were at their most vulnerable. Izzy hadn't found anything either – Beverley's record was spotless, the only items in her file were a pay history and letters of commendation. Izzy had gone through the names of every male who worked there but there was never going to be a note that said 'potential to attack other people in public'. The attacker could be a husband, brother, uncle, son or any other male friend related to any of the list of people working there too. If they were to continue the six-degrees train of thought, they really had very little to go on.

Reluctantly, the manager agreed to let them interview

Paula informally in his office – although he insisted they had to leave afterwards.

Beverley's friend was a timid woman in her forties, dressed smartly in her nurse's uniform. She was understandably anxious about why the police wanted to talk to her, twisting her watch in a full circle around her wrist over and over as she answered questions.

She seemed shocked that the police knew about Beverley's husband's affairs – even more so by the fact she was being asked about it. She insisted it was only ever something a small group of nurses talked about on their lunch, where they'd take a break from looking after terminally ill patients to complain about the state of their own lives. Substitute 'terminally ill patients' for 'shits and criminals' and you had the exact description of what everyone who worked for the police did in their canteen every dinner time.

Jessica apologised to Paula for using up her time and let her return to work. When they were alone in the office, she turned to Izzy. 'This hasn't worked out how we hoped, has it?'

'What was it like on your tour?'

'Awful. I was at my mother's residential home last night and that felt like a proper community of people doing their best to enjoy their lives. Everywhere you look here, there are all these wonderful nurses doing their absolute best, trying to make sure the patients are as comfortable as they can possibly be. In one way, it's the most morbid place I've ever been but in another it's inspiring to see that the people working here actually care so much. I couldn't do it.'

Jessica stared out of the window towards the gardens. The sky was blue, the grass green and lush and the sun was finally making an appearance. Through the glass, it felt positively warm. Summer was finally here, if only for a day. 'Did you find anything at all on the computer?'

Izzy shook her head. 'We can ask to print out the names of people who work here, even the patients, and then we'd have to go away and check everyone related to anyone here. But what could we do about friends? Or friends of friends? If Beverley told Paula and a couple of the other nurses that her husband was having an affair, they could have told anyone. It's the same with the other three – Luke Callaghan's wife's next-door neighbour's father was a patient here. How tenuous is that? He could have told anyone what he'd heard about Debbie. They could have told anyone else. Somehow, someone heard all four stories and acted.'

'It's more than that too – someone knew Humphrey was going to be at ParkFest.'

'Did his wife know?'

'Shite, I forgot to ask when I was at their house. I was put off by the yapping dog.'

Jessica called Beverley's mobile, only to be told she was leaving for work shortly.

'Just quickly,' Jessica said. 'We spoke yesterday and you said your husband wasn't as clever as he thought with covering things up – but you never said for sure how you knew he was having an affair.'

'I found a ticket for some festival thing in the drawer next to his bed while I was tidying up. I thought at first he might invite me but the day was getting closer and he hadn't said anything, so I assumed he was off with one of his fancy women.'

'Who did you tell?'

'No one really.'

'There must be someone?'

From the rustling in the background, it sound like Beverley was getting dressed. 'Just Paula and a couple of the girls from work – like I told you yesterday.'

'When did you tell them?'

'I'm not sure.'

'It might be important.'

Beverley sighed. 'You know he's home, don't you? He got back yesterday evening and has barely said a word. It's like I don't exist.' Jessica apologised but asked again if she could try to think of which day it was that she'd spoken to her friends. With another sigh, the answer finally came. 'I was off Tuesday and Wednesday last week, so it would have been Monday lunchtime.'

Jessica thanked the woman and hung up, turning to Izzy. 'She only mentioned the tickets to someone else on Monday – so there are five days between that and the park attack. That narrows it slightly. We can start by looking into her friends and the people they know and work backwards from there.' Jessica was ready to leave but she could see in Izzy's face that the constable had thought of something. 'What?'

'What were all the patients like when you were on the tour?'

'I don't know – ill.'

'There's different levels though, aren't there? Some people wouldn't be able to walk. Other people can have things like cancer and appear almost healthy until the end. I met a friend of one of my cousins who had leukaemia. They were wearing a hat and I didn't even know they were ill until someone told me. You have good days and bad days. Plus remember what we thought with that first attack at Piccadilly – why would you be so blatant in public?'

Jessica suddenly got it too, finishing the thought. 'If you're dying anyway and have nothing to lose, it doesn't matter if you get caught.'

38

The problem was that by spending all their time looking into the hospice's staff, Jessica and Izzy had tested the manager's patience to the point that he ordered them to leave. Without a warrant, he wasn't giving them access to confidential patient records. Jessica didn't blame him. He'd already gone a little too far out of his way for them as it was.

He led them to the front door and said that if they did get a warrant, he hoped they respected his patients' privacy and dignity. It was a nice way of telling them to get stuffed.

Jessica called Cole and talked him through their theory. He said he'd see what he could do about a warrant for the patient records but pointed out that on a day where they had television cameras camped at the front of the station, the press office in meltdown, and a senior Met officer starting an investigation into the entirety of Greater Manchester Police, raiding a hospice wasn't going to be too high on his agenda. Jessica didn't even get time to point out that a raid wasn't necessary, the records could simply be handed over, before the line went dead.

There was nothing for it but to walk back to Jessica's house, get changed, and then drive to work, hoping whoever the Met had sent up to investigate them didn't want a word with her.

The hospice's driveway zigzagged along the lawn up a slope to the exit. Jessica and Izzy followed it slowly, enjoying the morning sunshine and delaying their return to Longsight. As they reached the top, Izzy nodded towards a lone figure sitting on a bench, staring over the low wall towards the green on the opposite side of the road. It was a last resort but Jessica and Izzy sat on either side of the man. He was in his sixties or seventies, wearing suit trousers and a thick cotton shirt under a tweed jacket with a matching cap, walking stick hooked over the top of the seat.

'Hello,' Jessica said.

'Lovely morning, innit?' the man replied, still staring across the road.

'Are you a patient here?'

The man chuckled slightly. '"Patient" is the right word. They told me I had a month to live three months ago. Funny thing the old ticker, innit?' He patted his heart as if to emphasise the point. 'Poor daughter keeps coming around every Sunday – there's only so many times you can say your goodbyes.'

'Do you mind if I ask what's wrong with you?'

The man coughed slightly, more of a tickle than a heave. 'Heart disease. Bastards even took away my fags – as if it's going to do me any harm now. You don't have one on you, do you?'

He turned from Jessica to Izzy, hand out expectantly.

'Sorry, I don't smoke.'

'Good for you – it's a filthy habit. A filthy, wonderful, brilliant, beautiful, soothing habit. And those bastards have nicked my fags.'

Jessica spotted the corner of Izzy's mouth twitching into a smile. 'What's your name?' Jessica asked.

'Donald. Pleased to meet you. Be even more pleased if you could get some fags, like.' He grinned, showing off his yellow teeth, and then shook their hands as they gave him their names. After another cough, he smiled even wider. 'Jessica and Isobel. This is the first time I've had a woman either side of me since April '74. Christ, that would've been a way to go.'

'Do you mind if I ask you a few questions?' Jessica asked, suppressing a smile.

'You stay on the bench and you can ask anything you like. Don't get too close, like, my heart's not up to much and a girl like you gets the old pulse racing.'

He patted Jessica on the leg and she didn't even mind. Being chatted up by a terminally ill pensioner was likely going to be the highlight of her professional week.

'Do you know much about one of the nurses – Beverley Marsh?'

'Aye, she's the one who nicked my fags.'

'But what about her in general when she's not confiscating cigarettes? Is she nice around the hospice, does she look after you and everyone else?'

Donald nodded. 'Aye, everyone likes her. She puts an arm around you and listens to you moan about stuff.'

'What about a nurse called Paula – she's one of Beverley's friends.'

'Aye, she's all right too. They all are.'

'Were there any patients with whom either of them was particularly friendly?'

Donald puffed out loudly. 'I'm not sure – memory's a bit hazy, like. All those names, old guy like me can easily get confused. Nothing like a fag to refresh the mind, is there . . . ?'

Jessica leant backwards, peering behind Donald's back towards Izzy.

'Don't look at me,' the constable said innocently.

As Jessica crossed the road to the newsagent, she couldn't escape the feeling that this was a new low – buying cigarettes for someone dying of heart disease living in a hospice. She had to double-check the extortionate price three times before finally buying a box of ten, picking up a book of matches just in case, and then walking back to the bench. When she arrived, Donald had a hand on Izzy's leg and she was giggling like a pre-pubescent schoolgirl being felt up by her first boyfriend.

'Am I interrupting something?' Jessica asked with a raised eyebrow.

Donald held his hand out. 'I was just telling your girl here about what we used to get up to back in the day.'

Izzy was trying to hide a smile but Jessica felt charmed by Donald too. If he only had a few weeks left and he wanted to chat up younger women then good luck to him.

Donald starting patting his fingers into his palm, wanting the packet, but Jessica slid a single cigarette out and placed it in his hand, along with the matches. 'Just the one?' he protested.

'Get talking and I'll see what I can do. I'm already facing an ethics hearing if this ever gets out.'

Donald took a deep lungful of the smoke, held it and

then breathed it out, closing his eyes in satisfaction. 'Two girls and a cigarette, this really is like April '74 all over again.'

'All right, Prince Charming, get on with it.'

Another drag and Donald finally began speaking. 'Max Winward's your man – bit younger than me. He's got cancer and came here a few months back. He's been clinging on like me – all of the staff loved him. Good bloke – they've been letting him go home for odd days before he comes back because they're not sure what's going on with him. Some days you'd never know he had a problem, others it's like he's already in the coffin. He went home for good on Friday – decided he'd had enough of this place. Everyone tried to talk him out of it but his mind was made up.'

'What do you mean, he's our man?'

Donald puffed on the cigarette, giggling to himself. 'You're not very good coppers, are you?'

'How do you know we're police?'

Another deep drag and Donald flicked the remains of the cigarette over the wall, holding his hand out. Jessica plonked the packet in it.

'Let's just say Max is your man. He'd been wondering how long it'd take you all.'

39

Max Winward's bungalow on the edge of Droylsden would have once been a smart little property buried at the end of a cul de sac. The only reason it wasn't now was because someone who was terminally ill presumably didn't have time to mow the lawn, prune the bushes and trim the trees. Jessica had to duck to get under the overhanging branches and then walk on the lawn to get around the overgrown bush separating the bungalow from the neighbouring property. Jessica had called Rowlands to get an address for Max and given him the details – telling him to give them half-an-hour's head start and then pass up the rest of the information.

The once-white plastic door was covered in a thin layer of dirt but the handle was almost clean from where it had been opened recently. Jessica rang the bell and knocked, waiting for a minute before trying again.

'Shall we get the battering ram boys in?' Izzy asked.

As much as she enjoyed the sound of things being smashed, Jessica shook her head, side-stepping to the window. The curtains were wide open but the uncharacteristic appearance of the sun meant that she had to use her hand to shield the glare.

'He's in there,' Jessica said.

'Shall we—?'

'He saw me and was pointing towards the front door.'

Jessica returned to the door and pulled the unlocked handle down. She and Izzy entered the hallway slowly, still wary that they were entering the house of someone potentially dangerous. Because they weren't in their work suits, Jessica didn't even have her pepper spray or handcuffs but the cheery voice from the front room sounded as unthreatening as anything she'd ever heard. 'You can come on through,' the man's voice chirped. 'The door straight ahead of you is the kitchen – someone can put the kettle on. I'm on your right.'

Jessica glanced at Izzy and shrugged. It wasn't like the raids they usually went on. Slowly, Jessica nudged open the door into the living room and poked her head around it. Staring directly at her was a man in an armchair, grinning. 'Hi, I'm Max. I was wondering when you'd show up.'

From the information Dave had given them, they knew Max Winward was sixty-one years old but everything except his eyes looked older. He was huddled under a blanket, shivering slightly. The faint sound of Radio Four was in the background as Jessica slowly entered the room until she was standing directly in front of Max. He held out a hand for her to shake, which Jessica did – explaining that she had to check him for anything dangerous. She lifted the blanket, patted his pockets, and then returned his cover, telling Izzy to put the kettle on. Max removed his hat, showing his bald head.

'Cancer,' he said. 'Could be a few days, could be six months. What do doctors know?'

Jessica heard the plip of the kettle from the kitchen.

'Max, when you said you were wondering when we'd show up, what did you mean?'

'You're police, aren't you?'

'Yes.'

'It's taken you long enough. How long ago was Callaghan?'

'Just under three weeks.'

'Exactly – Saturday knackered me out; all those people. It takes a lot.'

Izzy entered through a second door at the back of the room holding a dark blue hooded top in a gloved hand. Jessica barely knew what to say – it was the strangest arrest she'd ever made. She read Max Winward his rights as he smiled along and then Izzy put the hoody back on the hook where she'd found it and brought in the tea. Max's eyes only left Jessica to sip his drink. Each time he lifted his arm there was a wince, as Jessica found it almost impossible to believe he was the same person who had outrun her in the park.

When they were all settled, Izzy took out her notebook. Strictly speaking, this should have been done at the station but Jessica sensed this would be the easiest confession they'd ever take.

'Can we start at the beginning,' Jessica asked. Max sipped his tea, nodding. 'To confirm – you're admitting to attacking Luke Callaghan, Alan Hume, Victor Todd and Humphrey Marsh.'

Max nodded. 'Yes.'

'Why?'

'Can I ask you a question first – was it Donald who sent

you here?' Jessica didn't answer but Max began laughing anyway. 'Silly old sod. Is he still going on about fags and women? You didn't give him any, did you? Fags I mean . . .' With that, he was laughing again until he dissolved into a fit of coughing that sent tea spilling over the top of his cup.

'Sorry,' he said when he'd recovered. 'I've been getting worse. Perhaps it's finally my time? The doctors gave me six months to live at Christmas. I moved into that hospice a few months ago but it's so—' He paused, swirling his hand around, searching for the word. 'I don't know, full of dying people. I felt great. There are horrible days which I won't tell you about – not young people like yourselves – but there are others where you think you can do everything you did when you were younger. I'd wonder what I was doing there, thinking the doctor had got it wrong. I'd come home for a while, then I'd have a bad day where I couldn't even get out of bed.' He looked directly at Jessica. 'Have you ever had anyone close to you with cancer?'

Jessica shook her head. 'Not cancer. My dad had a brain haemorrhage.'

'It's hard to describe. It's almost like you can feel it sometimes; like it's in your mind hurting you. Sometimes I'd wake up and not know where I was; who I was. Everything hurt. They give you things to make it feel better but you never know where you are. Half the time I didn't know if I was ill or well. On the days I was ill, I wanted to die to make it go away, on the others, I wanted to go and do things with my life.'

'What did you do?'

Max put his tea down and pulled the blanket up over himself. 'I know some people have these lists of things they want to do and places they want to go but I've never been that adventurous. It wasn't as simple as that. I just listened to people around the home. Everyone had so many things wrong in their lives, so I wondered if I could do a few things that would make it better for them. I'm not strong enough to act too often and it's hard to plan completely because I didn't know if I was going to have a bad day. But I was in the army when I was younger, so I know how to look after myself. It wasn't even that hard in the end. I never really wanted to hurt anyone, just bring them down a few pegs.'

'Tell me about Luke Callaghan.'

Max paused, waiting for Izzy's pen to stop scratching. 'Have you caught up?' he asked.

Izzy's awkward 'yes' echoed how Jessica felt. She'd never had a criminal ask if her notes were in order before, let alone stop speaking to make sure nothing was missed.

'Not long after I got to St Trinity's, I got talking to this old boy. He was a war vet – my old dad would've loved him. He'd lost his vocal cords and could barely speak but he'd croak his way through a conversation. He was telling me how his daughter was living next door to someone whose husband used to beat her around. He said the guy's name was Callaghan and that he was some sort of councillor. It wasn't hard to do a bit of digging – some of us codgers can use the Internet, you know – and so I found out all about him. One day I was in his room and he was saying how his daughter had heard all this banging on the door of the flat next door and we were joking that if we were thirty years younger that we'd do something about it.'

Max was short on breath and he stopped, breathing deeply and taking a drink of his tea. He nodded towards Izzy again. 'Are you all right, dear?'

'Yes, thank you.'

'Anyway, I was in bed that night and thought, "Why don't I do something about it?" On my good days, I'm as fit as I was years ago – maybe it's the drugs but I feel great. Plus, if I get caught, what does it matter? By the time you lot get me through court, I'll be dead anyway. At least that poor girl will get a bit of respite. While I was thinking about that, I kept hearing all sorts of other things. One of the other women was telling me about this grim flat where her daughter was living and how the landlord was trying to blackmail her to go to bed with him – horrible stuff. I thought I had to make a stand and so I started planning. Obviously it's hard because I'd forget things on my bad days. I wrote everything down.'

He started to get up, motioning towards an old-fashioned bureau in the corner of the room. Jessica told him she'd go – and sure enough, there was a stack of neatly written notes about all four of the victims.

Jessica put a glove on to flick through the top few papers, then returned them to the bureau. They'd need more evidence bags than the ones she had in her car. 'How did you know where Luke Callaghan was going to be?'

'He put it on the Internet, didn't he? It was only ever going to be him and I didn't think I'd get away. There's a big cupboard at St Trinity's where they keep all of the medicines and other controlled things. I was a bit naughty – waiting until it was unlocked and then telling the nurse Donald was having problems. She ran off and I took this acid stuff. I didn't realise it was as bad as it was. I thought it'd just scar the guy – y'know, teach him to keep his hands to himself. I didn't think it'd blind him.'

'So you went to Piccadilly on the tram.'

'I thought there'd be a big crowd of people but I guess no one's interested in these politicians. Afterwards I kept my head down and made a run for it – no point in making it too easy for you. I thought you'd come that day, either here or St Trinity's, but the knock never came – so I thought I'd have to act quickly.'

'Alan Hume was the next day, in the evening.'

'Exactly. I think the excitement and adrenaline gave me a bit of a spurt because I felt like a different person. I thought it was now or never, so I phoned him up about doing a job. I thought I'd lure him somewhere, maybe even here, I wasn't bothered – but he said he was doing some fitting job at the shopping centre. I thought it'd be as good a place as any – but I also realised there was a chance your cameras hadn't got me that first time, so I thought I'd be more careful.'

'Where did you get the mask?'

'Just some stall on the market – they're everywhere. I went looking around the car park for a van with his name on – you know what builders are like, it's a free advert, so it wasn't hard. Then I waited. I was sorry about that mother and her kids who saw it. That I do regret – perhaps I'll write them a letter.'

He genuinely sounded sorry at the prospect he might have upset the bystanders, although there was still something about that attack that was a little different from the others. 'With Alan Hume, he was actually beaten with a bat. No offence but . . . if it was you, how did you manage to overpower a younger man?'

Max smiled and began laughing until it again became a cough. He was almost bent over double in the chair, trying to apologise while still coughing. Jessica wasn't sure what she could do but Izzy disappeared into the kitchen and returned with a glass of water. Max took a sip and eventually the cough receded. 'If I'd known I was going to end up coughing like this anyway, I'd have never stopped smoking in my thirties.' He smiled again and it was impossible not to return it.

'I told you I was in the army, didn't I?'

'Yes.'

'In your jobs you must know that it's rarely about strength and size.' He nodded towards Izzy. 'I bet you've had to restrain some much bigger blokes in your time, haven't you?'

'Of course.'

'Outside of the bedroom too.' As Izzy blushed, Max burst out laughing at his own joke, launching himself into another coughing spurt. He was still grinning at the end of it. 'Sorry, love, you can't blame an old man for the odd dirty thought here and there.'

Izzy still seemed a little embarrassed, even though she was smiling. 'It's fine.'

'Anyway, my point is that it's not about any of those

things. I was always one of the smaller guys in the army but people learn pretty quickly who they can get away with picking on. I'd had this bat in the shed for years and never used it. It was a bit too heavy for me, so I sawed the end off. I took him by surprise with the first blow and it was fine after that. Like Callaghan, I wasn't trying to seriously hurt him, just teach him a lesson that he should treat people better. When I saw that woman and her boys, I felt terrible.'

'After that, it was four days until you attacked Victor Todd.'

Max took another sip from his water, then finished off his tea, nodding. 'I was really tired the morning after the Hume thing but it was getting in the papers and I was thinking they were really getting what they deserved. A couple of the nurses were talking and I overheard one of them saying how her daughter wasn't getting any money from the daddy of her baby. Apparently he had all these children with different mums and he wasn't paying any of them. It's just not right, is it – all those poor kiddies with such a shite for a dad. What chance have they got?'

'How did you know he was going to be in the shopping centre?'

'I didn't. He'd been in the papers about a year ago when he had another kid – some article about him being a drain on society. It gave the road that he lived in, which made it easy to get the actual address. I followed him for most of the Saturday but he never seemed to be alone, so I tried again on the Monday. I got on the same bus, got off at the same stop and followed him into the Arndale. When he went into the toilet, I thought it was time to do something. I'd kept one of my old needles and filled it with water, thought I'd give him a scare.' He winked. 'Worked, didn't it.'

Jessica knew she had to remain professional, even if the situation was anything but. 'After that, there were twelve days until you attacked Humphrey Marsh.'

Max asked for more water and readjusted himself under the blanket. Jessica knew their half-hour was up and that Rowlands would have told Cole where they'd gone and why. Backup would be on its way any minute – not that they needed it. After another drink, Max began again.

'After Todd, I had a couple of bad days. I honestly thought that was it, that I'd overdone it, lying in my bed barely able to move. As I was getting better, I just remember the nurse – Beverley – lovely woman, she'd do anything for anyone. She was talking to one of the other nurses about how her husband was cheating on her. She said he had tickets for some festival thing and that he was going without her. I thought that anyone who could treat her like that needed a right hiding but I wasn't up to it plus I had no idea where they lived. All I knew was that he was going to that ParkFest thing. On the days before, I was feeling better, so I went along to the park thinking it'd be this small thing and that I'd be able to find him easily. I didn't realise it'd be thousands of people.'

'How did you think you'd know what he looked like?'

Max smiled. 'It's not a common name, is it? Plus Beverley had been saying how her husband always buys these ridiculous new clothes whenever he's got someone on the go. I remembered this game from when I was a kid – me and my mates would go into the centre and yell out "John" or something like that just to see who'd turn around. Once we clocked a guy, we'd follow him for a short while, then one of us would go up close behind him and say something like, "Hello John". He'd turn around, not knowing who we were and we'd bluff it, pretending we lived down the road or whatever. While he was distracted, one of my mates would slide past him and get his wallet.'

He took another drink of water and peered down at the floor. 'I'm not proud of it – but we were only kiddies. It was just one of those things. It made me think that if I walked up and down the line—'

'*You* were calling Humphrey's name.'

'Right.'

'I was standing next to him.'

For the first time, Max seemed genuinely surprised, shuffling backwards in his seat, eyes wider. 'You're not . . . ?'

'I'm not the one having an affair with him, no, but I know the woman who was and she didn't know either.'

Jessica's interruption seemed to throw Max off his stride. He checked his empty teacup and then finished off the latest glass of water. 'I saw him turning in the pink jacket, so I knew he was the guy. I bought a ticket from one of the touts outside, then picked up a mask on the inside. It was really easy to follow him about for the day but I wasn't feeling too well around lunchtime. I think the music was too loud and I had to have a sit down in that food bit. If it had started to rain, I'm not sure I would have got through it.'

'Where did you get the pepper spray?'

'Had it a while. A few years ago, I was out in Turkey – before I started to get ill. I brought it back with me, not knowing what I was going to do with it. It's been at the back of a drawer ever since.'

'You knew what you were doing when you ran for the crowd.'

Max's smile acknowledged her without seeming to be too boastful. 'Always head for cover, always look to blend in. I knew I'd never outrun anyone and if I went for the exit, then people would have it covered. I just ran for the largest mass of people and didn't look backwards. When I could, I ditched the mask. My top is grey on the inside, so I turned it inside out and walked out. The guards didn't even look twice at me.'

The living room was suddenly bathed in a blue flashing glow, lights blinking through the front window. Jessica turned to Izzy. 'Do you want to go and tell them to take it easy?'

When it was just them, Jessica peered back to Max, who looked more worried now, his eyebrows meeting in the middle, a little of the sparkle gone from his eyes. 'What's going to happen to me?'

'Can you sit in a car?'

'Yes.'

'We're going to take you to the station and I'll ask you to repeat this on camera and tape. Your hood, notes and everything else will be taken as evidence and then . . .

honestly, I have no idea.' She paused for breath. 'I've got one more question for you: did anyone else know what you were up to?'

Max shook his head. 'They might have suspected but it was all me.'

Jessica helped him to his feet, hooking one arm around his waist, and then led him to the front door. A dozen PCs had turned up, their cars clogging up the end of the cul de sac, giving the residents a show like they'd never had before.

Standing in the middle with a photographer by his side was Garry Ashford. If anyone asked, then she had no idea who'd tipped him off but never let it be said that Jessica didn't repay her favours.

40

Three days later and Jessica was sitting in Cole's office waiting for him to get off the phone. He made a few notes on a pad on his desk, mouthed a 'sorry' to her and then finally put down the receiver. 'I said you could have gone to court if you wanted.'

'Not my kind of place.'

'Max Winward's been released on bail. He pleaded guilty to all four counts. Usually he'd have been remanded but given his condition the magistrate has sent him home on health grounds with an electronic tag and twenty-four-hour monitoring. He's basically under house arrest.'

'Did the CPS object?'

'Not a peep. Apparently even they draw the line at locking up someone who's likely to die some time soon. No one expects him to make Crown Court.'

With that, one of strangest cases Jessica had ever been involved with was officially in the solved pile. Considering they'd found two kidnapped kids – sort of, exposed one of their own and caught the person who'd been attacking people in public all in under a week, everything felt flat.

For one, Max Winward wasn't the type of hardened criminal any of them had signed up to catch. It didn't mean he hadn't committed serious offences, or that he shouldn't be punished – but it was still hard to get worked up about putting him away. Another reason was that anyone who'd had any involvement in the exposure of Niall Hambleton was being called into the main GMP headquarters at Moston Vale for official interviews. Jessica had already had hers, explaining how she had interviewed Colin Rawlinson's son, who had made the initial allegations. The entire process was taking place under the strictest of confidentialities, with everyone interviewed forbidden to talk about what had been said. Naturally, that meant that everyone and their dog knew exactly what was going on. Jessica couldn't remember morale ever being so low. The Met's investigator – Matthew Pratley – had a name that had been invented for piss-taking and no one was holding back.

Cole held up a copy of that morning's *Herald*, which had the headline 'MAD MAX?'

He was watching Jessica closely. 'Interesting how the local paper and the BBC got hold of information from Max's official police statement.'

'Lucky them.'

'More like lucky us – the steady drip, drip of information ahead of his court date has managed to push the inquiry into the Stretford Slasher's conviction off the news agendas. I didn't hear a word about it on the radio this morning and it's not in the first twelve pages of today's paper.'

'Funny, that.'

'It's almost like someone around here knew that journalists would be more interested in Max than anything else. If they hadn't had the information, we'd have spent the entire week fending off questions about a botched investigation from twenty-five years ago instead of getting on with everything from now.'

'We must have a guardian angel somewhere.'

'Indeed, *somewhere*. Pratley's gone berserk apparently. I think he thought he'd be up from the Met and on the front pages every day.'

'Niall deserves everything he gets but people actually going out of their way to stop us doing the job properly doesn't help anyone.'

Cole leant in, raising his eyebrows. 'Perhaps that's a view that should stay between us?'

'Of course, Sir.'

'Plus we shouldn't forget that someone lost their sight in all of this.'

'I know, Sir. Sorry, Sir.'

'Either way, all of our targets for May were hit, plus we're under budget on the overtime – perhaps because a certain someone keeps working even when they've been told not to.'

'I'll have a word with Izzy, Sir.'

This time Cole actually laughed, leaning back into his seat. 'I hope you realise how lenient everyone's been with you over the years.'

'I do . . . but we're still a sergeant short – at least one – and I was thinking perhaps if you put in your recommendation, pushed a few things . . .'

Cole stared at Jessica in the knowing way that he so often did; the 'what-am-I-going-to-do-with-you' look. It wasn't just with Thomas McKinney that Jessica was as subtle as a sledgehammer.

'Haven't you got work to do?'

'I was hoping to take a half-day. I know it's late notice but I'm up with my hours, Pat's half-asleep down there anyway, so he won't mind. We've got plenty in and—'

'Just go.'

Jessica didn't wait for him to change his mind, heading out of the door, passing Pat and his family-sized bag of chicken and thyme crisps, and making for her car.

There was one further promise she hadn't yet managed to keep.

The Northern Quarter was like a different place in the sunshine. Instead of the murky, cobbled alleys bathed in shadows and frost, it seemed like the pleasant throwback to another time that it was. Jessica parked her car close to the church hall at Ancoats and walked towards the familiar maze of back streets, enjoying the warmth on her arms. Everything was always better when the sun came out; she might even risk visiting her mother again – she had helped her solve a case, after all. First, she wanted to spend the afternoon doing everything she could to locate Tony. She'd promised his mother that she'd do her best to find him and because of everything that had happened, she hadn't had a chance.

Jessica started with the regular group of homeless people but, unlike before, this time no one even pretended to have seen him. She weaved in and out of the cobbled byways, looking for anyone who might have seen him, perhaps even some of that fluff that was falling out of his coat.

Nothing.

Jessica was ready to start another lap when she turned onto the road on which Tony lived. Parked on the opposite side of the road from his flat was a gleaming red soft-top sports car that hadn't been there when she'd passed the first time. The car would have been out of place in many parts of the city centre – but especially here. This was where arty-types lived; it was full of galleries, music bars, cafes, and craft shops. This wasn't a spot for fancy wine bars, it was cheap pints, yummy mummies and students. Jessica hurried along the street, but the glare from the windscreen prevented her from seeing if there was anyone in the driver's seat until she was so close that the alarm beeped a warning. The car was empty but she was directly under the lamppost where she had first seen Scott Dewhurst standing.

The street was quiet aside from a handful of mid-afternoon shoppers unfamiliar enough with the area that they weren't batting an eyelid at the sports car. Jessica crossed the road and could see Tony's slightly open front door. No pepper spray – she wasn't on duty – all she had was the handcuffs she often kept in her jacket pocket. Jessica thought about calling the station but what could she say? The person on whom she illegally had files might be up to something?

Quietly, Jessica edged inside, doing her best to stop the door squeaking. At the top of the stairs, she could hear some sort of clunking noise.

Whump!

Something hit the ground hard above and Jessica eased the front door back into the position it had been and made her way up the stairs, sticking to the edges to try to stop them squeaking. There was definitely more than one voice in the flat. One was higher-pitched, the other naturally louder. Jessica reached the top and rested against the wall. The door was slightly open but Jessica couldn't manoeuvre herself into a position that would let her see anything other than the inner wall. She could hear the voice clearly now though.

The louder voice, which she assumed was Scott's, was speaking calmly but with authority and an edge. 'Where's the rest of my money, Tony?'

Tony pleaded a whimpering reply. 'I can't get it. Me ma says I can't have any more until I go home.'

'You're lying.'

Jessica knew that Tony was – if he'd called home, his mother would have called her.

'I'm not!'

A sickening thwack echoed around the room and then there was the sound of scrambling. Jessica could feel the weight of the phone in her pocket. She could go back down the stairs and call the station – but no one would arrive quickly enough to help Tony.

Shite, shite, shite.

Jessica pushed the door open slightly, expecting to see a fight. What she actually saw was all the more shocking: Tony was prone on the ground, Scott straddled across his stomach. He was wearing the same type of smart suit in which she'd seen him before but his sleeves were rolled up for action, light gleaming off the top of his shaven head. Tony was limp but there was a needle hanging from his arm which Scott wriggled around slightly and then pushed the plunger.

'There, that's better, isn't it?'

Tony groaned, his mouth hanging open uselessly.

'Expensive stuff, this. I'm going to keep coming back until I get what I'm due.'

Scott let Tony's arm flop back onto the floor, the needle still dangling. Jessica wanted to turn, to run, to get help, but she couldn't move. It wasn't Tony who had got himself hooked on the drug again – it had been done for him by someone who wanted as much money as he could get. It didn't matter if Tony paid, he would keep asking for more.

No wonder he had taken to sleeping rough in areas unfamiliar.

As Jessica stepped backwards, the door creaked a high-pitched ominous groan. Scott turned, face screwed up in confusion. At his full height, he was massive – not just towering over her but wide too; thick shoulders and a powerful rhino-like chest.

'Who are you?'

The question hung in the air – he hadn't recognised her from either the alley, or the time she'd first seen him when leaving Tony's flat.

There was only one answer she could give: 'I'm Detective Inspector Jessica Daniel and you're under arrest.'

Scott's upper arms tensed slightly, eyes narrowing as he weighed her up. 'What's the charge?'

'Grievous bodily harm, possession of a Class A drug and being a big bald fuck-bag.'

He smiled slightly, holding his arms out to his side to show he was unarmed. Jessica's heart was thumping so loudly, she was convinced he must be able to hear it. She was trying to stop herself from shaking.

'I want you to put your hands on your head, turn around and kneel.'

'Do you now?'

'Hands on your head.' Scott did as he was told slowly, not taking his eyes from Jessica. 'Now turn around.'

This time he didn't obey. 'Can I ask which army it is you think you're going to take me in with?'

He ain't scared of you boys in blue.

Jessica ignored him, glancing quickly towards the ground. 'Tony, are you all right?' The only response she got was a slight groan from Tony and a wider smile from Scott. She turned her attention back to the man in the suit. 'I thought I told you to turn around and get on your knees.'

'And I asked which army it is you think you've got.'

'There are three patrol cars directly outside with both ends of the road blocked off. We've been following you for weeks – we were just waiting until we had you where we wanted you. Now turn around and get on your knees. I won't ask again.' She tapped her ear, tilting her head slightly away from Scott in the way Esther had done to her. 'Yep, that's the suspect's voice. We have a second man down too. Can you hear what's being said?' Pause. 'Roger that – firearms on standby.'

The smile evaporated from Scott's face and this time he

seemed rattled. He ran his tongue along his teeth, still staring at her.

'Knees.'

Thump, thump, thump. Could that really be her heart? Surely, he could hear it?

Scott turned around, fingers interlocked behind his head. He continued standing as Tony rolled onto his front, close to Scott's feet. He was still groaning with what sounded like pleasure, needle hanging out of his arm.

'Knees!'

Jessica realised she was holding her breath as Scott slumped forwards until he was kneeling. She unclicked the handcuffs and marched towards him, reaching for his hands. She was ready for him to react but he was far too quick for her. The moment she touched him, his fingers slipped out of each other and he grabbed her wrist, rolling sideways without letting go. Jessica heard the snap before she felt the pain. She lunged towards him with her free hand, going for the windpipe but he effortlessly kicked her legs out from her. Jessica fell sideways but Scott continued holding her wrist, his unflinching grip like a vice. There was a second snap and this time Jessica did feel the pain, screaming in agony. He was holding her where she already had the scars, running his fingers roughly along them, adding to the sting. She tried to kick up at him but his legs were like tree trunks and he didn't flinch.

Jessica finally pulled her wrist clear but Scott fell forwards onto her, straddling across her waist in the same way she'd seen him with Tony. He was so heavy that she couldn't wriggle out from under him. His saucepan hands swung back and slapped her across the face. Jessica's head bounced into the ground, leaving her with green and pink stars dancing in front of her eyes.

The next time she knew where she was, Scott had turned around, still straddling her but facing away. Jessica tried wriggling again but his ankles were pinning her arms to her side and she was out of breath from where he was sitting on her. All she could see was his backside but Jessica could feel him tugging at her shoes.

'What are you doing?'

'What happened to your firearms squad?'

'They're—'

'Yeah, they don't exist. Don't even try it – I'm not one of your usual idiots. You should've probably found out who you were dealing with before you stormed in: Little Miss Stupid without an army.'

Jessica could just about see the prone shape of Tony. He was still moaning.

'Scott Dewhurst.'

His body straightened but his grip didn't relax and Jessica suddenly felt the cooler air on her feet. He had taken her shoes and socks off.

'So you do know who you're dealing with?'

'You answer to Christian Fraser. He has a bunch of shit-hole clubs and pubs which he uses for dealing drugs and laundering money. You're under arrest.'

'Fuck me, I must've hit you harder than I thought – do you really think you're in a position to do anything about this?'

'About what?'

Scott twisted his body just enough so that Jessica could see one side of his face but he was so balanced that his weight didn't move at all. He reached into his pocket and took out a second needle that contained a light brown, almost yellow liquid. 'Fascinating stuff, opiate, don't you think?'

'No.'

'Do you know that the first time after you shoot this stuff, depending upon your make-up, it might only be six or seven hours until you start sweating and craving more. Take our friend over there, I reckon he's a six-hour man, don't you? It can be anything up to twenty-four hours but everyone has some sort of reaction.'

Jessica tried to struggle but her arms had gone numb and her legs were pinned. 'Don't do it.'

Scott leant back onto her wrists, making her squeal. He sounded so calm that even the tone of his voice was terrifying. 'I'm going to tell you a story about a little pit bull puppy I had as a teenager. He was called Bull and I loved that little dog. The thing was, he'd always come back for more. You'd throw it into the ring with the other dogs and he'd charge in, even when he was outnumbered and the other animals were much bigger. Even when he got hurt, he'd still come back to me. It got to the point where I was trying to see what I could do to him and still have him return. I took a lighter to his tail, threw him down the stairs, held him under the bathwater for minutes at a time. You name it and I did it to that little pup. Every time, he'd shake himself down and then be sniffing around my feet again, wanting more.'

He sighed wistfully, remembering the good old days.

'My point is that this stuff turns people into my little Bull. People think it does bad things to you but it really doesn't. It'll stop you having a shit but aside from that, all it does is make you come back for more. The only other side-effects are if it's been cut badly and you'll only get the best stuff from me. It's all about how you look after yourself. People fuck around with their arms and make a mess, so I'll give you a little lesson. Consider this a freebie.'

Jessica felt a stabbing sensation next to her big toe. She tried to scream but the sound was lost somewhere in between her lungs and her mouth. Scott hauled himself to his feet and rolled his sleeves down, straightening the rest of his suit. She tried to move but her body didn't feel like her own. As her head began to spin, Jessica heard Scott's final words. 'If you want more, he'll tell you where to find me. Talk to you soon.'

She heard the sound of glass crunching into the carpet nearby and then the rush came.

41

Jessica's stomach was on fire as she crouched over the toilet in Tony's flat feeling the contents of her bowels ripple up her throat and then blast the sides of the bowl.

Everything hurt.

She felt Tony behind her, pulling her hair aside, whispering something she couldn't make out. After two dry heaves, she rolled away, reaching up to flush the toilet but missing. Tony stretched across to do it and then helped her rest against the wall. She could see the outline of his face: the straggly hair, pale skin, thin, so thin. He took her hand and she realised she was shaking.

'You're sweating,' Tony said, running a hand across Jessica's forehead.

'I feel . . . I don't know how I feel.'

'It's warm.'

'Yes, it's warm.'

Tony drank some water and then passed the glass to Jessica. It tasted cold and beautiful, sliding down her throat and then—

More heaves.

'Ouch.'

'It's not like that every time. Everyone's different after the first time. Some are sick, some are barely affected. It depends on all sorts of things but mainly your own tolerance and how pure it is.'

Tony sounded completely coherent – the exact opposite of how Jessica felt.

'What time is it?'

'Four o'clock. He left around two hours ago.' Jessica groaned slightly and Tony pushed her hair away from her face. 'Why did you come?'

'I've been trying to help you.'

Tony seemed shaken by what she'd said, pulling away and leaning against the basin. 'I didn't want this to happen.'

'I know.'

'You don't have to be ashamed of how it felt – it's like that for everyone.'

Jessica's head felt cloudy. 'I'm not sure what you mean.'

He stared at her, almost through her, as if he was in her mind. He knew. 'Everyone thinks it's awful, that it hurts, but those first twenty minutes . . . the rushing, the swimming. It builds and builds and then it takes you. It's like you're being hugged so hard. Flying, falling and flying again. When I come down, it's like landing in bubble wrap. I can almost hear the pop, pop, pop.' He closed his eyes and breathed in.

Jessica didn't want to talk about it.

Tony pulled himself to his feet but didn't seem too steady either. 'Do you want some tea?'

'If I can keep it down.'

Tony helped her up and then closed the door behind him. Jessica realised she was still bare-footed and sat on the toilet, wrenching her leg around so she could see the small red dot in the webbing next to her big toe. With another grunt of effort, she hauled herself up using the basin and stared into the mirror. She was still the same, wasn't she? Her hair was drenched with sweat but her skin wasn't pale like Tony's. She could see herself clearly; her eyes were more green than brown today but the pupils hadn't shrunk like Tony's either.

Six or seven hours, Scott had said. That was how long before she started wanting more if she had a low tolerance. Two hours had already gone.

Tick-tock.

She knew the basics about addiction from the years in uniform; all those nights of arresting people who needed help, not incarceration. She knew that what Scott had told her about heroin was true – the only real direct side-effect was that it constantly made a person want more. The evil was in the simplicity because there was never enough. An addict would sell everything he or she had to get more, then steal whatever was around to keep the habit going.

I used to look at everything as a method to getting something else to drink, or go up my arms.

Tony knew what it was like. The only side-effects were the ones that tore everything about a person apart.

Jessica stared into the mirror and pulled her eyelids up to inspect the top of her eyeballs, then she looked up her nose, underneath her gums, poked, prodded and pulled each part of her skin.

'I'm still me.'

She looked herself in the eyes.

'I'm still me.'

In the living room, it was like nothing had happened. Whatever had crunched had been cleaned up and Tony had rearranged the chairs around the table. A steaming teapot was sitting between two cups and Tony poured a drink for her. The first mouthful scalded the back of her throat but that was good. Let it burn.

Jessica found her socks and shoes and put them on again, running her finger across the mark, remembering. She took another sip of tea, enjoying how it hurt her tongue. 'Did Scott get you hooked again?'

Tony nodded. 'Do you remember him on the other side of the road when you were here?'

'Yes.'

'That was the third time I'd seen him. He'd been offering me stuff for weeks but I kept saying no. I thought he'd go away but he wouldn't take no for an answer. He ended up pushing his way in here – he's so big. I was screaming but the pub's next door and no one could hear me over that. He stuck the needle in my arm and that was that.'

'You could have come to us.'

Tony shook his head, sipping his tea and looking away, embarrassed. He spoke softly. 'I enjoyed it.'

'Oh.'

'I still . . .' Tony took a deep breath and snatched a tissue from the table. He wiped his arm and then blew his nose. 'I know I shouldn't, I know what it does. I know . . .'

Jessica wanted to say something comforting but she

didn't know what the correct words were. Her head still didn't feel right.

'He came back the next day and said he had more but he wanted three hundred quid. I said I didn't have anything like that but he knew about my parents. They've got money and—'

'I know.'

'Right . . . I, er . . .' Tony blew his nose again before continuing. 'He said he knew all the people you can get stuff from and that no one would sell to me. If I wanted more then the only way to get it would be through him. I said I didn't want any and he walked away.'

'But then . . .'

'I could feel it inside of me, itching, scratching. I've got it under control now but it wasn't like that then because I'd been away from it. It felt like there was a worm under my skin and I couldn't get away from it. I called me ma and said I needed a bit more cash before I moved. She put it into my account straight away and I went to the bank and took everything out.'

That at least explained the bundle of money that had fallen from his pocket when Jessica had been with him in the alleyway at the back of Great Northern.

'So you've been paying Scott's higher prices?'

'He keeps wanting more. It's five hundred a time now. I say I can't get that sort of money but he knows my parents have it. I've not called them for any more because it's not fair, is it?'

Jessica still didn't have an answer, although the tea was at least helping the emptiness in her stomach. She could feel him staring at her and finally glanced across to meet his eyes. 'What are you going to do?' he asked.

'How do you mean?'

'I know what it's like, how it feels . . . How you want more.'

'I could just report him.'

Tony tilted his head to the side as if it was something he'd not considered. 'If you do that, how can you prove you didn't inject yourself?'

Damn.

42

Jessica stood in the alleyway hidden between the towering buildings at the back of Great Northern. The air was cool but nothing like it had been a few weeks before. Jessica only needed a jacket, not her heavy coat. Summer was on the way and it was definitely going to be a good one this year, it had to be.

At the end of the ginnel, the shiny red sports car came to halt, its sleek curves illuminated in the light from the street lamps. The whiteness caught the top of his head too, reflecting as he looked both ways and then began to walk towards her. She could see the swagger in his step; he was never going to let her go, the way he would never let Tony go. There was dampness around her hairline – it had barely disappeared in the three days since she had walked away from Tony's flat, constant beads of sweat pooling, matting her hair together. Her hands were in her pockets but they were shaking, her wrist still aching.

Jessica blew out, wanting to see her breath swirling away but there was nothing there. It wasn't even cold and yet her hands were still trembling.

Scott's footsteps boomed around the enclosed alley, the age-old cobbles providing a perfect platform for him to intimidate her one step at a time.

Clip-clop, clip-clop.

Tick-tock.

As he got nearer, she remembered how big he was, the thick legs, the wide, strong shoulders, the unmoving neck.

He bowed his head ever so slightly as he moved from the shadow into the light, keeping his own hands in the pockets of the long woollen coat. 'Detective Inspector.'

Jessica took a small step backwards and looked behind her at the empty alleyway.

He stretched out a hand towards her. 'Hey, hey – no need for that, we're both friends here. We know the score. It was very nice of you to contact me through your little friend and arrange this little meet. I'm surprised it took you three days. What's it been like?'

He reached further, stretching towards her face but Jessica batted him away.

'Hey, what did I say? We're both friends here – I'm concerned for you. Have you been sweating much, perhaps feeling your heart racing for no reason? You don't need to worry, I've brought what you're after.'

He patted his top pocket.

'I can see it in those pretty little eyes of yours that you want more. Come on, tell me, what did it feel like?'

Jessica didn't have to lie. 'Like an itch.'

Scott scratched his chin. 'That's what some of them say. Do you know, one of my favourite clients used to be a Shakespearean actor – doth this and all that. When I asked him that question, he said, "Out, damned spot". I didn't know what he was on about but I looked it up and it's from "Macbeth".'

'It's Lady Macbeth when she's sleepwalking.'

Scott nodded. 'Aren't you the clever one? Is that what it was like for you? "Out, damned spot"?'

'Sort of.'

Scott grinned, relaxing back, legs apart, in his element. 'That first dose was free but it's like anything in this world, the price goes up.'

'How much?'

'A hundred this time and I'll keep it quiet that you're a copper – but you should beware that prices keep going up and up. That's the market, I'm afraid.'

'Why did you go between my toes?'

Scott pursed his lips, having not expected the question. 'When you go into your arm, it's usually for ease or because you don't care. Some say it feels better in that instant but I wouldn't know. What I do know is that if you want to keep things quiet from those around you, then you need to find a spot where they'll never see. You could try the tops of your thighs . . .' He paused, licking his lips, eyes dancing down Jessica's torso. ' . . . But if I were you, I'd stick to between your toes. It might not be as intense but you won't get yourself into any bother.'

'Okay.'

Scott held out his hand again. 'So . . .'

Jessica took a handful of notes from her pocket and put them in his palm. He counted them from one hand into the other. 'Twenty, forty, sixty, seventy, eighty, ninety, one hundred. Very nice and I prefer twenties, for future reference. Never fifties.'

'I'll see what I can do.'

Scott pocketed the money and reached into the top flap

of his jacket, taking out a small foil packet and pressing it into Jessica's hand. She didn't look at it before putting it into the back of her jeans.

'Do you know about the heating and—'

'I know.'

'Good. I might ask you for a little favour here and there too. Nothing too tough but it's always good to have someone on the inside.'

'I can't compromise my job.'

Scott had begun to turn away, the back half of his head in shadow, his features still lit by the mix of moonlight and embers of the street lamp at the far end of the alley. He was nodding slightly and for a moment she thought he was going to walk away. In a flash, he was on her, slamming her into the wall, forearm pressed against her breastbone, other hand gripping her already-pained wrist. He was so close that she could smell his stinking aftershave and see the veins pulsing in his neck. She tried to press back against him but he was like a machine.

His eyes were narrow, glaring into hers. 'You'll do what I tell you to do. All it takes is an anonymous phone call and your bosses will have you taking a drugs test and where will that leave you?'

Jessica grunted, still trying to push back but Scott laughed in her face. He wasn't even using much force. Suddenly, as quickly as he had grabbed her, he stepped away again, smoothing down his suit. 'Next time it's two hundred and if you can't pay, we'll have to come up with something creative for you to do.'

He reached into his pocket and took out the cash,

followed by a lighter from his back pocket. With a flick and a flash, the notes were ablaze. Jessica could feel the warmth as he held them in front of her face before dropping them on the floor. 'That's how little your money means to me – now what are you going to do about it?'

Jessica could still feel the pain above her breasts from where he'd pressed into her. Each breath was heavy. 'Nothing,' she mumbled.

'Pardon?'

Louder this time: 'Nothing.'

He nodded, grinning. 'Exactly – nothing. There are no shades of grey here, this is black and white. When I call you up and tell you to jump, you say, "Yes, *Sir*, thank you, *Sir*, how high, *Sir*". If I tell you to get on your knees and do the one thing you sluts are good for, you look me in the eyes and say, "Yes, *Sir*, thank you, *Sir*, my pleasure, *Sir*". Got it?'

'Yes.'

Scott raised himself up onto tiptoes and then spun on the spot, turning and walking towards his car. His footsteps echoed loudly again, as he retreated into the shadows.

On the ground at Jessica's feet were the smouldering remains of the notes, flickering orange until they burnt themselves out. Jessica took the foil packet from her back pocket and dropped it onto the floor, using her foot to brush it and the larger fragments of the ashes into the nearby drain.

As she stared towards the car and Scott's silhouette at the far end of the alleyway, Jessica's heart was still pounding. It was hurting even more than the pressure he'd put on her chest or her wrist. This was what her career had come down to.

In the distance, Scott reached his car and started to walk around the front. The city felt empty, as if all of the traffic had stopped and the steady stream of people going home from the pubs had finished.

Shush.

Out of the shadows stepped a figure in a hooded top. Scott noticed him, turning at the sound of the noise but he was too late.

Blam.

Blam.

Blam.

Three shots from the closest of ranges. Jessica saw the spray of blood illuminated as it splattered out of Scott's head to the ground. She heard the gentle patter and then there was silence.

The hooded figure turned towards her but didn't say a word, his shape caught in the faded light. Jessica had no idea what would happen next but he turned again and sat cross-legged on the cold, hard floor.

Perhaps some things are black and white?

43

Jessica's phone rang at fourteen minutes past three in the morning, not that she'd been to sleep. She dressed, got in the car and drove to the station. By the time she'd arrived, she couldn't remember the journey; everything had happened on autopilot.

She went through the motions but it felt like somebody else was performing them. She was so good at being laughing, funny, cocky Jessica that that was autopilot too.

Hours passed until she was sitting in Cole's office, staring blankly at the wall. She could feel his eyes on her. 'You were brilliant in there.'

Jessica shrugged – she couldn't remember.

Izzy was in the room too, so was DS Cornish. Izzy was talking too quickly. 'We've been back to Max Winward's house and there's a floorboard that's been ripped up in his bedroom. The weapon he used to shoot Scott Dewhurst is an old one that was registered to him in the army. Somehow he must have got it away from the regiment – we'll have to look into it.'

Cornish cut in. 'I've been speaking to his doctor. He says Max has got a few weeks at most to live. He can barely stand – I have no idea how he managed to get to the centre; I can only think he had an accomplice.'

'Jessica?'

Cole was looking at her but she was thinking of Tony again. She'd watched him get into a car the previous evening with his mother and drive away. Had he really gone? She hoped so. Someone whose life would be better from now on.

'I'm not sure – we couldn't interview him for too long. He said he was working alone.'

Izzy's turn: 'We found his electronic tag at his house – it had been sliced off with bolt cutters. We searched his shed but there was no sign of them. He might have dumped them somewhere on the way to the centre, I suppose. I'll get onto taxi firms to see if they've had a pickup, as well as the trams and buses.'

Cole was nodding approvingly. 'Good. What about a link from Scott to the hospice?'

'Nothing,' Jessica replied.

Cornish was shaking her head too. 'The night crew were looking into it and then handed over to the day lot. We've checked everything. There's all sorts in Dewhurst's past and the SCD's drugs team have wanted him for ages but no links to that hospice. I'm sure there won't be too many people shedding tears at his passing, but wherever Max got his name from, it wasn't there.'

'Jess?'

Jessica shook her head. 'When I asked him in interview, he said he couldn't remember. We're not going to get near to talking to him again today, if ever. They've taken him to a secure hospital.'

Cornish shuffled through her papers. 'There's no CCTV at either end of the alley in which Dewhurst was killed and plenty of cut-throughs that aren't covered either. We've got no footage of Max arriving at the scene, let alone anyone else. All we have is some of Dewhurst on the traffic cameras nearby.'

Cole drummed his fingers on the desk. 'So that's it, then?'

He didn't sound so sure.

Izzy was as forceful as ever. 'I'll keep on at the transport companies – he obviously got to the centre somehow but by the time we arrived at the scene, he was lying on the floor himself, out of breath, barely able to move.'

Jessica felt everyone looking at her. 'Perhaps he's stronger than we think? It's amazing what someone can do when they're pushed hard enough.'

44

Jessica sat at the traffic lights watching the red burn through the windscreen.

'What do you want for your birthday, then?' Adam asked.

'I'm not having a birthday this year. It's getting out of hand, all this ageing.'

'How long is it until the big one?'

'Long enough.' As the light turned green, Jessica accelerated away, glancing down at the speedometer. 'This would be a lot easier if I had my glasses.'

'Where'd you leave them?'

'If I knew that, I'd be wearing them, wouldn't I?'

Adam laughed. 'Georgia got that flat, by the way. She's going in two weeks, so you can have the house back on your days off.'

'I don't mind, she's—'

'It's me you're talking to, remember. You don't mind her being there but you kind of do because you also like your space, but then you feel bad about not wanting her there, which means you don't say anything – you just moan to Izzy about it. I know.'

'Smart-arse.'

'I'll take that as a compliment. Anyway, are you feeling better?'

'I'm fine – I think there's been a bug going around.'

'How's your wrist?'

'Getting there.' Jessica indicated to go around the roundabout, following the signs for the superstore even though she knew the way. 'How is she about Humphrey?'

'All right but I'm not sure she'll be Internet dating any-time soon.'

'Caroline texted me to say she's off to Copenhagen with Hugo for one of his shows. If she gets out of the country without murdering some pretty blonde Danish fan of his it'll be a miracle.'

'They're the weirdest couple I've ever known – worse than us.'

'I'm not sure Hugo realises they're a couple. He'll prob-ably find out on their wedding day when he realises everyone's got a suit on and she's in a white dress.'

Jessica pulled into the supermarket car park and stopped towards the back where it was darkest. It felt like habit now. 'Did you think about that other thing?'

Adam nodded. 'I called that Shane guy of yours – he invited me down to help out with his kids at the church hall, so I'm going to give it a go. I've never thought about adoption before.'

'If it's any consolation, I don't know either. I just remember the look in his eyes when he was talking about them.'

Adam drummed his hands on the dashboard. 'Okay, let's get going, You've been up since silly a.m. and I've got tea to cook.' He reached into the back seat for the bags for life but when he turned around he seemed confused. 'Why are there bolt cutters in the footwell?'

He picked them up to prove the point.

Jessica stroked his arm and smiled. 'I needed them for something at work but it's all sorted now. Come on, let's go. I'm bloody starving.'

EPILOGUE

The PC scuffed her feet along the cobbles, eyes on the ground. 'Eight years on the force and this is what it comes down to: Joy Bag Fucking Jane. This is what they're going to be calling me for the next twenty years.'

The man next to her didn't look up. 'Oh, stop moaning – at least they're not accusing you of nicking all the pens. Just because I'm efficient enough to keep one on me, everyone's going around calling me PC Pen-Thief.'

'Oh, pipe down, that's nothing compared to Joy Bag. Maybe if you learned to spell, you wouldn't get so much shite.'

The man stopped, crouching to pick up a tissue and putting it in a see-through bag. 'Why are we even here? I thought they'd searched this area once? Some scumbag drug dealer gets himself shot and we're here a day later sweeping the alley for a second time.'

'The guv says he wants to make sure we did a thorough job – some bollocks about that Winward fella having an accomplice. If you ask me he did us a favour.'

Jane was about to take another step forwards when PC Pen-Thief put an arm across her. He crouched, peering at the ground.

'What's down there? I can't see a bloody thing in this light.'

PC Pen-Thief picked up the twisted metal frame with his gloves and dropped it into an evidence bag. 'Unless I'm very much mistaken, it looks to me as if someone's dropped their glasses.'

AFTERWORD

Manchester City Council don't like me very much. How do I know this? Basically, they've gone out of their way to completely screw me over.

I wrote this book and Jessica 9 – *Scarred for Life* – back-to-back in the spring and summer of 2013. You'll understand why when you read the next novel; they feed into one another, with not one but two of my favourite ever characters making their first appearances. (That's cheap plug #1.)

Anyway, I pottered my way through the rest of the year, writing the first two books in the Andrew Hunter private investigator series (cheap plug #2: book one, *Something Wicked*, is already out as an ebook), as well as doing a few other odds and ends. Then I got to the end of the year and Manchester City Council completely stitched me up.

How? They went and plonked a massive great Ferris wheel in the middle of Piccadilly Gardens. When I saw it, my heart sank. That wasn't because the attraction didn't appeal – who wouldn't want to be freezing cold, sixty metres in the air, with a wonderful view of the, er, car park and, er, bus station and, er, Burger King? No, it was because I'd already written the opening chapters of *Crossing the Line*, set in Piccadilly Gardens without the wheel.

I had a few options. Tampering with the wheel in an

effort to get it shut down seemed like an extreme idea, so that left me wondering whether I should rewrite the opening. I could have moved the politician scene to a different spot, or even written the wheel into the action. That only causes another problem, though. The wheel's on a two-year contract as a bit of a test to see if it's popular, meaning it could be temporary anyway.

So, ultimately, I changed nothing. These books are fiction and *Crossing the Line* could be set either before the wheel went up or after it comes down. Or it could be in an alternative reality where it never went up in the first place and Manchester City Council really like me. This afterword is just to let you know that I know that you know.

COMING SOON

SCARRED FOR LIFE

The next book in the Jessica Daniel series

DI Jessica Daniel is not having a good week. Her wallet's been nicked, the refurbished incident room is already falling apart, and a new football-mad constable is driving her crazy.

She also has bigger things on her mind. A student's body has been dumped in a wheelie bin at the back of a university building, with a vague link to an Olympic medallist and a theory that it could have been an induction that went wrong.

There's the tattooed shop raider who has her team stumped ——————— ng lone women; a chief inspector ————— oblem with her; and someone ————— front door insisting that she's

————— or Jessica – and, if she's not ————— er might not make it through in

ISBN 978-1-4472-4789-0

By Kerry Wilkinson

RECKONING

The Silver Blackthorn Trilogy

One girl. One reckoning. One destiny.

In the village of Martindale, hundreds of miles north of the new English capital of Windsor, sixteen-year-old Silver Blackthorn takes the Reckoning. This coming-of-age test not only decides her place in society – Elite, Member, Inter or Trog – but also determines that Silver is to become an Offering for King Victor.

But these are uncertain times and no one really knows what happens to the teenagers who disappear into Windsor Castle. Is being an Offering the privilege everyone assumes it to be, or do the walls of the castle have something to hide?

Trapped in a maze of ancient corridors, Silver finds herself in a warped world of suspicion where it is difficult to know who to trust and who to fear. The one thing Silver does know is that she must find a way out . . .

ISBN 978-1-4472-3530-9